THE SUN
AND
THE STAR

FROM THE WORLD OF PERCY JACKSON

THE SUN
AND
THE STAR

A NICO DI ANGELO ADVENTURE

RICK RIORDAN AND MARK OSHIRO

DISNEP • HYPERION   LOS ANGELES NEW YORK

First Edition, May 2023
1 3 5 7 9 10 8 6 4 2
FAC-004510-23076
Printed in the United States of America

This book is set in 12-pt Goudy Oldstyle/Fontspring
Design and illustrations by Alice Moye-Honeyman

Library of Congress Cataloging-in-Publication Data
Names: Riordan, Rick, author. • Oshiro, Mark, author.
Title: The sun and the star / by Rick Riordan and Mark Oshiro.
Description: First edition. • Los Angeles ; New York : Disney HYPERION, 2023. •
Audience: Ages 10–14. • Audience: Grades 7–9. • Summary: Nico, the son of
Hades, and his boyfriend, Will, the son of Apollo, travel to Tartarus, the deepest,
darkest part of the Underworld, as they attempt to rescue an old friend.
Identifiers: LCCN 2022023053 • ISBN 9781368081153 (hardcover) •
ISBN 9781368081344 (ebk)
Subjects: CYAC: Gods, Greek—Fiction. • Gay people—Fiction. • Adventure
and adventurers—Fiction. • Hell—Fiction. • LCGFT: Novels.
Classification: LCC PZ7.R4829 Su 2023 • DDC [Fic]—dc23
LC record available at https://lccn.loc.gov/2022023053

Reinforced binding
Follow @ReadRiordan
Visit www.DisneyBooks.com

SUSTAINABLE FORESTRY INITIATIVE

Certified Sourcing
www.sfiprogram.org
SFI-01681

Logo Applies to Text Stock Only

To all the Nicos, Wills, Pipers,
and everyone in between: this is for you.

May you shine as bright as the sun and the stars.

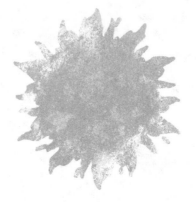

"Nico di Angelo, why don't you tell me a story?"

Nico bristled at that. A story? *Any* old story? That seemed too easy after everything they'd been through.

After all the suffering.

He looked to Will briefly, and his boyfriend arched an eyebrow. He looked tired. *Too* tired. And his bandages . . .

Nico's stomach rolled. The gauze strips were soaked through with blood again.

He turned back to Gorgyra. "A story about *what?*" he asked.

The nymph examined Nico's face, then Will's. Was she going to pull soul threads out of them again?

Nico felt something brush his knuckles. He glanced down and saw that Will was trying to hold his hand. He opened his fingers and let Will slip his in between.

Nico's heart sank. Will's grip was *very* weak.

Nico had to do this. He *had* to finish what they had started.

The whispers called out to him.

And then Gorgyra did, too.

"Tell me about the two of *you,*" she said.

CHAPTER  1

Nico faced the worst decision of his life, and he was certain he was going to mess it up.

"I can't do this," he said to Will Solace, the stunningly beautiful son of Apollo, who stood across from him. But it was Austin Lake—one of Will's half-siblings—Nico chose to focus on. He was pacing behind Will, which only made Nico more nervous.

"Stop moving, Austin," said Nico. "I can't concentrate."

"Sorry, dude," said Austin. "This is just so stressful."

"You gotta choose," Will said to Nico. "Those are the rules."

Nico frowned. "I'm the son of Hades. I don't live by most rules."

"But you *did* agree to these," said Kayla Knowles, another child of Apollo. She twirled a cherry lollipop in her mouth. "Are you a demigod without honor, Nico di Angelo?"

Austin kept pacing. "To be fair, I don't think this task requires any *actual* honor."

"Quiet!" said Nico, running his hands through his hair. What if he made the wrong choice? Would Will be disappointed in him?

But studying Will's face, Nico saw only anticipation. The good kind. Will was ready for whatever Nico would say, and no matter how this ended, Will would still think just as highly of him.

What did I ever do to deserve him? Nico wondered. He asked himself that question a lot.

"Okay, I've made my decision," said Nico.

"I might explode," said Austin.

"The world might end," said Kayla, now holding the lollipop at her side, her eyes bright with anxiety. "Like, *actually* end this time."

"So," said Nico, "if I had to choose . . ."

"Yes?" prompted Will. "You would choose . . . ?"

Nico took a deep breath.

"Darth Vader."

Will and Kayla groaned, but Austin looked like Nico had just given him a Ferrari as a birthday present.

"Dude!" Austin screamed. "That is the best answer!"

"It is the *worst* answer!" said Kayla. "Why would you choose Vader when Kylo Ren is *right there*?"

"*I* was hoping for a deep cut," Will mused. "Maybe someone like General Grievous or Dryden Vos."

"Hold on," said Nico. "I just finished watching all those movies *yesterday*. I can barely remember what happened in the prequels at this point." He paused. "Were those all actual characters in Star Wars, or are you joking?"

"Don't distract from your truth, Nico," said Kayla. "*Darth Vader?* You'd go on a date with *Darth Vader?*" She crunched on her lollipop. "I've lost all joy, Nico. All of it."

"Welcome to my world," Nico joked. He caught Will grimacing—a brief flicker of one, but he still caught it.

"This is a safe space," said Austin. "No judgment allowed for our answers, remember?"

"I take it back," said Kayla. "It's an all-judgment space."

"You're very quiet, Will," said Nico. "Especially as *the* number one Star Wars fan in the group."

"I'm considering all the reasons why you'd give that answer," he said. "You might be onto something."

"He's powerful," said Nico.

"And decisive," added Will. "He'd always know exactly where to go for your date. No arguing about that."

"Does he take off his helmet to eat?" said Kayla.

Nico laid his hand over his heart. "Imagine Darth Vader removing his helmet over dinner and then staring longingly into your eyes over the table. Now *that* is romance."

Will laughed hard, then flashed that brilliant smile of his.

Why, oh why, did it feel like such a victory to make Will laugh? For a long time, Nico had assumed he himself did not have a heart. He was the son of Hades, after all. Love didn't find people like him. But then came . . . Will. Will, who could melt Nico's iciness with a smile. Anyone could have guessed which god was Will's father—he radiated energy and light. Sometimes *literally*, as they had learned in the troglodytes' caverns earlier that year. Will was Apollo's son, through and through.

Maybe that whole saying about opposites attracting was true, because Nico didn't know a single person who was more his opposite. Despite that, they were coming up on a year. A year *together*. Nico had an actual boyfriend.

He still wasn't sure he believed it was real.

The four demigods continued their walk through Camp Half-Blood. There was no fire burning in the amphitheater. Maybe, since it was starting to cool down on Long Island, Nico and Will would light one tonight. No campers were rushing off to the armory or the forge; no one was visiting the Cave of the Oracle. The cabins were empty (aside from Hades's and Apollo's), and that was the clearest sign summer was over.

Nico didn't want to admit it out loud, but he was going to miss . . . well, pretty much all the campers, even though it was at times exhausting to be one of their counselors. He especially didn't want to say good-bye to Kayla and Austin.

As they passed through the strawberry fields, Nico sensed Kayla's and Austin's tension growing. They'd had to make a difficult decision about their travel arrangements earlier that day, and as the four of them climbed Half-Blood Hill, Kayla and Austin slowed.

"I'm thinking that maybe we should have chosen differently," said Kayla.

"You sure we'll be fine, Nico?" asked Austin.

"Yeah," he said. "I mean . . . no one has ever *died* or anything."

"That's not nearly as comforting as you think it is!" said Kayla.

"You'll be okay," said Will, and he put his hand on Austin's shoulder. "I've heard it's chaotic, maybe a bit nauseating, but you'll make it home safely."

They reached the summit of the hill, where the Golden Fleece glittered on the lowest branch of the pine tree. Below, Farm Road 3.141 curved around the base of the hill, defining the outer border of camp. On the gravel shoulder, next to a pile of boxes and duffel bags, stood Chiron, the Camp Half-Blood activities director, his equine lower half gleaming white in the afternoon light.

"There you are!" the centaur called out. "Come along, then."

None of them hurried. It was obvious to Nico that Kayla and Austin weren't in a rush to leave camp. Most everyone else had already returned to their "normal" lives, except . . . well, what was normal for someone like Nico?

Epic battles.

Constantly facing the threat of defeat and death.

The dead talking to him.

Prophecies.

The voice from his dreams bubbled up inside him again now, calling out for help.

Rachel Dare's words haunted him, too. Only he and Will had heard what the Oracle had prophesied a few weeks ago, and Nico hadn't shared it with anyone else yet, not even the other counselors. Why should he? It hadn't warned of any doomsday threats to Camp Half-Blood. The world was—as far as he knew—safe for now from angry gods or rebellious Titans. Resurrected maniacal Roman emperors were no longer a thing to worry about.

The prophecy merely concerned that lone voice in his dreams, begging for help.

Specifically, *Nico's* help.

"Some of the satyrs collected your things," said Chiron as the four demigods joined him at the road. "They wish you well on your journey."

"We might need it," Kayla grumbled. "Chiron, just tell us the truth. The Gray Sisters aren't going to kill us, are they?"

"What? No!" He looked aghast. "At least, they haven't killed anyone so far."

"You and Nico!" cried Austin, throwing up his hands. "Both of you think that's an acceptable thing to tell us?"

Chiron's smile lines crinkled around his eyes. "Now, now, you're demigods. You'll be fine. Try tipping them a few extra drachmas at the start of the trip, though. I've heard that helps make the experience less . . . intense?"

He fished in the pocket of his archery vest, pulled out a golden coin, and threw it into the road. "*Stop, O Chariot of Damnation!*"

No sooner had Chiron finished speaking than the taxi arrived.

It did not putter or cruise up to the group. It *appeared*. The coin sank into the pavement, tendrils of dark smoke curled upward, the asphalt twisted, and the Gray Sisters' taxi erupted into being. It *looked* like a taxi all right, but its edges swirled and wafted if you stared at it too long. Nico had heard all about Percy's, Meg's, and Apollo's experiences with this particular mode of transportation. They'd repeatedly told him that they even preferred his shadow-travel to the bumpy, vomit-inducing nightmare that was riding in that car. The Gray Sisters had a long history of detesting heroes, and at this point they viewed *every* inhabitant of Camp Half-Blood as a potential hero to be detested.

Nico didn't want to admit it to the others, but he had met the sisters several times on his own, and he kind of liked them. They were thorny. Difficult. Stuck in their ways. Chaotic, yet weirdly dependable. They wore their darkness on their sleeves. For Styx's sake, they all shared a single *eye*. How could Nico *not* appreciate them?

The sisters were in the midst of an argument as one of the rear doors swung open.

"I know exactly what I'm doing, Wasp," said the old lady sitting shotgun, her stringy gray hair swaying over her face. "When have I ever *not* known what I'm doing?"

"Oh, *oh!*" screeched Wasp, who sat up front in the middle. "That's lush. That's a real *lush* opinion, Tempest!"

"Do you even know what *lush* means?" Tempest shot back.

The driver groaned dramatically. "Are you two *children?* Will you please stop talking?"

Tempest threw her hands up and put on her best imitation of the driver (which confused Nico, since they all sounded identical). "Oh, my name is Anger, and I'm *sooooo* mature."

"I will eat the eye," warned Anger. "I'll do it."

"You *wouldn't,*" said Wasp.

"With salt and pepper and a little paprika!" Anger threatened. "I'll do it."

"Hi," said Austin, hoisting his saxophone case. "Is there any way you could pop the trunk? We have some luggage."

All three Gray Sisters spun toward Austin and spoke in unison: "NO!"

They fell back into arguing. Nico decided right then and there that these were his favorite people in the whole world.

Still, he sympathized with Kayla and Austin. As Chiron worked to open the trunk, both demigods looked more frightened than they ever had in the last year.

"You sure you don't want me to shadow-travel you to Manhattan?" Nico offered.

Will sighed. "Nico, you can't use shadow-travel like public transportation. It'll drain you dry."

"It's okay, Nico," Kayla said, sounding like she was trying hard to believe it. "We'll be fine."

"Plus, we're going to different places," said Austin. "My mom's meeting me uptown. I actually got into an academy up in Harlem, and she found an apartment for us close by!"

"Sounds like a good place to end up," said Will. "Not too far from here."

"And there's so much history in Harlem to explore," added Austin. "Apparently, one of the clubs where Miles Davis used to play has reopened!"

Nico nodded halfheartedly. He had no idea who that was. It was one of the downsides of not being in the "human" world for very long.

"What about you, Kayla?" asked Chiron, loading her archery gear into the trunk.

"Back to Toronto," she said. "Dad wanted me to come home, and it's actually been a while. I'm pretty excited, to be honest." Her eyes glinted. "Especially to prove that I'm now better than him at archery!"

Austin turned to Nico and Will. "So . . . you two are really staying here?"

Nico hoped Will would answer first. The sun falling behind the western hills made Will's curly blond hair look like it was aflame. For a moment, Nico wondered if Will was using his glow-in-the-dark power.

Either way, it made Nico a little annoyed. Why did Will have to be so beautiful all the time?

"I think we are," said Will, taking Nico's hand. "Mom's touring for her new album this fall, and I don't know if I want to bounce around the country in the back of a van."

"Could be fun," said Austin. "I hope I get to travel because of my music one day."

Kayla nodded. "I wonder what it would be like to see other places without worrying whether some murderous statue is going to kill you."

"Oh, come on," said Nico. "Where's the fun in that?"

"Are you going to get in the car?" Tempest growled. "Or are you paying us to listen to your boring conversation?"

She was hanging out the window with an open palm extended toward them. Austin paid her with three drachmas, tipping her heavily as Chiron had suggested. Tempest examined the coins for a moment—Nico didn't know how, as she had no eyes behind that thick gray curtain of hair—then grunted. She pulled herself back into the car.

"Get in," she said.

There were quick hugs and cheek kisses, and then Austin and

Kayla climbed into the back seat of the Gray Sisters' taxi. All the while, the sisters continued to argue.

Kayla looked around the cab. "We've been on worse adventures," she said to those outside the car.

"*Have* we?" asked Austin.

"Anyway, hope to see you soon," said Kayla. "And don't get into any trouble, you two."

Austin leaned across Kayla to poke his head out the window, a mischievous excitement on his face. "But if there *is* trouble . . ."

Will waved at them. "You'll know. Promise."

"Be safe yourselves!" Chiron called out.

"Drive, Anger! Drive!" screamed Wasp. "Isn't that what you *do*? Honestly, why do you even sit in that seat if you don't—"

Her words were lost as the taxi jerked forward and disappeared in a blur of gray.

Yep. Nico loved the sisters.

"So, that's it," said Will. "They were the last, weren't they?"

"Indeed," said Chiron. "Aside from some of the staff, the satyrs, and the dryads, Camp Half-Blood is actually . . . empty."

The old centaur sounded a bit lost. As far as Nico could recall since he'd started coming here, this was the first time that there were no demigods present. Aside from him and Will, that is.

"This is weird," said Nico. "*Really* weird."

"A lot has happened over the past few years," said Chiron wistfully. "I understand more than ever why campers would want to go home to be with their families, or to see the world."

"I guess . . ." said Nico.

"Now, gentlemen," said Chiron, dusting off the front of his vest, "I've got a meeting with Juniper and the dryads about tree rot. Exciting stuff, I assure you. I'll see you at dinner?"

They nodded, then waved as Chiron galloped off.

"So," said Nico, "what do we do next?"

Will, still holding Nico's hand, guided him back up the hill. "Well, we don't have any monsters to slay."

"Boo. I could raise a skeleton army to perform a choreographed dance. I bet I could teach them 'Single Ladies,' if you like."

Will chuckled. "We don't have any Roman emperors to locate and dethrone, either."

Nico flinched. "Ugh. Don't remind me. If I could go the rest of my life without even thinking Nero's name again, I'd be happy."

"That's a funny joke," said Will as they reached the summit.

"What is?"

"You," said Will. "Being happy."

Nico rolled his eyes.

"My grumpy little ball of darkness," added Will, poking him in the ribs.

"Ew, gross," said Nico, dancing away from him. "We are *not* making that a thing."

"Did you already forget that I was once your—and I am quoting you here, Nico—'significant annoyance'?"

"Oh, you're *still* that," said Nico, and then Will was chasing him down the hill, back into camp. In that moment, Nico allowed himself to enjoy the sensation. Will was right: there were no threats whatsoever on the horizon. No Big Bads. No lurking demigod traitors, no hidden monsters waiting to destroy Camp Half-Blood.

But then dread prickled across Nico's skin. His body was warning him, wasn't it? *Don't get too comfortable*, it was telling him. *He's waiting for you in Tartarus. Or have you forgotten about him like everyone else did?*

Maybe this period of rest wasn't such a good thing. If Nico didn't have some terrible monster or villain to fight, then what excuse did he have to ignore the voice any longer?

The truth was, he couldn't ignore it even if he wanted to. He'd been visited by so many ghosts over the years. The dead wanted to be heard, and who better to listen to them than the son of Hades?

But *this* voice . . . it did not belong to someone who had passed on. And Nico had never heard someone sound as desperate for help.

So his mood was muted by the time he and Will made it to the dining pavilion after stopping by their cabins to freshen up first. It felt strange to be in this place that was normally so alive. Now there were only a few staff dryads and harpies spread unevenly around the various tables. The camp director, Dionysus—Mr. D to all of them—was lounging at the head table with Chiron, who had somehow beaten them to dinner. The two administrators were so deep in conversation that they barely acknowledged Will when he waved.

Even the satyrs who served Nico and Will didn't seem all that thrilled to be doing so. "This whole place feels like my soul," Nico joked to Will. "You know, empty and dark."

Will swallowed some chicken kebab pieces. "You're not empty," he said, then pointed the skewer at Nico. "You are definitely dark, though."

"Dark as the pits of the Underworld."

Will looked down, focusing on his food like it was the most interesting thing he'd ever seen.

"We don't have to talk about it if you don't want to," said Nico.

Will managed a smile. His warmth was genuine—like it always was, since he was basically a *literal* ray of sunshine—and it softened Nico just a bit. "We can," he said. "Just maybe not now, Nico. Austin and Kayla just left. The camp is calm. Serene. *Quiet.* Let's just appreciate the break, okay?"

Nico nodded, but he wasn't sure how he was supposed to do what Will had requested. When had he *ever* gotten a break before? If it wasn't dead Roman emperors, it was his father. Or Minos. Or his stepmother, Persephone. It had been years since that particular incident had happened, but he was *still* annoyed about being turned into a dandelion. A *dandelion*! It was an affront to his aesthetic!

And there were other things he didn't want to remember. Darker things. Ghosts who would probably visit him eventually. Nico stuffed it all down—making a grumpy little ball of darkness inside his chest. Then he forced a smile as he listened to Will talk about all the things they could do that fall while they stayed at camp.

It would be fine. Everything would be fine.

CHAPTER  2

It always came rushing back to Nico in his dreams.

When he'd first confessed to Will that he was hearing a particularly haunted voice from the Underworld, Nico worried he shouldn't have said anything. Sometimes, Will didn't seem to understand what it meant for Nico to be . . . well, *Nico*. The Underworld spooked Will, to be frank, but Nico needed to tell *someone* what was happening to him.

Months earlier, Nico had sensed his friend Jason Grace's death, which had sent him into a tailspin of grief and rage. By the time Lester and Meg had arrived at Camp Half-Blood at the start of summer, Nico's emotions were so volatile that he'd raised the dead more than once by accident. (There is nothing more disconcerting than waking in the morning and finding a freshly incarnated zombie standing over you, ready to take your breakfast order.)

Will had listened to him attentively, like he always did. Afterward he'd posed a few questions, mostly about whether the voice had anything to do with the flashbacks Nico had *also* been having lately. Will had stayed quiet for a while and then asked, "Are you sure it's not post-traumatic stress disorder?"

Sometimes, Nico's brain thought of a joke and it came out of his mouth a second later without any sort of filter at all. That's exactly what happened when he blurted out, "My whole *life* is a disorder!"

Will hadn't laughed at that.

Instead, he'd suggested that maybe Nico should talk to Mr. D. For all Dionysus's faults, he was an Olympian god with experience in these matters: dreams, visions, and altered states of consciousness.

He's also the god of madness, Nico thought. He tried not to dwell on that, or the implications of Will making such a suggestion.

"I'd rather do almost anything else," Nico countered. "Can the guy even make it through a single conversation without sarcasm, an insult, or a combination of the two?"

Will grinned. "Can you?"

Nico had spent the rest of the day trying to recover from Will murdering him with those two words. Still, there was some truth to what Will had said. This wasn't the first time Nico had dealt with flashbacks or PTSD. He remembered coaching his sister Hazel Levesque through her own devastating flashbacks after she'd spent time in the Underworld. He'd even had a frank conversation with Reyna Avila Ramírez-Arellano about post-traumatic stress and how it related to the memories of her father. Yet he'd never really turned that gaze inward. Was *he* dealing with the same kind of thing? Honestly, how could he not be? But he was sure the voice was something else.

After dinner on the day he'd confided to Will, Nico got up the nerve to speak with Mr. D. He told the director about his flashbacks during the day, the repetitive dreams, the voice from deep within Tartarus. (He did not, however, tell Mr. D the details of the Oracle's prophecy. That still felt too raw, too personal for a first conversation.)

Mr. D sat back in his deck chair, turning his can of Diet Coke in his fingers. With his unkempt black hair, blotchy complexion, and wrinkled leopard-pattern camp shirt, Dionysus looked more like a hungover Vegas conventioneer than a god.

To Nico's surprise, Mr. D didn't tell him to go away, or make any snarky comment at Nico's expense.

"We need to get to the bottom of this." Mr. D's violet eyes were unsettling, like crystallized wine . . . or blood. "I want to see you each morning at breakfast. You are to report on your dreams and keep me apprised if anything new comes up."

The ball of darkness in Nico's chest pressed against his stomach. He would've preferred Mr. D being dismissive and rude. Seeing the god so serious was disturbing.

"Every day?" he asked. "Are you sure that's necessary?"

"Believe me, Nico di Angelo, I'd rather not have my breakfast spoiled with your silly mortal problems, but yes, it *is* necessary if you'd like to keep your consciousness intact. And try to have some interesting dreams, will you? Not the usual boring *I was flying, I was being chased, I was singing onstage in my underwear* tripe."

So it had become a routine. Mr. D talked to Nico each morning, the god's plate piled high with sausage and eggs while Nico's was usually empty except for a few strawberries. That too concerned Mr. D, who, as the god of festivity, disapproved of anyone not enjoying food. "I know you've got the whole gaunt-and-pale-son-of-Hades thing going on, but you're still human. You need to eat."

Nico shrugged. "I guess I'm used to being hungry. It doesn't really bother me."

Mr. D grunted. "But your appetite is getting worse. Along with the flashbacks, and the voice in your dreams—"

"It's nothing I can't handle," Nico insisted.

Mr. D pushed his plate away. He turned his whole body toward Nico. "Look here, boy. After living in exile at Camp Half-Blood all these wretched years, I've learned that you mortals are surprisingly resilient."

"Exactly—" Nico began.

Mr. D held up a hand. "I'm not done. You may be resilient, but you're still *human*. There is no need to punish yourself with hunger just because it's what you're used to. For your mind to heal, your body must also."

Nico grumbled. Then his stomach followed with some grumbling of its own.

Some days, Nico couldn't share his dreams with Mr. D. They were too painful, too vicious, dredging up old memories he didn't want to examine. But other times, Nico had to admit that talking helped. He found that he didn't have to sugarcoat *anything* with Dionysus. The same crudeness he'd found annoying in the camp director was actually really helpful when Nico was recounting his flashbacks.

"My goodness," Mr. D once said after Nico described a spate of dreams that had less to do with singing in his underwear and more to do with simultaneously being burned, drowned, and crushed inside a giant bronze vase filled with ants. "That's marvelous! I must remember to give my worst enemies that nightmare."

But none of the talks got to the heart of the matter: Why were these visions happening to Nico?

Did he *deserve* them?

CHAPTER 3

On the night after Kayla and Austin left, Nico stayed awake long after Will had retired to Apollo's cabin. His mind was still buzzing, and he was dreading sleep. Demigods always had vivid—and occasionally prophetic—dreams, but when he slept, the voice became almost unbearable.

Help me, please! it called out. *I need you, Nico di Angelo. I need you.*

Well, so did *every* ghost who visited him. The dead just wanted to be heard, especially if they hadn't been listened to during their time on earth. The Underworld was full of souls wandering the Fields of Asphodel, crying out for attention.

But this voice wasn't dead. It felt farther away than even Asphodel, and more tortured than any ghost's. This voice was calling out from Tartarus, the darkest and deepest area of the Underworld. And *nobody* called out from Tartarus.

It had to be Bob the Titan.

Nico remembered their first meeting: Christmas Day nearly three years ago, when Nico, Percy Jackson, and Thalia Grace were tasked by Persephone to retrieve Hades's missing sword. To do so, they'd had to battle Iapetus, a Titan unleashed from the depths of

Tartarus. The Titan might have killed all three of them, but with the last of his strength, Percy had pulled Iapetus into the River Lethe, wiping him of all his memories. Then Percy renamed him Bob and convinced the Titan they were good friends. Strangely, the new identity *stuck.*

Nico had visited Bob several times since then down in the Underworld. The newly gentle Titan had taken a janitorial job in Hades's palace and seemed quite happy to spend his time sweeping up bones and dusting sarcophagi. He and Nico struck up a strange friendship. Both felt disconnected from their pasts, uncomfortable around others, and melancholy about their mutual "friend" Percy Jackson, who never seemed to remember they existed.

Then, a year and a half ago, Percy and Annabeth had fallen into Tartarus. Bob had sensed their peril and plunged into the abyss to help them. He had held off an army of monsters to give Percy and Annabeth a chance to return to the mortal world. No one was sure what happened to Bob after that—whether he had died or somehow survived.

But almost every day for the last three years, Nico had thought about Bob. He felt *guilty.* They should have saved him. Someone should have rescued him from Tartarus. How could they have just *left* him there after he'd saved Percy and Annabeth and . . . well, pretty much the entire world?

Maybe Will and Mr. D were right. Maybe Bob's voice was a false echo, a manifestation of Nico's own PTSD.

But that didn't explain the prophecy.

That's what Nico was thinking about when sleep finally came for him.

Nico was in darkness. What else was new?

He'd had this dream so many times he thought he knew where it was leading.

Except . . . not this night.

In the void, Nico heard his name.

Nico.

A different voice than before, but so familiar . . .

Caro Niccolo.

He stirred as shadows wrapped around him. No one *ever* called him Niccolo. No one except . . .

Niccolo, vita mia . . .

The shadows pressed tighter against his face. He couldn't breathe.

He hadn't heard that voice in years. Decades.

Mamma.

I'm here! he tried to call out. *Please, don't go!*

Vita mia, she repeated. *Devi ascoltarmi.*

Nico struggled to understand what she was saying. He was *Italian*, yes. This was his native language. But his mind moved sluggishly, as if the darkness had seeped into his skull.

Finally, the meaning came to him.

"I *am* listening, Mamma!" he answered.

He thrashed, trying to free himself from the thick cocoon of shadows.

ASCOLTA! the voice cried.

LISTEN!

Nico fell.

He plummeted into a soft, warm nest of blankets. Was he back in his bunk at camp? He sat up and—

Light. On a lacquered brown nightstand, an ugly steel desk lamp cast a yellow glow over an oddly familiar room. Thick blackout curtains. A flatscreen TV. Striped gold-and-cream wallpaper like gilded prison bars.

Wait. No. Was this—?

He grabbed a laminated card from the nightstand.

LOTUS HOTEL AND CASINO: IN-ROOM BREAKFAST OPTIONS

No. No, no, no!

He turned slowly in the gigantic king-size bed, remembering how the mattress made hollow, tinny creaks whenever he moved.

He sensed her before he saw her, asleep in the bed next to him.

His sister Bianca. She looked so peaceful there, her chest rising slowly with her breath, her dark hair fanned across her pillow. Nico tried to open his mouth, tried to call to her, but his voice didn't work. There was something poking out from the edge of the duvet at Bianca's shoulder. Was that . . . her *quiver*? Nico ripped back the covers and saw that his sister was dressed as if ready for battle, complete with boots, jacket, and arrows.

This was all wrong. Bianca hadn't become a Hunter of Artemis until *after* their time in the Lotus Casino. Then she'd taken the pledge . . . and left Nico for the last time. If he could just warn her, keep her from making those choices—

Wake up! he tried to yell, but his lips wouldn't open. His right hand flew up to his mouth. Fear curdled in his stomach.

He bolted out of bed, tripping as his legs tangled in the duvet, and then staggered into the harsh fluorescent light of the bathroom. He braced his hands on the makeup mirror. Once his eyes adjusted—

Nico wanted to scream, but he couldn't. He *literally* had no mouth. Beneath his nose, where his lips had been, was a pale line of scar tissue.

This is a dream, he told himself. *A dream. Wake up, wake up, wake up!*

His terrified, marred reflection continued to stare back at him. For the thousandth time, Nico wished he had inherited Hades's dream magic. Then he could control what he saw. He would already be awake. He could tell Will or Mr. D about his nightmares, downplay their importance, and revert to being in denial about the voice from Tartarus. That would be *so* much easier.

Instead, he stumbled back into the room. The bed was now empty.

Bianca? Where did you go?

But he couldn't yell it. He couldn't say anything.

Nico took another step toward the bed and plunged through the floor.

Again he fell.

This time when he landed, he smacked against something *very* solid. The air rushed out of his lungs, and he opened his eyes to find himself looking at—

Sky.

Bright blue *sky*, framed by rows of steel suspension cables.

What? he thought. *Where am I?*

His hands pushed against the surface beneath him. It was warm and scratchy. Asphalt. A road. Then he saw the cars on either side of him. Nico scrambled to his feet in a panic, certain that he was about to be run over.

But the cars remained still.

He hesitantly approached one and was further confused to discover that the driver's seat was *empty*. All the cars seemed deserted—two frozen lines of traffic, and in the distance, the Manhattan skyline. The wind buffeted Nico's clothes. The asphalt swayed gently, while above him the gray-blue metal support cables thrummed like giant guitar strings. Pedestrian paths on either side of the road were blocked off with dull red barriers. But there were no people anywhere. Far below, the East River rippled in the sunlight.

"Okay, dream," he muttered to himself. "Why am I on a New York City bridge?"

As soon as he said it, Nico had two realizations.

First, he could talk again. His mouth was no longer fused shut.

Second, this was the *Williamsburg* Bridge.

Oh, no, he thought. No, I *won't* relive this day.

There was a roar behind Nico, and his blood ran cold. He turned and saw the impossible.

The figure was tall and golden—but not in an attractive way like Will, more in an unnatural, terrifying, *I'm going to kill you* sort of way. He stood nine feet tall, with a cruel ageless face, molten-gold eyes, and shining armor. In his hands gleamed an enormous scythe.

Kronos.

"This doesn't make sense." Nico edged back, his pulse racing as the Titan strode toward him, a horde of monsters and allied demigods at his back. Dreams rarely made sense, but this one . . . Nico hadn't even been on the Williamsburg Bridge during the Battle of Manhattan. He'd only heard how Percy had collapsed the center of the bridge to keep Kronos's invasion at bay.

Kronos locked his eyes on Nico. The Titan smiled hideously, as if he could read Nico's thoughts. He raised his scythe.

"No!" Nico turned to run toward Manhattan, away from Kronos's advancing army.

But *they* stood in his way.

Percy.

Michael Yew.

Annabeth.

Will . . . looking so much younger, and so terrified.

Nico froze, trapped between the lines of battle. The bridge swayed beneath him.

"This isn't real," Nico told himself. "I'm not here."

"Listen." Percy stepped forward, forcing Nico back in Kronos's direction.

"Percy, what is this?" Nico held up his hands defensively. "What are you doing?"

"You have to listen," said Michael Yew, his intense brown eyes brimming with tears. "If you don't, you will share my fate."

"Ominous much?" Nico snarled. He spun around, but Kronos was nearly on top of him, wielding the scythe like a guillotine blade.

"Listen!" commanded the Titan.

"I *am*!" Nico was furious. "Whoever is trying to reach me, just *tell* me what you want!"

Kronos's scythe hurtled toward his face.

Nico was in darkness. *Again.*

By this point, he was just irritated. A person could only take so much terror and misery before it started to get really annoying. This weird dream-jumping through memories and events seemed so unnecessary.

I get the message! he thought. *I will listen! Isn't that good enough?*

A light appeared, soft and purple.

"What the—?"

Nico grabbed his Stygian iron sword and let its glow illuminate his surroundings. He was wedged into an egg-shaped space barely large enough to hold him. The gleaming metallic walls were cool to the touch. In front of him, etched into the bronze, were three long hash marks.

"No," he said aloud, and the sound of his own voice echoed back at him. "You've *got* to be kidding me."

Nico's dream had taken him back to the jar that the giants Ephialtes and Otis had stuffed him into so he could serve as bait for the seven demigods of the prophecy. It was, all things considered, not exactly Nico's favorite memory.

"Here?" Nico called out. "Why are you making me relive this?"

He shut his eyes and smacked the side of his head. *Wake up, Nico! Wake up!*

He opened his eyes again. He was still in the jar, and there, at his feet, was one lone pomegranate seed. His stomach contracted. Panic swelled in his throat. He remembered his endless hours in this jar, racked with hunger and thirst, wondering how long he could hold out before eating that pomegranate seed—his last bit of sustenance.

"Hey, subconscious?" said Nico. "If you're trying to get me to realize something, this is a terrible way to go about it."

He was met with silence.

Suddenly, a terrible screeching sound filled the vessel as the lid was pried open. Harsh light spilled in. Nico winced and covered his eyes. This hadn't happened in the real world. The jar hadn't been opened until it tipped over, just before the fight with Ephialtes and Otis.

Nico tried to uncover his eyes, but the light above was still too bright. Given the strange logic of this dream ride, he wouldn't have been surprised if Cookie Monster appeared over the mouth of the jar, reached inside, and gobbled up Nico like the chocolate-chip cookie he was.

Cookie Monster did not, in fact, show up.

Percy Jackson did.

Nico gazed up into Percy's face, which was framed by tousled black hair. His green eyes looked stormy, his mouth twisted down in concern.

There was a time when just the thought of Percy had made Nico feel an intense pit of desire in his gut. It was an unrequited desire, of course, because Percy was *never* going to have the same feelings for Nico. It had torn up Nico for a long, long time. After a while, though, he became used to the idea that he wanted things he couldn't have: Percy, Bianca, his mother, stability . . . it was all the same. Getting over Percy was easier than Nico expected. What was one straight boy when you spent your whole life longing for the impossible?

As bizarre as this dream was, the sight of Percy was comforting to Nico. He missed his friend and was eager to get out of this stupid jar. He remembered how frail and sickly he'd been when Piper had rescued him in real life. This time felt just as difficult. He tried to untangle his stiff legs and stand so Percy could help pull him out.

The other demigods must have defeated Otis and Ephialtes already. Nico couldn't hear anything outside the confines of his bronze prison.

Nico reached up to take Percy's hand.

But Percy was now *farther* away. Even standing with his arms outstretched, Nico couldn't reach the mouth of the jar.

Nico looked down, and his heart leaped into his throat. Either that pomegranate seed had swollen to the size of an apple . . . or Nico was *shrinking*!

He cast another glance at Percy. . . .

No, *no*! His friend was even farther away! The mouth of the jar now seemed like a skylight at the top of a cathedral's dome, and Percy was the size of a Titan, peeking in to see what the little mortals were up to.

Percy reached in with his gigantic hand. Nico jumped high, desperate to grab hold of one of Percy's fingers, but he just kept shrinking smaller and smaller, the walls of the jar looming around him.

"Stop it!" Nico cried out.

Percy pulled his hand out of the jar. His face disappeared for a few seconds. When it returned, his eyes were red and glassy.

He was *crying*.

"Nico," he said. "Nico, listen!"

Nico wanted to scream. "I have literally been doing nothing else!" His voice came out tinny and high-pitched, like he'd sucked down the helium from a million balloons. It only sounded worse as it echoed throughout the jar.

"You have to go," Percy said.

Nico's heart seemed to be shrinking at a slower rate than his rib cage. It pressed against his sternum, hammering with each beat.

"Go *where?*" he asked, though he dreaded the answer.

"We made a mistake," said Percy. "You have to fix it."

The jar shattered.

Again, Nico fell.

CHAPTER 4

Nico slammed hard into a stone column. Then he tumbled to the ground, breathless, and grasped for his blade. But it wasn't there.

He groaned, and the sound reverberated in a long, haunting echo. His skin felt sticky and damp. Was that sweat? *Blood?* He decided he didn't want to know.

As his eyes adjusted to the low light, he saw a smoke-stained ceiling overhead, barrel arches stretching between rows of limestone columns.

He rolled to his side. Bright bands of sunlight filtered through a row of high-set barred windows, making stripes of shadow across the floor. It was that image that triggered Nico's memory and revealed where he was.

Nico had never dreamed about this before. In fact, he'd done everything in his power to avoid thinking about that day *ever* again.

He slowly pushed himself to his feet. "Brain, if you're doing this, this is the *worst* mental vacation of all time," he said bitterly.

Nothing.

"If this is a god or a demigod or something else," Nico added, "you're really starting to annoy me."

Still no response.

So here he was, back in the basement of that cathedral whose name he did not remember, looking for . . .

Right. The scepter of Diocletian.

Except . . . someone else had been here with him.

Oh.

Jason Grace.

A new pit opened in Nico's stomach. Most of the time, emptiness was his best friend, but there was a vacancy in his heart that had never been filled since Jason . . . Ever since he . . .

Nico gulped. Even in this ridiculous dream, Jason was gone.

Nico wiped a tear from his cheek. "Okay, this has to stop," he said. "Please. Just let me wake up."

"You still think this is a dream?"

Nico spun toward the voice. "Who's there?"

"Come now, Nico di Angelo. Don't you remember?"

He inched forward until the voice's source came into view.

A marble bust of Diocletian, sitting atop its pedestal, staring right at Nico.

The emperor's head was still on his shoulders, no signs of it ever having been broken. Which made sense in the weird logic of this dream. Without Jason here to smash it, the bust would still be in one piece. Nico's memories of this day poured over him, a waterfall of images and sensations that he had kept locked deep in his mind.

One of them rose to the surface.

Jason, grabbing Nico and lifting him in the air while they chased down Favonius, the strange winged man who had been buying an ice cream cone in Dalmatia. Things had seemed so much simpler then. When you saw a wind god buying ice cream, you chased him.

When anyone tried to touch you, you lashed out. Nico had always hated being touched. As soon as Jason set him down that day, Nico had barked, *Don't ever grab me again.*

Now, staring at that unnerving bust of Diocletian, Nico wished for nothing more than to feel Jason Grace's protective arms around him.

But Jason wasn't here.

Behind Nico, a different voice said, "Are you ready?"

Nico spun once more, and there, leaning against one of the columns, stood Favonius, the Roman god of the West Wind. He was dressed exactly as he had been that day: a red tank top over an aggravatingly bright set of Bermuda shorts and huarache sandals.

"*You,*" Nico snarled. "Get out of my dreams."

"Oh, Nico," said Favonius, shaking his head. "If only it were that easy."

"Nothing is easy for me," Nico said. "I've come to expect that."

"Then you know I have to take you to see someone."

There was no joy in the god's face, none of the excitement or eagerness that Nico had seen last summer.

Favonius looked *scared.*

"Please, *no,*" Nico began.

"You have to fix it, Nico."

Nico's heart hammered even harder against his ribs. What came next in the real world had been . . . well, truly one of the worst things Nico had ever been through, which was saying a lot for him. He'd had to endure Cupid, who was no adorable little winged cherub. The intense, intimidating god of desire had forced Nico to confess his crush on Percy Jackson *in front of* Jason, all so they could acquire the scepter.

The ordeal had proved vital to winning the war against Gaea.

It had also torn a wound in Nico that still hadn't healed.

"Whatever this is," said Nico, "I get the message. I need to listen. I *am* listening. So I don't need to go through this again."

"You have to talk to him," said Favonius. "But not for the reason you think."

Nico tried to steady his breathing. He forced himself to ask, "Will Jason be there?"

He wasn't sure which answer would be more painful: yes or no.

The god's expression darkened. "No, Nico. He's gone." Then he added softly, almost to himself, "They'll all be gone eventually."

Without another word, Favonius dissolved into a swirl of dust and sunlight. The wind wrapped around Nico and lifted him off the floor. Even in a dream, Nico *hated* this sensation, like his entire body was being torn to atoms. They zipped through the smallest cracks in the church windows, then raced across the Croatian countryside without regard for gravity or mass or his stomach. All Nico's thoughts and feelings collided with one another, vying to exist simultaneously in his mind. He had *literally* fallen apart into a mess of emotions.

At least I am #OnBrand in my dreams, he thought. Then: Will would *hate* that joke.

The wind deposited him on a hill overlooking the ruins of Salona. Put back together again, Nico's thin body trembled with nausea. He felt like he had Sisyphus in his throat, eternally pushing his stone up the steep incline. "Ugh," he coughed. "That feeling is just as bad in a dream."

Favonius's disembodied laughter floated around him. "Look at you, still thinking this is a dream. You are *so* cute when you're delusional, Nico di Angelo!"

Nico really, *really* hated being called cute. He had no time for retorts, though. The wind faded, and Favonius was gone.

Nico scanned the ruins. They looked exactly as they had before:

crumbling, decaying shells of buildings, moss-covered lines of stone—a once-great Roman city reduced to a field of rocks. Nico *still* wasn't impressed. He'd seen too many ruins just like these over the years, reminders of how quickly mortal creation could turn to rubble.

He raised his hands. "Let's get on with it, then! Cupid, I'm here!"

Nico waited. But there was nothing. No booming, rushing voice taunting him, coercing him to reveal his most painful secret.

Then, suddenly, Cupid's voice was everywhere: *You know what you need to do.*

The words whizzed past Nico's ear.

Nico tried to act unfazed. It was just a dream. About a god who had left Nico wounded, shattered, and exposed . . . but still a dream. This time, he would *not* be Cupid's chew toy.

He crossed his arms. "I get it," he said. "I don't need convincing anymore! I'll go to Tartarus!"

That's not enough, Nico di Angelo. Look upon me.

"Look upon you? But I thought no one could see you in your true form!"

Unseen, Cupid slammed into him, hurling Nico backward into a broken column.

Look upon me!

Cupid was now so close that Nico could feel his breath on his face.

"I *can't* see you!" Nico screamed. "Stop with these games!"

I AM HERE.

The voice came from behind him now, and all the hair stood up on Nico's arms. It was an instantaneous reaction—a fear so primal that without even thinking it, without issuing the command, Nico called forth skeletons. They rose from the earth beneath his feet, moss and dirt and decay hanging from their bones. They ringed

Nico, their sticklike arms in defensive postures, ready to fight for him.

Turn around, Nico. Look upon me.

The voice had shifted direction again. Nico did not want to look. He had no rational reason to believe this, but he was convinced that if he actually *did* see Cupid, he would die.

"Please, Nico. Look at me."

The voice had changed. It was warm, like honey, like a late-summer sunset, like the first rush of heat from a campfire.

It was Cupid.

No.

It was *love.*

Nico turned slowly, and there stood Will Solace, his golden hair lit oh-so-perfectly in the dreamlike daylight of Salona. He wore the red smiling-sun T-shirt that Nico had bought him as a joke, and that pair of camouflage shorts with the frayed hems. He strode barefoot over to Nico.

Deep inside, Nico suspected that this was still Cupid, playing games with him, but his anger softened anyway.

"Will," said Nico. "I don't understand. What is this?"

"Listen," said Will, stepping closer.

"I've *been* listening! Why won't anyone tell me what I'm listening for?"

Will reached out and Nico did, too, but just before Will's hand touched Nico's, he pulled back.

"You have to do something, Nico," said Will, his eyes soft and sad.

"I know."

Will shook his head. "It's more than you think. When the time comes, tell me the truth."

Nico laughed. There was an edge of hysteria to his voice, but laughter was the only reaction that made sense at this point. "Sure, Will. Cupid. Cwill? Wupid? What do I call you?"

Will's face elongated like putty, his mouth opening wide, wider, so that Nico could see sharp, needlelike teeth lining his gums. Nico tried to back up, but the *thing*, whatever it was, leaped forward and screamed one last command:

WAKE UP!

"Nico!"

He opened his eyes with a jolt but couldn't make out the figure looming over him. Nico kicked out with his right leg, unfortunately landing a foot square in his boyfriend's stomach.

Will howled and tumbled off the edge of the bed, then curled up on the floor of Hades's cabin. "Nico, I *swear*," he groaned. "How do you pack all that energy into your body?"

"I'm sorry, I'm sorry!" said Nico. "You scared me!"

Will winced as he sat upright. "I think you have that backward. I could hear you screaming bloody murder from my cabin!"

Nico put his head in his hands. "I—I had a bad dream. Bad dreams, plural. *Really* bad dreams."

Nico felt a weight settle on the bed next to him, and he looked up to see Will there. "I'm really sorry about the kick in the gut."

Will smiled, and warmth washed over Nico. "Can I hold you? Would that be okay with you?"

Shame burned Nico's cheeks. He didn't like Will seeing him so vulnerable, but he nodded because what he needed overrode his pride. Will pulled him close, and Nico quietly cried into his boyfriend's chest.

"It's all right." Will ran his hand up and down Nico's back. "They were just dreams."

But were they? Nico thought. Before he could tell Will any of the details, the door to the cabin burst open. Chiron stood there, his eyes wide. "Oh—oh, no, have I interrupted something?"

Nico pulled away from Will and wiped his face with the back of his hand. "No, no, it's okay," he said. "We were just talking."

"Well . . . uh, that's fine," said Chiron awkwardly. "I'm sorry to barge in so late at night, but we have an emergency."

Nico grimaced. "Was it my screaming? Did I accidentally summon a battalion of skeletons while I was sleeping?"

"What? No!" Chiron hesitated. "At least, I hope not. Let's revisit that in a bit. First, we have a visitor who urgently needs to speak to you."

Chiron stepped aside, and Nico's heart twisted with dread as Rachel Elizabeth Dare, the current Oracle of Delphi, entered the cabin.

She pulled back the hood of her sweatshirt, and her long, gorgeous red hair spilled out. She looked flushed and exhausted, as if she'd run here all the way from Brooklyn.

"Nico," she said. "Thank the gods. You have to listen."

Before he could protest that he'd already received that particular message loud and clear, like, a MILLION times already tonight, dark green smoke began to pour out of Rachel's mouth.

CHAPTER  5

The smoke had a bitter, sulfuric smell, and Nico, Will, and Chiron all started coughing.

Rachel's pupils dilated. Then her eyes turned completely black as the words slithered out of her mouth in the rasping voice of the Oracle:

> "Go forth and find the one who calls out your name,
> Who suffers and despairs for refusing to remain;
> There leave something of equal value behind,
> Or your body and soul no one will ever find."

Rachel's knees buckled, and Will dashed forward to catch her before she hit the floor.

Chiron gripped the doorframe with one hand. His face looked as pale as the gray flecks in his beard.

"After all these years," he said grimly, "I have *never* gotten used to hearing those. Nico, are you all right?"

Nico nodded, his heart thumping.

Chiron clopped into the cabin, lowering his head to fit. "I know these prophecies can be hard to understand when you first hear them," he said. "Take all the time you need. We don't have to discuss and dissect it now."

Nico caught the sharp, chastising look that Will cast his way.

"Well, this is awkward," Nico muttered.

Chiron tilted his head. "Why? Do you know what this prophecy is about?"

Nico exhaled, trying to purge the last remnants of his dreams. He wondered if he could still be trapped in a nightmare.

"Chiron, I wanted to tell you and Mr. D at some point, but . . . well, I just never found the right time."

"It's not a new prophecy," Will explained. "We've already heard it."

Chiron glanced at Rachel, who was now breathing more steadily in Will's arms.

"I'm sorry," the centaur said. "Are you telling me that Miss Dare just rushed here in the middle of the night to give you a *rerun* prophecy?"

"They're telling the truth," said Rachel, sounding miserable. "This prophecy . . . it *keeps coming back*. Again and again."

Nico's heartbeat stumbled. "*Keeps* coming back . . . You mean this isn't just the second time?"

Rachel winced, then started to cough.

Will helped her sit up. "I'll get you some water."

He dashed to the bathroom and came back a moment later with a cup that Nico really *hoped* was clean.

Rachel took it gratefully. "I guess someone *really* needs your attention, Nico." Her expression was strained but sympathetic. "The previous times, I thought maybe I was just caught in a feedback loop or something. Maybe a glitch left over from Apollo's fight with

Python. I didn't want to worry you. But this time . . . the urge overwhelmed me. I had to come find you."

Will placed his hand on her shoulder. "How many times has the prophecy repeated?"

Rachel's cheeks flushed. She took a sip of water. "Twelve."

"Twelve times?" said Nico. "Are you serious?"

Chiron scowled. "This is an alarming situation. In all my years, I've never heard of something like this."

Rachel nodded and took another sip. "It's like a constant reminder that the quest needs to be fulfilled—that it hasn't been undertaken yet."

Nico frowned. "So, you've basically become like one of those annoying notifications in a video game reminding me to complete a side mission."

She glared at him.

Nico silently cursed himself. "That came out wrong. I'm sorry. You're not annoying, Rachel. You know what I meant."

Rachel mustered a weary smile. She nodded her thanks to Will as he helped her to her feet. "This prophecy is definitely annoying. Whatever you need to do, Nico, it would be great if you could get started. Then maybe I can turn off my notifications."

Nico glanced at Will. "It's him. There's no way it's not."

"Who are you talking about?" said a new voice.

Mr. D stood in the doorway. He had on a leopard-print tank top, bright yellow board shorts, and pink flip-flops. Basically a typical outfit for the god of partying. In one arm, he was cradling a large metal mixing bowl.

Nico sniffed the air. "Is that *popcorn?*"

"I figured there might be a show happening out here." Mr. D tossed a kernel into his open mouth. "What's a good show without popcorn?"

Nico bit back an angry comment. "A repeating prophecy isn't exactly a *show*."

Mr. D's eyes widened. "Oh, there's a repeating *prophecy*? Perfect!" He walked over to Nico's bed and plopped down at the foot. "And here I thought it was going to be a boring fall at camp. I was even thinking about staging a cage match for the dryads."

Chiron glared at the camp director. "We've talked about that, Mr. D."

"You can participate if you like, Chiron," the god said cheerfully. "I'd love to see you go hoof-on-fist with a few feisty mulberry bushes."

Chiron sighed. "Could we please focus on the problem at hand?"

"Absolutely!" Mr. D shoveled popcorn into his mouth with glee. "Tell me about this repeating prophecy. Is it about me? Do I finally gain my freedom from this miserable camp and once more become the toast of the gods, preferably with a bottle of 1945 Château Mouton Rothschild?"

"Dionysus, please," said Chiron. "I don't think this is a joking matter."

"I'm not sure about that," grumbled Nico, "given that Rachel has been more or less forced to become a prophecy voicemail system."

"Nico . . ." said Will in a warning tone.

"Well, he isn't wrong," said Rachel. "It's like all those annoying calls my dad gets about renewing his car warranties."

"Except . . . this is Bob," said Nico, finally saying his name out loud. "That's who the prophecy is about."

"You mean the Titan Iapetus?" asked Chiron. "I thought he was still in Tartarus."

"Tartarus, eh?" Mr. D grabbed another fistful of popcorn. "This is getting better by the second."

Chiron ignored that. "Do you think Iapetus has become a threat again? A rogue Titan would certainly be cause for concern."

"Bob isn't like that anymore," said Nico. "He *changed* after his dip in the River Lethe. He's nice now. Considerate. He wants to be helpful."

The others regarded him in silence. The scent of their skepticism was almost as pungent as Mr. D's popcorn.

Nico wanted to believe what he was saying, but doubts gnawed at him. What if Bob had died helping Percy and Annabeth? If he'd regenerated from the primordial landscape of Tartarus, the way monsters did, would he be Iapetus again?

The prophecy had called him the one *who suffers and despairs for refusing to remain.* Could this be some sort of trick, luring Nico down to the worst place in the cosmos only to help a hostile Titan escape?

"He's my friend," he said, mostly to himself. "I've been hearing his voice for months, even before the prophecy. He needs my help."

"Or it could be a trap," suggested Mr. D. "Which would be very exciting. By which I mean it would be terrible, of course."

Chiron frowned. "Must you be so negative, Dionysus?"

"Must you ignore the obvious?" the god shot back. "I'm not saying it's the only explanation, but we have to consider the possibility." He turned a kernel of popcorn in his fingertips as if it might hold the answer. "Nico and I have been talking about some things he's been experiencing: dreams, waking visions, a voice calling out to him from Tartarus. Now I learn there is a repeating prophecy? I haven't even heard it yet, and I'm already skeptical. I don't want to see him get hurt, Chiron."

Nico felt an unexpected surge of gratitude. He'd never heard Mr. D come so close to admitting that he cared about another person.

"Does that mean I can share your popcorn?" Nico ventured.

"Absolutely not."

"Aren't we ignoring the bigger issue?" Will asked. "Because I feel like we're ignoring it."

"You mean me going to Tartarus," said Nico. "You've already made your feelings about that clear many times."

Will stared at the ceiling as if wondering why he had to be the voice of reason. "Whether or not it's a trap," he said, "it's still a trip to *Tartarus*. And I'm not a fan of those lines in the prophecy: *There leave something of equal value behind / Or your body and soul no one will ever find.*"

"Bit of a forced rhyme structure there," Mr. D noted between crunching.

Chiron shot him a dirty look. "I'm not ignoring that part," he said to Will. "And I agree, without more information, we could never sanction such a dangerous quest."

"I don't need a quest." Nico stood. Hearing Rachel's prophecy again, hearing it discussed aloud, made him feel suddenly resolved. Or maybe he was just feeling contrary and cranky after enduring *Nico's Greatest Nightmare Hits*, vols. I and II. "I *have* to go."

Chiron's expression was heavy and sad. Perhaps he was remembering all the other heroes he had trained over the centuries, who had said *I have to go* and then never returned. "Nico, we are in a period of relative peace. In recent months, we have learned at great personal cost that prophecies can be manipulated or just plain malicious. . . . No offense to Miss Dare."

"None taken," Rachel muttered. "I'm just happy to be spewing green gas again."

"It would be better for you to enjoy this time off," Chiron continued, "to heal instead of running after—"

"You're not the one being tormented in your dreams!"

Nico immediately wished he hadn't blurted it out like that. If

Bob really was in danger, doing whatever he could to reach out for help, then *he* was the one being tormented. No matter how painful Nico's dreams were, Tartarus was worse.

On the other hand, if something were tormenting an immortal Titan like Bob, a being older than the gods, what chance would Nico stand against such a force?

"Is that what you were dreaming about?" Will's voice stirred him from his thoughts. "Bob in Tartarus?"

"Not exactly," said Nico. "At least . . . not directly."

He decided to tell them *everything*. He started with the long summer of frequent flashbacks and nightmares. Clearly, Mr. D wasn't as interested in that part, since he'd heard all about it already. Instead of listening, he continually tossed popcorn into the air and tried to catch it in his mouth. (He missed. A lot. Which Nico took as proof that he was not the god of hand-eye coordination.)

As soon as Nico got to last night's greatest-hits parade of trauma, though, Mr. D hung on every word.

"Fascinating," Mr. D said once Nico had finished. "I know that mortal dream worlds are confusing, elaborate, and vivid, but that marathon sounds absolutely *absurd*."

"Thanks . . . I guess," said Nico. "Look, the point is that every memory, every thought and emotion in my head is screaming at me to *listen*. And Bob is the one who's calling out. It could be a trap, but I don't think so. Bob is suffering down there. He needs my help. And Rachel's prophecy getting stuck on repeat . . . I think that means the situation is getting worse. Bob is running out of time. I have to try to help him."

Dionysus picked a fleck of popcorn from his godly teeth. "I thought your father made it so *no one* alive could enter his realm anymore," he said. "You know, after that whole Doors of Death business."

"That doesn't mean I shouldn't go," said Nico. "There's always a way into the Underworld, and my father doesn't need to know. I have to try."

Rachel shivered. "But *leave something of equal value.* That's the part I can't wrap my mind around. Equal to *what?* Bob's life?"

Will's blue eyes fastened onto Nico. He had that slightly worried, slightly exasperated expression he got when one of his patients didn't follow doctor's orders. "Nico, you *can't* trade one life for another. Please tell me you'd never consider abandoning someone else in Tartarus to save Bob. Or even worse, sacrificing yourself."

Nico tamped down a wave of irritation. Of course that thought had occurred to him, too. And his parade of nightmares, all featuring people he had lost, only heightened his fears. But he had to help Bob. He had delayed as long as he could.

"You're assuming this is a rescue mission," he said. "What if Bob needs my help with something but *also* wants to stay in Tartarus?"

Mr. D cackled. "Who would want to *stay* in that realm of nightmares?"

"Or maybe the 'equal value' thing isn't a life for a life," Nico suggested weakly. "Maybe Bob wants to bring something back with him . . . like his broom or something. And he needs . . . a broom . . . of equal value."

Will gave Nico a look that said *Come on. You don't really believe that, do you?*

"And anyway," Nico forged ahead, "a mortal life wouldn't be equal to the life of a Titan, would it?"

Mr. D nodded thoughtfully, then glanced at Chiron. "The boy makes a good point. We immortals are clearly bigger-ticket items."

Chiron frowned. "We know so little about all this, Nico. And Tartarus . . . Well, it's not a place where any of us should venture, mortal or immortal."

"But I've *been* there," said Nico. "Did you all forget that I'm one of only three demigods who's ever come back from that wretched place alive? And I survived there the longest. If anyone can help Bob, it's me. I can do this on my own."

Will marched over and grabbed Nico's hand. "Yeah, that's not happening. If you go, I'm going with you."

Nico actually laughed. "No, you're not. That's the one thing that makes me okay with this quest—that I am *not* putting you in danger."

"Excuse me, Noble McSacrifice," Will said. "We're *both* perfectly capable of survival."

Chiron's hooves clopped nervously on the floorboards. "But a child of Apollo in Tartarus?"

Will's face fell. "I can manage."

Nico squeezed his hand. "Will, you're a child of the sun. Where I'm going . . . There's *no* sunlight down there. I know that seems obvious, but it's a lot worse than what you're probably picturing. The true nature of Tartarus . . . I never want you to have to experience that."

"So your clever plan," said Will, "is to sneak into the Underworld by yourself, hoping your father doesn't notice, then slip down into Tartarus and . . . what? Bring Bob back here?"

Nico shrugged. "I just want to give him a choice. He could go anywhere in the world. Or if Bob wants to stay at camp, why not? He could build his own cabin or—"

"Oh, could he?" Mr. D interrupted. "You're talking about releasing an *allegedly* reformed Titan into the world! And I am putting a great deal of emphasis on *allegedly*. You can't just make a decision like that without consulting the camp leadership, which would be . . . Oh, yes, me!"

"For once," said Chiron, "I agree with Mr. D. This is an extraordinarily dangerous idea."

"What options do I have at this point?" Nico growled. "Wait until my nightmares get so bad my head explodes? Wait until Rachel is spewing that prophecy twenty-four hours a day?"

"Would not be my first choice," Rachel admitted.

"I must say, however," Mr. D interjected, "this is better than any human film I've ever seen. The *drama*! The *twists*! I should have made a second bowl of popcorn."

Nico turned to face Chiron. "I can't let this keep happening. Someone is *begging* me for help, and I can't just sit here and ignore it."

The old centaur bowed his head, as if he were already contemplating the words he would have to write on Nico's tombstone. "I can see that I won't be able to dissuade you, no matter how foolish your plan. But even if I grant a formal quest, you're forgetting a very important detail: to succeed, a quest needs *three* people. That is tradition. That is the sacred number."

Nico shook his head. "I thought about that. Percy and Annabeth went through Tartarus, just the two of them." He glanced at Will. "If my stubborn boyfriend insists on going—"

"I do."

"Then Will and I can do the same. We're just as good a team. Besides, when we do find Bob, that'll bring the number up to three."

"A fair point," Chiron conceded grudgingly. "But . . . if you *do* need to leave something behind? Or someone?"

It was second nature for Nico to assume the worst, but at the moment, he wished that his brain was wired for a little more optimism. If saving Bob truly required Nico to leave something of equal value behind . . .

He looked at Will.

Nico's mouth dried up instantly. No, that couldn't be it. That would be so *cruel*.

But wasn't that Nico's whole history? Wouldn't this just be the cherry on the ice cream sundae of his life?

"Hey." Will squeezed his hand. "This isn't some hero play I'm trying to make. I promise you right here and right now, Nico, I'm not going to trade myself for Bob. And you're not going to have to make that choice."

Nico's jaw dropped. "I– What?"

"That's what you're worried about, isn't it? You think the prophecy is suggesting that one of us will have to stay behind to save Bob, right?"

Nico's mouth was still hanging open.

"I *do* know you, Nico," said Will. "And I'm telling you: that's not going to happen."

"Wow," Nico said. "I feel like I'm standing in front of all of you in my underwear."

Nico scanned the faces of the others: Mr. D, Rachel, Chiron. There were no more objections, no more debates about the ethics of rescuing Titans from Tartarus or trading lives to fulfill prophecies. They seemed to have accepted Nico's destiny, which scared Nico more than a little. This was really happening.

"You know," Mr. D said, breaking the silence, "I've changed my mind. You've earned my respect, Nico di Angelo." He handed over his nearly empty bowl of popcorn. "It's not hot anymore. But knock yourself out."

Nico's curiosity got the better of him. He scooped out a handful and gave it a try. To his surprise, even at room temperature, the buttery, herbed popcorn tasted like the ambrosia of the gods.

"You *made* this?" He tried not to sound too incredulous. "Like, magically?"

"Oh, no magic," Mr. D said. "I watched some videos on that

YouTube thing. Some fellow named Alton Brown taught me the perfect recipe."

Nico stared at him, but the god didn't seem to be joking. "Look at you, learning new things."

"I may be older than this entire country, but I've still got a few tricks up my sleeves."

"I don't think I've ever seen you wear anything that *had* sleeves."

Mr. D winked. "Exactly."

"Anyway," Will broke in, "before I change my mind, are we good here?" He turned to Chiron. "Is this quest official?"

The centaur took a deep breath. "Nico di Angelo."

"That's me," Nico said.

"Do you accept this quest that's been laid before you?"

Nico hesitated. So much for bravado. He wasn't sure what it would be like to return to his father's realm, or to visit the terrifying, draining reality of Tartarus. Also, between the recurring prophecy, the relentless dreams, and the voice of Bob crying out from Tartarus, it didn't feel like he had much of a choice. This was all inevitable, wasn't it?

On the other hand, he *was* sure he couldn't leave Bob down there any longer. Bob deserved help after everything he'd done and everything he'd had to endure.

"I accept," Nico said.

Mr. D clapped. "Bravo! Nico, you have yourself a quest. More importantly, you've given me the most entertaining night I've had in Camp Half-Blood in *months.*"

Chiron looked much less excited. Will squeezed Nico's hand, but Nico could feel the way his boyfriend's fingers trembled.

Rachel hugged herself. "I hope this works. For your sake, of course. But also because I'm supposed to leave for Paris next week.

I'd love to be able to make it there without prophecy smoke billowing out of me on the plane ride over."

"It'll work," said Nico. "I know it will."

But a small pit of dread settled at the bottom of Nico's stomach. He hoped he hadn't made the wrong decision.

"The two of *us*?" Nico turned to Will, who still wore a haunted look on his face. "What do you want to know about us?"

"Anything," Gorgyra said. "Tell me a story in exchange for a boat. That is all I will ask of you."

"There are so many stories we could tell," said Nico. "How do I narrow it down to just one?"

The nymph smiled. "Would you tell me how you two first came into each other's lives?"

"And if we do that," said Will sluggishly, "you'll help us?"

She nodded. "If it is satisfactory to me, yes."

Nico gazed at Will and shrugged.

Then he took a deep breath and began.

CHAPTER 6

Nico was doing his best not to get annoyed at how much preparation was swirling around him at the current moment.

He had accepted that Will was coming with him on this journey. The prospect still left Nico's nerves tingling around the edges, but he was also excited to show Will . . . well, his other home. Even if he didn't have the closest relationship with Hades, and despite the many difficult moments he'd had in the Underworld, Nico still had a fondness for the place. He wanted to get going.

But Will and Chiron were rummaging around Apollo's cabin in a state of high anxiety. The two were treating this like Will and Nico were about to go to war with every Titan, all the Roman emperors, *and* a reconstituted Gaea.

"Do you think I'll need warmer clothes, too?" Will asked Chiron. "I mean, it's cold in the Underworld, isn't it?"

"I don't really know," said Chiron.

In unison, they both turned to Nico, and their expressions made them look like confused puppy dogs.

"You might need a hoodie," he said. "At most."

"Okay, I'll pack an extra in case the first gets dirty," said Will.

Nico glanced down at Will's legs, which were, unsurprisingly, bare from the knees down. As usual, Will had on a pair of cargo shorts.

"Will," said Nico, "how are you worried about it being cold in the Underworld but you're still wearing shorts?"

He shrugged. "My legs don't really get cold. Plus, cargo shorts are so handy! You never know when you might need to store something in a pocket."

"I swear," Nico said with a sigh, "you're making this way more complicated than it has to be. All we need is water, *maybe* a change of clothes, and that's it."

"What about food?" said Will. "We're demigods, not ethereal spirits. We still have to eat."

"I've got that covered," said Nico with a sly smile. "Besides, if we run low, our friends in the Underworld will help us."

Will narrowed his eyes at Nico, but he didn't say anything. He stuffed another hoodie in his knapsack—Nico was certain that was the third one—and then crossed the cabin to the doorway. "Okay, I'm done this time," Will said. "Promise."

"Did you bring extra socks?" Chiron said, trotting over to them.

"Chiron, you don't even own socks, do you?" said Nico.

"No, but that doesn't mean I can't appreciate them. Nothing wrong with having an emergency pair of socks."

"I have enough of those, thank you," said Will. "Plus, if I hold up Nico one more minute, I think he'll send me to the Underworld the old-fashioned way."

"Like you said yesterday," said Nico, "you know me well."

"What are you bringing, Nico?" Chiron asked.

Nico grabbed the lapels of his leather bomber jacket. "This," he said, opening the jacket wide. He had on a black shirt with a white skull sitting beneath a red line and the letters AFI. Then he patted the weapon at his side. "And my trusty sword."

Will frowned. "Nothing else?"

"What else do I need?"

"Well," said Chiron, "at least allow the dryads to pack some ambrosia and nectar for you as a safety measure. What if one of you—or *both* of you—gets hurt?"

Nico groaned. "Fine. But then we leave after that, okay?"

"Deal," said Will.

They did not leave after that. Juniper insisted on providing a *fresh* batch of ambrosia squares. While those were being prepared, Grover the satyr called in via an Iris-message and demanded to give a little pep talk to Nico, which Nico begrudgingly sat through. It *was* sweet, but Nico thought everyone was overreacting. Extra hoodies, ambrosia, and well-meaning advice weren't going to make much difference once they got to Tartarus.

The thing that finally got Will to stop delaying the inevitable was when Nico told him that they were going to miss their train if they didn't get going.

"Okay, okay!" Will said, stuffing Juniper's ambrosia and nectar into his knapsack. (Nico wondered if that knapsack was somehow limitless, because no other bag could fit this much stuff.) "The taxi is coming soon?"

Chiron nodded. "A regular human taxi, as requested."

Nico gritted his teeth. "We'd get to Manhattan faster if we—"

"No!" said Will sharply. "No, after seeing Kayla and Austin off, I'm good with this."

"I think you're missing out, frankly," said Nico. "Those three old ladies are a million times cooler than we'll ever be. Or I could call Jules-Albert. That would be free."

"No zombie chauffeurs, either." Will's eyes were pleading. "Please grant me just a bit of normal, boring human travel before the Underworld."

Nico sighed. "Fine."

Which is why, a few minutes later, Nico and Will packed themselves into a boring yellow taxi on Farm Road 3.141. The driver was hunched over in the front seat. He had on a gray cardigan and a black driver's cap, and his car smelled vaguely of something smoky and dead.

The driver twisted around to stare at them. "You boys going to the Long Island Rail Road station in Montauk?"

"Uh, yeah," said Will. "Our train leaves in fifteen minutes. Will we be late?"

The man smiled, and he had a gold cap on one of his front teeth. "Not in this car you won't."

The engine revved, and the car seemed to jump forward as it sped away from Camp Half-Blood. There was no Gray Sisters magic at work here. No, this was just the beauty of a Long Island cabdriver on a tight schedule.

Nico had a blast with the window rolled down. As the traffic whizzed by on the Sunrise Highway, the driver regaled them with a story of how he once got a movie-star client from Sag Harbor to the Islip airport in under thirty minutes. As for Will, he was not doing as well. He had a white-knuckle grip on the door, his eyes were wide with terror, and he was obviously trying to get a handle on his breathing.

The driver got them to the station with six minutes to spare.

They raced up the steps to the platform, Nico easily outrunning his boyfriend, though that was mostly due to Will having to get his land legs again. "Was that worse than the Gray Sisters?" Will panted. " 'Cause it felt like it was worse than the Gray Sisters."

"You were the one who wanted to travel like a normal human," said Nico.

By the time the train arrived, they'd fallen into an uncomfortable silence. The doors opened, and they quickly moved inside. The car they'd chosen was about a third full, so they headed to a part where there were fewer people. Will struggled to fit his knapsack on the luggage rack above the seats.

"I'm telling you," said Nico, sliding into the seat closest to the window, "you won't need half that stuff on the journey."

"We'll see about—" Will began, and then something toppled out of his bag and smacked him in the face. "Ow!"

Nico restrained himself, because he knew laughing wouldn't make the situation better, even though it was very, very funny. Will rubbed at his face and then crouched down to pick up the thing that had fallen—a white sphere about the size of a softball.

"Will, what is that?"

"Nothing," he said, and stuffed it back into his knapsack.

"Oh, no. I must know what that is."

Will sighed, brought it back down, and handed it over. When Nico gripped it, the entire thing lit up so blazingly bright he almost dropped it.

"Sweet Hades, what is this?" Nico blinked repeatedly as little white spots appeared in his vision.

"Don't laugh," Will warned.

"I can't guarantee that I won't."

"It's a battery-powered sunlamp."

"A *what?*"

"Look," said Will, "I don't know what it's like down in the Underworld, and plenty of people use these things to help them get through the winter months when the sun is weak. It's a form of light therapy. I used to have one when I traveled with Mom."

Nico was actually impressed. "Okay, that's kind of amazing. And maybe it'll delay the effects of the Underworld on you."

"That's the idea." Will returned the sunlamp to his bag and sat down next to Nico. "I brought extra batteries, too."

"What *didn't* you bring on this quest, Will Solace?"

Will didn't answer. Moments later the train crawled forward, and soon the various Long Island neighborhoods were whizzing past them. Nico enjoyed the panorama: the woods, the industrial parks, the run-down strip malls and rows of cozy brick houses where normal mortals lived normal lives. Will, however, was clearly nervous. He bounced his right leg up and down as he glanced around the train car.

Nico reached over and placed his hand on the bobbing thigh. "Will, you can't do that the whole train ride."

"Sorry," he said. "Just trying to focus."

"I don't think you have to worry quite as much as you are," said Nico softly.

Will raised an eyebrow. "Nico, we're going to *Tartarus*. Are you seriously trying to tell me that it *wasn't* that bad when you were there?"

"I mean . . . Yeah, it was awful, okay? But I know a lot more about navigating it now than I did then. Plus, I'm *choosing* to go this time rather than being pulled down there and getting kidnapped by a pair of attention-seeking giants."

"I still think you're underselling the trauma," said Will. "But can you at least appreciate that I have *no* experience with the Underworld in general, let alone Tartarus? So this is freaking me out a lot more than it is you."

"Okay, okay," said Nico, reaching for Will's hand. "That's fair."

Will closed his eyes and leaned back in his seat. His breathing slowed, and Nico watched his chest rise and fall. Will did this sometimes when he needed to calm down, so Nico let him be.

Nico's gaze wandered over the train car. A couple of businessmen in plain black suits were having a muted conversation a few rows up. A woman with dark brown skin and locs was laughing at her young daughter, who was standing in the aisle without holding on to anything, trying to keep her balance.

"Subway surfing," said Will, which startled Nico.

"What?"

"You try to stay upright while the train moves without holding on to anything," he said. "Though I bet it would be much harder to do in the city. Those trains are way lurchier."

"How do *you* know about that? Do they even have subways in Austin, Texas?"

Will smirked. "There's a lot you don't know about me, Nico."

Nico scoffed. "Like what?"

"I love Golden Oreos, for starters."

"Oh, please. That's obvious. They're basically Apollo's version of an Oreo anyway."

"And the morally superior choice."

"We'll come back to that," said Nico. "What else don't I know about you, Will Solace?"

"I first visited New York City when I was . . ." Will counted on his fingers. "I think I was nine?" He gazed out the window as the train rolled into the next station. "Mom was on tour, and she was really excited because she was playing some big club in Manhattan a few nights in a row. But what I remember most about that trip was that she parked our van in this big, cavernous lot and said we would not drive a single second while we were in the city."

"Why?"

"She told me you don't really get to see New York unless you're on the subway. So, everywhere we went, we took the train. We rode it up and down Manhattan. We took it out to Coney Island one day to go on a bunch of rides. We went out to Queens, too, to see the place where the World's Fair was held a long time ago. We even made the most amateur mistake possible."

The train picked up speed again, and a conductor asked them to show their tickets. As Nico handed his over, he said to Will, "I'm afraid to ask what your mistake was."

"Well, it was very hot that summer," said Will. "It's not the same out at Camp Half-Blood. In Manhattan especially, the heat gets trapped between all the buildings, and it's like a giant oven. So we'd just come out of the Met, and by the time we'd walked the two or three blocks to the train, we were sweating buckets. So we were super excited when the train arrived, because one of the cars was completely empty! Guaranteed seats in a perfectly air-conditioned car during the summer are so rare. Usually all the cars are jam-packed and humid."

"Okay," said Nico. "But . . . the empty car was a good thing, right?"

Will's smile faltered. "Well . . . no. Turns out if an entire train is packed except for one car, that's actually a warning sign."

Nico twisted up his face. "A warning for . . . *what?*"

Will wrinkled his nose.

"Oh, gods. What, Will?"

"Let's just say that when the doors closed, a very pungent and recognizable smell filled that car. Someone had, uh, made a deposit on the floor."

"NO!" Nico grimaced. "Are you serious?"

"It happens," said Will. "I guess someone couldn't wait?"

"I would pass away," said Nico. "Right on the spot."

Will laughed at that, which felt like a small victory to Nico. "We just moved cars at the next stop. And that was when Mom taught me about subway surfing."

"Wow. I didn't get to travel to New York until the Battle of Manhattan."

Will grimaced. "Not a great introduction to the city. Did you know that years before that, my mom and I were actually in Manhattan when my satyr found me and brought me to Camp Half-Blood? Monsters attacked me downtown."

"No!" said Nico.

"Remind me to tell you that story someday."

The way he said it, Nico got the message that he wasn't quite ready to share the details.

"Sometimes I forget you've been all over this continent," said Nico. "I mean, I've been a lot of places, too, but mostly since coming to Camp Half-Blood. Do you ever miss traveling?"

"Occasionally," said Will. "But I think it was more that I liked being with my mom. She has such an adventurous spirit. It's hard not to feel the same way when you're around her and she wants to go see the world's biggest ball of twine or something."

Nico tried to imagine the world's biggest ball of twine. He found the concept vaguely terrifying.

He glanced a few rows up at the woman and her kid, who now sat in her mother's lap. He leaned against Will's shoulder. "Did you ever want like . . . like a normal childhood?"

He could feel Will fidget. "I don't think so," said Will after a moment of silence. "Maybe sometimes I wanted the things I saw other kids experience. But I also got to travel all the time! My mom is basically like my best friend, and I wouldn't trade that for the world."

Nico considered that. Some days, he struggled just to picture his mother's face. He remembered her voice in his nightmares: *Vita mia.*

"Do you ever think about what life would be like if you weren't a demigod?" he asked.

Will jerked away from him. "What? Why would you say that, Nico?"

"It's just a question."

"No, I don't ever think about that." Will gazed into the distance. "I think about all the wonderful experiences I've had because of who I am. I've gotten to help people—to save their *lives*, Nico!—and I've protected the world from imminent danger."

Then he gave Nico one of his soul-warming smiles. "I can heal people. I can glow in the dark. And . . . well, I met *you.*"

"Oh, *gods*," groaned Nico. "No cheesiness! It's too early in the day, Will!"

Will snuggled up to him. "But it's true. I'm very thankful we're in each other's lives."

"You cheated with that answer," said Nico, "but I'll allow it."

Will planted a kiss on Nico's temple. "My grumpy ball of darkness."

"The world's *largest* grumpy ball of darkness, thank you very much."

They spent the rest of the train ride in silence. At some point, Will began to doze. Nico watched the world go by outside. At Woodside, the last stop before Manhattan, the mother and daughter got off. The young girl skipped alongside her mother on the platform, and her carefreeness made Nico's heart sink.

Will was right. There was so much about being a demigod that Nico would never want to give up, and he certainly didn't want to even *imagine* a world without Will. But there was more to what they'd been born to than just abilities, demigod friends, and ridiculous adventures.

The images from Nico's dream last night swirled around in his mind. There were . . . darker aspects. Loneliness. Pain. Isolation. And all those things made up who Nico was. Did Will not see that? Or did he only focus on the positive things about being a demigod, the things full of light and promise, the things he *wanted* to see?

Sometimes Nico wasn't sure. Did that make him a bad boyfriend? He had nothing to judge this against because he'd never gotten as close to anyone as he had with Will. How did other couples do this? Did Annabeth and Percy ever doubt each other?

At the thought of his friends, Nico realized that there was a possible solution to *some* of his anxiety over this trip, and maybe Will's, too. Who else knew more about Tartarus?

When the train finally pulled into Penn Station, Will was quick to rouse. He yawned. "Didn't expect to fall asleep. Where to now?"

"A little last-minute detour," said Nico, shaking off the nerves that had crept over him. "Humor me, and I promise it will be worth it."

As Nico explained that they had to catch another train uptown, he noticed Will reaching under the collar of his blue T-shirt and running his fingers along the gold chain he wore.

The chain Nico had given him.

And like Will's smile, it warmed Nico. Maybe he was overthinking all of this. It was clear Will cared deeply for him, and Nico let that one little gesture push away his worries as they headed into the maze of Penn Station.

CHAPTER 7

Parts of Penn Station had been renovated recently, but it was still nowhere near as picturesque as Grand Central Station, a fact that Nico always found disappointing. The lower level was dimly lit, crowded, and claustrophobic. As they navigated their way from the LIRR terminal to the subway, Nico grumbled to Will about the station's dismal design.

"It's not that bad!" said Will, pointing to a nearby food stand. "Those pretzels smell delicious."

"I don't think the scent of baked dough counts as a positive architectural feature," said Nico.

"You're just upset that I didn't let us shadow-travel or use the Gray Sisters or your zombie chauffeur."

"Any of which would have been easier *and* more fun!"

"What have I told you about shadow-travel?" Will chided him. "It's not good for your health. You should only use it for emergencies, and this is not an emergency. Yet."

As soon as he said this, a woman who was *definitely* a tourist walked straight into him, spilling her iced coffee down the front of Will's shirt and jeans.

Once again, Nico had to hold back a laugh. The poor woman was incredibly apologetic and offered to buy Will a shirt from a gift shop. Personally, Nico would have *loved* to see Will in an I ♥ NY tee, but Will muttered that it was fine, accidents happen, and they continued on their way.

"Is it an emergency yet?" Nico asked as they waited at the platform for the E train, a puddle of beverage forming around Will's feet.

"It's coffee," said Will matter-of-factly. "We'll be in the warm open air soon enough, and it'll dry. Still not an emergency."

It wasn't an emergency when the E train they were waiting for didn't show up for thirty minutes due to a signal problem somewhere downtown. It *also* wasn't an emergency when the 6 line they'd transferred to sat in the tunnel outside the Ninety-Sixth Street station for another ten minutes, Will's clothes still damp, making the subway car smell like the dumpster behind a Starbucks.

"This train is now out of service," the conductor announced when they *finally* pulled into the station.

"I can literally hear you saying *I told you so* in your mind, Nico," said Will when they emerged on the Upper East Side. "You're basically yelling at me through telepathy."

Nico laughed super hard. "I said no such thing!"

"Exactly. But you're *thinking* it."

Nico mimed a zipper across his lips. "I am nothing if not supportive of you, Will Solace."

Will turned his face to the early-fall sun and breathed in deeply. "All right, Nico di Angelo. So what's this detour you had in mind?"

"Right this way," Nico said.

The two of them dodged pigeons and some slow-walking tourists in a neighborhood that was very much alive and very much unaware of the gods, demigods, and monsters who called it home. The Mist prevented most humans from ever seeing that magical side of the world. To a mortal, a glowing sword might look like a baseball bat, because that's what their brain could accept. A ravenous harpy might look like a bad-tempered chicken. Even a celestial fight between gods and Titans might be written off as a freak thunderstorm. This was a good thing, considering how many wars for humanity had taken place here in Manhattan. But the Mist sometimes deceived demigods, too, obscuring the truth of the immense, primordial powers at play, and that's why Nico was taking Will to a small apartment on 104th and First Ave.

Because only two other demigods had ever survived a journey through Tartarus, and for Will's peace of mind as well as Nico's own, he wanted to compare notes.

Will did not figure out where Nico was taking him until they were in front of the building. Then he stopped cold.

"What are we doing here?" he asked. "Recruiting Percy? I thought he was in California."

Nico scowled. "Not recruiting him. Hades *no*. I wouldn't dream of that. He more than deserves time off."

"Then—"

"You'll see." Nico led the way inside and up the stairs.

When the apartment's front door opened, Sally Jackson smiled, her daughter, Estelle, firmly attached at the hip.

"Hello, boys. Been a few months since I got a demigod visit," she said, and Estelle cooed. "Come on in."

It was strange being in Percy's home without him. Sally set Estelle in her playpen and then headed for the kitchen. She returned with a plate of blue sugar cookies. "You know," she said, setting them down on the dining room table, "I *could* make cookies in any other color. But it's mostly habit at this point."

"Thank you, but we don't want to put you to any trouble," said Will. He glanced at Nico. "Do we?"

"No . . ." said Nico, though he considered Sally's cookies a really great kind of trouble. "I just wanted to contact Percy and Annabeth, and I thought, well, this might be the best place to do it from."

"Contact him?" asked Sally, taking the empty chair across from them. "About what?"

As best as he could, Nico briefly summarized the story of Bob and the prophecy.

Sally turned down a corner of her mouth. "You're not thinking of asking Percy to go with you, are you? Because he's just gotten settled at college, and this is the closest thing to normal he's—"

"Not at all," Nico cut her off. "I promise."

"Good." Sally crossed her arms over her chest. "Because I would *never* want Percy or Annabeth to have to face that place again. You shouldn't go either, dear, no matter who is in danger."

"It's different for me," Nico assured her. "As the son of Hades, I know my way around. But Will . . ."

Will leaned back, understanding dawning on his face. "Oh, I get it. You want *me* to talk to Percy. So he can discourage me from going?"

"No," Nico protested, though maybe that thought had been in the back of his mind. "But I know you're nervous about it. And you worry I'm underselling the danger. So I thought it might help to hear from someone who isn't related to Hades *and* who still survived Tartarus."

"Barely," Sally murmured. "Percy doesn't tell me the details of everything he's been through. I think he believes he's protecting me. But I *do* know that his worst nightmares are about Tartarus."

Will gulped. "Wow, this is already helping so much. . . ."

Nico tried to push down his rising frustration. "Will, just *talk* to Percy, okay?"

Will managed a smile. "Yeah, of course. It'll be nice to see him.

And Annabeth, too, if we can . . . Wait, how exactly are we contacting them—Iris-message?"

Nico turned to Sally. "I was hoping you might know their schedules? I don't want to send them a glowing hologram when they're in the middle of a lecture or something."

Sally smirked. "I'm not saying I have their college schedules memorized, but this time of day, West Coast time, I imagine they're both at Percy's dorm . . . hopefully studying for their English exam."

"Perfect." Nico pulled a golden drachma out of his pocket. "Next question, Ms. Jackson. Do you have a standard way of sending him Iris-messages? Like, so I don't have to spray water all over your apartment?"

"Very thoughtful," said Sally. "I have just the thing. Come on."

She gathered up Estelle and led them down the hallway, Nico and Will both grabbing some cookies on the way.

They ended up in Percy's old bedroom, which again, Nico found very strange. He remembered years ago, coming in through that fire escape window and, to his surprise, being offered some of Percy's birthday cake. It had been one the first glimmers Nico had ever felt of true friendship.

"Here we are," said Sally, gesturing to a contraption on Percy's dresser.

Will laughed with delight. "That's actually kind of brilliant."

Nico had to agree. Percy had rigged a humidifier next to a desk lamp, so when Sally turned it on, a veil of steam bloomed upward, the water droplets breaking the light into shards of color—just what you needed to ask a favor of Iris, the rainbow goddess.

Nico held up his gold drachma. "O goddess, accept our offering," he prayed. Then he tossed the coin into the steam, where it promptly disappeared. "Show me Percy Jackson at New Rome University."

Seconds later, a familiar face took up most of the image of the Iris-message. Percy's green eyes looked like blotches of algae floating in the steam. "Nico?" he asked. Then he stepped back and took in more of the scene. "*Mom?* Is everything okay?"

Estelle squealed with delight at the sound of her brother's voice. Sally laughed. "Yes, Percy, everything's fine. Your friends just stopped by for a visit!"

From what little Nico could see in the background, Percy was indeed in his dorm room. There was a small unmade bed to the left and a desk covered in books and papers. Percy himself looked somewhat disheveled, too.

"Nico!" said Percy. "Oh, man, it's so good to see you!"

Annabeth loomed into view, pushing Percy out of the way. "What's going on? Do we need to come fight someone?" Then her expression brightened. "Oh, hey, Nico. And is that Will? Will Solace! How are you?"

"We're good," said Will, beaming. "How's college life?"

"Shockingly normal," said Annabeth. "Aside from the stray monster or two, the biggest worry we've had is getting to class on time."

"Only *I* seem to have trouble with that," grumbled Percy.

"You're not missing classes, are you?" said Sally.

Percy's eyes went wide. "No! Definitely not. Never missed a class in my life."

"Didn't you set your high school on fire once?" said Annabeth. "I bet you missed class that day."

"I— You know that isn't what happened! They were *empousai!* How was I supposed to know that Hecate was setting me up?"

Annabeth smirked at the others. "He's so easy to wind up."

Percy grunted. "Anyway . . ." he said, peering at Nico and Will. "What's up?"

"So, we wanted to get your advice," said Nico. "About a quest."

"Whoa, you guys got one?" said Annabeth. "Oooh, tell us about it!"

"Well," said Nico, grimacing, "we're going down to Tartarus."

There was a long silence. If it wasn't for Annabeth and Percy blinking, Nico would have believed there was some type of problem with the Iris-message connection. They'd recently gone almost a year without magical communications because of the evil Triumvirate, so it wasn't like that was impossible.

Still . . . Nico should have anticipated their reaction.

Finally, Annabeth turned to Percy. "He said Tartarus, right?"

"Maybe it's a quest for tartar sauce," Percy said. "Something low-stakes and delicious."

"Yeah, I'm going with that." Annabeth looked back at Nico. "So, a tartar-sauce quest. Good for you. Goes great with fish and chips."

"Come on, guys," said Nico. "I'm being serious."

"Oh, we know," said Annabeth. "So are we! You should *definitely* take up a tartar-sauce quest. Maybe consider a nice lemon aioli? That could be exciting."

"Annabeth, please—" Will began.

"I saw a kid in the dining hall the other day mix every condiment available into a masterful nightmare of a sauce," said Percy. "He called it the Explosion."

"Because it would be an explosion in the mouth," said Annabeth. "Makes a lot of sense."

Nico groaned, and Estelle giggled in her mother's arms.

"Sounds like you all need to discuss this among yourselves," said Sally, bouncing Estelle gently on her hip.

"There's nothing to discuss!" said Percy.

"Love you, Percy!" Sally called out. "Stop missing classes!"

There was another awkward bout of silence once Sally and Estelle left the room.

Nico sat on the edge of Percy's bed. "Will and I are going whether we discuss this or not," he said. "I was hoping you two could give Will something in the way of advice so that the journey isn't as hard on him."

Annabeth shook her head. "It's Tartarus, Nico. You almost lost your mind there once before. We weren't even in Tartarus that long, and it nearly destroyed us."

"I practically lost myself in that place," said Percy. "The things I saw . . . The things I *did*." He shuddered. "I still have nightmares about Akhlys."

"Well, this *definitely* doesn't make me feel any better," said Will, plopping down next to Nico.

"And you two are *willingly* going there?" said Annabeth, her voice pitched high. "What is this quest? What possible reason—"

"Bob!" Nico shouted, louder than he'd intended. "I'm going back for *Bob*."

Now it was Percy and Annabeth's turn to look uncomfortable. Percy closed his eyes for a long moment. "Oh, Nico," he said. "I'm sorry."

"I know this is going to sound terrible," said Annabeth, "but I wasn't even thinking of him. Gods, how could I forget?"

Will reached over and grazed the back of Nico's hand with his fingertips. "We know this quest is a bad idea, but . . . there've been some developments. Nico, tell them."

And so Nico did, as carefully as he could. When he recounted his most recent string of nightmares—the voice calling for help, the apparitions all telling Nico to listen—Percy and Annabeth became visibly upset.

"We shouldn't have left Bob down there," said Percy softly. "I knew this would come back to haunt us one day."

"I suspected it would, too," said Annabeth. "But . . . why *you*,

Nico? I mean, no offense, but wouldn't Bob reach out to me and Percy as well, since we were the ones who saw him last?"

Nico didn't answer, though one theory lurked in a dark corner of his mind: *Maybe because Bob thought I would help, but he wasn't sure about you two.*

Will seemed to pick up on his brooding thoughts. He hooked his finger around Nico's. "Guys, I agree it's troubling that this prophecy seems geared only for Nico. We don't know what Bob's situation is. We don't know if this is some kind of trap—"

"I don't care if it is!" said Nico. "Because Bob is really in pain. I *know* it. I need to do something to help him. We can't leave him down there to suffer."

Will squeezed his hand. "Exactly. We have to try. So if there's anything you guys could tell us that might help . . ."

Percy's gaze became unfocused, as if he were staring into the past. "Well, Bob *is* a former Titan. That means Tartarus itself doesn't affect him the way it does us. At least he has some mental protection against the place. If he survived that battle with Gaea's minions . . ."

Nico could tell Percy was grasping at reasons for optimism, but they all knew Tartarus was the bleakest, most dangerous, most toxic environment in creation. Even if Bob had some resistance, even if he was an immortal being . . . there were plenty of things down there that could make a Titan wish he *could* die. Nico was beginning to wonder if this Percabeth pep talk had been such a good idea after all.

"Is there any protection I can bring?" Will asked. He let go of Nico's hand and rummaged through his knapsack. He pulled out a sun globe. "I do have this."

"Why would you need—?" Annabeth began. "Oh, *duh*. Child of Apollo. That's actually really smart."

Percy frowned. "Yeah, no sunlight . . . I didn't consider that.

Tartarus is going to be worse for you than anyone else." When Annabeth gently slapped his shoulder, he winced. "What? I'm not wrong."

Will's whole body seemed to deflate. "So there's nothing else I can do?"

"Now, wait a second," said Annabeth. "That's not what either of us said. In fact, I would say that you and Nico have one *big* advantage."

Percy nodded. "You two have *each other.*"

Nico squinted at him. "Um . . . okay? What does that mean? Besides sounding like a cheesy Hallmark card."

"It's exactly what it sounds like," said Annabeth. "Because that cheesiness is what's going to make the journey survivable."

"Okay," said Will. "Meaning what, though?"

"Tartarus wears down your sense of self," said Percy. "It honestly feels like it was *designed* to make mortals suffer. The more time you spend down there, the worse it gets."

"I remember that," said Nico, a familiar coldness creeping into his limbs. "It's like . . . an endless dark voice in your head, telling you that you're the worst."

Percy was nodding. "And then there's the Cocytus—the River of Lamentation—which is like that times ten."

Will ran his fingers through his blond hair. "So . . . how is this supposed to help, exactly?"

"Nico went through Tartarus alone," said Percy. "Well, maybe not totally alone, but he certainly didn't have someone alongside him who cared about him and was invested in making sure he survived the journey. Honestly, I don't know how he did it."

Nico's ears burned. He wasn't sure if the awe in Percy's voice made him feel pleased or resentful.

Annabeth wrapped her arm around Percy. "Being together is what made the difference for the two of us." Her gray eyes fixed intently on Nico, then Will. "We reminded each other about the world above. We did what we could when one of us was suffering to try and lift their spirits. Told jokes. Stories. Anything. Having a companion makes all the difference down there."

"And who knows, Will?" Percy added. "Maybe you'll find that being the son of Apollo gives you some kind of advantage. It's possible that your powers will actually be *stronger* down there."

"But don't depend on it," said Annabeth. "We both felt drained all the time. If it hadn't been for Bob . . ." She gazed at Percy, a regretful sadness on her face.

"We wouldn't have made it," he said, finishing her sentence.

Nico was now more certain than ever that he had to complete this quest. It wasn't right that Bob had gotten left behind, and he would do pretty much anything to fix this.

"Thanks," said Will. "That actually does help to know." But he didn't speak with much certainty. When his eyes met Nico's, they betrayed his fear.

"Well, thanks, guys," said Nico. "We should let you go."

"Be careful," said Annabeth. "I know it goes without saying, but we don't want to lose either of you."

"We've all lost so much already," said Percy. "Honestly, though? If any two people could survive a journey to Tartarus and back, I think it's you two."

Warmth spread through Nico's chest. He remembered why he'd been drawn to Percy Jackson in the first place. Like Will Solace, Percy had an inexplicable, stubborn faith in other people.

"Thanks," Nico said. "That means a lot, coming from you."

"One last thing," said Annabeth. "I don't know if it's possible, but see if you can find Bob's cat."

"Small Bob!" exclaimed Percy. "Oh, man, I hope he's survived, too."

"A *cat?*" said Will.

"Not just any cat," said Annabeth. "He's a *spartos*, created from the fang of a saber-toothed tiger. He looks like a calico cat, but he's so much more."

"Bob and that cat were inseparable," said Percy. "Bring them *both* home if you can."

"We'll do our best," said Nico, nodding. "Promise."

They said their good-byes, and the Iris-message faded.

Will and Nico sat in silence for a few moments before Sally Jackson returned. "You get what you needed?"

"Yes, thank you," said Will.

"I take it Percy couldn't talk you out of it?" asked Sally.

"He tried," said Nico. "You would've been proud."

"But we're still going," Will said, and Nico heard resolve in his voice.

Sally Jackson sighed. "Well then, you boys want some snacks for the road?"

Nico got the sense that this wasn't the first time she'd had to deal with despondent demigods in her home. She seemed unfazed by it all.

Will helped her pack some blue sugar cookies in his bottomless knapsack while Nico wandered into the living room. Displayed on a bookshelf were various photos of Percy through the years. Nico picked up one of a young Percy, maybe eight years old, standing next to his mother, arms around her waist, his mouth open in a wide smile. They looked to be in Central Park, and snow was falling around them.

"Sometimes I need reminders of the normal, good times," said Sally as she came up behind Nico. "What with all the chaos in our lives. Despite it all, we actually *did* get to do some fun family stuff together."

Nico turned to her. "You're not afraid."

"Hmm? What do you mean?"

"All this talk here today . . . you didn't bat an eye. Doesn't it ever freak you out?"

"It has," she acknowledged. "And I've seen some terrible things. There were certainly moments when I wasn't sure my son would come back. He disappeared for *months* that one time, remember?"

Nico nodded. "Yeah, I was the first Half-Blood camper to find him in Camp Jupiter after he was swapped with Jason Grace."

"But at the same time, he's part of something wonderful now, and honestly, that makes it a lot easier."

"Part of what?" asked Will, rubbing blue crumbs from the corners of his mouth.

"Did you leave any for me?" Nico said.

Will just smiled.

"Percy's part of a great big family," said Sally. "He's got friends like you and Will, and many others across the globe. And all of you, at a moment's notice, would do everything in your power to save the people you love. What more could a mother ask for?"

As Will and Nico left Sally Jackson's home, Nico kept thinking about Sally's words.

Family.

I guess Camp Half-Blood is basically one big super-dysfunctional family, he thought.

He wasn't sure what awaited him and Will in the coming days, but he grabbed Will's hand as they walked back to the subway. If they were going to survive Tartarus, then it was time to believe what Annabeth and Percy had told them.

They'd have to do it *together.*

CHAPTER 8

After an uneventful ride south on the 6 train, Nico and Will made their way to the southernmost edge of Central Park. Some of the leaves on the trees were beginning to turn yellow, and a light breeze rustled them. Joggers and cyclists zipped along the main road as Nico guided Will toward the woodland. When Nico stopped in front of a large grouping of boulders made up of Manhattan schist, Will raised an eyebrow.

"Where do we go next?" he asked.

Nico pointed at the rocks. "Through there."

Will regarded the giant gray slabs. "Am I missing something? Nico, they're just rocks. What are we supposed to do?"

"Oh, *I* am not doing anything," said Nico proudly. "I need you to sing."

Will looked around him. "Is this a prank? Did you and Mr. D come up with this? Are there hidden cameras?"

"I'm honored that you think I'm capable of orchestrating a prophecy to pull off such a thing, but no, this isn't a joke. This is the *literal* Door of Orpheus."

"Oh," said Will. Then: "*Oh.* So it's . . ."

Nico nodded. "One of the only remaining secret entrances into the Underworld."

"Which Orpheus opened with music," said Will.

"Exactly," said Nico. "You think you could give it a try?"

Will took a deep breath. "Yeah, I can. And then . . . that's it?"

"That's it," Nico agreed. "Our journey can begin."

Will turned around slowly, taking in the gorgeous Central Park trees that rose above them. "I don't know how long this adventure is going to take," he said as he spun, "so first I just want to get a last look at everything. To recharge my internal battery."

"You're cute when you're nervous." Will came to a stop, and Nico reached out to bring him into a hug. When they let go, Nico said, "We're going to be fine. Just keep in mind what Percy and Annabeth said. We'll stick close together, okay? I know the Underworld well."

"I'm not that worried about *you*," said Will. "I'm more freaked out about how *I'm* going to react. It's going to be dark, scary. I'll be surrounded by death and sadness and misery."

"It's not *all* bad," said Nico. "Besides, our friends will help us."

"The troglodytes, you mean?"

Nico smiled, picturing the small froglike humanoids who had helped them defeat Nero. "We'll be in good hands. Little webbed hands with lots of pointy claws."

Will scratched his head. "Okay, I guess it'll be nice to see them. Are you sure they'll help us again, though?"

"Why wouldn't they?" said Nico.

"Well . . . we kinda destroyed their home, didn't we?"

"That was an accident, first of all. We had no idea the *tauri silvestres* had followed us!"

"I know, but *still*. Wouldn't you be mad if someone accidentally destroyed Camp Half-Blood by allowing mad bulls in to trample it?"

"Second of all," said Nico, "I helped the trogs find a new home."

It took Will a moment to put the pieces together. "So . . . you're expecting them to help us. . . . You found them a new home. . . . You relocated them to the *Underworld?*"

Nico nodded. "They're even farther underground now, and less likely to be found. As long as they stay out of my father's view, they'll be safer."

Will shook his head, clearly mystified. "I don't understand how anyone could live down there."

A burst of irritation jolted Nico's heart. He pressed his lips together so as not to blurt out his initial reaction, which wasn't very kind. "The Underworld isn't what you think it is," he said quietly. "There's a lot more to it. You'll see."

"Okay," said Will. "I trust you."

This time when he smiled, it didn't really make Nico feel better. So Nico just stepped aside and gestured at the rocks. "A song, please."

Will approached the mass of boulders. He took another deep breath and started into a soft, winding melody. It was a familiar one to Nico—he'd heard Will sing it when he was using his healing abilities on someone. As Will's voice rose and fell, Nico saw small green shoots sprout up from the ground around him. A few of them bloomed yellow flowers.

"Well, *that's* new," Nico said aloud to himself.

No sooner had he uttered those words than the rocks groaned and shuddered. Will stopped singing and moved back, his eyes full of wonder, as a triangular crevice appeared, just big enough for a person to squeeze through. Inside, steps led down into deep darkness.

Will covered his mouth and nose. "Ugh, what's that *smell?*"

The odors hit Nico then: mildew, decay, dust . . .

Home.

"That's the Underworld." He drew his Stygian iron sword. "I'll go first."

Will grabbed his arm. "Shouldn't I use my glow-in-the-dark power for more light?"

Nico shook his head. "Save that for later. No sense draining yourself."

There was a sheen of sweat on Will's forehead. "If you're sure . . ."

Rather than draw this out any longer, Nico reached down and grabbed Will's hand. "Come on," he said, and he led his boyfriend into the stairwell. After the first few steps, Nico glanced back to see the shape of Will's curls in the bright light of Central Park behind him. Then, with a loud groan, the crevice closed, and darkness swallowed the two demigods.

Only the blade of Nico's sword cast any light: a dim purple glow that made the shadows feel even thicker.

"Oh, wow," Will said. "It's *really* dark down here."

Nico was ready to crack a terrible joke, but right then a sensation of dread trickled over his skin. He raised his sword and peered into the gloom. The passage continued down as far as he could see, silent and empty.

"Nico, what is it?"

Something rustled in the darkness, but *behind* them, where the Door of Orpheus had just closed.

Nico spun, gently pushing Will to one side, and stuck his sword in that direction.

There was nothing.

"What's happening?" Will demanded.

Nico brought his sword back close to his body. He turned to Will. "I think you got me all amped up, is all. I'm imagining things."

Will didn't look convinced. Unfortunately, Nico wasn't sure *he* believed it, either.

"Okay," Will said. "But is it going to be this dark the whole time?"

"Oh, no, not at all. We have to descend these steps for a while, but once we emerge in the Underworld, it's . . . Well, you'll see. This is the only part without any light." He paused. "At least, before we get to Tartarus."

"Good to know," Will muttered.

Nico headed down the narrow stairway, and Will followed. The steps were much steeper than Nico would have liked, but that was mostly because he was worried for Will. He could hear his boyfriend's footsteps echoing around him—Will was tapping his feet on every step as if to make sure it was solid. After a few minutes, Nico paused.

"You're nervous," he said. "Just take the steps like you normally would. It'll be all right."

Will started to answer, then stopped and looked behind him. "Did you hear that?"

"Hear what?"

"Is something following us?"

Nico didn't hear anything this time.

"Maybe it's your imagination?" said Nico. "This place can feel very strange the first time."

"Okay," said Will, his voice shaky. "Lead the way, then."

They continued. Will had Nico stop a few more times, but in each instance, Nico couldn't hear whatever it was his companion had. So they kept going, descending deeper and deeper. Nico knew that the stairway was lengthy, so he tried to remain as calm as possible as he put one foot in front of the other, careful not to slip on the slimy steps.

It wasn't long before impatience began to creep along Nico's spine. He remembered descending these same steps years ago when he had led Percy to his father. The memory stung a little; he hadn't really wanted to betray Percy, but he'd needed to know more about his own childhood, which he'd lost in the River Lethe. But Nico recalled that it had maybe taken an hour or so to traverse the entire set of steps.

Had it been an hour since Will parted the stones? Or had it been longer? Weren't journeys supposed to feel shorter when you'd done them before?

Will echoed Nico's thoughts. "How much farther do we have to go?" he asked. "I feel like we've been going down forever."

"I think we've got a bit more," said Nico, panting. His arm was tired from holding out his sword; the last time he'd made this journey, Percy had been the one to light the way. Funny how the older Nico got, the more he saw things about Percy differently.

"Like, I get that it's the *Underworld*," said Will. "So we have to go under the earth. But this—"

"Shhh." Nico froze so suddenly that Will ran into him.

"What is it?" whispered Will.

"Do you hear that?"

They both stood still. From somewhere ahead came a muted roar, like a rainstorm against a metal roof.

"What is that?" asked Will.

Nico smiled. "That's the River Styx. We're almost there."

The two of them forged ahead. Nico began to take the steps two at a time. He nearly slipped on one of the stones, then steadied himself and waited for Will to catch up.

Soon, a dim gray light filled the tunnel. Nico did his best to keep his cool as they continued their descent. The roar of the Styx turned from muted to thunderous. The steps started to level out. When Nico reached the bottom of the stairwell, he emerged into a large cavern lit by glowing stalactites overhead. To his right, the River Styx spilled over the edge of a towering climb and cascaded down a set of rocky rapids.

And in the distance . . . the Underworld.

Fires guttered on the ramparts of Erebos, the kingdom of death. Masses of ghosts converged on the great iron gates like a fog bank, clamoring to get in. Beyond those walls, Nico knew, lay the ghosts' final destinies: Elysium for the lucky few who had been virtuous in life, the Fields of Punishment for the wicked, and the bleak Fields of Asphodel for the indifferent and the neutral, which was most of humanity. Beyond those fields would be Hades's palace, all sharp angles and shadows. Nico was glad they were too far away to be able to make out any of those details. Will didn't need to see the fates of the dead. He was already nervous enough.

Nico's head spun with exhaustion. For a moment, he thought he saw a dark shape in his peripheral vision, something strange and menacing, but when he turned, there was only Will.

"Welcome to the Underworld," Nico said.

Will frowned, then put a hand behind his head. He was still breathing heavily. "Is this a joke?"

"A *joke?*" Nico was stunned. "Why would you call my father's home a *joke?*"

"What are you talking about?"

"What are *you* talking about?"

"You said we were here," said Will.

"We are!" Nico spread his arms wide.

Will fixed his eyes on the distance. "Um, no, we're not."

Nico turned to look again and—

What?!

They were back in the stairwell. The cavernous vista of Erebos was gone. The steps before them seemed to continue endlessly down into darkness.

"No!" screamed Nico. "What is happening? We just made it and—"

"Can you hear that?" asked Will, cutting him off. "The river? Because I can."

They fell silent again. Sure enough, the distant rush of the River Styx echoed up through the tunnel.

"I don't understand," said Nico. "I *saw* the Underworld. I saw the River Styx and . . . and . . ."

Will sat down on the steps. "There wasn't anything, Nico. It was just . . . more stairs."

"That's impossible. That's not how this is supposed to work."

"Regardless, we're still not there. Do you think your father is trying to prevent us from entering the Underworld?"

"No!" said Nico. Then: "I don't *think* so. He shouldn't even know that we're here."

"You sure about that?" said Will.

Nico hesitated. "Let's keep going. If I see the end of the tunnel again, I'll ask if you see it, too."

He helped Will up, and then they pushed on. Nico wasn't positive, but it seemed like another hour passed before the sound of the Styx finally got louder and the tunnel filled with gray light once more. Nico reached back for Will, and his boyfriend's hand slipped into his.

"There," said Nico. "Do you see that brightness ahead?"

After a short pause, Will said, "Actually . . . yeah, I do."

"Okay!" said Nico. "Good. Let's keep moving."

Moments later, as the darkness receded, Nico spotted the base of the steps.

"Can you see *that*?" said Nico, pointing.

"Yes!" said Will, breathless. "It's the end!"

They rushed down the remaining steps and into the cavern. As before, the Styx's waterfall roared to Nico's right. Across the river loomed the burning ramparts of Erebos.

Nico had this whole plan in his head to explain the geography of Erebos to Will so he'd have some idea where they were heading, but when he turned to speak, his heart sank.

It wasn't just Will's panicked expression that terrified him. Somehow, their surroundings had changed again. Nico couldn't believe it, but they now stood in the woods of Central Park in the dead of night.

His heart racing, he pivoted and stared at the blank gray wall of schist that marked the Door of Orpheus.

There was a *thump* behind Nico. Will had fallen to his knees in the wet grass.

"Nico," he said desolately. "What's happening?"

"If I remember correctly," said Nico, "the first time I met Will was during a battle."

"Which one?" Will narrowed his eyes. He still looked so weak and tired. "Oh, wait—was it when Octavian's faction attacked the camp?"

"Uh, *no*," said Nico. "Wasn't that only, like . . . a little over a year ago? We've known each other a lot longer than that."

"Oh." Will rubbed his face. "Sorry, you're right."

Nico felt another twinge of concern. "Is your memory getting worse?"

Will grunted but did not answer the question. "You were around . . . before that," he said hazily. "Long before. Back around the time when . . . when the Battle of Manhattan . . ."

Nico smiled. "Yeah, I was. I wasn't staying at Camp Half-Blood much, though."

"I remember that! And even when you *were* at camp, it was so hard to pin you down. You wouldn't stay put. You were . . . afraid. Afraid of getting close to anyone."

Nico was silent for a moment. "Sometimes I still am," he said. "Like earlier, when you were complaining that I wasn't telling you things."

"Sort of." Will pressed his hand against his stomach. "I don't know if I was being fair to you—"

"That's not important now," said Nico. "Let's get through this."

"I hope you do not feel that I am something to 'get through,'" said Gorgyra. "I am not trying to make things difficult for you boys."

For a moment, Nico had almost forgotten the nymph was there. He tried to tamp down his fear and frustration, his urge to scream *Just let us go!*

"It's a trade, right?" he said. "We give you our story, and you give us a boat."

"If you must see it that way," she said. "Yes."

"I remember . . ." Will coughed softly, and Nico ran his hand over his boyfriend's back. His eyes traveled down to the gauze on Will's leg.

It was completely soaked through with blood.

"What do you remember?" Gorgyra asked.

"I remember how sad I was when you left to go find Percy," Will said to Nico. "When he disappeared."

"You were sad? But . . . did we even know each other then?"

"Maybe not as close friends or anything, but . . . but I was drawn to you. Maybe it was because you were so mysterious. Maybe it was because you kept pushing everyone away whenever they tried to be your friend."

"Not a lot of people tried to be my friend in those days," said Nico.

"That's not true!" said Will, and for a moment his energy seemed to come back. "Plenty of us tried to be friendly to you, and you always had an excuse or a mean remark ready for us."

"That doesn't sound like me," Nico said, trying to play it deadpan, but Will gave him a stern look. Nico laughed. "Okay, okay, fine. *Maybe* that sounds like me."

"We met . . . way before the Battle of Manhattan, actually," said Will, leaning against Nico. "You . . . You came into the Big House, remember?"

"What?" Nico scratched at his head. "When was this?"

"Back when I was still training to be a field medic, with Michael Yew. . . ."

Will fell silent, unable to finish, and that's when the fragment of memory came back to Nico.

"The sword fight," he said. "I'd only been at camp a couple of days. Chiron had me training with the other campers, and I went too hard."

"You sliced your own leg," said Will, smiling weakly. "If I remember correctly, you missed the target dummy completely because you were arguing with Chiron."

"I love that you seem to remember all the most embarrassing moments of my life," said Nico. "Way to go, Will!"

"I only remember that because of what came after. The part that's more striking . . . was you. In the Big House. You wouldn't sit still, and Michael was barking commands at you because you were bleeding everywhere, and . . . and—"

"You calmed me down," said Nico, and the image bloomed in his mind: a young Will Solace, his blond hair bushy and slightly unkempt, holding Nico's leg still, Will's blue eyes boring into his own.

"At least I *tried*," said Will. "I don't think it worked."

"It did," said Nico. "Even if it was only for a moment. I was . . . a little difficult when I was younger."

Will grinned. "Oh, *only* when you were younger?"

"Shut up."

"That's news to me. You've *never* been difficult since."

Nico shifted uneasily. He glanced over at the old nymph, who was studying the two of them with a wistful look.

"So, is that *it*, Will?" Nico asked. "Is that really how we met?"

"I think so. I'm pretty sure I saw you running around Camp Half-Blood when you were originally rescued by Percy and Annabeth, but that was our first face-to-face moment."

Nico shook his head. "I didn't even realize that was *you* back then. But . . . well, I also don't remember much about my first few weeks at the camp. I felt so out of place."

Gorgyra sighed. "It seems you two have a complicated and labyrinthine connection."

"Would really love to never think about a labyrinth ever again," Nico muttered.

She smiled. "I find this fascinating. Sometimes mortals are not aware of the threads that bind them. You could both be wrong about the first time you met, and yet the two of you have orbited each other for so long, like heavenly bodies in the sky."

Will squeezed Nico's hand. "I like how that sounds."

Nico studied Will's broken fingernails, the cuts on his knuckles. He certainly felt like he was spinning through space . . . like he would go shooting off into the void if it weren't for Will's gravity.

"Well," Nico said at last, "maybe we don't remember the first time we *actually* met, but I do remember when I considered you a friend."

"Tell me," Gorgyra said.

Nico heard the yearning in her voice: insatiable, like the three-headed dog Cerberus begging for bones. *Just one more. Just one more.* Nico worried Gorgyra would keep demanding stories, pulling on string after string, until their whole lives were unraveled at her feet.

Nevertheless, he wanted to talk about it. He looked into Will's tired blue eyes when he spoke, not Gorgyra's. "It was at camp. After . . . after Octavian. When he . . . you know."

Will's face drooped. Nico knew he hated that memory: when

Nico and Michael Kahale had allowed Octavian to launch himself to his own death. "I remember."

"We had defeated Gaea. You were standing in the doorway of your cabin."

Will laughed softly. "I remember that, too. I think I scolded you pretty hard."

"You did," confirmed Nico. "But it was the *way* you did it. You made it clear that you wanted me around. You said you wanted me to come to the infirmary and help, because . . . because you could use a 'friendly face.'"

"It was true. And you did help."

"You brought me closer instead of rejecting me," Nico said, his voice cracking. "I'd never been called a friendly face. Ever. You made me rethink everything—my place in camp, my crush on Percy, my future. It took you scolding me like you were the camp director to make me realize that I was . . . wanted."

Gorgyra sniffled, then wiped her eyes. "You'll have to excuse me," she said. "It is hard not to react to something like that."

Will swayed, and Nico steadied him.

"You okay?" asked Nico.

"This place," he said. "I'm so tired."

"I know," Nico said, watching apprehensively as the blood seeped across the gauze bindings on Will's leg. He turned to Gorgyra. "We need to go if we're going to reach Tartarus."

"Wait," said Will. "I remember something else. I know we need to go, but . . . you remember what Percy and Annabeth said, about how important it is to remind each other of the world above?"

Nico frowned. "But we're not even in Tartarus yet."

"It feels like we are," said Will. "And I know you're worried. But just . . . give me this. It *does* make me feel better."

Nico gazed at Gorgyra and the whispers in his mind returned: voices telling him what he already knew about himself, all his worst fears and failures.

"All right," he said to Will. "If it helps."

That brought a bit of color back into Will's face. "I remember when I realized . . . when I *knew* that this was more than a friendship."

That made Nico smile despite himself. "I remember my moment, too."

Will's eyes filled with tears. "I think mine is different than yours."

"But I *know* mine happened first," Nico said.

"Tell me," Gorgyra said, moving closer to Nico and Will. "Tell me one more story."

And Nico felt another string start to unravel.

CHAPTER  9

Nico rushed to Will and pulled him to his feet. "Are you okay? What happened?"

Will dusted himself off. "I suddenly felt *sleepy* . . . like I hadn't slept in a million years." Then he looked around. "Uh, Nico . . . why are we back in Central Park?"

"I don't know," he admitted. "It shouldn't be possible."

And yet he could hear leaves rustling in the wind and the distant sound of traffic.

"But . . . we went down all those steps!" said Will. "Like, *twice.*"

"Maybe you were right," Nico said. "Maybe my father *is* preventing us from going into the Underworld somehow."

He walked up to the massive rocks that made up the Door of Orpheus. He placed his hand on them. They felt very real: rough, solid, and cool to the touch. "Can you try to open this again?"

Will shook himself like a wet dog. "Just trying to wake up."

He approached the door and began humming the same melody as before. Slowly, the schist rumbled and split apart, revealing the dank, dark steps again. Will plugged his nose. "I don't think I'll ever get used to that smell."

Nico held his purple-glowing sword in front of him as he led the way down the steps. As before, the door closed behind them, filling the space with terrible silence.

"We're going to have to do this all over, aren't we?" said Will. "I'm already so tired. . . ."

"It doesn't make sense," said Nico, descending. "I've never had anything like this happen before, which makes me think it *isn't* Hades. He wouldn't toy with us like this."

Will gave him a skeptical look. "Then what is it?" he asked. "Is there someone or something else that could make this happen in the Underworld?"

Nico sighed. "Are you asking me if there are terrible creatures who can do awful things to us down here? Sure. But I don't know if you really want me to list them all."

He turned to face Will, but . . .

Will wasn't there.

Nico stared at the empty space behind him. No Will, no stairway, no tunnel, just . . . darkness.

His heart climbed into his throat. "Will?"

"I'm right here," said Will.

Nico jumped. Will was, in fact, standing right in front of him—exactly where he *hadn't* been a moment before. The steps, the tunnel . . . were where they should be.

What is going on? Nico wondered.

He remembered an old stereoscope his mother had owned back in the 1930s. At the time, it had seemed like magic to Nico. He would put his eyes in the view-mask as his mother changed 3-D photo cards at the other end of a guide stick. One moment Nico was in Paris; then, in the blink of an eye, he was at the Great Wall of China, then the Grand Canyon.

Nico felt like that now: stuck in a stereoscope he couldn't control. And he wasn't sure who was changing the cards.

"Are you okay?" Will asked. "You looked panicky there for a second."

"You . . . You weren't there. *Nothing* was. It was just me in the darkness."

In the purple glow of Nico's blade, Will's face seemed to float in and out of focus. "But I've been here the whole time. I didn't see anything change."

Nico tried to think. It wasn't easy with the adrenaline buzzing through his system.

"Something doesn't want us to make it to the Underworld," he decided. "Will, I think you were right from the start. Can you . . . do the glowing thing? Maybe a better light source will help us see what's actually going on."

"Okay," said Will, his voice trembling ever so slightly. "Whatever you say."

His skin began to glow like rice paper lit from behind by a candle. Nico found the sight both beautiful and unsettling, as if his boyfriend were about to burst into flames.

They descended once more. For the third attempt, the dim light of the Underworld began to shine at the end of the long passage, but it seemed to happen much more quickly this time. Maybe Will's glow was helping? Nico could make out the roar of the River Styx below. Finally, the steps gave way to the uneven ground of the cavern, and Nico reached back for Will's hand.

"Don't let go of me," he said, holding his Stygian iron sword before him. "No matter what happens."

Will clutched him tightly. "I got you."

Nico managed a few steps toward the river's edge, and that's when a wave of exhaustion rolled over him, and an uncontrollable desire to curl up and sleep.

It was an unusual sensation for him, because he wasn't much of a sleeper. He'd spent many a night at Camp Half-Blood wandering the grounds instead of lying in bed. Anything to avoid the dreams he'd been having. And if his dreams in the mortal world were so terrible, he thought with a shudder, what would they be like in the Underworld?

"Will, keep your eyes open," he said. "Don't close them."

"Why do I feel so sleepy?" Will's grip on Nico's hand was already loosening. "Should we rest?"

Nico forced himself to look across the river to the black ramparts of Erebos. *Was* this his father's doing? Had Hades somehow discovered that Nico was trying to cross his realm and deliberately enter Tartarus? Maybe this was his way of saying *No way, Jose*.

"We can't rest yet," said Nico. "We have to follow the river and make our way down those cliffs. It's not too far. Then we can find the troglodytes and rest, I promise."

Thump. Will's hand slipped out of Nico's, and when Nico turned, he found that his boyfriend—whose illumination was much dimmer—had fallen to the ground again.

"No!" Nico cried. "Not here, please!"

"I can't," said Will. "I can't be here."

"Please, get up," begged Nico, his arms under Will's armpits, trying to lift him, but it was hopeless.

"This place," said Will. "It's not meant for someone like me."

"Do you need your sunlamp?" Nico's heart raced faster. "Why is this happening so *suddenly?*"

Nico looked up and—

No. *No!*

Darkness was seeping into his field of vision. The world around him—the cavern walls, Erebos, the River Styx—began to fade away.

"Not again!" Nico called out. "Stop it!"

When he looked down at Will, his boyfriend's internal light had extinguished, and he seemed to be completely asleep on the—

What?

The grass. Will was curled up on a bed of wet *grass*.

With a rising wave of horror, Nico scanned his surroundings.

They were back in Central Park.

Again.

A voice floated through the trees: *Help me, Nico!*

Bob.

It was *Bob.*

Why won't you help me, Nico?

Nico screamed in frustration, his eyes squeezed tight, and then—

CHAPTER 10

Will was relieved to have his feet on something other than the slimy stone steps, even if it was the banks of the Styx. The air here was thick with . . . something; he wasn't sure what, but at least they were out of that dark tunnel.

Nico had been right about the Underworld having some light. Its sky—could he call it a sky?—was a glowing hazy red, punctuated with flashes of orange and veins of dark shadows. Where was the light coming from? The air seemed polluted, even worse than he'd experienced in cities like Houston or Los Angeles while touring with his mom. In the distance, across the river, towering stone walls with black battlements stretched as far as he could see, blocking off access to . . . the land of the dead? Hades's home? Will didn't want to find out. The fortress was *terrifying*.

"Welcome to the Underworld," Nico said, sweeping his arm toward the horizon like he was showing off something he was proud of. He actually looked *happy* to be here.

Well, this *was* his home, technically.

Will couldn't escape the sense of dread crawling over his skin as he peered around. He had a confused feeling that he had been here before. . . . But he also didn't remember how he'd gotten here. His instincts told him this was all wrong. He should run. But he had to endure it. . . . He had to *try* if this quest was going to succeed.

"Impressive," he said weakly. "Where do we go now?"

"This way." Nico tucked his sword away and ran off to the right, bounding over the boulders that jutted along the river's edge.

Will hesitated. He was enjoying *not* moving, and his limbs felt like lead. How did Nico have so much energy? Will wondered if this was what *he* looked like to Nico in the world above.

"Hey, wait up!" Will called out, pulling the straps on his knapsack to keep it tight against his back.

He chased after Nico, who moved like a mountain goat over the jagged rocks. Will wasn't sure that Nico had even heard him yell, as the roar of the River Styx was impossibly loud here, the churn of the rapids booming off the cavern walls. Nico stopped at the top of a boulder, where the River Styx widened into a swirling back eddy fifteen feet below.

Nico turned toward Will with a crooked smile, waved, and then—

"Nico, no!"

Nico *jumped in.*

By the time Will made it to the boulder top, Nico's head was bobbing along in the middle of the river. He was dog-paddling along in the inky water, grinning as if he was *enjoying* his dip, which . . . gods, wasn't that impossible? Will remembered Percy talking about his brief plunge into the Styx: how it was like acid to the human soul, eating away your very identity. It had almost destroyed him in a matter of seconds. Was Nico somehow immune to the river's effects?

"Nico!" he screamed, running along the rocky bank as fast as he could. Why hadn't Nico talked to Will about this? Why did he always have so many *secrets*? Didn't he know by now that he could trust his own boyfriend?

The muscles in Will's legs screamed at him to stop, and despair ripped through him. He couldn't keep up with the raging and turbulent current; Nico was getting farther and farther away, heading toward the next set of cataracts. Didn't Nico see the danger?

His chest burning, he managed to scream Nico's name one more time.

Before Nico plunged over the edge of the falls.

Will's cry was lost in the terrible sound of the Styx. He forced himself to keep going until he stood at the top of the cataract, a lower tier of the Underworld stretching out impossibly far beneath him. He scanned the water, terrified that he might see Nico's lifeless form, but in the pool below, illuminated by a purple glow, Nico was bobbing along just fine.

Will was furious. What was Nico *thinking*?

Nico glanced up, saw him, and waved his sword like a racing flag. "Just jump in!" he yelled, his voice strangely close, as if he were standing right next to Will. "The water's fine!"

These words made even *less* sense to Will than what he had just witnessed.

The water's fine?

Which got Will thinking. . . . Had he ever *seen* Nico swimming? Did Nico even know how? In Will's exhaustion and terror, an absurd image popped into his head: Nico wearing one of those old-timey one-piece men's swimsuits while floating in an inner tube. In Will's frazzled state of mind, that seemed hysterically funny. Too bad no one else was around for Will to share it with.

"Don't hold me back!" Nico shouted up at him. "We have to keep moving."

"What's gotten into your head, Nico?" he asked softly, not expecting Nico to hear him.

"Don't you want to save Bob?" Nico yelled. "Or are you giving up on our quest already? I *knew* you would."

"What?" Will felt punched in the gut. Nausea threatened to overwhelm him. "No, of course not! But what am I supposed to do? Is this part of the plan?"

"Jump in," said Nico. "You'll be fine. I promise."

Will had done any number of ridiculous things since learning he was a son of Apollo. Sure, demigods possessed abilities that pushed the limits of what human bodies were capable of. He'd seen incredible leaps, tumbles, tackles, and other feats over the years. At the same time, demigods were all still heartbreakingly mortal, and they could definitely get seriously hurt. As one of the main field medics in camp, Will had seen it firsthand.

And in no way was he prepared to jump into a soul-destroying, toxic river of damnation.

"Stop giving up on me," said Nico, and this time Will swore he could feel his boyfriend's breath on his neck. "Come on! Don't be a coward."

That comment sent a burst of anger through Will. How could Nico be so cruel? Why would he *ever* think of Will as a coward?

A new theory started to coil around the base of Will's brain: What if the Underworld was already changing Nico?

All that talk from Percy and Annabeth . . .

What was it Percy had said? *I practically lost myself in that place.* He'd meant Tartarus, but what if that process had started happening even before? What if Nico didn't even realize how much he was changing? Will had to get him out of that water before it was too late, whatever the cost.

He flipped his knapsack around so that it was over his chest, clasped it tightly, and jumped.

Will had braced himself for a jolt of cold water.

Instead, the River Styx *burned*. Even that was an understatement. As pain ripped through his body, his mind drifted to the memory of sitting under a tattoo gun, the needle pressing into his skin on his pectoral as his mom held his hand. She had taken him to the shop and helped him choose a design to honor his father. But once the process had begun, he'd been surprised that the sensation had felt like burning, like he was skinning his knee from a fall over and over again.

Except the River Styx was a billion tattoo guns running over every inch of his body, and the ink was made of acid, and also, everything was on fire, including the fire.

Yes, he decided as he bobbed to the surface, gasping for air, down here, the *fire* is on fire.

His skin felt like it was melting off, and he wished he hadn't filled his knapsack with so much stuff. It was hard enough to swim without that extra weight.

His head went under, and a mouthful of the River Styx actually *went down his throat.*

If that water felt awful all over the *outside* of his body, it was even *worse* on the inside. He kicked as ferociously as he could, his muscles aching from the overexertion, and his head broke the surface again. His throat burned so badly even breathing hurt. He twisted around, looking for Nico. Where had he gone?

"Hurry up, slowpoke." Nico's voice wafted past Will's left ear.

Will turned. His vision was hazy, but he saw a purple glow moving across the shoreline. How had Nico gotten out of the water so fast?

Will flung his arms toward the bank, then paddled frantically until the water was shallow enough for him to stand in. By the time he flopped onto his back on the rocky riverbank, trembling and wheezing, he felt like he'd just taken a long bath in his mom's favorite ghost-pepper salsa. Will imagined he could bottle Styx water and sell it as the hottest hot sauce in the world. Mr. D would probably be his celebrity sponsor for a hefty percentage.

He laughed. He laughed because everything hurt, because he shouldn't be alive, because he was delirious from the pain and total absurdity of plunging into the River Styx.

Wait. Was he . . . invulnerable now? Wasn't that what happened if you survived a dip in the Styx? That couldn't be right. It couldn't be that easy.

He rolled over and pushed himself up to his hands and knees. He coughed out more acidic black water, which burned on its way out, too. Well, at least it was consistent.

"Nico," he croaked, swaying as he stood up. "Nico, where are you?"

No one was there.

Then Will turned and glimpsed the familiar purple glow disappearing behind an outcrop of stalagmites.

He tried to yell "Nico, stop!" but his lungs were on fire. His skin felt . . . Oh, gods, was this what a sunburn was like? Being a child of Apollo meant he had never gotten one, and if it was anything similar to this sensation, he had immense sympathy for all the lobster-red campers he'd seen and healed over the years.

The purple glow was getting dimmer in the distance.

"You're just slowing me down," his boyfriend's voice whispered in his ear.

How was this possible? Was Will's mind dissolving?

"I won't, Nico," he said, sobbing. "I promise."

"You already are."

Will watched in despair as the faint purple glow slipped into the shadows and disappeared.

He crumpled to his knees, tears prickling his eyes. This wasn't happening. This *couldn't* happen. Nico would never do something like this to him!

"Nico!" he cried out. "Come back!"

But this time, Nico didn't answer. Behind Will, the Styx rushed past. Will's skin and clothes steamed. Will kept staring into the darkness, hoping to see that purple glow reappear.

Then a heavy shadow fell over him. Will didn't have the strength to fight as it enveloped him like a burial cloth.

CHAPTER  11

When he came to, Nico wondered if he'd passed out from exhaustion.

He was back at the bottom of the stone stairwell, his cheek pressed against the rough, rocky floor of the cavern. His body was sore all over, so he stayed still for a moment, trying to get his bearings. He'd fallen asleep, hadn't he? The endless repetition of walking down the steps behind the Door of Orpheus must have drained him of his energy.

This was unlike him, though. Nico generally had *trouble* falling asleep, unless he had shadow-traveled a long distance. The memory of the gigantic Athena Parthenos statue flashed in his mind, and he shuddered. That summer had involved a lot of sudden, long-lasting naps in order to manage transporting the Parthenos via shadow-travel halfway around the world.

But this was different. His mind was even more tired than his body, which didn't make any sense. He couldn't seem to string his thoughts together. He had a vague feeling that something was wrong, but he couldn't identify what or why. He blinked a couple of times, his eyes adjusting to the dim light of the Underworld, and that's when he saw the shadow.

A dark mass flickered in the near distance, swaying back and forth. Nico's heart began to thump so loudly he worried that this *thing* would hear it.

Appendages of some sort swirled and twisted about its body. It moved unnaturally, quavering and jerky, and Nico remained as still as he could. Maybe it thought he was dead; he certainly wasn't going to give it another idea. But where was . . . ?

He shifted his head just a bit, his breath even and slow, and his gaze fell upon . . .

Will.

Nico's pulse quickened. He would have recognized that bushy blond hair anywhere. Will was splayed on the ground about twenty feet away, completely still aside from the gentle rise and fall of his back as he breathed.

And that shadowy *thing* was looming above him, its appendages— almost like tentacles—swaying over Will's body as if casting some kind of spell. "Sleep, demigod," it said in a slimy, slippery voice.

Nico acted without thinking. He pushed himself up with one hand, and with the other he drew his sword.

"Get away from him," said Nico.

His dark blade glowed fiercely as he held it toward the monster, pointing the tip toward . . . well, this creature only had the vaguest shape of a body, so Nico just guessed where its head might be. For all Nico knew, he was targeting one of the being's armpits.

Nico probably didn't look all that threatening anyway.

The creature shifted toward him, pulling in all its appendages. As it did so, the darkness encasing it drifted away like birthday-candle smoke, leaving some*thing* behind. A vaguely humanoid shape with arms, legs, a chest, a head (which *was* in the place Nico had guessed), and . . .

A face. Beneath a black spiked helmet of Stygian iron was a visage as shiny and slick as tree sap. Other details fell into place: half a dozen milky-white eyes, a chiseled V-shaped jaw, and a triangular bone-like protrusion that might have been a beak or a nose. Their emaciated body was wrapped in inky, formfitting cloth, and their appendages folded elegantly behind them so it looked like they were wearing a cape.

Nico didn't want to tell the creature that they were supercool, but . . .

They were supercool.

"Nico di Angelo," they said, and their words seemed to slither under his skin. "Finally, you might put up the kind of struggle I was expecting."

"I'll do more than that." Nico jabbed his blade toward the creature, though it was hard to look intimidating when he was propped up on one arm and his legs felt like wet sandbags. "What have you done to Will?"

The creature smiled—at least Nico assumed that's what the jagged line of pointy black teeth indicated. "I only pushed him toward what he wanted. His mind did the rest."

"What he wanted?" Nico's stomach twisted. "If you hurt him, I swear . . . Who even *are* you?"

The creature's smile shriveled and died. "Who *am* I?"

"Well . . . yeah. I don't recognize you. Do you work for my father?"

"As *if!*" the creature roared. "Ew, why would I *ever* do that?"

"I don't know. You're down here, you aren't in Tartarus, and I've never seen you or your kind before. You haven't exactly given me a lot to go on."

"Honestly, I'm offended," they said. "I know who *you* are. Do you not do your own research into demons?"

"I— What? Research?"

The demon dropped and sat cross-legged in front of Nico. "It's ludicrous," they said. "Just ludicrous. Here we are, roaming the Underworld, sending our choicest monsters and spirits back to the upper world to give you demigods something to *do*, and you can't even muster up the slightest bit of interest in who we are?"

Nico blinked. "I'm so lost," he said. "*Should* I recognize you?"

"I would hope so!" The demon threw their hands up in despair. "I visit you *all* the time."

"No, you don't!"

"*I just did!*" they hissed.

Nico lowered his sword. *Just* visited him?

The answer came to him suddenly, and it was so *obvious*.

"The time loop on the stairs," Nico said. "None of that happened. That was you."

"Well, *duh*," said the demon. "I mean, your brain and your body probably *thought* it was real, but nope."

Nico glanced at Will, still passed out cold. If his boyfriend was trapped in a dream, then . . . Not great, but at least fixable, if Nico could figure out how. Maybe Will would wake up on his own if Nico could just keep the demon's attention away from him.

"I'm impressed," Nico told them. "I'm usually really good at knowing when I'm in a dream."

At this, the demon puffed up with pride. "Well, I do good work," they said. "But sometimes it would be nice to get a little acknowledgment."

Nico had an idea. Slowly, he sheathed his sword and sat upright. This was the Underworld. He had more weapons at his command than just a blade, if he could only gather enough strength. . . .

"You're right," he said. "That's on me. You did a wonderful job. You had me believing *everything*."

To Nico's great shock, the demon appeared to blush, the dark skin on their face turning red. They waved a tentacle dismissively. "Aw, thank you! You have no idea how much it means to hear that."

"So, could you tell me your name? Obviously, I need to correct this oversight in my research."

The demon's appendages fluttered behind them in what Nico could only interpret as a happy dance. "Well, my mother always wanted to go for the dramatic, so she decided on Epiales."

"Ephialtes?"

The demon frowned. "No. *Epiales*."

"Ah. Sorry. It's just . . . I once knew a giant by the name of Ephialtes. Terrible guy. Your name is so similar."

"It's *hardly* similar!" said Epiales, back to being offended again. "There are *two* whole letters added to it!"

"My bad! I promise to get it correct."

Nico placed his right hand on the ground. He would need to be *very* delicate if he was going to pull this off without Epiales noticing. He dug his fingers into the dirt, carefully sending his consciousness downward . . . looking for bones.

"So, earlier, you said *we*," Nico continued, trying to split his attention. "How many demons like you are there?"

Epiales crossed their arms over their chest. "Oh, let's see . . . to count just my own siblings would take more appendages than I have, but demons, total?"

Nico leaned forward. "Yes?"

Epiales leaned forward, too. "If I had to hazard a guess, probably ten thousand."

"Ten thousand."

"Indeed."

"And you're all down here . . . What did you say? Roaming the Underworld?"

"Not *all* of us," they said. "Every so often, a few of us get lucky and are sent topside to wreak havoc for a while . . . at least until one of you demigods sends us right back down. Then it's back to centuries of busywork, cataloging monsters, filling out performance reviews, waiting for our next chance."

"Sounds exhausting," Nico said, leaning back. He dug his left hand into the dirt, his mind searching the ground for— *There.* A nice cluster of dormant skeletons, just waiting to be weaponized.

"You have *no* idea," said Epiales. "You demigods are always so *sneaky.*"

"Not *always.*" Nico pushed downward with his power, willing those skeletons to rise . . .

. . . when two of Epiales's appendages shot forward and wrapped around Nico's wrists. They yanked him toward the demon, making him cry out in pain.

"Yes, ALWAYS!" the demon shrieked. "Did you believe you could fool me? You truly don't know me, Nico di Angelo!"

More tentacles wrapped around Nico, holding him fast against the demon. Their breath smelled like dry rotted leather. Nico jerked back hard, but Epiales held him tight.

"What do you *want* from me?" Nico screamed.

"I just want you to sleep," the demon said gently. "Don't you want that, too?"

Suddenly, Nico's eyes felt heavy. "No!" he said. "I don't want to go to sleep."

"Nico?"

Both Nico and Epiales turned their heads.

Will was sitting upright, his eyes wide. "What's going on? Who is this guy?"

"Um, *excuse me!*" said Epiales, their body pluming angry black smoke. "I am not a guy!"

Will gulped. "Oh, sorry."

"Like, do you think that demonkind, in all our glory, would stick to the completely archaic notion of there being only *two* genders?"

"Not at all." Nico shot Will a look that hopefully said *Stay calm,* though it might actually have said *Help!* "I mean . . . how boring would that be?"

Epiales smiled. "You understand me, Nico! You might not *know* me, but you *see* me, don't you?"

"I promise it won't happen again," said Will, nodding. "Just let my boyfriend go."

"Oh, he's not going anywhere," said Epiales. "And neither are you, demigod!"

Will, still groggy from his slumber, was unable to dart out of the way before the demon's shadowy appendages shot out and held him in place, too.

"Will!" Nico cried out. "Leave him alone, Epiales!"

"You are both right where you are supposed to be!" the demon said giddily. "Oh, Mother will be *so* proud! I am Epiales, the demon of nightmares, and you two will *never* wake up again!"

As more appendages wrapped around both boys, smoke billowed from the demon's body, stinging Nico's eyes and filling his lungs. Nico thrashed in the demon's clutches, but it was no use. Epiales blasted him with their powers, and Nico gave in to the darkness.

CHAPTER  12

Nico found himself at Camp Half-Blood.

He stood outside the front door of the Big House, hand raised, cheeks stinging from the cold. As his knuckles rapped the door, he realized which moment he was reliving. He knew what waited for him on the other side of that door: another memory he very much preferred not to visit. But like in all his nightmares, he had no choice.

He pushed his way inside.

His gaze jumped anxiously from Chiron to Annabeth, from Silena Beauregard to Charles Beckendorf, from the Stoll brothers to . . .

Percy Jackson.

All of them were gathered in the living room, staring glumly at the carpet or the fire crackling in the hearth.

Nico didn't want to ask what was wrong. He already knew the answer. Still, the words spilled from his mouth. "Hey! Where's my sister?"

The air seemed to leave the room, just as it had on the actual day. The blood drained from Percy's face.

He stood, putting out his palms, as if Nico were a feral cat he was trying to approach. "Hey, Nico . . . listen to me, okay?"

The memory was so raw, so agonizing. But Nico managed to regain control, wresting himself from the grip of the dream logic. "NO!" he screamed. "I am not reliving this nightmare again!"

Chiron swiveled his wheelchair toward him. "You have to, young demigod," he said, but his voice was wrong. It now belonged to Epiales. "You can't escape this."

Nico sneered. He marched across the room, pushing aside Percy Jackson, and loomed over Chiron. "*You've* been behind all the horrible dreams I've been having for months, then. Why do you keep telling me to listen? What does it have to do with Bob?"

Chiron's face twisted in confusion, and Epiales spoke through him again. "For *months*? But—"

"You can't manipulate me." Nico unsheathed his sword. "This isn't real, and you can't hold me here forever."

Chiron/Epiales scratched their chin, apparently unfazed by the Stygian iron blade in their face. "Wait, can we go back to you claiming I've been sending you dreams *for months*? I certainly wish I had been. That would have been so fun! But no, Mother only required that I intercept you and Will Solace once you passed through the Door of Orpheus. Also . . . who is Bob?"

Nico's sword hand wavered. Around him, the images of his fellow demigods flickered like faulty lightbulbs.

"You know exactly who I'm talking about," he said, though he couldn't muster much conviction. "Who is Mother?"

Epiales smiled through Chiron's face. "Oh, some questions you don't want answered, Nico di Angelo. . . ."

Then the floor split, and Nico fell into the void.

Will's eyes fluttered open.

It was dark, which didn't tell him much; all the Underworld was dark. But as his vision adjusted to the shadows, he realized he was lying on a thin stretch of brickwork at the edge of a sewer trench.

"Jump the cow?" said a voice to his right. "*That* was your plan?"

Will turned his head, and there she was: Meg McCaffrey, her dark hair unkempt and her face sweaty. Her rhinestone-studded cat-eye glasses sparkled in the gloom.

"Meg?" he said. "How did you get here?"

She scowled at him. "Same way as *you*, Sun Boy. Your boyfriend helped us."

Will's heart dropped when he looked where Meg was pointing. Nico was curled up asleep in the tight space they were sharing. Will crawled over to him.

"Nico!" He cupped his hands around his boyfriend's face. "Nico, are you okay?"

"He'll be fine, assuming you can heal him."

Will looked up at a bedraggled teen boy with acne and ill-fitting clothes.

Lester Papadopoulos. Aka the Ex-God Formerly Known as Apollo.

AKA *Dad*.

But how was he back? Apollo had been returned to godhood at the end of the summer, and Will had expected that it would be years before he saw his father again, if ever.

Will's head was full of a terrible fog, something thick and soupy that made it difficult to sort between the present and his memories. He had lived through this moment before, hadn't he? So why was he living it again?

He vaguely remembering being in another place . . . a dark smoky figure towering over him—

"Help him." A third voice broke through Will's thoughts. Rachel Elizabeth Dare was staring at him expectantly. "I thought you were a healer."

"And *I* thought you were one of my children," said Lester, crossing his arms. "My children are supposed to be the *best* doctors."

"What use *are* you," Meg asked, her voice sharper than before, "if you can't even fix your own boyfriend?"

No, Will thought. This isn't right. There was a prophecy. . . . His mind grasped for it. Was he . . . Was he supposed to leave something behind? But his companions were all staring at him, waiting for him to do his job.

Will dug in his pockets furiously. Where was his supply of Kit Kats?

He pulled his pockets inside out.

They were empty.

When he looked down at Nico again, he seemed even paler than usual.

"Nico, wake up," Will pleaded. "You *have* to be okay."

"Does he?" jeered Rachel, her red hair falling over her face. "Come on, Will Solace. Heal him."

"*Heal him!*" Lester ordered, and it was the command of a god, not of a seventeen-year-old.

The melody escaped Will's lips. He sang in Greek, caressing Nico's forehead, hoping beyond hope that color would return to his boyfriend's face.

"You're supposed to be *good* at this," Meg grumbled.

Will's hands began to glow, dully at first, then brighter, until his body illuminated the sewer culvert. He pressed his fingers into Nico's cheeks, tears running down his face, but Nico wasn't responding. In fact, the color in Nico's whole body was disappearing, so he looked like he belonged in an old television show.

"I can do this!" Will said, sobbing. "I can save you!"

Nico's eyes opened, but they were milky white.

"No," he said, smiling coldly. "You can't."

He grabbed Will's wrist. Will yelped in protest. His light began to drain away, flowing into Nico's body. As Nico's color returned, he sat up and pushed Will to the ground while the others looked on approvingly.

"Finally, you're good for something," Lester said. "You make an excellent spare battery."

Will was unable to breathe, his life draining away, his colors vanishing until his fingers were as gray as ash.

He tried to cry out, to plead with Nico, but he made no sound. . . .

Then Nico released his grip, and Will tumbled into darkness.

As Nico fell, he could sense something waiting for him below in the darkness, much like he could sense the dead lurking beneath the soil. This time, instead of waiting to land in another dream, he lashed out, grabbing the presence with both hands, and was rewarded with a startled, piercing shriek.

The dream world fractured.

Nico opened his eyes and found his fingers clamped around Epiales's throat. Nico was *free.*

Epiales thrashed, two of their appendages flinging Nico across the ground. Nico rolled, avoiding another set of appendages that were trying to grab him. His hand found the scabbard of his sword, and he yanked it free, pointing the glowing blade at Epiales.

The demon roared. "Why are you making this so *difficult?* Who *doesn't* want to sleep all the time?"

"Your mistake was thinking you could keep me down in my own home," Nico said with a sneer.

Then he jammed his sword into the dirt.

All around him, the dead rose—flesh and rotted clothes clinging to the skeletons, dim light glowing in the eye sockets of the cracked skulls, rusted swords clutched in bony fingers. But there were more than just humans here. This was the Underworld, after all. A pack of skeletal wolves snarled at Epiales. A dragon-like creature the size of a car flicked its vertebral tail, snapping its long jaws.

"I can summon as many of them as I need to," said Nico. "This won't go the way you want."

Epiales *laughed*, a high, giddy sound. "Nico, you're not thinking correctly."

The demon waved their right hand, and in an instant, every skeleton crumpled onto the ground, fast asleep.

"I'm the demon of nightmares, silly," said Epiales. "And the dead can dream just like everyone else."

They raised *both* their hands, and the ground cracked beneath Nico's feet. He scrambled backward as more of the dead clawed their way to the surface—humans, beasts, monsters. But these hadn't been summoned by Nico, and they weren't skeletons. These beings flickered in and out of view, drifting over the ground like they were both there and *not* there.

"How could you even think to frighten or harm me?" Epiales continued. "I bring darkness to the minds of others. I can summon anything—dead, living, real, imaginary—to torment you!"

There was a terrible, terrible roar behind Nico, and when he spun around, he saw an impossible creature.

A manticore, with the body of a lion, the tail of a scorpion, and the face of a man.

But this wasn't just *any* manticore. This one had the short gray hair, the mismatched blue and brown eyes, and the hawkish face of Dr. Thorn, Nico's old vice principal from Westover Hall. Suddenly Nico felt like a helpless little kid again. He backed away, unable to master his fear.

Epiales laughed, their mouth full of black teeth. "You can't defeat me, Nico di Angelo. I *am* darkness. Yours, Will's, *everyone's.*"

Their every appendage rose into the air, then whipped toward Nico and his lifted sword.

Will rolled onto his stomach, his hands now free, and the stench of the Underworld hit his nose. He nearly gagged, but there, just ahead of him, he saw the demon Epiales, surrounded by a host of terrible creatures.

He saw the manticore and knew exactly who it was from the stories Nico had told him.

He heard Epiales's warning: "You can't defeat me. I *am* darkness. Yours, Will's, *everyone's.*"

Epiales's horrible appendages rose and . . .

Will understood.

Of course Nico had *not* abandoned him at the River Styx, or drained the light out of him when Will tried to heal him.

They were just nightmares—Epiales playing on his worst fears, just as they were now doing to Nico.

And Will wasn't going to lie there and let *anyone* hurt his boyfriend.

Will didn't think. He rose to his feet and shouted in defiance, and when he did so, his skin glowed brighter than ever before. Light erupted from his chest, slicing through the dark appendages that whipped at Nico.

He watched in shock as they fell to the ground and flopped there.

Epiales looked just as shocked. As the manticore *poofed* out of existence, the demon of nightmares stared at their severed appendages, which wriggled like long, lanky eels out of water.

"Ow," they said, staring at Will, eyes wide. "Did you just—?"

"Will?" Nico pushed himself up on one elbow. "What was *that?*"

"No, seriously, what *was* that?" said Epiales, folding their remaining appendages protectively behind them. "Mother never told me about . . . whatever that was."

"It's light," said Will, breathing heavily, a line of sweat trickling down his left temple. "You said you were darkness. Well, I'm the opposite."

Epiales inched back, whimpering pitifully. Suddenly they seemed more like a scolded child than a demon. "Mother is going to be so disappointed in me. She already thinks I'm not as powerful as I could be. Now you're probably going to defeat me, aren't you?"

"I kinda have to," Will said. "We have a quest to complete, you know."

The demon stomped a foot. "You demigods always have to ruin things! And no one appreciates what *I* offer the world."

"For what it's worth," said Nico, struggling to his feet, "your nightmares . . . they're *really* good."

"Totally," said Will. "I believed they were real until about two minutes ago."

At that, Epiales perked up, their appendages fluttering. The ones Will had severed were already starting to regrow. "Really? You think so?"

Nico nodded. "Definitely high-grade material."

"Well, shucks," said Epiales. "No one has ever told me that."

"And you're sure you weren't the one sending me nightmares *before* we entered the Underworld?"

"Very sure," said Epiales. "I would claim it in a heartbeat if it *had* been me."

Will frowned at his boyfriend, wondering what conversation he'd missed, but a different question rose to the surface of his thoughts. "Who is your mother?" he asked the demon.

Epiales merely smiled. "You'll find out soon enough. Just go ahead and blast me with your light. Get it over with."

Will hesitated. It somehow seemed wrong to blast someone on request. But Epiales *was* a demon. They'd regenerate down in Tartarus anyway, starting the cycle all over again. They were a monster; Will was a demigod. That's how it worked, right?

Epiales must have sensed his reluctance. They raised their appendages and roared at Will, and just like that, it happened again. Will's fear guided him: light burst from his chest, smacking Epiales in the face, and with a piercing scream, the demon dissolved.

Nico stared at him in disbelief. "Will . . ."

Will drew a shaky breath. His eyes were swimming with exhaustion. He worried that he'd finally done something that would make Nico realize they were simply, irreconcilably too different. "Yes?"

Nico didn't seem able to talk at first. Then: "You are a legitimate demigod Care Bear."

Will's top lip trembled. He fell to his knees. Then he bent over in loud, raucous laughter until tears poured from his eyes.

"You're so weird." Nico crawled over, pulled Will to him, and silenced his laughter with a tender kiss. "Please keep being my own personal Care Bear, though."

"Always," said Will.

And then he promptly passed out.

CHAPTER 13

Will's newfound heart-light power—which Nico still didn't understand—must have really drained him. Nico sat on the ground and rested Will's head on his thigh, absentmindedly stroking his boyfriend's curly blond mane while Will slept.

Nico wondered if the Care Bear anti-demon display meant that their main worry—that Will's powers wouldn't work in the Underworld—was moot now. But what had made this one ability materialize at that particular moment? Fear? Desperation?

Will snored softly, providing no answers.

It struck Nico then how surreal all this was. In the distance, beyond the River Styx and the walls of Erebos, was his father's palace, usually a place where he would be welcomed. Now he'd have to avoid Hades at all costs on his way to Tartarus. Still, a part of him wanted to take Will into Erebos, teach him to play fetch with Cerberus (Will loved dogs), then stroll into the throne room and introduce Will to his father—to show Hades that Nico was trying, that he hadn't forgotten Hades's wish that Nico be the one child of his who was happy.

That was the most surreal thing of all. . . . *Was* he happy?

Nico wasn't very familiar with the sensation, but he couldn't deny that he felt wonderful in Will's presence. He even *longed* for the son of Apollo when they were apart. A funny thing had happened as the two grew closer: Nico suddenly understood all those cheesy, sappy love songs he'd always hated. They'd always seemed like such a ridiculous exaggeration. And it wasn't *only* that, of course. He'd grown up in a time and place where people like him . . . well, they just didn't have love songs. In a roundabout way, his experience in the Lotus Hotel had allowed him to end up *here*, where *this* was possible.

Nico had a boyfriend.

But that was the dichotomy of his life. The seventy years they'd spent at the Lotus Hotel had protected Bianca and Nico, but by then they'd already lost their mother due to Zeus's rage, so it wasn't like Hades's plans were infallible. They'd had to move all over the country. They found Camp Half-Blood, and friends, and then Nico experienced loss once again: Bianca, taken from him. . . .

It was a constant pattern for Nico: find some sort of solace and comfort, only to have it ripped away.

Now here was Solace in his lap, sleeping like a baby. What would come and tear *him* away?

Nico wanted to believe it would be different this time. He wanted Will to understand and accept the darkness that was a part of him, but he also wanted to be seen as a complex person who was *more* than that—not just a child of Hades. Still, how could Will understand if Nico couldn't understand it himself? He couldn't seem to escape the darkness any more than he could defeat Epiales. It always came back, always claimed him, always reminded him of who he was.

Was it possible for him to choose a different destiny? Or was he cursed to suffer every time he found a crumb of happiness?

Nico reached out and grazed the scabbard of his Stygian iron sword. This was far from his first trip to the Underworld, but he felt as nervous now as he did that first time, long ago. He was thankful that Hades hadn't been the one trying to keep Nico and Will out of the Underworld, at least. Nevertheless, something was coming for them. Someone down here didn't want Nico and Will to reach Bob.

Someone called *Mother*.

An inkling of an idea started to form in his head, but then Will stirred. His eyes darted around and found Nico.

"Hey." Will smiled. "My grumpy little ball of darkness."

Just like that, Nico's brooding sense of doom evaporated. It was ridiculous what Will could do to him with just a smile.

"Don't move," he ordered.

He dug around in Will's knapsack until he found the ambrosia squares Juniper had made them. As he fed one to Will, he silently conceded that they *had* been a good idea. The color soon came back into Will's face, and he was able to sit up.

"Well, that was an experience." He wiped some crumbs from his chin, then gave Nico a guarded look. "You okay?"

"I'm perfectly fine," said Nico. "So . . . are we gonna talk about it?"

Will's face flushed red. "Do we have to?"

"Demigod Care Bear."

Will reached into his knapsack, retrieved a metal canteen, and took a swig of water before handing it to Nico. "You're not going to let me hear the end of that, are you?"

Nico had a drink, then gave the canteen back to Will. "Why would I? It perfectly describes the fact that *light just erupted from your chest*."

"Don't Care Bears shoot their energy from their stomachs?"

Nico waved that off. "An unimportant detail. Have you been holding out on me? Did you *know* you could do that?"

"Not really," Will said. "But ever since I found out I could glow, I've been thinking that if my skin could emit light, maybe I could eventually project it outward."

"You sliced off some of Epiales's weird tentacle things!"

"You're welcome?"

Nico laughed. "Well, at least we know your powers still work in the Underworld."

"I'm *still* pretty tired, though," Will said. "So I shouldn't use it often."

Will it still work once we reach Tartarus? Nico wondered.

He really hoped so.

After helping Will to his feet, Nico guided him to the bluffs that overlooked the River Styx. Will froze there, seemingly transfixed by the rushing water below.

"Will?" Nico asked, his hand on the small of Will's back.

Will shook his head. "In the nightmare that Epiales gave me, you jumped in the river."

"*What?!* There's no *way* I would do that."

"I should have realized it was a dream once you *did*," Will said. "You basically pressured me into doing it as well. It was . . ."

He didn't finish.

Nico grabbed his boyfriend's hand and guided him toward the edge of the cliff. As they approached the brink, Nico could sense his reluctance.

"We're *not* jumping," Nico assured him. He brought Will closer and pointed down. "Look."

Right at the very edge, a small recess was cut into the rock. The indentation continued downward, snaking along the side of the cliff, widening into a ledge no bigger than a goat path, only a few feet above the raging current.

"We're taking *that*?" Will asked, his pitch rising with anxiety.

"We are," said Nico. "It's the safest way to stay out of my father's sight."

"Safest, huh?"

"It's also the only way to get to the troglodytes' new home."

Will took a moment to survey the world before him. He spent a long time staring at the black walls of Erebos dotted with torches, and the crowds of smoky gray figures pushing toward the main gates.

"So many dead people . . ."

Nico nodded. "They have to go somewhere. Like I said, most will end up in Asphodel. They'll be bathed in the River Lethe, forget their mortal memories, then just wander around. Forever."

"And that doesn't disturb you?" asked Will.

"Not really," Nico said. "Most of them wandered through their lives anyway. It's what they chose."

Nico could tell that Will wanted to say something else, but whatever it was, he kept it to himself. Nico reached into his own pocket. He touched the bronze coin he always kept there—a keepsake Will had given him as a token of his dedication. He wondered if Will's commitment would always be that durable, or if he would eventually decide that Nico was just too alien, coming from this realm.

Nico shook off the thought. He led Will down the narrow, twisting path. If either of them made one wrong move, it was entirely possible they might slip and fall into . . .

Actually, Nico didn't really want to think about that, either.

Thankfully, it wasn't nearly as long a descent as their initial one from the Door of Orpheus, but as they hiked along the river, Nico worried about what would happen when they reached the troglodytes. He was sure his subterranean friends could help them get into Tartarus. He was also certain that whatever plan they concocted, it wouldn't be a pleasant experience for Will. They were still in the upper reaches of the Underworld, and they'd already been nearly bested by a shadow-squid nightmare demon with mommy issues. Once they reached the depths of Tartarus, things would get so much worse. . . . Well, they'd just have to deal with that when the time came.

Nico stopped often to allow his boyfriend to catch up on the trail. The first time this happened, Will seemed convinced that something was following them again.

Nico saw nothing. Plus, the trail was so narrow that nothing of significant size could have hidden from them.

"I swear I heard little rocks falling down," said Will. "Like something had accidentally knocked them over the edge."

This didn't seem likely to Nico, given that the roar of the Styx would drown out most other noises, but he decided to humor Will and remain still for a minute. They both heard nothing.

Nico shrugged. "We're both on edge after Epiales and their nightmares. Don't let this place get to you."

"And . . . you're sure we're not still in a nightmare?"

Nico inched closer and gave him a quick kiss. "That feel like a nightmare?"

Will smiled. "No."

"Correct answer. Now come on. Just stick close and watch your step."

They stopped a few more times, though, because Nico kept getting ahead of Will.

"You're so good at this," Will said, his steps careful and controlled, while Nico was now walking backward down the trail. "How many times have you taken this trail before?"

"Oh . . . A few."

Will's eyes brightened like he'd just had an epiphany. "All those times I couldn't find you over the past couple of weeks—this is where you've been disappearing to."

Nico nodded. "I wanted to make sure the troglodytes got settled in their new home. There were some challenges, but . . . well, you'll see what I came up with."

The corner of Will's mouth rose. "I'm glad you thought about helping them."

"Well, that's what this quest is all about, isn't it?" said Nico, facing forward. "We have to fix what's been broken."

"I love that about you, Nico di Angelo."

Nico's face flushed. He wasn't sure he'd ever get used to Will being so open and . . . *nice*. But he was definitely willing to try.

The ledge continued downward, gradually leveling out until it was no more than a narrow path running along the water, the rocks slick with spray from the rapids. As they neared the end of the trail, Nico slowed. "You're going to need one of those hoodies you brought," he told Will. "We're not going swimming, I promise, but you'll want to get as little of the River Styx on your skin as possible."

Will didn't argue. He slipped into a pale blue hoodie that read CAMP HALF-BLOOD COUNSELOR across the chest.

Nico pulled the hood on the collar of his leather jacket up over his head. "Just follow my lead."

He moved ahead cautiously, hugging the cliff on his right, his face practically rubbing against the dark stone. And then: a reprieve. A wide cave mouth opened up in the side of the cliff, and Nico darted inside, away from the water. Will followed, the hood of his sweatshirt pulled *very* tight, so that all Nico could see was the tip of Will's nose and his eyes.

"That's a good look on you," he said.

Will pushed his hands out of the ends of his sleeves and shuddered. "I feel like a turtle."

Nico unsheathed his sword. Its dim purple glow didn't do much to illuminate the cave, but Nico knew the way from here. "You ready, Will?"

Will pushed back his hood and let his bushy blond hair loose. "Ready for what, exactly?"

Nico grinned.

"Troglodytes!" he called, his voice echoing deep into the cave. "It is Nico di Angelo, son of Hades! I have returned with my glow-in-the-dark boyfriend, Will Solace!"

CHAPTER  14

The answer came almost immediately. One moment, they heard the sound of shuffling feet from somewhere far away, and then, suddenly, they were surrounded by troglodytes.

There were too many to count, but Nico was so happy to see them.

The troglodytes looked like humans if humans stood only a few feet high and had evolved from frogs. They had paper-thin lips over wide faces, recessed noses, and bulging eyes like amphibians'. Their skin tones came in a seemingly limitless assortment of colors. Even in the dim light, Nico could see greens and blues and browns. One of the trogs—dressed very much like an aerobics instructor from the '80s—had skin that glittered as if covered in yellow gems.

Troglodytes had a penchant for costumes, and they were dressed in every conceivable outfit you could imagine: sweaters on top of overalls; double-breasted suit jackets over sweatpants; skirts and dresses and blouses, all haphazardly assembled and layered on top of one another. One trog wore nothing but neon pink: high-waisted leather pants, a jacket with cropped shoulders over pink mesh, and an audacious cowboy hat, all of it studded with gold.

The hats were . . . Well, if anything was expected of a trog, it was that they loved hats. Rarely had Nico seen a troglodyte wear only one at a time. Indeed, every trog in Nico's field of view had stacked multiple chapeaus on top of their head. Beanies under Stetsons under newsboy caps under snapbacks under crowns. If it went on top of a head, the troglodytes wore it.

The trog Nico knew best, Screech-Bling, stepped forward, decked out as usual in his miniature George Washington costume, complete with a white wig under a leather tricorn.

"We see you, Nico di Angelo and Will Solace!" Screech-Bling cried.

Of course, his actual speech was punctuated with the constant clicks, growls, and screeches the trogs used to communicate.

"Thank you—*grrr*—O great *Screech*-Bling, CEO of the troglodytes!" said Nico. "I—"

Will stepped forward. "We come bearing—*click*—gifts, O great—*screech*—troglodytes!"

Nico watched in horror as Will unknowingly told the audience that he came bearing "rotten" gifts to the great "fermenting" troglodytes. Then his boyfriend set down his knapsack in front of a couple of jittery, nervous trogs and pulled out the other two hoodies he had packed. He held them high and asked, "Do these gifts—*grrr*—you?"

The troglodytes looked uncertainly at Screech-Bling.

"Will, what are you *doing*?" Nico whispered.

"I thought I'd at least *try*," Will said.

"You just asked them if your hoodies 'devour' them."

"No, that's not what I said!"

Nico nodded. "It totally is."

But the trogs seemed to have understood the gesture. Two of them had already slipped inside the pale blue hoodies, which dragged on the ground due to their short stature.

Screech-Bling doffed his triangular hat. "They do devour us," he said. "Come, Nico and Will—*screech!*—and join us in our new home."

Will smiled at Nico. "Guess I did okay."

Nico chuckled. "Yeah, I think so." He took Will's hand in his. "Thank you for trying."

They began their trek through the dark cavern with Screech-Bling in the lead. Soon they entered a side passage lit by clusters of bioluminescent mushrooms—the trog version of wall sconces—and Nico could see well enough to put his glowing sword away. One of the trogs who had snatched a hoodie danced a little jig in front of Will, clicking and screeching before darting away.

"I think that trog in particular is happy with you," said Nico.

Will scanned the crowd, which was chattering and clicking fiercely in their colorful fashion ensembles. "They've really improved their clothing options since we last saw them."

"That was part of the appeal of this place," said Nico. "They're right by the River Styx."

Will tilted his head. "I don't get it."

"The Styx carries the remains of broken dreams."

"Which means—?"

"Well, when the dead cross the river, they abandon their mortal lives. A lot of times, they discard the last of their precious memories in the water. You can see all sorts of debris floating in the current: the pages of unfinished manuscripts, paintings that went unsold, photographs of loved ones."

Will winced. "That is *so* sad."

Nico hadn't really thought of it that way. To him, it was just the nature of the Underworld, but he nodded in sympathy. "Anyway, a *lot* of clothing ends up there, too. The trogs have a great time fishing it all out."

"And . . . Hades doesn't mind?"

Nico shook his head. "I doubt he's ever going to notice or care that there's less"—Nico stopped himself; he'd almost said *garbage*, but Will would probably find that a harsh way to describe the remnants of people's lives—"less stuff in the Styx. This is the perfect place for the troglodytes to be. No one is looking for secret caves on this side of the Styx, and no one from the world above is ever going to come down here willingly. So, there's, like, zero chance that their home might . . . well, you know. Accidentally get trampled by a bunch of tauri silvestres."

"Ugh," said Will. "I don't even eat beef anymore because it reminds me of them."

The tunnel twisted sharply to the left. Nico and Will fell silent as the light ahead of them grew, along with the echoes of what sounded like a boisterous party. Their trog escorts rushed forward, clicking and hissing excitedly, and the tunnel opened into a cavern even larger than the first.

"Sweet Hades," muttered Nico.

He'd seen the earlier stages of the construction, but the sheer scope of what the trogs had accomplished since his last visit took Nico's breath away. If their previous home had been akin to a subway platform, this was Grand Central Station. The troglodytes had carved the cave's ceiling into an elaborate dome, with friezes of trogs chasing giant lizards and bulls, then repurposed the largest stalagmites and stalactites into looming support columns, reinforced and decorated with all manner of garbage. To the right, the trogs had set up a massive staging area, where they organized all the human objects they'd found into house-size piles, though Nico couldn't see any rhyme or reason to the way things were sorted. Toward the back of the cave, an archway led into an even more bustling area, with trogs coming and going like rush-hour traffic: more trogs than

Nico had ever seen in one place. But even that wasn't the most overwhelming thing about Trog HQ.

On the left side of the cavern, the trogs had excavated an *enormous* hole in the wall, about fifty feet off the ground, from which cascaded a midnight-black waterfall. The water crashed into a gigantic pool before being channeled through a series of canals, where troglodytes sat on the banks with rudimentary fishing poles and nets, grabbing out all sorts of detritus and tossing it behind them to other trogs, who sorted the refuse and laid the best bits on racks to dry. Farther down, the current turned giant waterwheels that seemed to be powering grindstones, bellows, and other strange contraptions.

"What *is* this?" Will muttered in awe.

"You are bearing witness to a new age of the troglodyte," said Screech-Bling. "This is a most effective operation."

"You . . . diverted the River Styx," said Nico, and he rubbed at his eyes. "For hydraulic power. And you've basically introduced the Underworld's first recycling system."

"Yes, we did," said Screech-Bling.

"It's so brilliant I can barely stand it," said Nico.

Screech-Bling puffed out his chest. "You have helped us greatly, Italian son of Hades."

Will frowned at the troglodyte trash-pickers. "But isn't Styx water dangerous?"

Screech-Bling made a derisive clicking sound. "To trogs? No."

Another troglodyte ambled by with a large goblet of smoking dark liquid, decorated with miniature paper umbrellas. "It is spicy, however." He belched and continued onward with his Styx-water mocktail.

Screech-Bling grinned at Will. "It is good to see you again, Texan son of Apollo. Please give your father our regards the next time you see him."

"Um, thanks," said Will. "I've got to admit, your new headquarters are *very* impressive."

"You have seen nothing!" Screech-Bling said, lifting his chin. "Come. We shall feed you and hear stories of your quest!"

"Oh, I'm okay for food," said Will hastily. "I just had some ambrosia."

"You speak gibberish to the troglodytes," said Screech-Bling. "All beings must eat! Come feast with us!"

The trog leader pushed ahead through the crowds, not waiting to see if his guests were following.

Will gave Nico a worried look. "The last time we ate trog food, it was lizard soup."

"Which was not that bad," Nico said. "Honestly, live a little, Will! Let's get some food and rest before our journey *really* begins."

"And if they're making their food with Styx water now—?"

"I'll let them know we have, uh, dietary restrictions. It'll be fine. Besides, you need some nourishment after your Care Bear reveal."

Will did not look convinced, but he followed Nico into the flow of trog foot traffic, trying to keep an eye on Screech-Bling's tricorn hat in the distance. They passed numerous tunnels that branched off from the main thoroughfare, and Nico hoped they'd have a chance to explore.

At the same time, a voice nagged in the back of his mind: *No. Don't waste time. Go save Bob.*

Finally, they arrived in the trogs' communal eating area—a huge recessed pit like an amphitheater, with a cooking fire and a collection of salvaged kitchen appliances in the center. Nico felt like he was about to be in the studio audience for a television bake-off. As they made their way to the front row, the trogs' master cook strode toward them, a huge grin on his face and a much-too-tall white chef's hat canted on his head like the Leaning Tower of Pisa. Click-Wrong (pronounce the *W*) looked overjoyed to see Nico and Will again.

"I have improved our recipes!" he exclaimed. "Today, I have a human dish for you!"

"Oh?" Will looked like he wanted to ask whether that meant a dish made from humans, but he didn't.

As Click-Wrong scurried off to prepare, a small troglodyte dressed like a Tour de France cyclist ran up and offered Will a large yellowish triangle that kind of resembled a block of cheese.

"What is this for?" Will asked.

The child pointed at Will's head. He then offered Nico a brown bowler hat.

Nico couldn't contain his amusement. He put on the bowler, then turned to Will. "Where's your team spirit? You know the trogs expect their guests to wear hats. Don't be shy."

With a look of irritation, Will placed the foam cheese wedge on his head. "Why can't I ever get a *normal* hat?"

"Who likes normal?" Nico said. "I much prefer the weird."

"Says the guy with a normal hat!"

Click-Wrong returned with a steaming black stone cup in either hand. "Please provide feedback," he said. "I accept a rating between one and five stars."

Nico peered into the cup. The broth was a dark red color, with pieces of some sort of animal protein floating in it. "Er, looks great, though I should have mentioned we can't ingest Styx water—"

Click-Wrong waved aside the comment. "I am aware of human digestive weaknesses! Do not worry. Bon—*screech*—appetite!"

Nico took a sip and was pleasantly surprised. It was a little tart, very savory, and actually quite good, though he couldn't identify what human recipe it was supposed to be.

"Not bad at all, *Click*-Wrong!" said Nico.

Will followed his cue and took a sip. He contemplated for a moment, then gave a thumbs-up. "Yeah, this is tasty! What is this?"

"Tomato soup," said the chef. "I am glad you enjoy it! This gives *Click*-Wrong pride."

Nico stared into his bowl. Tomato soup would not have been his guess. "Where do you get tomatoes down here?"

Click-Wrong smiled coyly, as if this were a trog state secret. "It also contains green anole lizard and some noodles. Those are my contributions!"

Will froze with the bowl halfway to his mouth. "Lizard. Again?"

"A delicacy among trogs," Nico reminded him, so as not to offend their host. "Lots of human cultures eat lizard, too. We are honored, *Click*-Wrong!"

To show he meant it, Nico slurped down a chunk of lizard meat. It was less chewy than he'd expected.

Will took another sip from his cup. "And . . . what kind of noodles did you find?"

"The most common kind you humans use," said Click-Wrong.

Will frowned, then pinched a long dark "noodle" out of the broth. A look of horror grew on his face. "Um, would that be the kind of noodle we wear on our shoes?"

"Exactly!" said Click-Wrong, delighted. "They are quite tasty."

Nico covered his mouth to hold in the laughter. On the end of the "noodle" was a small sheath of plastic—an aglet—that only appeared on one thing in the human world.

Will sighed. "Well, thanks, *Click*-Wrong. Humans can't actually eat shoelaces, but . . . they add a real kick to the soup?"

Click-Wrong, clearly pleased, skipped off to serve other trogs.

Nico was lucky enough that his cup didn't have a single shoelace in it. He was about halfway through his soup, and wondering how anoles could be so tasty, when Screech-Bling reappeared, heartily chewing on a bootstrap. "It is good to see you feasting with us!"

"I'm glad you've made so much progress with the new headquarters," said Nico.

"There is more to do. Our hat-storage room is already overflowing."

"Maybe you could collect *fewer* hats?" Will suggested.

Screech-Bling stared at him.

"Or not!" Will said, adjusting the block of cheese on his head. "More hats for everyone!"

Screech-Bling turned back to Nico. "Now please—tell me of your journey."

Nico updated the troglodyte on everything that had transpired so far, from the voices and the repeating prophecy to the fight they'd had with Epiales.

By the end, Screech-Bling was scratching nervously at his powdered wig. "We have only been here a few months," he said, "yet we can sense something has changed in the ground beneath us. Something is stirring."

"I don't like the sound of that," said Will.

"What do you think it is?" asked Nico.

"We do not know." Screech-Bling clicked his tongue a few times. "We lack wisdom of the Underworld and its many strange creatures."

"That's understandable," said Will.

"But I do know this." Screech-Bling sniffed the air. "The change has a strong smell. . . . And that scent is on you."

"I'm sorry, *what?*" said Nico.

"It is on both of you," said Screech-Bling. "A smell of . . . I do not know."

Will sniffed his blue hoodie. "Is it from our run-in with Epiales?"

"No," said the troglodyte. "I know the scent of demons. This is similar . . . but stronger. Related? It perplexes me." The trog CEO turned to the crowd in the dining area and shouted, "Trogs, come and smell these demigods!"

Suddenly, Nico and Will were swarmed by other troglodytes pressing their noses against them.

"Excuse me," said Will, trying to push one away who was smelling his knees.

"Yes, yes!" The troglodyte grinned up at him from beneath their sideways baseball cap. "The smell is all over you."

"On you as well!" said another one, sniffing Nico's shoes. "Very strong. Like fish rot."

"No, like truffles," said another.

"Bug goo," suggested a third.

"It is the changey smell!" said a trog in a cowboy hat, and the others murmured their assent.

"Yes, the changey smell!"

Nico's skin crawled. Whatever "the changey" was, he didn't want to smell like it.

A fierce chorus of clicks and growls broke out nearby, and Screech-Bling excused himself to deal with a group of young troglodytes who were fighting over a set of matching wizard hats.

As he walked away, Nico's thoughts began to race.

Epiales had mentioned *Mother.*

Screech-Bling said the smell might be *related* to demons.

Nico's theory from before resurfaced, but he didn't want it to be true.

It couldn't be.

"Nico?" Will nudged him. "You okay?"

"Yeah . . . just thinking."

Nico must have been sending out strong *I don't want to talk about it* vibes, because Will didn't ask for details.

"At least the troglodytes seem happy down here," he offered. "I didn't expect that."

Nico raised an eyebrow. "Why not?"

Will shrugged. "You know, just . . . the Underworld, land of the dead. I thought they might find living here . . . depressing?"

"Death is a part of life," said Nico. "We *always* live next door to it. I don't think that fact should be called depressing."

"Okay, sure, but living in *this* place . . ." Will scanned the cavern, like he was looking for something that just wasn't there.

Nico took a deep breath. He reminded himself that Will had been through a lot today. . . . They both had.

"Not everything here is the worst in the universe," he said. "My father lives in the Underworld. And lots of living people keep his palace running. Bob was a janitor there, remember?"

"Yeah, I remember," said Will. "I'm just saying . . . living people, like Bob or the troglodytes, they're the exception to the rule, right?"

Nico scowled. He wished Will could be a little more open-minded about the Underworld. The troglodytes may not have been born here, but they fit right in. Couldn't Will see that?

But Nico didn't want to fight anymore. He also supposed their encounter with Epiales hadn't made for the best first impression of his father's realm.

He was trying to figure out how to say that, how to spin his irritation into something more positive, when Screech-Bling reappeared, having successfully mediated the wizard-hat dilemma.

"Now, Nico di Angelo," said the CEO, "where were we?"

Unfortunately, Nico remembered: the smell of change, of something stirring. Mother . . . Epiales had warned they would meet her soon enough.

"I know what is stirring," Nico said. "Or at least I *think* I know."

Screech-Bling examined him, his eyes moving quickly back and forth. Then his pinkish tongue flicked in and out of his mouth. "How would you know this, Nico di Angelo?"

Nico hesitated to say. He didn't even want to speak her name. But if the troglodytes could sense her—*smell* her presence even at this great distance—then they deserved to know. They all might be in danger.

"You should summon your council," Nico told the trog leader. "We need to talk." Then he faced Will. "I think I know who sent me those terrible dreams. And why Bob's in trouble."

CHAPTER 15

Screech-Bling summoned one of the younger trogs, hissed and clicked some instructions to them, and sent them off on an errand. Then he looked up at Nico.

"Follow me," he said.

He led the way—very badly, Nico thought, since he didn't seem to care if Nico and Will kept pace with him—back into the main cavern, then through a series of side tunnels. They passed a row of sleeping quarters where younger trogs were napping on beds of woven bioluminescent moss.

"You know, before this trip," said Will, struggling to keep up, "I didn't know if the troglodytes slept at all, since there's no day or night underground."

"We all must eventually!" Screech-Bling called out. "We are not so different from you, son of Apollo."

Nico caught a glimpse of Will's face as they scurried along, and he was sure it was a little redder.

Screech-Bling cut a sharp right into a small circular room dominated by a round conference table. Three other troglodytes were already there, milling about anxiously. As soon as Will and Nico passed through the entrance, a fourth trog—wearing a thick parka and at least three separate beanies stacked atop one another—pushed a large boulder across the doorway with her shoulder, sealing them all in.

Will raised an eyebrow. "*Screech*-Bling, what is this?"

"This is our council," said the female troglodyte. "And I am *Howl*-Smith, its leader." She bowed.

The others introduced themselves as well. There was Clack-Jones, who wore a Stetson on top of a baseball cap, then Shriek-Vibes, who appropriately wore an orange bucket hat with a jack-o'-lantern on it. The fifth member of the council was a scrawny troglodyte named Hiss-Majesty. Their name was absolutely the greatest Nico had ever heard, but he was surprised that they were *not* wearing a hat at all.

Nico pointed to the trog's bare head. "Missing something?"

Hiss-Majesty turned away. "I am sensitive about it," they said. "I—I have not found the right hat for me."

Screech-Bling patted them on the shoulder. "In time, *Hiss*-Majesty."

Hiss-Majesty sniffled, then glanced at Nico. "Thank you for helping us find a new home."

"Indeed!" said Howl-Smith loudly.

"It is perfect for us," agreed Shriek-Vibes. "I am confused, though. Why have we called this council meeting?"

Screech-Bling raised his hands. "I called this meeting at the request of our demigod friend Nico di Angelo! He has important information to share. About the changey smell."

The other council members muttered apprehensively, then took their places around the table. Nico and Will were seated to the left of Howl-Smith.

"Speak, Nico di Angelo," Howl-Smith said. "Though our new headquarters is located where few could ever find us, we are still in the Underworld, where many creatures, monsters, and spirits could prey on us. We must always be vigilant! If you know the source of the change we have smelled, you must share!"

Nico swallowed his nerves. "It's a theory," he said, "but I think I'm right. I believe what you are sensing . . . *who* you are sensing, is Nyx."

At the utterance of her name, the troglodytes let loose a frenzy of clicks and clacks, hisses and shrieks, snarls and pops.

"Wait," Will murmured to him. "Are you talking about . . . the goddess of night? *That* Nyx?"

Before Nico could answer, Howl-Smith whistled for the group's silence. "If true, this is most serious, Nico di Angelo." She glanced at Will. "As for your question, son of Apollo, Nyx is no mere god. She is a *protogenos*."

Will looked nervous, like he'd been caught in a pop quiz. "Um, I feel like I should know that word, but remind me again?"

"A *protogenos*," said Nico. "A primordial goddess, born before the Olympian gods or even the Titans."

"They are the constants of our existence," added Shriek-Vibes.

"The fundamental powers of the cosmos!" Hiss-Majesty said.

"They are really awful!" said Clack-Jones.

"And we've actually already met one," Nico reminded Will. "Gaea."

Will frowned. "Oh, great. So we're dealing with Gaea two-point-oh?"

"Well, no . . ." said Nico.

A spark of hope kindled in Will's eyes, which was why Nico hated what he had to say next.

"I think Nyx may be worse," he grumbled.

Will's mouth dropped open. "Worse? How is that even possible?"

"She is the goddess of pure darkness," said Howl-Smith.

"Mother of hellhounds," added Clack Jones. "And demons."

"And . . . I've met her," said Nico.

"When?" Will asked sharply.

Nico watched him come to the realization that there were still things . . . *big* things . . . that Nico had never shared, and dread filled his own heart.

"I never told you," he admitted, his voice soft. "I never told anyone. Not Chiron, not Mr. D, not Percy or Annabeth, or . . ." He couldn't bring himself to add Jason's name—not so close to the land of the dead.

He felt the gaze of the troglodytes as they watched him in anticipation.

But it was Will he focused on. Nico was used to people looking at him with a mixture of sadness, awe, and maybe a touch of pity in their eyes. How could he blame them? There was such a relentless darkness to Nico's story. But Will didn't look at him like that. . . . He looked hurt, and that was worse.

"I just couldn't talk about it," Nico said. "I . . . tried to tell people the minimum about what happened to me in Tartarus. I only hinted at what *actually* happened down there, kind of hoping no one would ever ask me for more."

And they hadn't, Nico thought.

Even his closest friends had respected his silence . . . or maybe they were just too terrified of learning the details.

Will's expression softened. He ran his fingers through Nico's hair. "I get it. You don't have to tell me. You're the only one who can decide whether talking about it will help. And if it won't, I don't want to re-traumatize you."

Nico marveled how Will could shift from being hurt to being a caregiver so quickly. He was like one of those dent-resistant cars that just popped back into their original shape no matter how bad the fender bender.

Nico wanted to believe that he could choose not to share. He wanted to disappear into Will's light and warmth, to purge the memory that was awakening in him.

But he shook his head. "No, Will, I think I *need* to tell you this."

Nico wiped his face, annoyed that it was already wet with tears. He faced the trog council.

"You *all* need to hear what really happened to me the last time I was in Tartarus."

CHAPTER  16

N ico had walked for a few hours over the grim and lifeless terrain, past his father's palace and the Fields of Asphodel, before he'd found the cave.

He wasn't sure what he'd been expecting. The entrance to Tartarus looked like . . . well, a hole in the ground. Nothing special. Surrounded by enormous boulders, the pitch-black entrance sank into the earth at a steep angle. Maybe the air coming out of it was a little warmer than the rest of the Underworld, like the exhalations of a living creature. Otherwise . . . yeah. It was a cave. Very cave-like, all things considered.

So this was it. For the entrance to the worst place in all existence, it felt oddly anticlimactic. But if the Doors of Death were down there, then maybe Nico could close them and stop Gaea before things got worse.

Things always get worse, he thought. *Don't let your guard down.*

The irony, of course, was that as he stood there, worried about what lay ahead of him, he didn't sense the thing coming up behind him.

By the time he heard its hiss and spun around to meet it, the Chimera was upon him.

It was twice Nico's size, its lion's maw caked in dirt and blood. Its shaggy goat body swarmed with blow flies, and its scaly tail lashed back and forth like a diamondback rattlesnake.

Nico whipped out his Stygian iron sword, but it didn't matter.

It was the tail of the *other* monster that caught him across the chest.

Nico slammed against the nearest boulder, the breath knocked out of him.

"Nico di Angelo," said a gloating voice. "This time, you don't have anywhere to escape to!"

He tried to suck in air, but it was like a giant had clasped their hands around his chest. He pushed himself upright, pointing the tip of his sword toward . . .

Nonna?

Nico immediately felt ashamed for making that comparison, but the creature looming over him *did* look a lot like his grandmother back in 1930s Venice. Her coiffed hair was gunmetal gray, her stout upper body clothed in a faded flower-print dress and a hand-knit sweater. But Nico's grandmother hadn't had eyes slitted like a reptile's, a flickering forked tongue, or a massive snake's trunk instead of legs.

"You know," said Nico, "you could just say hello instead of trying to kill me."

"I am the Mother of Monsters," she said, her voice thick with bile. "You will address me as Echidna!"

"Like that hedgehog animal?"

She cast a baleful glare at her Chimera companion. "Every time! Why do they say that *every time?*"

"Well," Nico said, "you *did* name yourself after the animal."

This seemed like a reasonable point to Nico, but judging from the way Echidna bared her fangs, she did not agree.

"First of all, it's not a hedgehog," she said. "It's related to the anteater. Secondly, *Australia* named *it* after *me*. Do you honestly think I would allow myself to be linked to such a lowly creature?"

"Hedgehogs are pretty cute," he said, his mind running calculations on how he could get out of this mess without being slaughtered. "I'd be flattered."

"This is why I hate demigods," she said. "You think you can joke and distract your way out of everything. That Percy Jackson also thought he could escape me."

At the mention of Percy's name, Nico's heart skipped a beat. "From what I heard . . . he didn't 'escape,' because you never actually captured him."

She sneered. "A mere technicality."

"I don't know. If you look up the definition of the word *escape*—"

"Enough!" Echidna roared. "If I wanted you dead, Nico di Angelo, I would have already killed you. We are only here to bear witness, and to make sure you don't lose your nerve."

The Chimera stepped forward, forcing Nico back toward the cave's entrance. The warm breeze from the chasm seemed to wrap around him, pulling him closer.

"Do you sense it now?" asked Echidna, her forked tongue darting between her fangs. "That is your destiny. . . ."

Nico's feet slid against the dirt as if he were already on an incline. He tried to take a step forward, but it was pointless. His feet slipped out from under him and he nearly cracked his jaw on the ground.

Echidna laughed. "You're right where Gaea wants you!"

Nico dug his fingers into the dirt, but he was moving too quickly.

"Say hello to all my monster friends!" she called.

The terrible gravity of Tartarus grasped Nico, and he plunged into the pit.

He fell.

Not for long.
For an eternity.

At last, he crash-landed against a hard surface, and for the second time that day, he got the wind knocked out of him. Every bone in his body should have been broken, but somehow he forced himself to move.

He got to his hands and knees. His muscles screamed in protest. Something slithered past him in the darkness, grazing his shoulder. He swung his sword in that direction, hoping to strike something. A piercing shriek was his answer.

He hoisted himself up, scrambling for purchase on the rough ground. In the purple glow of his blade, all he could see were shadows dancing around him.

"Who's there?" Nico yelled.

He was met with laughter—a sick, phlegmy sound. As he moved forward, his sword held aloft, something brushed his neck. He screamed and swatted at it. Then a voice giggled in his other ear. It sounded like a demonic toddler.

Knowing his luck, it probably *was*.

Nico pressed on until he perceived a dim light in the distance. Still, he could see nothing of his surroundings. He'd thought he understood darkness, but now he realized he'd been thinking of the shadows here all wrong. They didn't recede in the glow of his blade. Instead, they thickened stubbornly, clinging to him like some sort of mist or fog.

It was as if Tartarus were alive, sending antibodies to attack him as a foreign invader. He trudged forward toward the distant red glow. The scent on the breeze turned sharp and bitter.

Finally, he staggered out of the shadow fog.

Nico nearly collapsed at what he saw.

Spreading to the horizon was a bloodred landscape of hills and crags, dotted with twisted, blackened trees. Noxious green clouds drifted through the air and clung to the valleys. And just below him, on a flattened plain of crushed rock and volcanic glass, Gaea's army was preparing for war.

Hyperborean giants towered above the other troops like living blue siege towers. Legions of Cyclopes rummaged through mounds of armor and weapons, looking for the best-quality gear. Packs of wolves prowled the perimeter, occasionally surrounding some unfortunate monster straggler and taking them out for lunch. A herd of drakons wove in and out of the ranks, trampling anything too slow to get out of their way.

"Oh, Hades," Nico murmured.

Which was exactly when three basilisks raised their heads to look at him. Nico knew what they were instantly—not many creatures look like cobras with miniature deer antlers—but he knew better than to meet their yellow lamp-like gaze.

Instead, he turned and ran.

He heard their blood-chilling screeches behind him, but he refused to look back. Whatever he was running toward, it had to be better than the ten-thousand-to-one odds behind him.

The ground gave with each step like spongy turf. Off to his left, a green bank of fog drifted across a marsh. He thought of heading into it, for cover at least, but he didn't know what that fog was made of. It could be acid, or poison, or some monstrous gaseous life-form with a taste for demigods.

Behind him, a beast snarled. Nico instinctively swung his sword back, and the blade connected with flesh. The creature howled in pain. Another lunged in front of him: one of the massive black wolves. Nico sliced off its head without even slowing, and its body disintegrated immediately.

Nico kept running. Sweat poured down his face. His lungs burned. He glanced back just long enough to see more wolves racing after him, slavering for a di Angelo snack plate.

Absolutely not, he told himself.

But there was nowhere to go, nothing to hide behind. About a hundred yards away, he spotted a ridge with some strange black ovals protruding from the surface. Volcanic outcrops, maybe? Perhaps something there could give him a bit of coverage, but he'd never make it before the wolves tore him apart.

Then he glanced to his right and nearly tripped over himself in surprise. Someone was waving at him.

Nestled between the nearest two hills was a white house with red trim, big bay windows, and a sloping, shingled roof. Unlike everything else in Tartarus, it didn't appear dead, rotting, or poisonous. It was just . . . a house, like you might see anywhere in suburban America. On the front porch stood a human-looking figure, beckoning to Nico. He knew in his heart this was probably a trap, but where else was he supposed to go?

His lungs burned.

His eyes watered.

He was losing hope as the wolves gained ground.

So Nico cut to the right and pumped his legs. He could hear the wolves' paws thumping behind him. He pushed himself harder, until the person on the porch was fully in view. They had shoulder-length black hair and a striking red jacket that matched the surrounding landscape. As Nico got closer, they turned and walked through the front door, which began to close. . . .

"Hey!" Nico yelled. "Wait!"

He was running so fast he almost flew through the doorway. It slammed shut, just in time for the wolves to crash into it.

They howled and whined outside while Nico sat panting on the floor, his back wedged against the door. Why did his lungs hurt so badly? Maybe he'd cracked his ribs in the fall. Or maybe the atmosphere in Tartarus just wasn't fit for demigods. Maybe he was *supposed* to struggle to survive here.

He glanced around at the empty room: nothing but a bare, dusty hardwood floor and blank white walls. No other exits. Even the bay windows seemed to have disappeared from the front wall.

"About time you found me."

The voice startled Nico so badly that he jumped and banged his head on the doorknob. Clutching the tender spot on the top of his skull, he squinted at the person who had materialized across the room.

She didn't look like a monster, which concerned Nico, given that he'd fallen into Tartarus. Then again, monsters came in all shapes and sizes. Her jeans and leather boots were the same dark tone as her hair. A single gold chain looped across the front of her white blouse. Her red jacket glistened disturbingly like fresh blood. Behind her was . . . nothing. The back wall had simply vanished, replaced by a dark void.

She stared at Nico appraisingly. "Well? Aren't you going to ask me who I am?"

Nico rubbed the knot forming on his head. "I'm going to guess you're a goddess, seeing as you have a house in the middle of Tartarus. Is this, like, your vacation home, or . . . ?"

"It's not really my home," she said. "Think of it more as . . . a shrine, if you will. A safe haven. And until recent events, I was not allowed even that."

As she said this, her irises flared red. "My only true home is in the heart, the spirit. When balance is achieved."

The flare went out.

"Impressive," said Nico. When she rolled her eyes, he laughed. "I'm serious! That was actually pretty cool."

"Leave it to Nico di Angelo to tell a goddess that they're 'cool.'"

He examined her sharp, angular face. The dark eyes. The dark hair. The obsession with balance.

"You're Ethan Nakamura's mother," he decided. "Nemesis."

She opened her arms wide. "In the flesh. Or not, depending on how you view godhood."

Nico got to his feet. He wasn't usually one to feel starstruck—or godstruck—but an unfamiliar sensation was creeping through him: awe.

"Why are you here?" he asked. "Why did you save me?"

"Can't a goddess do something nice for a demigod?"

Nico barked a laugh. "Yeah, but it always comes with a catch. I'm not a fool, Nemesis."

She stepped toward him, and the field of darkness came with her, drifting behind her body like the train of a dress. The house *changed*. No longer was Nico in an empty room. He stood on the parapets of Erebos, the walls of impenetrable darkness marching off in either direction. He gazed across the Fields of Asphodel, toward the spires of his father's palace.

"Why have you brought me here?" he murmured.

But when he turned for the answer, Nemesis was gone. Instead, his father stood before him.

Hades's robes swirled with ghostly afterimages of the damned. His dark beard was longer, which startled Nico, since he had seen his father only a day or so ago. But of course gods could look like whatever they wanted, and *this* god wasn't his father at all.

"What is this, Nemesis?" Nico demanded. "Why do you look like that?"

The false Hades spoke with Nemesis's voice. "I know what you really want," she said. "I know the imbalance that exists in your heart."

As if to prove her point, Nico's heartbeat stumbled. He wondered how deeply Nemesis could see into his feelings, and why she'd chosen to stand in judgment in the guise of his father.

"I don't know what you mean," he said.

Nemesis/Hades chuckled. "I have taken a greater interest in demigods since Percy Jackson advocated on behalf of us so-called *minor* gods to those snobs on Mount Olympus. I have come to believe that you heroes may be more . . . interesting than I thought. And you in particular wish to right what was made wrong."

Nico's mouth tasted of ashes. "But why show me this? Why my father?"

Nemesis swept her hand across the landscape of Erebos. "To demonstrate what you already know. Your father tries, but even here, in the place of final judgment, true fairness is so rarely achieved. The good suffer. The bad are rewarded. The gods' great system is a creaky machine, a lopsided wheel. At times, we must act individually—*you* must act—to achieve a proper justice. Just as you are doing now."

"Enough," Nico said, heat flushing his cheeks. "If you want to help me, get me to the Doors of Death."

Nemesis's smile faded. Darkness swept around them, and suddenly she was back in her original form, staring at Nico across the bare room of her suburban Tartarus sanctuary.

"There are limits to how much I can help you," she said, "especially in Tartarus."

She moved closer to Nico, her stare burning into him. "I am the goddess of retribution," she said. "This is the realm in which monsters regenerate after they've been disposed of by gods or demigods. All of them desire *nothing* but retribution, Nico."

"So wouldn't that make you more powerful here?"

She frowned. "It's the opposite. Each moment I spend here, I am torn in every direction. I can feel my body ripping apart right now."

"I can relate," Nico grumbled. His lungs hurt with every breath. He found himself leaning on his sword just to stay up.

There was a brief flash of pity in the goddess's eyes. "You have a terrible journey ahead of you, and in the short term, I sense it will cause even more injustice and misery."

"Great," groaned Nico.

"But listen to me, demigod." Her voice turned sharp and chiding. "You *must* endure." She grabbed Nico's hand, and he was shocked by how warm it was. She pressed something into his palm. "Keep these with you all the time. You will need them."

He looked at what she had given him: three glistening red seeds— *pomegranate* seeds.

"From your stepmother's garden," Nemesis explained.

"I know what they are." Nico could feel their power radiating along the lines of his palm.

He knew that as a child of Hades, he could use each one to put himself into a daylong death trance, a sort of hibernation, if necessary. But . . . why? Why was she giving him these?

There was a loud *THUD* behind him. The front door shuddered on its hinges. Outside, he could hear the wolves snarling, preparing for another assault.

"We are almost out of time," Nemesis said. "Follow the River of Fire, Nico. Follow it downstream, through the mist and the forest. There you will find the Doors of Death."

Nico jumped as the door began to splinter. Through one of the cracks flashed the baleful yellow eye of a wolf.

"I will get you away from here, Nico," said Nemesis. "But one day, you will need to deal with the imbalance in your heart."

Nico closed his fingers around the pomegranate seeds, then tucked them away with the others he kept. There was much more he wanted to ask, but he also wanted to be far, far away from this place as soon as possible.

"Thank you," he said. "I appreciate the help."

Nemesis raised her hands, and the darkness began to swirl around them. "One last thing . . . Beware of my mother. She only comes out during the daytime and . . . let's just say she is not as sympathetic to demigods as some of her children are."

"Daytime?" Nico asked. The concept made no sense to him down here, in the darkest depths of Underworld.

But the house disappeared, and Nemesis with it. Nico found himself standing on a ridge, the spongy red ground once again under his feet. There were no wolves or other monsters in sight, but spread across the hills in every direction were the strange black oval outcrops he'd seen from a distance. He edged closer to the nearest one and peered down at its surface. . . .

"Ugh, *gross*," he said.

It was as if the land itself had a pimple. The substance wasn't rock, exactly—more like a dark translucent membrane covering an area the size of a bathtub. And underneath, some sort of sickening yellow-green fluid was *pulsing* around a shadowy figure suspended within.

"What the—?" Nico made a terrible mistake, but he couldn't resist. With the tip of his sword, he poked the Tartarus zit.

Predictably, the membrane burst, unleashing a geyser of goo that splattered him from head to toe.

"You've got to be *kidding* me!" Nico stumbled backward, landing hard on his tailbone. He watched in horror as something very much alive crawled out of the goo pit.

It shook its sticky wet hair, which began to smolder and then caught fire. Its form was human, but with mismatched back legs: one shaggy and hooved like a donkey's, the other constructed of bronze.

An *empousa.*

Nico's grip tightened on his sword. He'd been kidnapped by one these vampiric spirits after foolishly following Minos into the Labyrinth, and he was in no mood to be charmspoken to death.

Taking advantage of the creature's disorientation, he scrambled forward and drove his blade through its chest.

The creature wailed. "I *just* regenerated!" she screamed. "Come on!"

Then she crumbled into clumps of dust that broke apart in the goo. Immediately, the fluid began to ooze back into the pit, and the membrane began weaving itself together.

Wonderful, said Nico to himself. *Monsters regenerate even faster in Tartarus.*

He scanned his surroundings with a mounting sense of dread.

The landscape was *covered* with these regeneration zit pits. He had to keep moving.

The only thing that gave him a *little* bit of hope was the sight of a glowing red ribbon of flames in the distance, threading across the plains. At least Nemesis had deposited Nico within sight of the river he was supposed to follow: the fiery Phlegethon.

Nico pulled his leather jacket tighter and started walking.

CHAPTER  17

Nico had no idea where he was relative to the staging area he'd stumbled on before, but he figured Nemesis must have dropped him someplace far, far away.

Because this part of Tartarus was *empty.*

The land seemed to stretch on forever. Nico was thankful that Nemesis had given him some guidance, because if he hadn't kept himself to the left of the River Phlegethon, he would've had no idea where to go. After hours of walking on the strange marshy ground, Nico was exhausted. Hungry. His feet ached, and his lungs burned from the sooty air.

Something else was happening to him, too.

The world around him . . . It seemed to be shifting. That was the only way he could describe it. He'd be staring into the distance, where mist clung to a dark expanse of forest, and for the briefest of moments, the horizon would leap backward like a mirage. The landscape before him took on sharper edges, with colors so terrifyingly intense that they hurt his eyes. The land itself seemed to be rising and falling, as if it were breathing. Or was Nico imagining that?

He had no one to compare notes with, so he kept walking. The river flowed smoothly past him, and if it hadn't been made of pure fire, he would've wished for a boat—anything that could keep him moving toward the bottom of Tartarus and closer to his goal.

Sometimes, he heard cries in the distance: definitely not human, full of rage and defiance. Perhaps they were creatures awakening in the darkness, crawling from their regeneration pits, ready to head back to the world above, or to join Gaea's army. He remembered what Nemesis had said: *All of them desire* nothing *but retribution.*

He forced himself to keep walking. The fate of the whole world depended on him finding and closing the Doors of Death.

As the forest grew closer, the temperature dropped. Nico zipped up his leather jacket and kept his hands in his pockets, but soon he was shivering. This shouldn't have been possible with a flaming river literally right next to him, but somehow the closeness of the Phlegethon didn't cut through the cold. If anything, it made things worse. A part of Nico's mind begged him to jump in, to experience the warmth it would provide for a few seconds before he burned up.

"Stop that," he told himself out loud. "Don't let this place break you down."

But it *was*, wasn't it? The deeper Nico went into Tartarus, the more it sanded off the edges of his sanity. He was now convinced he was full-on hallucinating. The ground beneath him was definitely breathing, albeit very slowly, and those dark regenerating blisters were now spread so thickly in his path that he had to squeeze between them in order to keep moving. He felt like a mite crawling across a giant's stubbly face. Once, he heard the sickening *pop* as a blister burst open somewhere nearby. He stopped, his sword glowing gently at his side, but whatever monster had emerged, he heard it scampering away, heading upriver.

Nico's throat was so dry that his tongue was stuck to the roof of his mouth. He had to reach in with a finger to pry it off, which only caused him to break out in a deep cough.

And meanwhile, the River Phlegethon just kept rolling along.

It *moved* like water. To Nico's delirious mind, it had even started to look like water. But . . . it was fire. Right?

Nico searched his memories for information about the Phlegethon. For the first time in years, he thought about his old Mythomagic cards. Was there any lore in that game about what would happen if a mortal drank from the River of Fire?

He couldn't remember. He couldn't believe he was even considering it.

Then Tartarus *shuddered*. The ground shifted sideways, throwing Nico off his feet.

He tumbled to the bank of the Phlegethon, his hands digging into the fine sand. Ash and cinders swirled around him, making him cough up sour mucus. Huh. The Phlegm-a-thon, he thought. Bet I'm the first person to think of that.

Up close, the sound of the river was less like roaring fire and more like gentle babbling. It seemed to call out to him, as if begging him to drink.

No. No, he couldn't. He hauled himself upright. When he turned again toward the dark forest, it was *much* closer, no more than a stone's throw away. And in the green fog, between the twisted dark branches of the trees, thousands upon thousands of tiny, glowing eyes stared back at him.

He couldn't have cried out if he wanted to. His throat was too parched. He blinked away the soot, and when he looked up again, the forest's eyes had vanished. The ground beneath him, though, was still heaving restlessly. Like it was alive.

He froze.

Oh.

Oh, Hades.

He tried to gulp down his fear. He knelt and put his hand on the ground, his fingers sinking into the fine sand. Underneath was a layer of . . . not soil, exactly. Not marsh. More like *hide.* It all came to him suddenly—Tartarus was not just a place. Tartarus was a living *being*—the sleeping body of a primordial god, and here Nico sat, right on top of its skin.

He sobbed, overwhelmed by how far he was from home. The thought made him cry harder because he wasn't even sure where home *was.* Camp Half-Blood? Camp Jupiter? At this point, he would take either one, because they were both better than this.

High above him, a dark shape soared through the poison clouds, heading north. Its wingspan had to be forty or fifty feet. More creatures followed it, like colossal geese in formation, and Nico assumed they were going to join up with Gaea's forces.

What had Nico been *thinking*? Why had he come down here alone? No one even knew that he'd ventured into Tartarus, and even if someone did, they couldn't help him. Tartarus wasn't the kind of place you just strolled into.

He was going to die down here, wasn't he? What happened to a demigod who died in Tartarus? Could they even reach the afterlife, or would they be trapped here forever, maybe drowning in one of those covered goo pits, unable to break free?

The ground rose again, shuddering, as if the entire landscape was tossing and turning in its sleep. Nico was so thirsty. . . . He stared at the burning water. He wanted to drink so badly. . . .

For some reason, his mind went back to Dante's *Divine Comedy*, which his mom had read to him when he was younger. Being Italian, she'd insisted that Nico learn at least some Dante by heart. She'd read those poems to him at bedtime—stories about descending into the Inferno and clawing your way up again into the light of Purgatory. Almost like she'd been preparing him to know the truth about his father, or preparing him for this journey . . .

Somewhere in those cantos, there'd been a moment when Dante faced a wall of fire. His guide Virgil had convinced him to walk through it, despite his fears: *Qui può esser tormento, ma non morte.* Here you can be tormented, but not die.

It was wishful thinking that the Phlegethon would work like that. Then again, Tartarus would eventually kill him anyway, wouldn't it? Monsters he could fight. But thirst . . . that would be slower, more painful, and just as lethal.

Nico knelt. Hesitantly, he touched the surface of the "water."

It was *freezing.* He yanked his fingers back, only to discover that his skin was still very much intact and very much *not* on fire. He waited a few seconds, certain that his pain receptors would kick in, or that he would combust.

But no. His hand ached from the cold, but there were no burn marks.

He removed his jacket and set it aside.

Here goes nothing, he thought.

Then his thirst took over.

He cupped his hands, dipped them in the icy flames, and brought the water to his lips.

The effect was instantaneous. He choked and gagged, the fire raging down his throat and into his belly. He clutched at his stomach. His vision doubled, and he was certain this was the end. This was how he'd go out: curled up next to the River of Fire. From which he'd DRUNK like a fool.

But the pain began to fade. Nico lay there, gasping, and his exhaustion began to slip away. The soles of his feet no longer ached. His head felt *clearer.*

Nico sat up, and the burning . . . was all gone. Not only that, he no longer felt thirsty.

Had just a small sip of the Phlegethon done all that?

He decided not to question it any further. It was a win-win. He wasn't dead, and he'd just figured out that he could survive if he drank from a *literal* river of fire. Nico grabbed his leather jacket and slipped it on, then stood up and brushed himself off.

The forest awaited him. As did the Doors of Death.

So the son of Hades kept going.

Days passed.

Or maybe it was hours. Or weeks. Or months, for that matter. Nemesis had warned him about her mother, who only came out during the day, but Nico had no sense of when one day might be passing into another down here. The light did not change. The weather was always hellish with an 80 percent chance of noxious clouds and scattered monsters. Tartarus simply pressed down on his spirit as Nico moved deeper and deeper, following the Phlegethon as it cut through the forest.

He went as long as he could between sips from the river. He had no idea if there were any long-term effects from drinking fire, but the river water seemed to heal any exhaustion or pain that Nico was experiencing. It did *not* help him with the mental ramifications of being in Tartarus. He missed the sun. And solid food. He missed Camp Half-Blood and the satyrs and Chiron's stern fatherly voice, and even the way Mr. D whined and complained as if he were being murdered continuously day in and day out. Nico missed the other demigods, like Percy and Annabeth and Jason, even if he wasn't sure they missed him.

It didn't help that the forest—thick with a smelly, sulfurous fog— was so thoroughly unlike any woods Nico had ever been in. The trees contorted around one another, and the branches seemed to bend ever so slowly in Nico's direction, even though the trunks looked completely dead, rotten on the inside and falling apart. Nico could not see above the treetops because of the impossible fog, but he heard creatures flying above, whooping and shrieking. Bushes like tumbleweeds—but with much sharper thorns and burrs—clogged the forest floor, and Nico often had to use his sword to clear his way, which sent small lizard-rat creatures scurrying away from him.

The glowing eyes were back, too: always floating in the shadows at the edge of his vision, always watching him. He wondered why the owners of those eyes never approached or attacked. What were they waiting for? There were far more of them than there was of him. Nico stayed on constant guard, awaiting the inevitable, and the anticipation was perhaps worse than if he'd actually been attacked.

He was so focused on the eyes, he barely realized that he'd reached the far side of the forest. The fog suddenly lifted, and he was met with an unending and impenetrable wall of darkness. It stretched in every direction, as far as he could see. Even the River Phlegethon made a sharp left turn and wended off to the north, as if it didn't want to deal with that darkness. Nico stopped and stared, uncertain of what to do. How could Tartarus just *end* like that?

The ground below him continued for a few feet, so he took a step. Then another.

Then a narrow rift appeared in the darkness: a vertical fissure that revealed a dirt pathway sloping down gently until it ended at a black stone archway, not unlike the masonry on the parapets of Erebos. It looked like . . .

A doorway.

Was it *the* doorway?

The idea was appealing. What if the Doors of Death weren't some huge gates guarded by countless monsters from Gaea's army but just a simple arch hidden in the middle of nowhere?

Nico didn't want to get too excited, yet it was hard to contain himself. He moved forward onto the dirt path. He tested it with a single footstep. It did not give way. The walls of darkness on either side did not close in on him.

Okay, he thought. Feels real enough.

Another step. Another. He was halfway across when he felt compelled to look behind himself for a second. The Phlegethon cast an eerie glow over the trees. Nico was afraid to leave the only source of water that had been keeping him alive, but . . . he had to. He felt sure this was where he was supposed to be.

Near the end of the path, he noticed something about the archway that he couldn't have seen from a distance.

The black stone was *moving*.

Not shifting as a whole, but the arch appeared to be made of millions of tiny . . . well, he didn't know what he was looking at. Particles of dust? Quicksand? He reached out to touch it, then jerked his hand away.

No, he thought. *Don't do that. Something is wrong.*

Maybe he wasn't at the Doors of Death after all. He turned again, looking wistfully back up the trail. Should he drink once more of the river? Maybe rest a while and think about this? The forest didn't seem quite so creepy now.

The voice he heard forced his hand. It came from the rift at the top of the trail—an indistinct grumbling, getting closer, and definitely headed in Nico's direction. Whatever it was, Nico estimated it was only seconds from appearing, seeing him, and blocking his only exit.

With no other option, he darted through the archway, ducking to one side behind the nearest cover he could find: a tall tree with bark as black as night. Beyond, in the gloom, was an area that looked like an overgrown garden.

The voice got louder. Nico hid behind his tree just as something emerged from the archway. It was as if all of Nico's blood instantly chilled, and when he slowly let out a breath, he could see it condensing in the air.

"Mother, she's intolerable!" said the voice. "Why do we have to listen to her?"

From deeper in the garden, another voice answered. It must have been Mother—and her tone was harsh and unforgiving.

"I don't know why my children are so disobedient," she said. "I created you. I gave you life, I gave you purpose, and what do I get in return?"

There was a terrible pause.

Then the first voice said, "Love and affection?"

"Disrespect!" shrieked Mother.

Nico moved slowly, turning his head until his right eye could just peek around the edge of the trunk. What he saw twisted his heart around his stomach.

Mother was enormous, at least three times the size of an adult human. She was swathed in smoke and ash that swirled around her like she was the eye of a hurricane. Her dress was the deepest black Nico had ever seen, glittering with the twinkles of entire galaxies.

Her face was an indistinct mass of darkness, but her eyes burned with the fury of twin supernovas. She sat on a Stygian iron throne at the center of a circle of black trees. Dark gravel paths wended between topiaries that looked like clouds of ink—every branch, leaf, and flower competing to be the darkest thing in the garden. And in the distance, at the edge of Nico's vision, rose some kind of onyx structure—perhaps a temple or a palace.

The other figure stood before Mother's seat.

He was tall but more human size, with a dark skin tone and shoulder-length black braids. He wore a sweeping black coat that shimmered in mesmerizing patterns, making Nico's eyes feel heavy. "No one is disrespecting you, Mother," he said, his tone guarded. "But Gaea is not our master. Why should we—?"

Mother unfurled a set of wings that stretched from one end of the tree circle to the other. Their leathery surface swirled with shadows. "Must you always disagree with me? After that last debacle with Kronos—which I *told* you not to get involved in—you wouldn't even be safe if I hadn't let you stay here, Hypnos!"

Involuntarily, Nico grunted with surprise. The god Hypnos—who had put the entire island of Manhattan to sleep during Kronos's assault on Olympus—apparently lived here now, in his mother's basement?

Mother's wings quivered, dripping liquid shadow from their spiny tips. "We are being watched," she said.

Her terrible eyes scanned the area where Nico was hiding. He jerked back and dropped to the ground, his heart racing.

He couldn't get caught. Not this close to the end. And he *had* to be close! He'd done as Nemesis told him and followed the River Phlegethon. Unless Nemesis had guided him into a trap . . .

Nico stayed as still as possible. The archway he'd entered was only a few steps away. Maybe, if he sprinted, he could get through it, back up the path, and into the forest.

He never got to find out. Tendrils of smoke wrapped around him and abruptly lifted him into the air.

"No!" he cried as he was yanked backward across the garden, then spun around to find himself face-to-face with *her*.

Up close, her visage wasn't just dark and indistinct. Except for those piercing eyes, it was a churning void, a black hole devouring all light and matter. It was pure hopelessness made real.

"Now, who are *you*?" Her supernova eyes seemed to be peeling back Nico's soul layer by layer. Her swirling debris-cloud of darkness held him fast, but Nico didn't struggle—he suddenly didn't *want* to. He was paralyzed.

"I asked you a question," she said, and her voice had *gravity*, as if it might pull the answers right out of his skull.

"Mother, leave him alone," said Hypnos with a tired sigh. "It's clear that he's harmless."

"Harmless," Nico echoed, exhaustion spreading through his bones. "Definitely harmless."

"Hypnos, stop feeling sorry for him!" Mother commanded. "Why are you always taking pity on every stray you find?"

"Sorry," Hypnos said, lowering his head.

Mother pulled Nico closer, and he swallowed a scream. He'd never been so terrified, and yet he couldn't fight, could barely even think.

"You aren't a monster," she cooed softly. "And you aren't a god."

"I could be . . ." he said dreamily.

"The god of bad decisions, perhaps?" Mother sounded amused by her own joke. "Because you made a mistake coming into *my* home."

Nico felt his rage stirring until he thought his heart would burst. He hated being confined, and he hated being ridiculed. But he couldn't move. His eyelids were made of lead.

"How did you get here?" Mother mused, looking him over like he was a specimen of some invasive species. "This realm is protected from all who don't belong. Unless . . . ah, a demigod."

Nico smiled weakly. He tried to look smug and unconcerned, but he doubted he was pulling it off.

"You got me," he said.

She cackled, her voice radiating malice. "You are terrified, child. As you should be. Fear is the highest form of respect you can give me."

"It is best to stay afraid of Nyx," grumbled Hypnos from somewhere behind him. "I've certainly learned that."

Nyx.

Nico hadn't heard that name in *ages*, but he knew her by reputation. She was the goddess most other gods were terrified of. No one ever risked making her angry; even Zeus refused to mess with her. She was the goddess of night, born from Chaos, and one of the original inhabitants of the universe.

Now he understood Nemesis's warning to be wary of her mother. Nico had come to Tartarus looking for a way to stop Gaea from rising . . . and he'd walked straight into the lair of a goddess who was just as old, powerful, and dangerous.

"I see you are putting the pieces together," said Nyx, her voice thick with amusement. "No need to explain your parentage. I've already figured it out. There is only one father whose children could survive this long in Tartarus. And there is only one reason the entrance to my home would reveal itself. It sensed a kindred spirit. . . ."

The darkness swirled tightly around Nico, pushing all the blood to his head.

"What an interesting case you are," Nyx continued. "A son of Hades, yet you live in the mortal world, don't you? I can smell the stench of daylight on you."

Hypnos tutted. "Oh, Mother doesn't like that."

"I *don't* like that," she confirmed. "Do you know why, son of Hades?"

Nico had to use nearly all his energy just to shake his head.

"We are all born into our own natures," she said. "I, created from Chaos, was given unto the night. It is what and who I *am*. Who are you, Nico di Angelo?"

He gasped softly. "How—?"

"How do I know your name?" Nyx feigned outrage. "We are in Tartarus, you silly child. Everything here is stripped to its truest, rawest form. The longer you remain with me, the more clearly I can see you . . . and the less you can hide."

She brought Nico so close he thought he would pitch forward into the void of her face.

"Have you ever looked at yourself, Nico? Because *I* see the truth. You *belong* down here in the darkness. It is your nature, and yet you fight it every day. Must you be so obstinate? Must you ignore the obvious?"

"No," he said, squirming against Nyx's hold. "I know where I'm supposed to be."

A terrible laughter echoed from the empty space where her mouth should have been. "You are hopelessly confused. Those who are confused end up with me."

"They do," said Hypnos. "They always do."

"Night is when all beings stumble and go astray," Nyx said, her voice now soothing, "but it is also when you can face the darkest truth. You must stop entertaining this notion that you can escape who you are. I will help you choose, Nico di Angelo. I will make things so much simpler. . . . *Choose.*"

Her last word was a blast of darkness, and Nico could feel his soul breaking into dust, his identity being shorn away and pulled into Nyx's gravity. He couldn't breathe; hopelessness radiated through every part of his body; he believed this was the end.

Which was precisely when the giants arrived.

CHAPTER 18

"Excuse me!" a voice called out. "Is there any way we could borrow that demigod?"

Nico forced himself not to pass out, even though he wanted to chase after unconsciousness. He tried to twist around to see who was speaking, but he didn't need to. Nyx promptly dropped him, and his back hit the ground, knocking the air clean out of him.

He turned his head to see two nearly identical giants—both twelve feet tall and with snakes where their feet should be, but otherwise much more like humans than he expected. They were dressed in identical tie-dyed overalls—who made overalls for giants?!—on top of white T-shirts. Both of them had their hair tied back in thick braids that glittered with coins, though the giant on the left had green hair and the one on the right had purple. Nico thought they looked like Tartarus versions of Pokémon trainers.

Nyx hissed. "Who do you think you are, barging in here? I am Nyx, the goddess of night!"

"Oh, we know who you are," said the giant with purple hair. He pointed at his twin. "That's Otis, and I'm the Big F."

Otis made a face. "Dude, I don't know about that stage name."

"The Big F?" said Hypnos. "What does the *F* stand for?"

The purple-haired giant put his hands on his hips and raised his chin proudly. "Ephialtes."

Hypnos looked up at his mother, whose supernova eyes flickered as if she were short-circuiting.

"Does it not make sense?" said Ephialtes. "You know, because the way you say my name is—"

"No, no, we understand," said Nyx.

"Yeah," Hypnos said, "there's certainly a logic to it, but . . ."

The giant looked down at Nico.

The demigod shrugged. "It could use some more thought."

"I told you to workshop it more," said Otis. "How are we supposed to get our big break if everyone thinks your name is ridiculous?"

"Dude—"

"Dude!"

"Pardon me for interrupting this clown show," said Nyx, "but what are you two doing here?"

"Right!" said Ephialtes. "We're here for the demigod."

The air around Nyx turned several degrees colder. "Not now," she said. "He's . . . occupied."

"Gaea wants him," said Otis.

Hypnos frowned at his mother, as if to say *See, I told you she was trouble.*

"Gaea," Nyx repeated.

"Yep," said Ephialtes.

"For what possible reason?"

Ephialtes smiled from ear to ear. "Oh, we're trying to trap the seven demigods from the prophecy."

Nico pushed himself up on his elbows. "What?"

"We're gonna kidnap you and use you as bait," said Otis. "Then, when your friends come to rescue you, we'll just wipe out everyone at once."

"It's brilliant," said Ephialtes. "And it will *definitely* help us go viral!"

Nico looked at Nyx in panic. Then back at the giants. He thought about trying to make a break for it, but he was deep in Tartarus, surrounded by four immortals, with barely enough energy to stand. Maybe if he could goad them into fighting one another, he could sneak away. . . .

"I can see you plotting, Nico," said Nyx, her voice syrupy. "But there is no escape for you."

"I thought you resented Gaea." Nico turned to Hypnos. "You called her intolerable. Why do you take orders from her?"

Hypnos shook his head. "It's pointless to try dividing us, demigod."

"Does that mean we can have him now?" asked Otis. "Gaea will reward you for your cooperation, Nyx."

Nyx didn't frown, exactly, since she had no mouth, but Nico could sense displeasure in the darkening churn of her face. "I do not *need* rewards. And it is one thing for me to support my primordial sister's awakening. It is another thing for you to barge into my home and demand—"

Nico wasn't going to wait around for the result of this negotiation. He sprinted for the archway. Hypnos shouted. The giants cried out in alarm as Nico dove between Otis's snake legs and came up running. He was almost to the exit when two new shapes closed ranks to block his path—horses with bodies of pitch-black void just like Nyx, their disturbingly sharp silvery teeth gnashing at Nico. Giant vampire horses.

"Nope!" Nico cried, and veered into the woods.

The horses whinnied. The giants bellowed, "Get him!" and "No, dude, you get him!" but Nyx's voice rose above the din.

"Let him try," she said. "Go ahead, Nico di Angelo. Try your best to escape."

Nico knew she was toying with him, but he didn't have much of a choice. He ran as fast as he could, following the perimeter of the garden. A dark wall hemmed it in—much too tall to climb, made of seething ash particles like the archway. Nico considered trying to shadow-travel through it, but even if he'd had the concentration and the energy, something told him shadow-travel in Nyx's sanctuary would be a very bad idea.

He kept running, his clothes snagging on briars and tree branches, until he stopped short, staring at a house that should not exist.

Nico had seen so many terrible things over the course of this journey through Tartarus, but this? This was what broke him.

The *living* house towered above him—its many gables and overlooks and bay windows shifting from one shape to another, each one like an *eye*, dilating, constricting, swiveling to focus on him. Nico could sense them inspecting him, peering deep into his soul. The black shutters snapped hungrily. The double doors yawned, inviting him in past bristling rows of black teeth.

He dropped to his knees. As the house shifted and shuddered, Nico realized what it was made of. Like the archway, like the garden wall, the house was constructed from black particles—but these particles weren't dust or ash or stone as Nico had thought. Each and every speck was an insect. Billions of tiny wings, pincers, and stingers swarmed together, somehow forming the shape of the mansion and not collapsing. Nico knew deep in his heart that he should not be looking at this, that *no one* should be looking at this.

Suddenly, he felt a cool hand under his chin. Nyx lifted Nico's head and tenderly wiped the tears from his cheeks.

"I told you there was no escape," she said gently, almost as if she *pitied* him.

"What . . . What is this place?" he asked.

"The Mansion of Night. It is my home."

Nico whimpered. "Why? Why design something so awful?"

"You have seen nothing but the smallest part. You mortals have a phrase for that: the tip of the iceberg. It is the purest expression of who I am."

He sobbed and shut his eyes, but he could still envision it in his mind. He imagined himself breaking down, crumbling into a billion swarming insects that would slowly be absorbed by that house.

"Your filter has burned away," Nyx said softly. "Few demigods have ever entered Tartarus. . . . Fewer still have seen my home. The Mist clings to you, trying to protect your sanity from the true appearance of things. . . ." She caressed Nico's face. "But now you can see it all, can't you, child?"

"Yes," he said, wishing it wasn't true. Suddenly, it didn't seem like such a bad thing to be drawn into the black hole of Nyx's gaze, to be crushed into nothingness by her gravitational pull. It might hurt less than seeing the world like this: nothing but swarms of dark, ravenous bugs, pushed into whatever patterns pleased the goddess of night.

Nyx lowered herself until her head was level with Nico's. "Good . . . I am going to give you over to the giants, because I believe in what Gaea is doing. But if there is any future in which you survive—in which you and your little demigod friends aren't destroyed—then we will continue this conversation, Nico di Angelo. . . ." She rose and spread her smoky wings to their full span. "I will make you choose your true nature. You won't be able to escape it."

Nico may have whimpered. He was too terrified to even be ashamed.

Nyx turned to the giants. "Take him."

Behind Otis and Ephialtes, the massive fanged stallions snorted and pawed the ground.

Nyx raised her hand. "Settle down, Shade, Shadow. . . . There will be other flesh for you to devour."

Hypnos took their reins and led them away, as Otis loomed over Nico. The giant's huge hands wrapped around the demigod's rib cage and lifted him from the ground, but Nico was too tired, too scared to resist.

"Did you bring it?" Otis asked his brother.

Ephialtes scoffed. "Of course I did. What kind of giant do you think I am?"

The Big F snapped his Big Fingers. An enormous bronze jar *poofed* into existence on the gravel path. As Ephialtes pried open the lid, Nico realized the jar was just the right size to fit . . . well, *him*.

"Thanks for making this so easy, kid," Otis said, lifting him over the mouth of the jar. "I can't promise this won't hurt."

"Good-bye, Nico di Angelo," Nyx called. "You may not remember our meeting. Your tiny mind may crack under the strain of what you have seen. But if you somehow survive . . . it will be delicious to see what you become."

Otis stuffed him inside the jar, and Nico's hand closed around the pomegranate seeds that Nemesis had given him. Had she known this would happen?

Maybe she'd been part of the trap—the trap that would end them all.

The idea that his friends might try to rescue him brought him no comfort. As Nico was sealed in the darkness of the bronze jar, only one thought persisted in his shattered mind:

I failed them all.

CHAPTER 19

After Nico finished his story, there was a long silence in the trogs' council chamber.

Will stared at some faraway place as he absorbed what he had just heard. The trog councilors frowned at one another, as if wondering who would be brave enough to speak first.

Nico felt exposed and vulnerable. He had never planned to share what had happened to him after getting dragged to Tartarus; it was simply easier to bury it deep within his mind. And in fact, there were parts of it he had forgotten, just as Nyx had warned him might happen. Maybe his mind had done that to keep himself safe, but as he recounted the story, it all came back in terrifying detail.

Maybe that whole PTSD thing had a lot more merit than he'd previously accepted.

He reached in his pocket. His trembling fingers touched the coin from Will. Usually, this gave him a reprieve from his grief and pain, if only temporarily, but this time it wasn't enough. When the tears spilled and his body shook, Nico turned to Will and cried into his shoulder.

Nico wasn't sure how long they stayed like that. He imagined Will would've held him for an eternity if that's what he'd needed. But after his initial burst of sorrow, Nico began to feel self-conscious, aware of the trogs waiting around the table. He pulled away and wiped his face.

"Okay, okay," he said. "No more feeling sad. It is what it is."

"You're allowed to have feelings, Nico," said Will. He was doing that concern thing again, where he knit his eyebrows together. "What you went through . . . That was *a lot*."

"I have to move past it if we're going to reach Bob."

Screech-Bling scratched at his powdered wig. "So it is Nyx we have sensed? She has begun to stir?"

"But why now?" Howl-Smith gave Nico a resentful glance. "We just moved in!"

Hiss-Majesty clicked reproachfully at Howl-Smith. "It is not the son of Hades's fault. He has always helped us!"

"Yes," agreed Shriek-Vibes. "And I'm sure he will help us now—with answers, will he not?"

The trogs all looked at Nico, their large amphibian eyes full of anxiety. Nico wanted to help, but he feared his suspicions weren't going to make them feel any better.

"You think it's all connected," Will guessed. "Nyx starting to stir. Our quest to find Bob. Because that's what all this is leading to, isn't it? You think she's imprisoned him somehow. My question is *why?*"

Nico studied the rough stone tabletop. "I'm not sure you're going to like my answer."

"Please try," said Will.

Nico took a deep breath. "I think . . . Nyx's whole purpose in life is to shape things into their purest possible form—personifications of a single negative emotion, or feeling, or state of being. Look at her children, for example: Keres, the god of violent death. Geras, the god of old age. Eris, the god of strife. Nemesis, god of retribution. Akhlys, god of misery."

"Sounds like a real party," Will grumbled.

"And we met another one earlier—Epiales, god of nightmares."

"This isn't very comforting," Will said. "Epiales said their mother had *ten thousand* kids?"

"It is a lot," Nico said. "There's actually a funny word for what they are."

"I'm ready," said Will. "Give it to me."

"Cacodemons."

He shook his head. "Yeah, I wasn't ready for that."

"Cacodemons aren't *all* bad," Nico continued. "If we had time, I'd introduce you to Charon, who works for my father. Technically, all hellhounds are Nyx's children, too, so that would make Mrs. O'Leary one. And I met Akhlys in a dream once."

"Sweet Apollo! That had to be a terrible nightmare."

Nico grimaced. "Actually, she said she couldn't do anything to me because I was already so full of sorrow."

Will frowned at that. "So . . . thousands and thousands of cacodemons. I barely beat back Epiales with all the power I had. And we're not even in Tartarus yet! If we have to wade through armies of Nyx's children . . ."

"We may have to face some of them," Nico admitted. "Or maybe we'll find some like Nemesis who want to help us."

Will raised his eyebrows. "None of this explains why Nyx is so interested in Bob . . . or in luring you to Tartarus."

"Or threatening the troglodytes' new neighborhood!" said Howl-Smith, eliciting a fresh round of screeches, clicks, and growls from the other council members.

Nico thought about that horrible garden of darkness in Tartarus . . . that mansion made from insects. The idea of Nyx interfering with the trogs' newfound happiness broke his heart . . . and made him angry.

"Nyx is . . . obsessive," he said. "I faced her only briefly, and she was downright *offended* by who I was."

"Right," said Will. "That whole bit about escaping who you are."

"She's a primordial goddess of night and darkness. There's nothing she despises more than someone who leaves their darkness behind. She doesn't like beings who reject the form they were 'destined' for."

Will hit his forehead with his palm. "Oh, I get it now. *Bob.* Bob, who is a *former Titan.*"

Nico nodded. "A former Titan whose memories were washed away in the Lethe and who now *chooses* to be someone different."

"So he's basically like . . . evil catnip for Nyx."

Nico wanted to laugh at that—technically, Will was spot-on—but a terrible feeling came back to him. The third line of the prophecy ran through his mind: *There leave something of equal value behind.*

If Nyx despised all that was light . . .

"Nico?" Will put his hand on Nico's shoulder.

Nico shook his head. "Sorry. It's still a lot to think about."

It was a small white lie, one amid a very real truth, but Nico couldn't vocalize his worst fear. If he broke down in tears again, he was afraid he might never be able to put himself back together.

"So you think Mr. D was right?" asked Will. "The dreams, Bob's cries for help . . . it's all a trap to lure you back to Tartarus?"

"I don't know," said Nico. "Though . . . if she wants me to reach Tartarus, why would she send Epiales to attack us?"

Will brooded, which couldn't have been easy while wearing a foam cheese-wedge hat. "Some sort of test?"

Screech-Bling clicked at Will. "Explain, son of Apollo. Trogs do not like tests. Especially essay questions."

The other council members hissed in agreement.

"Well, think of it this way," Will said. "Nyx believes that everyone is destined to be *one* thing. Nico, like Bob, has defied that. Epiales was trying to prove that Nico couldn't escape his nightmares. . . ." He turned to Nico. "That you couldn't even *make* it to Tartarus before giving in to your darkness."

"And he was almost right," Nico said. "If you hadn't been there . . ."

Will squeezed his hand. "I'll *always* be here. But if the tests get harder the deeper we go . . . I hate that idea a *lot*."

"You must face her," said Howl-Smith.

In her fluffy parka, with a stack of beanies on her head like multicolored pancakes, she didn't look like your typical government official, but she sat forward, her hands laced, and fixed Nico with a stare of absolute authority. Suddenly, Nico understood why she'd been made leader of the council.

"If you do not," she continued, "Nyx will torment you and Bob the Titan *forever*. And any who care about you."

Nico understood her meaning. The trogs were his friends. By moving them into the Underworld to protect them, he'd unwittingly put them in the path of Hurricane Nyx.

Nico made a fist. "I just don't understand why she cares so much about *me*. I'm one demigod."

Trogs don't have eyebrows, but Howl-Smith arched the skin where her eyebrows would have been. "You are Nico di Angelo."

The other trogs murmured and nodded.

"You show new ways through the dark," Clack-Jones added.

"You see the trogs," said Screech-Bling. "You see Bob the Titan."

Will smiled and squeezed his hand. "Nyx hates what you represent—change."

Howl-Smith nodded wisely. "Or at least the potential for it."

Nico was uncomfortable with the way they were looking at him: with trust and pride, like he was someone who deserved a spotlight. Being a son of Hades, he didn't do spotlights.

"I'll fix this," he promised. "I'll save Bob and convince Nyx to back off."

"*We* will," corrected Will of the Magnificent Cheese Hat. "And hey, if Nyx wants your darkness so bad, you can just leave some of it with her! That wouldn't be so bad."

Nico knew he was joking, but the comment didn't sit well. "Ha-ha. You're hilarious."

"Then it is settled," said Howl-Smith. "We troglodytes will guide you past Erebos to the far side of the Underworld, where you may descend into Tartarus. We will do our best to keep you hidden from Hades *and* Nyx. Does the council agree?"

All five troglodytes clicked in unison.

Howl-Smith beamed at Nico and Will. "Excellent! Now you should rest. At mushroom-glow, *Screech*-Bling and *Hiss*-Majesty will escort you through the pathways."

"Mushroom-glow?" Will asked.

"It's their dawn," Nico explained. "When the mushrooms start . . . glowing."

"And the pathways?"

"We do not travel out in the open," said Shriek-Vibes. "For our own protection, we have found hidden trails."

"To avoid the attention of Hades's minions," said Hiss-Majesty. "And the ghosts."

"Ghosts?"

"This is the land of the dead, Will," said Nico. "Not all souls make it across the River Styx or into my father's kingdom. Some get lost, or turn aside for whatever reason. . . . They wander around as ghosts."

"They are usually not dangerous," said Hiss-Majesty. "But they are often sad. It is hard to hear their wails. We want to help them, yet we cannot!"

Will turned to Nico. "This isn't disturbing to you? All those lost souls?"

"Why would it be? It's just part of how things are. The Underworld is my second home, Will."

Will shivered. "I could never live here."

Nico bit back the urge to say *No one's asking you to*. He took a deep breath and addressed Howl-Smith. "We are thankful for your help," he said, channeling his frustration with Will into gratitude toward the troglodytes. "I owe you many rare skinks for your troubles."

That sent the council into a new frenzy of excitement until Howl-Smith was able to calm them down. "We help you because it is right, son of Hades," she said. "Not because we expect tasty skinks."

"But we will not refuse tasty skinks!" added Screech-Bling. He stood so quickly his tricorn almost fell off. "Now come! I will take you to our nap cove, where you may rest with our young ones."

Will smiled weakly. "Nap time with baby troglodytes?"

Screech-Bling nodded. "They will cherish the opportunity to share blankies with heroes!"

The CEO led the way out of the council room, and Nico stayed in the rear, his thoughts simmering. He knew Will meant well; he'd never met anyone as kind and understanding of the world around him. But after less than a day in the Underworld, the place was already exposing a part of Will that felt different, more judgmental. Sure, Nico often struggled with how other people saw him, and he'd certainly had to correct Will's perceptions before. But was it getting *worse*? Will didn't seem very open to appreciating either Nico's second home or the troglodytes. On the other hand, nothing in Nico's story about his time in Tartarus had made it sound *good*. Could he really blame Will for thinking everything in the Underworld was bad after hearing all that?

As they moved through the cavernous main area, it was Will's joke about Nyx taking some of Nico's darkness that bothered Nico the most. If only it were that easy. If only someone *could* just remove all the dark and scary and sad parts of him. But at the same time . . . they made up who Nico was. He wouldn't be Nico di Angelo without his past. But did it make him less appealing to Will?

Ugh, this was so confusing to think about. Nico wished he wasn't so sad all the time, but he also didn't like the idea of giving it up. What was someone like him supposed to do?

He was surprised, then, as he and Will snuggled up on two bedrolls laid side by side in the trogs' nap cove, that sleep came to him quickly. Normally, when his mind was buzzing, he would be up for hours.

But not this time. He was too exhausted, and his body desperately needed the rest.

He dreamed he waded knee-deep in a sea of shadows. Shapes floated within the darkness, but . . . what were they? They were small, barely coming up to his shins, and they scattered every time Nico took a step. Out of curiosity, he bent down and tried to touch one.

A mouth lashed out, full of glowing, sharp teeth.

Nico yanked his hand back, and the scene before him changed. He found himself standing before a long pit dug into the earth. Some sort of horrible-smelling liquid gurgled at the bottom. Nico pinched his nose.

A blue shade began to form out of the noxious gases at the bottom of the pit. Nico knew what was happening, knew it was just a dream, but that didn't alleviate his sense of dread.

The spirit took shape in front of him. Bianca wore her Hunter of Artemis outfit—a glistening silver parka, a bow strung across her shoulder—though she was still illuminated by a ghostly blue glow.

"Hello, brother," she said.

"You're not my sister," he said bitterly. "Nyx, get out of my dreams."

"You must choose, Nico." Her face was so lovely, so soft, so warm. Gods, he missed her. "Can you tell Will the truth?" she asked. "The truth of who you are?"

Nico refused to be a part of this. He turned and started walking away, but suddenly Bianca was once again in front of him.

"I really hate dream logic!" he screamed.

"Choose," said Bianca.

"Message received!"

Bianca pulled an arrow from her quiver. "Choose, Nico."

"Leave a message at the tone!" he snarled. "BEEEEEEEEEEEEP!"

She nocked the arrow and drew it back.

"It's a dream, Nyx," he said. "You can't hurt me here."

This time, the goddess's bone-chilling voice came out of Bianca's mouth: "You sure about that, son of Hades?"

Bianca's arrow pierced Nico's sternum, and pain exploded through him. He couldn't breathe as he pitched backward. Then Bianca was standing over him, cackling as she fired another arrow point-blank, then another, each of them setting Nico's body on fire.

"I'll be waiting for you," she cooed.

Nico melted into darkness.

He awoke in a rush, his hand clutched to his chest. His face was damp with sweat. A phantom pain throbbed in his sternum, so sharp that it took a while for his breathing to return to normal. He forced himself to endure it all quietly, since he didn't want to interrupt Will's snoozing next to him.

The nap cove was completely empty—just piles of bedrolls and blankets where the young trogs had been sleeping before. As carefully as he could, Nico rose and moved to the entrance so he could feel the cool air that moved through the entire underground system. He took a deep breath, trying to steady his nerves.

He knew that demigod dreams were always worse in the Underworld, but Nyx had reached out from Tartarus and *actually* hurt him. Would her powers increase as they got closer?

He looked back at Will, still sleeping peacefully. At least, he hoped Will was free from nightmares.

Nico resolved right then not to share his newest dream with Will. His boyfriend was a natural caretaker—which was why he was such a great healer—but in this case, what could Will do to help *him*? Maybe it was time for Nico to help Will for a change. So Nico stood by the entrance, bathed in the dim light from the torches outside, and watched Will sleep. When he finally crawled back into his own bedroll, he remained wide-awake.

He refused to let Nyx get to him that easily.

"It was all 'cause of Leo, wasn't it?" Will said.

Nico's mouth dropped open. "Wow, you *knew?*"

Will brought a small piece of ambrosia to his lips and chewed on it. Even that much effort seemed to pain him. "Not at the time," he said after swallowing. "But I know it *now.*"

Nico turned to Gorgyra. "Leo is our friend, but there was a time when we all thought he'd died."

"But he had not?" she asked, confused.

Nico shook his head. "We were so sure. . . . We saw it happen. He literally exploded in midair."

"It's complicated," said Will. "It involved a magical cure and an automaton dragon."

Gorgyra smiled. "Such wonderful tales you both weave. Continue."

"Well, Nico can sense when someone is dead," explained Will.

"Child of Hades," Nico added.

"Of course," said Gorgyra.

Will took a sip of nectar. "So, Nico had definitely felt Leo die—"

"But I also had this strange sense he wasn't completely gone." Nico frowned. "Then, a few days after Leo 'died,' I got this magical scroll from him telling us he'd actually survived. He'd come up with this whole plan for cheating death, but he hadn't shared it with any of us ahead of time, which made me *furious*. I was so angry about him keeping me in the dark that I couldn't think about anything else."

Nico looked directly in Will's blue eyes. "Until you, that is."

"I remember," said Will.

"One night after dinner," Nico continued, "Will took me into the forest outside camp. Just marched me out there with no explanation. I thought he was angry with me. And an angry Will is a scary Will."

Will laughed weakly. "It wasn't anger. I was just determined."

Gorgyra sat forward. "Determined to do what?"

Will's eyes went glassy again. "Once we were in the middle of the forest, I told Nico to start screaming."

"Screaming?" Gorgyra's face twisted in confusion. "Whatever for?"

"To let the anger out," said Nico. "I didn't want to do it at first, not until he turned to the forest and screamed at a tree."

"It was a very big tree," said Will. "I was sure it could take it."

"You scared that poor dryad half to death."

"I didn't know she was there!"

"I've never seen a dryad run so fast in my life."

They both fell into giggles, and Nico was glad to see Will's spirits rise, even temporarily.

"So I screamed, too," Nico said. "It felt silly the first time, but then I was full-on *yelling* at the trees about how annoyed I was with Leo."

"Much later, when Leo returned and invited us to sock him, I think the punches he got from Nico were significantly less powerful than they could have been." Will smiled at his boyfriend. "All because you screamed at the trees."

Nico laughed. "Well . . . it did made me feel better. And *under-stood*. No one had ever done something for me like that before. That's when I started looking at you differently."

Will stared into the fire. "For me it was that week in the infirmary."

Nico nodded. "That's how I knew your moment came first."

"I do not understand," said Gorgyra.

"Right after Gaea's defeat, there were a lot of injured demigods," said Will. "And one thing the Apollo cabin is responsible for is medical care and rehabilitation. We help other demigods recover, whether it's from cuts and broken bones, or from injuries that have left them permanently disabled."

"Will told me that he wished I could help out in the infirmary, so I did," said Nico.

Will laughed, though it made him wince. "I remember turning around and seeing Nico asking Dakota where the antiseptic cleaner was. Dakota is—*was*, I mean—a child of Bacchus from Camp Jupiter." Will smiled sadly. "He wasn't all that knowledgeable about the infirmary, either, so I got to witness both of them running around the room, desperate to find something neither one knew how to find."

"I tried," said Nico. "That week was *painful*. I constantly felt lost."

"But you never gave up," said Will. "And I don't know . . . Your dedication just felt so beautiful to me. That's all it took for me to see you differently."

Nico blushed. "Wow, we are *such* softies."

Will narrowed his eyes. "Wait, how did you know *my* moment came before yours?"

Nico gave Will a mischievous smile. "Because I *caught* you looking."

"What?" Will said. "No, that's not possible."

"It was the last day you needed help in the infirmary," he said.

"Before you sent me away. I was with Connor Stoll, and he nudged my shoulder and said you were staring at me. I thought I was gonna turn around and find you glaring at me angrily because I'd done something wrong.

"But instead, you were sitting next to Chiron, who was chatting your ear off, and you were looking at me with this whole puppy-dog-eyes thing going on."

A slight redness rose in Will's cheeks. "Oh, gods, I don't even remember that."

"If you hadn't looked at me that way . . . well, later on, I don't think I would have had the courage to come out to you and tell you I wanted to go on a date."

Gorgyra clapped her hands together lightly. Nico noticed that her skin tone had changed from light blue to something closer to lavender. "Excuse me for my excitement," she said. "I am so used to hearing stories of isolation that I am overjoyed at hearing one of connection."

Apparently, these stories weren't just giving Will some fortitude, they were affecting Gorgyra, too.

"Can I tell you another?" Nico asked, surprising himself.

Gorgyra placed her hands over her chest. "Please! It may be a long time before I see anyone else."

Will nodded in confirmation, and the son of Hades began again.

"I want to tell you how I asked Will on a date."

CHAPTER 20

Curled up in the trog's nap cove, Will dreamed of Maron.

He was ten when the satyr had first appeared to him, and it was no different in his nightmare. Will held his mom's hand as the two of them entered Washington Square Park, passing under an enormous stone arch. There were street performers and buskers everywhere. A group of college students danced near the fountain to music blaring from a set of speakers, while a skateboarder did a kick-flip over four people lying on their backs on the asphalt path.

Will wasn't sure what to look at. It seemed like this everywhere in New York, no matter how many times they'd been here before. And after nearly a week in Albany, Will welcomed the chaos of the city over the sleepy, overcast vibes upstate.

He knew how this dream would unfold: Will would point out to his mom how many pigeons there were crowded around the fountain. She'd say that no other US city had more of them than New York. Then one of the pigeons would land a little too close for Will's comfort, and he would shy away from it, only for more of them to flutter over, until he and his mom were surrounded.

Will had had variations of this dream before, but this . . . this felt too real, as if he were reliving the memory itself rather than seeing it through the magic of a dream. When the first pigeon pecked at his foot, its beak was *sharp*. When his mom expressed concern that these pigeons were too aggressive, he could *feel* the fear in her voice.

And when the swarm hit, he couldn't breathe.

It's a dream, Will! he told himself. *You're a demigod. You have these all the time.*

But he couldn't control this one. His memory of the Stymphalian-bird attack was dialed up to eleven—his mom's screams all the more piercing, her hair unkempt and wild as she threw her arms around him, trying to protect him.

Maron arrived from out of nowhere, just as he had in real life, leaping in front of Naomi and Will Solace and opening an enormous black umbrella to repel the birds. He wore obnoxiously neon-green pants with pink suspenders over a white T-shirt.

As the birds rained down on the umbrella, Will felt again the terror of being shrouded in darkness, his mother screaming, unsure whether they were going to survive.

In real life, they had escaped with Maron's help to their East Village hotel, where the satyr had told Will the truth about his heritage. Maron was the one who had brought Will to Camp Half-Blood.

But that didn't happen in the nightmare. Under the umbrella, what was once a heroic moment took a dark turn when Will looked up into Maron's eyes and saw that they were bloodred.

"He will leave you," Maron said, his voice deep and frightening. "When the time comes, he will choose to leave you behind."

Maron laughed as the Stymphalian birds pelted the umbrella, pushing it closer to the ground. Will and his mom crouched down as she held Will tighter.

"I love you," she said.

"I love you, too, Mom."

Then her face contorted. She sneered, her glowing red eyes boring into him. "He's going to leave you behind, you fool."

Will woke in a panic. When he saw Nico's bedroll empty, he worried that he *had* been left behind, just like in his nightmare. But then he sat up and saw the silhouette of his boyfriend appear in the doorway.

Relief rushed through him. "Nico," he said. "Where'd you go?"

Nico walked over and handed him a strange bronze cup that was warm to the touch. "Drink up."

Will balked. "This isn't more of that shoelace soup, is it?"

Nico chuckled. "No, just broth."

Will reluctantly brought it to his lips. He let a small bit of it touch his tongue, and a burst of savory goodness filled his mouth. He finished it off in less than a minute while Nico watched, a look of satisfaction on his face.

"Okay, that was good," Will admitted, wiping his mouth. "But please don't tell me this is broth of troglodyte armpit. I feel like you're going to."

He meant it as a joke, but Nico looked irritated.

"It's not," said Nico. "Troglodytes *do* eat a lot of stuff that humans do."

His tone sounded almost accusatory, as if Will should *love* stewed shoelaces and armpit broth. Ever since they'd passed through the Door of Orpheus, Will had felt like he was walking on thin ice with Nico. Will always seemed to be doing and saying the wrong thing, even if he was just trying to lighten the mood.

Even that term, *lighten the mood*, seemed like a biased statement here in the Underworld, but Will wasn't sure what else to do, how to act.

He lay back down, images from the nightmare swirling in his head. He didn't feel rested. Here it was *always* night, so his circadian rhythms were off. Then there was the warning from his dream: *He's going to leave you behind, you fool.*

How much worse would all this get once they entered Tartarus?

Nico sat next to him. "You're worried."

"Bad dreams," Will muttered, which was a half-truth, at best. There was so much else that worried him.

"Me too." Nico lay beside him, and Will was grateful for his boyfriend's head on his shoulder. If only they could stay like this, and not think about what came next. . . .

"We should reach Tartarus today," Nico said, shattering that hope. "*Screech*-Bling was just telling me they found a shortcut."

Will glanced over. "A shortcut?"

"One that won't require us to enter the way I did last time. Which I'm thankful for. I'd rather not fall in darkness for an indeterminate amount of time again."

"That's good," said Will. "I'll take anything to help us at this point."

Nico shifted next to him. "Are you still sure you want to do this? We're at a point where you *could* turn back."

"Absolutely not," said Will. At this point, it was more of a stubborn, involuntarily reflex than a conscious thought.

Nico studied him. "I can't tell how you're really feeling. I know you want to help, but you've seemed a little . . . different since we got here."

"I'm scared," admitted Will. "I don't know what's coming, and . . ." He faltered, remembering Maron's nightmarish voice: *He will leave you.* "And I don't like that I can no longer feel the sun. I'm cut off from it for the first time in my life."

Nico reached over to Will's knapsack. He pulled out the sun globe, flicked it on, and tossed it over.

Will couldn't help but smile. It was a cute gesture, and he always considered it a little victory when Nico did something adorable. He was also surprised at how quickly the globe worked. By the time they'd packed up to leave, Will's spirits were definitely improved. The light wasn't a substitute for the sun, but he was glad he'd brought it with him.

He clicked it off and stowed it when Screech-Bling and Hiss-Majesty arrived.

"Demigods!" Screech-Bling said. "Shall we begin?"

Will glanced past the CEO and was surprised to see Hiss-Majesty wearing a foam cheese hat identical to his own. A warm feeling spread through Will, almost as good as the sun globe.

"You found a hat!" he noted. "I like it."

Hiss-Majesty was perhaps the most bashful troglodyte Will had ever seen. They blinked a few times, then ducked behind Screech-Bling.

"It is a good hat," Hiss-Majesty mumbled. "A hero's hat."

Screech-Bling grinned. "You have made an impression, son of Apollo. And do not worry about Hiss-Majesty. They are brave when they need to be."

"Well, so am I," said Will. "You can't judge a book by its cover."

He caught Nico scowling at him.

What? he mouthed.

Nico merely shook his head.

Will sighed. Sometimes it was hard to tell what Nico was feeling, too.

Screech-Bling adjusted his hot-pink rucksack across his shoulder, which clashed magnificently with his George Washington outfit. "Today we venture through the southern tunnels. We will bring you to the shortcut swiftly, so you may rescue Bob the Titan from the clutches of Nyx, goddess of night!"

Will wasn't sure his life could get any weirder, but then Screech-Bling paraded them through troglodyte headquarters, much to the delight of the shareholders. The appreciative onlookers clicked and clacked, which sounded like applause if all the clapping hands were made of dominoes.

Like an Underworld-style graduation, many of the troglodytes tossed their hats into the air, then immediately started fighting over the ones they liked best. Even when the expedition had left HQ for the wider caverns of the Underworld, Will could still hear the joyful chaos of the crowd echoing behind them.

"The troglodytes are special, aren't they?" he said to Nico.

He finally got a smile out of his boyfriend. "Very much so," Nico said.

As they followed the path along the roaring River Styx, with dark clouds hanging over the walls of Erebos in distance, Will kind of missed the crowd.

Screech-Bling led the way, and Hiss-Majesty brought up the rear. Not long after veering away from the Styx, the troglodyte CEO brought Will and Nico to a sizable hole in the ground, partially covered with large rocks. He and Hiss-Majesty moved the rocks out of the way quickly, which was another reminder for Will of how fast and strong the trogs were for their size.

"We move deeper underground," Screech-Bling said. "Do you require a source of light?"

Nico looked to Will with an eyebrow raised.

"Maybe," Will said. "How dark is it?"

"There is no light below," said Screech-Bling.

Will tried to imagine what *no light* meant for a troglodyte, since *pitch-black* was their *sunny afternoon*.

"Nothing to worry about." He swung his knapsack around and fished out the sun globe. When he switched it on, Hiss-Majesty gasped.

"Does the child of Apollo carry the sun with him everywhere?"

Will laughed. "It's artificial," he said, handing it to them. "Powered by batteries."

"I don't know what batteries are," said Hiss-Majesty, holding the globe in their hands as if it would burn them at any second. "Surely this is some type of demigod magic, yes?"

"Sure," said Will. "And now *you* may wield it!"

Hiss-Majesty looked like a kid in a candy store. "Allow me to lead the way, *Screech*-Bling! I shall provide light for our companions like a child of Apollo!"

Screech-Bling nodded and let Hiss-Majesty go first. "Thank you," he said to Will. "It is important that *Hiss*-Majesty feels they can contribute in meaningful ways."

"Of course," said Will. He glanced over at Nico, who had a strange, wistful look on his face. "What?"

"It's just nice seeing you give that responsibility to *Hiss*-Majesty."

Will shrugged. "They're just trying to help," he said. "None of the troglodytes have to, so it's the least I can do."

Nico still had the same look on his face.

Will squinted at his boyfriend. "I don't know what that expression means, so I'm just going to ignore it. Let's get going."

Will faced the tunnel entrance and took a deep breath, his nerves tingling. Then he ducked down and crawled into the hole.

Despite the fact that Hiss-Majesty was just in front of him, the darkness and closeness of the tunnel made Will's heart race. This reminded him too much of their descent from the Door of Orpheus, except here, the ground felt softer and warmer beneath his feet, which made him think about Nico's story of the living landscape in Tartarus. The trogs had no trouble walking upright in the tunnel, but Nico and Will had to crouch and even crawl in some places. It wasn't long before Will wished that *he* was holding the sun-therapy globe. Hiss-Majesty kept getting farther in front of the group, and Screech-Bling had to remind them multiple times that humans could not move as fast as troglodytes.

"Yes, I will go slower," they said. "I am sorry, son of Apollo and son of Hades."

"It's okay," said Will. "You're just excited."

So they pressed on. Nico had been silent since they'd entered the tunnel, and Will wondered if he was starting to freak out a little bit, too. Or did he naturally adapt to places like this? Did he not feel like the earth was pressing down on top of him?

The tunnel twisted often, and Will couldn't escape the sensation that they were crawling down the esophagus of some massive creature. He was so disoriented. He wasn't sure what direction they were even heading, aside from *down*. Always down.

He slowed, and Nico bumped into the back of him.

"You okay?" asked Nico.

Will bent over and put his hands on his knees, his breathing labored. "I need a moment."

Screech-Bling clicked his tongue a few times, and Hiss-Majesty came running back. "Yes?"

Nico held out his hand, and Hiss-Majesty reluctantly dropped the glowing orb into it.

Nico knelt in front of Will. "Take this for now," he said. "The trogs don't actually need it to lead the way, and it'll make you feel better."

"I just wish we didn't have to be underground," Will said. "It's so dark."

He knew that sounded silly. *Of course* they were underground. This was the Underworld. Still, he felt like a little boy again, trembling under the protection of Maron's umbrella.

"We don't have many options," Nico said. "It would be faster to go overground across Erebos, but . . . well, you know. My father."

Will clutched the globe under his left arm while he used his right hand to rub his eyes. There was a slight pressure building behind them. His thoughts felt hazy.

"What about your father?"

Screech-Bling and Nico traded a worried glance.

"You remember," Nico said. "We don't want my father to know we're traipsing around down here, or that we're heading to Tartarus."

"Right," Will said, wondering why the tunnel seemed to be swaying beneath him. "Because he'll stop us."

"We do not cross Hades," said Screech-Bling. "We like our new home, and we would like to keep it. So we must take the hidden paths."

"Okay." Will stood with difficulty, his mind still foggy. "Then let's keep going. But . . . you said this way is longer? I thought it was a shortcut."

"No," said Nico, a hint of impatience in his voice. "I said the troglodytes found a shortcut *into* Tartarus. We're heading there now."

An unfamiliar feeling was bubbling up inside Will. Why was Nico irritating him so much? He clutched the globe tighter.

"Sorry," he said. "I think I'm still tired, that's all."

"It should not be much longer, Will Solace," said Screech-Bling. "I shall lead the way."

He moved to the front with Hiss-Majesty. After Will took a few deep breaths, he followed the troglodytes.

"Just let me know whenever you need a break," said Nico. "Don't feel bad about it. I want to reach Tartarus *with* you, okay?"

"Yeah . . ." Will tried to un-tense the muscles in his shoulders. He had no reason to feel irritated; Nico was just trying to help. "Tartarus. Together."

As they continued, Will's mind drifted in the darkness. What would Tartarus be like? He had nothing to help him imagine it except for Nico's descriptions from the day before.

The day before. Will wasn't even sure if it *was* a new day.

Will tried to cope with that thought. Gods, he'd always relied on the rising sun to introduce him to a new day. But he wouldn't have that down here. For all he knew, it had been one hour in the mortal world since they'd entered the Door of Orpheus. Or maybe a *month* had passed.

He missed . . . a lot of things. Not just the sun. He missed campfires, too—being under an open night sky, eating s'mores, and singing with his friends at Camp Half-Blood. Right then, a melody came to him, and he started humming. Low at first, and then he increased the volume until his voice echoed through the tunnel. To his surprise, the tunnel actually seemed to get *lighter.* . . . Or were his eyes just adjusting? He could see the tiny grooves in the rock where the trogs had used their hands, or some sort of digging tools, to excavate the passage. Will picked up his pace, a sudden burst of energy filling him.

"What is that tune?" Nico asked softly.

"Something my mom wrote a long time ago," Will said. "I only realized recently that it was probably about my dad. The crowds would go absolutely bonkers for that song. It was about love as a brightness of the spirit."

He started the melody again, but Nico grabbed his arm.

"Will," he said, "do you realize you're *shining?*"

Will looked down at his own hands. Sure enough, his skin was illuminated, casting a warm glow.

"Wow," he said. "That wasn't on purpose."

"Should you maybe stop?" asked Nico. "Is it draining you?"

At that, Will's skin slowly dimmed until the only light came from the sun globe.

"Probably a good idea," he agreed, though he wasn't sure.

The music seemed to be helping him. Will wanted to hum the melody again, but Nico was right—he had to conserve his energy, and if he glowed himself to death before they even reached Tartarus that would be bad. On the other hand, the darkness . . . gods, it felt like it was getting *worse*. And was the tunnel shrinking, too? Was it trying to close in on them?

Focus, Will, he told himself. *Keep moving.*

He was sweating profusely by the time he saw the end of the tunnel: a ragged circle of dull, reddish light maybe fifty yards ahead.

"*Screech-*Bling, is that it?" Will asked. "Are we close?"

"We are," the trog said. "But once we emerge from the passage, there will be one more obstacle to deal with. Stay close, and you'd better turn off your magical orb, Will Solace."

Will obeyed, then stowed the globe.

Nico kissed the back of his neck. "I'm proud of you," he whispered. "I know this is hard."

A warmth spread across Will's cheeks. He wasn't sure he was

doing a good job. He felt guilty for being irritated with Nico earlier, but Nico's little gesture of affection made him want to try harder.

He clasped Nico's hand in his, and the two of them headed into the reddish unknown.

CHAPTER 21

Nico was worried.

When they emerged into the arid, smoky air of the Underworld, Will came to a stop, his hands on his hips, his breathing uneven. Will looked . . . Well, it felt strange thinking that Will was paler than usual. Nico usually cornered the market on having a ghostly pallor. But Will *had* lost some of his color. Was this what he looked like without exposure to sunlight?

It wasn't just that detail, though. Will had been a little loopy and forgetful in the tunnel, and Nico believed that what everyone had been concerned about was starting to happen. Deep in the Underworld, a child of Apollo would be affected more than anyone else. And they hadn't even made it to Tartarus yet!

"Take a moment to catch your breath," Nico told him.

Will rubbed at his eyes, as if willing them to adjust faster to the light. "I'm glad to be out of that tunnel," he said. "Where to next?"

Nico pushed down his fears because there was nothing he could do about them at the moment except care for Will. Even that role reversal was starting to grate on him, mostly because he wasn't used to it. Will always ran around camp (or any battlefield, really) doing whatever he could to assist those in need. Now, though, Nico had to step up and assist Will, and it was a lot harder than he'd expected.

That didn't stop him from trying, though. "First, sit and rest," he said. "I want you to drink a little nectar."

Will didn't argue. He plopped down on a boulder and lay back before partaking of the nectar Nico offered him.

"Guess I'm more tired than I thought," he said.

"It was a long journey," said Screech-Bling, but Nico could tell the trog was also concerned about Will. "We will give you some time," he continued. "Come, *Hiss*-Majesty. We shall hunt for lizards."

The troglodytes darted off in an impossible blur, leaving Nico and Will alone on a low ridge overlooking the broken hills of Erebos. They had somehow navigated under the Styx and across the borders of the land of the dead, coming up deep inside Hades's territory, in an area Nico was pretty sure he'd never visited.

"What is it like?" Will asked.

Nico followed his gaze to Hades's shadowy palace, its obsidian fortifications still dominating the landscape even at this distance. Above the turrets, dark shapes swirled—perhaps the Furies, or skeletal pegasi from Hades's stables. Nico felt a pang of longing. He was so close to his Underworld home—to safety and comfort—but it was the one place he couldn't go right now.

"Father modeled his palace after Olympus," he said, his hand on Will's shoulder. "He felt so left out by the other gods, he basically made a mirror image of their headquarters. It's very different, though. I don't know if this will make sense, but it's . . . less pretentious?"

Will tilted his head. "I'm not sure I get that, but I like the idea of it."

"I think it's because it's just for *him*. So there's this genuineness to everything. He may have copied Olympus, but he put his own spin on it."

Will gazed at the distant towers. "But you didn't spend much time there growing up, did you? I'm not sure I could."

No, Nico thought. *You couldn't*.

"Bianca and I traveled all over with our mother. Hades visited us, though. So no, I didn't grow up in his palace, but he was in my life."

"Wow," said Will. "I didn't even know about my heritage until I was ten, and I didn't meet Apollo for years after that."

"He didn't reveal himself after you got attacked by pigeons?"

Will scowled. "They were Stymphalian birds!"

"Which looked exactly like pigeons."

"*Anyway*," continued Will, "maybe if we get through this quest . . . *when* we get through this quest"—he took a deep breath—"we should visit your father's palace sometime?"

Nico raised an eyebrow. "Are you joking?"

"No. Why would I be? I think maybe it's time."

A smile grew on Nico's face. He recalled the relief he'd felt when Will had been kind to Hiss-Majesty before entering the tunnel. Will *was* making an effort, wasn't he?

"I suppose it's only fair," said Nico, "after I spent all that time hanging out with *your* dad."

"To be *actually* fair, my dad was a teenager at the time, so I don't know how much that counts."

Nico hesitated. "But do you really want to meet mine?"

Will looked up at him. "Of course. He's important to you . . . so he's important to me."

In moments like this, the harder parts of being in a relationship with a child of Apollo were easy to forget. Will was so quick to be kind. There wasn't an insincere bone in his body. So Nico sat on the ground in front of Will and leaned against him, comforted by his presence and loyalty and warmth.

"Okay, then," Nico said. "Next time, we'll visit my father."

"The son of Apollo wishes to meet Hades?" said Screech-Bling, startling both Nico and Will.

The CEO and Hiss-Majesty had rematerialized as quickly as they'd vanished, each now clutching fistfuls of dead lizards. Nico had no idea where they'd found them.

Screech-Bling tossed one in the air, then caught it in his mouth, swallowing with gusto. "This is fascinating to me," he continued. "We troglodytes are not afraid of Hades, of course. CLICK! We are brave and fierce. But—"

"We prefer to be brave and fierce from a distance," finished Hiss-Majesty.

The two trogs sat next to Nico and Will and gazed at Hades's palace while they finished their meal. It was . . . nice, actually.

A nice moment in the Underworld. Even Will seemed to relax, though he turned down Hiss-Majesty's offer to share their dead lizards.

Finally, Hiss-Majesty straightened their foam cheese hat, making sure it was sitting at the same angle as Will's. "I think we should continue," they said. "If you're ready, GRRR. We just have to make it past one more obstacle before we reach the shortcut to Tartarus."

"One more obstacle?" Will squared his shoulders. "Well, I can do *one* more. What is it, exactly?"

"The farm," said Screech-Bling. "We have to make it through the farm."

He said the word *farm* as it were a new form of torture in the Fields of Punishment.

"People *farm* here?" said Will. "How? There's no sunlight."

And just like that, Nico's creeping dread reappeared. It was two-pronged: First, he was annoyed that, once again, Will couldn't seem to imagine life in the Underworld. Second, a memory started to surface from the depths of Nico's mind . . . a vague recollection of something Hades had told him about a farm, during the same trip when Nico had found Hazel Levesque, his half sister, wandering the Fields of Asphodel.

What had Hades warned him about? Nico wished he could contact Hazel—she'd probably have the answer. She had a better memory.

As Nico and Will followed the trogs, he thought about how much he missed Hazel. He was learning to make peace with that feeling. It was okay for him to miss people because that meant he wanted them around in his life. That idea was *very* new for him—he was used to either pushing people away or watching them recoil from his presence. There was a time when he'd even tried to push Will away. Where would he be now if he'd actually followed through with that?

Screech-Bling led the way, following a ravine that snaked between granite hills like a dry riverbed. Nico quickly lost all frame of reference. He knew his father's palace was to the north, beyond the Fields of Asphodel, but this landscape looked totally unfamiliar. No spirits drifted across these hills. No wails of the damned filled the air—just the crunch of their feet on the gravel. The only illumination came from patches of blue lichen on the hillsides, which made Nico feel like he was walking through a crime scene being inspected under UV light for blood splatters. Ugh. He'd been listening to too many of Will's beloved true-crime podcasts. (Another thing Nico didn't understand about his sunny-natured boyfriend.)

Will shuffled along behind him, his pace slower than before. He was humming again, and the melody floated over to Nico, wrapping itself around him, almost as if Will were sending out his energy as a way to stay connected even while they were just a few feet apart.

Though Nico wanted Will to preserve his energy, he was perfectly fine with the comforting sensation of the music. He guessed he would just have to monitor Will for excessive glowing.

At last, they crested the ridge of a hill. Below, a sprawling patchwork of fields and orchards stretched to the horizon, and then the whole "farm" thing started to make sense.

Rows of towering gray trees bristled with scarlet flowers. Ghostly farmhands wove through the orchards, some hammering syrup taps into the trunks while others carried buckets on yokes across their shoulders. In the pastures, herds of jet-black cattle grazed on yellow grass.

"Cows," Will grumbled. "Those aren't related to tauri silvestres, are they?"

Before Nico could answer, he was distracted by movement in the nearest orchard. From the shadows of the trees, an enormous humanoid creature emerged.

Nico's heart sank.

Now, too late, he realized where they were and who they were facing. The creature had the head of a red Angus bull, the shirtless torso of a muscular man with crimson skin, and black leather pants over dark work boots.

"Minotaur!" Will yelped, assuming a defensive stance. "Should we run?"

"That's not the Minotaur," said Nico. "And no, we should not run."

The bull-man sprinted up the hill, charging straight toward them.

"Um, you sure about that?" Will asked.

"He will not attack you!" Screech-Bling promised cheerfully. "It is much worse than that!"

Nico sighed. "He's a demon, Will, and he doesn't want to fight us. He wants—"

The bull-man skidded to a stop right in front of them, panting heavily.

"Oh, good!" he bellowed, his voice so deep it rattled Nico's teeth. "I am *so* glad I spotted you, because you are not going anywhere!"

"I want to make it clear that I didn't actually know what I was doing," said Nico. "Like, we have to establish that."

Gorgyra tilted her head. "There is no judgment here."

"I was mostly saying that to Will, because he *loves* teasing me about this."

"Only every once in a while!" said Will. Then he raised his hand to the side of his mouth and stage-whispered to Gorgyra, "I do it all the time."

"Look," said Nico, "you know what Camp Half-Blood *really* needs to be teaching us?"

Gorgyra shook her head.

"We need courses on *human emotions*," said Nico. "Classes on how to come out, how to talk about feelings, how to ask a cute boy on a date—"

"You did just fine," said Will.

"Well, I definitely didn't intend to come out *and* ask you on a date in front of the whole camp!"

Will started laughing, but it quickly turned to a deep, shaking cough. Nico put his arm around his boyfriend's waist.

Will held up a hand. "I'm fine."

"No, you're not." Nico frowned at Gorgyra. "He's getting worse. We need that boat *now*. We've wasted too much time!"

The lines tightened around Gorgyra's eyes. "Stories are never a waste of time, son of Hades. We are all of us made of stories."

"Just keep going," Will said, waving his hand.

Nico sat back down with a grunt. "Anyway," he said, looking back to Gorgyra, "I was terrified to tell Will the truth. Every time I was around him, I thought I was gonna burst into flames."

Will wiped his forehead. "You had me fooled. I thought *I* was the one who was obviously a mess."

Nico shook his head. "Not at all. Even though I sensed there was something there, it was still frightening to think about . . . I don't know. Declaring it. And not knowing how anyone—not just Will—would react."

"Not that Camp Half-Blood is full of bigots or anything," Will said, leaning toward Gorgyra. "It's just that . . . well, in our world, you learn to tread carefully. You never know if someone's feelings will change toward you once you tell them who you really are."

Nico let the silence grow before he spoke. "It happened to me once, a long time ago," he said. "All because of a harmless thing I said about my Mythomagic cards."

"Wait, really?" Will asked. "You never told me this."

One side of Nico's lip curled up. "Well, I have to start sharing sometime, right? I can't keep my whole past a mystery from you."

"Nico, you don't—"

He raised a hand. "I actually want to tell you."

Will scooted closer. "Okay."

"It was right after we'd moved to the States from Italy," Nico said. "We were living in Washington, DC, and I had a deck of Mythomagic cards with me at school—"

"You had Mythomagic cards back in the 1940s?"

Nico sighed. "Yes, Will. We didn't have cell phones or the Internet, but we *did* have Mythomagic cards."

"Wow, Grandpa."

"Shut up."

Will chuckled, snuggling closer.

"Anyway," Nico continued, "thinking about it now, I don't even know that I recognized my own feelings about being gay. It just . . . happened? But I was playing with this kid, Henry Whittaker, and I made a comment about how pretty Ares looked on his card."

"Ares?" Will raised an eyebrow. *"Really?"*

Nico rolled his eyes. "I was, like, eight years old, Will."

"At least I had the foresight to find Hermes attractive."

"Hermes? Are you kidding me? Who goes for *Hermes?"*

"I do," said Will.

"Wow, you really do like underdogs," muttered Nico.

"Boys . . ." said Gorgyra, bowing her head toward them in a slight admonishment.

"Sorry," said Nico, but then he shook his head at Will. *"Hermes."*

"I thought this was a safe space," Will said, smiling.

"Hmph." Nico was glad to see Will smile, but his heart still fluttered with nerves. "So once I said that about Ares, Henry looked at me funny. He told me I was weird. He didn't call me names or anything, but he never hung out with me again. I got the message loud and clear: Don't do that. Don't feel that. Don't even *think* that."

"Wow," said Will. "I had no idea."

Nico let out his tension in a long breath. Anytime someone suspected that Nico wasn't straight or every time he shared too much about himself, he felt like this—like a ticking bomb, or a draft of air that teased at a fire.

But with Will . . . he was safe. Will wouldn't turn on him, or abandon him, or start saying nasty things behind his back.

Thinking about that, Nico made a connection. For the first time, he realized something about a part of himself, and instead of stamping it out, instead of shoving it down into the darkness to fester, he shared it.

"That's why I had such a negative reaction to Cupid," he said.

He gave Gorgyra a brief summary of what had happened a couple of years earlier, how Cupid had forced Nico to come out as some twisted form of honesty. "I was terrified that Jason was going to leave me there in Croatia," he said. "I completely believed it, too. Why wouldn't he? In that moment, I think Jason knew more about me than any other person on Earth."

"But he stayed," said Will softly. "He stayed, and so did the rest of us."

"Yes," he said. "But that experience still hurts. I know it would have been a while before I felt comfortable enough to come out to Jason, but it still should have been left up to me. It should have been my choice."

"It is unfair when we are coerced to reveal ourselves," said Gorgyra. "This is why it is important that whatever souls share with me is freely given."

"Consent," said Will, nodding. "It helps people feel safe."

Gorgyra tipped her head to the side. "Nico, I wonder . . . why are you telling *me* all this? You do not know me at all, and you are corporeal. You are not a lonely soul in the Acheron."

"Well, I figured you could be trusted," Nico said after some thought. "I mean, most gods and immortal creatures aren't homophobic. How *can* they be after being alive for so long?"

"Like my dad," said Will. "He's fallen in love with people of all genders."

"Exactly," said Nico. "Plus . . . you're all the way down here, Gorgyra. Homophobia? In the land of the dead?" He scoffed. "It just seems silly to judge a person's sexuality when they're dead."

Gorgyra's face glowed with satisfaction. Her dress flowed and whispered, like voices calling out. What were they saying? What were they asking of Nico?

He thought he knew.

"I finally got to make the choice myself," he said. "I mean, it came about because of a misunderstanding, but still, I chose."

Will squeezed his hand. "The date."

Nico looked at Gorgyra. "I asked the satyrs and nymphs at Camp Half-Blood to set up a picnic for me and Will. I thought that's how you were supposed to do it! That's how it is in the movies. You make these intimate romantic gestures, and everything goes as planned, and—"

"And then the satyrs accidentally orchestrated a camp-wide coming-out party for Nico," finished Will.

Nico groaned. "Gorgyra, I thought they were going to set up the food in some out-of-the-way grove in the woods, so imagine my surprise when I pass the dining pavilion on a regular Thursday afternoon and there are flower wreaths hanging everywhere. Picnic baskets at every table. The nymphs are dressed up in their finest greenery, and Juniper greets me with a crown of holly!"

"You looked so cute in that," said Will.

"And then they sat me at the head table, and I still didn't get what was going on. I worried I was going to be late to my picnic with Will!"

Nico glanced over and was surprised to find his boyfriend glowing again. Not as brightly as before—more of a soft aurora flickering over his body. Nico worried that Will might be wasting precious energy, but Will's skin no longer looked waxy. His face was no longer sickly and pale.

So Nico kept talking.

"When all the campers had gathered, Juniper announced that it was a special day. I had an announcement to make. Mind you, I was *terrified*. I had finally realized what they'd done, and even though it was an honest mistake, I was still upset. This wasn't what I'd wanted!"

"But you went through with it," said Gorgyra. "Why? What changed?"

Nico was quiet for a moment. "I decided I could own it," he said. "Do it my way. I could not only tell Will that I was gay and that I liked him, but I could tell *everyone*. If I was going to stay at Camp Half-Blood, I needed to know that I could be myself there, that I didn't have to hide in the shadows all the time."

"You do like the shadows, though," joked Will.

Nico nudged him with his shoulder. "Shush. This is *my* coming-out story, Will."

"I mean, it's technically mine, too!"

"That's true." Nico smiled at the memory. "Some of your cabin-mates were *very* shocked by the revelation."

"Not Kayla or Austin, though. They were thrilled, but they'd both noticed me staring at you multiple times."

"What was it like, Nico?"

The question from Gorgyra caught him off guard. "What was what like?"

"The moment. Revealing your truth."

He gazed back at Will, into his warm blue eyes.

"Terrifying," he said. "The whole dining pavilion went silent, and I remember standing up and clearing my throat, and then I didn't say anything for like . . . half a minute. And then . . . it was like a dam had broken. I just *talked*."

Will nodded. "I remember you being kinda defensive at first," he said. "Telling us all that you knew everyone talked about you, that you knew you hadn't been around all that much. It was like . . . like you were anticipating every possible argument or criticism."

Nico's eyes welled with tears. "But none of those worst-case scenarios happened. Instead, I told the whole camp I was gay, that I was sick of hiding the truth, that I liked Will Solace and wanted to go on a date with him. And there were no meteor showers or explosions. No mass exodus from Camp Half-Blood."

He turned to Will. "Do you remember what you said, Night Light?"

Will rolled his eyes. "I do, Death Boy. I told you that you didn't have to throw a party. I would have said yes if you'd just asked me."

"Again, I did not throw a party on purpose!"

"But I didn't know that at the time," said Will. "I was so impressed. You didn't seem like the party type, and you'd gone through all that just to tell me you liked me? It helped, Nico."

"Helped what?"

"Helped make it easier for me," he said. "To be able to say who I am. Me agreeing to go on a date with you wasn't just me saying I thought you were cute. Which is very true!"

"Ew, gross," said Nico, but he couldn't suppress his smile.

"It was my chance to stop hiding as well." Will's glowing skin brightened. "Do you know how many others have felt comfortable coming into their own because of you, Nico?"

"What? What are you talking about?"

"Paolo. Malcolm Pace. Jake Mason. And it's not just in Camp Half-Blood! Piper is just as thankful for you as the others. None of them would have been able to be out if you hadn't gone first."

Heat rose in Nico's cheeks. He hadn't ever thought of it that way—he'd just been trying to be himself.

"We often don't see the effects we have on others," said Gorgyra. "In the moment, all that matters is ourselves. But you, Nico di Angelo . . . Do you not see what you are surrounded by?"

The whispers rose again, and this time, Nico sensed a desperation in them.

No, that wasn't right.

It was *envy.*

"Come," she said, rising from her rocky seat. "I have promised you a boat, and you have given me more than enough stories."

Nico helped Will stand, and his boyfriend swayed a bit before steadying himself against Nico.

Gorgyra's silver eyes seemed sad. Did she not want them to go? Nico imagined that this had to be hard for her, knowing her nature, and a burst of pity hit him.

He glanced over at Will, who had stopped glowing. Even so, he definitely looked better than he had before they'd begun telling stories. Nico examined the gauze on Will's leg. The bleeding seemed to have stopped.

Nico didn't quite understand it, but the stories had somehow accelerated Will's healing.

They walked toward the river, Will limping. Before they reached the shore, Will stumbled. Nico sat him down on at the edge of the dock. Maybe another story would help?

"Hey." He put his face close to Will's. "Do you remember the first time you kissed me?"

CHAPTER 22

Nico raised his hand to the bull-man. "Menoetes, meet Will, *Screech*-Bling, and *Hiss*-Majesty. Everyone else, this is Menoetes."

Menoetes grabbed his horns and started jumping up and down in excitement. "Oh, the gods *definitely* answered my prayers today! I've been waiting *ages* for a demigod to show up, and now I actually get *Nico di Angelo*?"

Will's jaw dropped open. Nico reached over and gently shut it. The troglodytes, however, didn't seem fazed at all.

"Greetings, Menoetes!" said Screech-Bling proudly. "We have not actually met before, but I am *Screech*-Bling, the CEO of the troglodytes, at your—SHRIEK—service! And this is my comrade, *Hiss*-Majesty."

Hiss-Majesty bowed, doffing their cheese hat with great finesse.

"Wow, *four* people who can help me?" Menoetes clapped his beefy hands. "This is the best day of my life."

"I'm so lost," said Will. "Who are you?"

Menoetes flared his bovine nostrils. "Menoetes? No? Has Nico told you *nothing* of me?"

"I've been . . . kind of busy?" said Nico sheepishly. "You know, between finding my half sister down here, and falling into Tartarus, and then all those pesky Roman emperors? You know, all that."

"Yes, yes, I *did* hear such rumblings from Hades," Menoetes said. "But surely you told your friend here about me at *some* point!"

Will grimaced and shook his head.

"Well, I will try not to be mortally offended," said Menoetes. Then he offered his hand to Will. "I work for Nico's father. I tend to his cattle and oversee the farm."

"Tell me," said Will, taking Menoetes's hand, "what is the farm *for?*"

Menoetes laughed. "Oh, you're *silly*. Surely you know—"

Will shook his head again.

Menoetes glared at Nico. "Do you not tell him *anything?*"

"Sometimes!" Nico said. And then he thought, Sometimes I'm afraid to tell him more.

Menoetes grunted. "Well, let me make it easy for you . . . uh . . . What's your name?"

"Will. Will Solace."

Menoetes narrowed his eyes. "Child of Apollo?"

"Yep."

"Hmph. Don't know what *you* are doing down here, Night Light."

"Hey!" said Will, scowling.

Menoetes swept his hand to indicate the landscape behind him. "All that you see exists so the Underworld can nourish its helpers and keep the machinery moving. There are many living beings who work for Hades, either in the fields, or in the palace, or in Elysium. They must be fed. Did you think ambrosia and nectar come from *nothing?*"

"Of course not," said Will. "I help manage the infirmary at Camp Half-Blood."

"It doesn't just *exist*," said Menoetes. "It is *grown*. I'm sure your satyrs or dryads up in Camp Half-Blood manage your fields and orchards."

"Menoetes has been working for my father since . . . well, for a very, very long time," said Nico. "He's really good with the cattle."

The bull-man waved off the comment. "Oh, *stahp*," he said, and then, in a lower voice, "But it's true. I can show you around if you'd like."

Nico squirmed. "Menoetes, it's good to see you, but we're on a quest, so—"

"Not a *quest*! How exciting! Well then, let me lay down the red carpet for you!"

Nico watched in discomfort as Menoetes sprawled on the ground. "Go ahead, O great demigods!" he said.

"Please don't do that," said Nico.

"Do you get it? I'm a red carpet."

"I got that."

"Because I'm red."

Nico sighed. "Please stand up, Menoetes."

The bull-man did, then dusted himself off. "The world doesn't come to a standstill just because you're demigods."

"No one said it did!" said Nico. "We just need to pass through for . . . uh . . ." He looked down at Screech-Bling.

"For the shortcut," said the troglodyte.

"The shortcut?" Menoetes snorted. "The shortcut to *where*?"

Before Nico could reply, Hiss-Majesty blurted out, "Oh, they're going to Tartarus!" The trog's eyes glowed with admiration.

"*Tartarus?!*" Menoetes burst into laughter. He doubled over, clutching at his ripped abs. "Oh, this is perfect. Thank you so much, my young troglodyte! You've given me exactly what I need!"

"What does that mean?" asked Will.

Menoetes snapped back to attention. "It means I will *absolutely* tell Hades that you two are traipsing around his realm without his knowledge. He won't be too thrilled about that, will he, Nico?"

Nico could feel the sweat breaking out on his forehead. "Don't do that, Menoetes. You can't."

"I can't?" Menoetes shrugged. "I could call on him right now. Or even write him a *letter*."

"Please! He can't know—"

"'Dear Hades, how are you?'" said Menoetes while he mimed writing. "'Hope you're doing swell. Your cows are *lovely*, and the nectar reserves are overflowing this season. By the way, your son brought another demigod into your realm—a child of Apollo, no less!—and they're totally walking into Tartarus. Yes, that's right, the place you expressly forbade anyone else to enter. Love you! Signed, your faithful and loyal cattle driver, Menoetes.'"

To cap off the performance, the bull demon pretended to fold up the letter, stuff it in an envelope, and seal it with a kiss.

"Are you done?" Nico asked.

"Maybe," Menoetes said. "Depends on what you're willing to offer me *not* to tell your father."

Nico tried not to groan. "What is it you want this time, Menoetes?"

"Me? You're asking *me*?" He feigned surprise. "Well, that's so sweet of you to think of my needs!"

"This demon is very dramatic," noted Screech-Bling.

"Every day of every year of the last two thousand seven hundred years!" said Menoetes. "Get used to it!"

Nico pressed his lips together. "Okay, let's make the usual unfair trade: we complete some inane task for you; you let us pass without interference."

Menoetes giggled, which was a strange sound coming from a

giant bull-headed man. "Isn't that what heroes are for, Nico? You're always out there pointlessly retrieving items for some misguided moral goal. Why can't *I* take advantage of it?"

"What do you *want*?" Nico said sharply.

"Fruit," he said. "Specifically, fruit from Persephone's garden."

Nico's heart dropped to the bottom of his stomach. "You know that's not possible."

"And you know it's not possible for you to enter Tartarus," said Menoetes. "So we're at an impasse already. Wouldn't you like to resolve this?"

Screech-Bling folded his arms. "You ask too much, bull-man farmer. The troglodytes would never visit Persephone's garden."

"Never," agreed Hiss-Majesty. "Despite how shiny it is."

Screech-Bling gazed dreamily into the distance. "Yes. So very shiny . . ."

"Hold on," said Will. "Would someone explain to me why this a big deal?"

"Yes, Nico." Menoetes's voice dripped with mock sweetness. "Why don't *you* explain it?"

Nico dug his fingernails into his palm. "My stepmother's garden . . . There's no place like it in existence. It's beautiful. And if I'm being honest, it's one of my favorite spots."

"I'm not hearing the problem," Will said. "If you know it so well, why can't we just visit and ask Persephone not to tell her husband?"

"Because she's not going to let me take anything from her garden! *No one* is allowed to do that. It's full of some of the rarest plants ever. There are bushes of diamonds, Will. Trees with flowering rubies. And I'm pretty sure she'll know the *moment* we take something, which means she'll tell Hades immediately after that. Then we're toast."

"You don't have many options," said Menoetes. "You can take

the chance and *maybe* not get caught. Or you can refuse to help me, and you *will* get caught."

"Why?" said Nico. "Why are you always asking things of others? Do you have a collection of stuff people have retrieved for you?"

"No!" said Menoetes, and this time, his offense didn't seem fake. "No, it's for . . . Well, I like to share."

"Share?" said Will. "With whom?"

"With my boyfriend!" he blurted out. "Fine, I said it. Are you happy now?"

Nico and Will looked at each other, shocked.

"Oh, so you have a problem with a male demon being in a relationship with a male giant?" Menoetes scraped the ground with his human foot, like he was going to charge them.

"What?" said Nico. "No! It's just—"

"I expected better of you, I guess," said Menoetes. "It seems so—"

"Menoetes, calm down," Nico interrupted. "I'm *gay*."

"And I'm bisexual." Will pointed to Nico. "He's *literally* my boyfriend."

"Oh," said Menoetes. "Well . . . sorry. I get a little defensive sometimes."

"That's okay," said Will. "But back up the Boyfriend Train a second. You said . . . a *giant*?"

"Yes," said Menoetes proudly, puffing up his chest. "Although he's not a *giant* giant, mind you. He's more my size. His name is Geryon, and we've been going steady for a while now."

Nico immediately started coughing so hard that Will pounded his palm on Nico's back.

"GERYON?!" Nico demanded. "Black hair? Tiny little mustache? Three bodies?"

"That's him," said Menoetes dreamily. "You know him?"

"He tied me and my friends up! He tried to kill Percy Jackson!"

"That was his old life!" claimed Menoetes. "Ever since the Doors of Death were closed . . . well, he's been *different*."

"Different *how?*" demanded Nico. "Because he was awful! He helped Kronos. All he cared about was money!"

"And now he *doesn't*," said Menoetes. "Which is why I want to give him something nice. He doesn't have anything anymore. He lost his ranch business. He started reevaluating his life, and I'm so proud of his growth! If I can get him just one pretty thing . . . Well, gift-giving is my love language," he said bashfully. "But I never have a chance to *find* gifts. I'm always working here."

Will nodded. "That . . . actually sounds really sweet."

"Sweet?" Nico scoffed. "You didn't meet Geryon. You don't know what he's like."

"*Was* like," said Menoetes. "*Was.* Because now you don't know what he *is* like."

Nico was left speechless.

"Maybe we should give him a chance," said Will. "We both know people who were once terrible and then turned things around. Like Ethan. Or Luke."

When he put it that way, Nico had to concede the point. And wasn't that the whole purpose behind this quest, after all? They were rescuing someone who had dared to be different.

"Fine," he said. "Menoetes, we'll find a way to get you that fruit, as long as you promise to let us pass afterward."

Menoetes put his hand on his red chest. "I swear on the Styx."

"That's good enough for me," said Will.

"Me, too," Nico decided.

A flurry of hissing and clicking passed between Screech-Bling and Hiss-Majesty.

"We cannot go with you, demigods," Screech-Bling announced. "It is too dangerous, even for brave troglodytes. If we were caught, our whole people might face the wrath of Hades!"

"Shiny though the garden may be . . ." Hiss-Majesty added dreamily.

"I understand," Nico said. "You've done plenty already. It'll be difficult enough for just *two* of us to sneak into the garden."

"Which brings me to another question," Will said, his legs wobbling. "Isn't Persephone's garden next to Hades's palace? Do we have to walk all the way back there?"

"Stop fretting and follow me," said Menoetes. "I have a solution."

The bull-man led the group down the hill, through pastures filled with black cattle that seemed utterly uninterested in them. Nico tried to dampen his racing thoughts, but he was drowning in worries about how to avoid his father's detection—and Persephone's.

As they passed through the orchards, Menoetes patted one of the enormous, thick-trunked trees. "Have any of you ever had nectar straight from the source?"

Will stared at one of the spirits, who was sticking a spigot into a trunk. "Is that what these ghosts are harvesting?"

"They're *souls*, first of all," said Menoetes. "Sometimes souls in the Fields of Punishment want to work off the horrible things they did in the mortal world, so Hades allows them to come here. Which is perfect for me, since handling too much nectar at once is toxic."

"Wow," said Nico. "I knew about your cattle, but I guess I never asked Father what else you did on this farm."

Will nodded. "How did no one at Camp Half-Blood ever teach us about this?"

"A lot of gods and demigods just take it for granted," said Menoetes. "Nectar and ambrosia are so plentiful that most folks don't ask where they come from."

"I think we should have a conversation with Chiron when we get back," said Will.

That warmed Nico's heart.

To their left, spirit workers were pulling ambrosia chunks from the ground like giant tubers and piling them in wheelbarrows. Menoetes waved at them as he brought the group to a hitching post where half a dozen smoky jet-black donkeys were tied up.

"Donkeys?" said Nico. "Aren't they pretty slow?"

Menoetes laughed. "You could walk instead."

"Donkeys sound great," said Will quickly. "Please, Nico."

Nico noticed the dark circles under Will's eyes. He looked *exhausted*. It was the reminder he needed that he couldn't ask too much of Will in a place like this. It wouldn't be fair.

"Demonic donkeys it is," said Nico.

Menoetes threw saddles on two of the donkeys and then stepped aside. "This is how we deliver ambrosia and nectar to the mortal world. As far as I'm concerned, there's no better way to travel."

Will narrowed his eyes. "You mean these things deliver *all* our nectar and ambrosia?"

"No," admitted the bull-demon. "Like I said before, I'm pretty sure the dryads manage the grove at Camp Half-Blood. But there are many customers who require it elsewhere, and this is where it comes from."

With a little help from Nico, Will climbed onto the back of a donkey, and then Nico leaped up onto his.

"I'm still not sure about this," he said. "My father is . . . well, he's very perceptive. I don't know how we're going to avoid his notice."

"You're creative," said Menoetes. "You know your father and the palace grounds."

"If anyone can do this, it's you," said Will. His eyes sparkled with that very Will-like sincerity that Nico loved. He was constantly amazed how powerful it felt to have someone by his side who believed in him.

Nico thought for a moment. "We'll have to approach from the north. There's hardly ever any activity on that side of Erebos, so the walls aren't well maintained. If we can find a break in the defenses, we could ride right up to my father's palace."

Menoetes nodded. "An excellent idea."

"Then, if we can sneak into the garden . . . Hmmm. I have an idea for the perfect fruit."

"Don't tell me!" Menoetes cupped his hands over his ears. "It must be a surprise!"

Nico put up his palms. "Okay, okay!"

"We're just happy to help you," said Will.

Nico still wasn't sure about that, but they *had* to do it if they were going to reach Tartarus before it was too late—for Bob, but also for Will.

Menoetes laid his hands on the heads of the respective donkeys, then murmured something to them in ancient Greek. When he was done, he stepped aside.

"They'll bring you right back when you're done." The bull-man turned and regarded the troglodytes. "As for you, my small friends, you are welcome to stay with me while you wait."

Screech-Bling's eyes gleamed. "We shall do so. We have much to learn from one another."

"Perhaps a trade could be arranged," Hiss-Majesty added. "The lizards and grubs in your farmlands, in exchange for"—they touched their cheese-wedge hat—"fashionable haberdashery?"

Menoetes fluttered his long bull eyelashes. "Oh, that would be amazing!"

Before Nico could even process the idea of Menoetes wearing a stack of trog hats, their donkeys rocketed forward. Will let loose a scream of both terror and joy. As he clung to his donkey's neck, he repeated the same phrase over and over: "OHMYGODSOHMY GODSOHMYGODS."

And the two of them zipped over the land of the dead on the backs of demonic donkeys.

CHAPTER 23

When they dismounted near the gates of Hades's palace, Will was certain he would never experience anything so thrilling ever again.

Sure, his muscles were sore, his breath was shallower than usual, and his mind felt like it was being mixed in a blender . . .

But if he had to conserve his energy, there were worse ways than riding a demonic donkey. Their steeds had zipped across the Underworld without a single incident, easily evading packs of hellhounds, skirting the sentried towers of Erebos at just the right moments to avoid detection, and finally bringing them through a break in the walls, straight up to the palace perimeter. If they hadn't been trying to sneak in, Will would have let loose a joyful whoop and asked the donkeys to do it all over again!

However, as they crept closer to the palace gates, a chill passed through him. It wasn't just the imposing obsidian doors that disturbed him. It was what was carved *into* them.

The intricate engravings were all death tableaux: planes dropping bombs on crowds of people, enormous mushroom clouds etched in a distant horizon, lines of officers in riot gear, their batons raised against panicking masses. Will wondered if these depicted historical events, or if they were prophecies of the future. Were they meant to be a commentary on the circular nature of death?

Will didn't really want to know the answer.

Fortunately, Nico didn't lead him through the gates. That would have been unwise, given the half dozen zombie guards in ancient Greek armor. Instead, Will followed him along the northern wall, through a gap in a thicket of briars, to a small hidden gate of Stygian iron.

Nico rummaged through his coat until he found a finger bone. (Will still wasn't used to the fact that his boyfriend kept random bits of human bone in his pockets for emergencies, but he guessed everyone needed a hobby.) Nico shaped the bone into a key—a literal skeleton key—and quietly unlocked the gate.

Will was about to peek through when Nico held out a hand to stop him.

Wait, he mouthed.

Nico twisted his body, stole a quick glance inside, then pressed his back to the wall. "We have a problem," he whispered. "She's here."

Will's pulse quickened. He'd been hoping they'd finally have some luck. Maybe Persephone would be traipsing around the upper world painting daisies or something. But if she was *here*, how were they supposed to get Menoetes any fruit?

Nico held a finger to his lips. He peeked through the gateway again, then gestured to Will that it was safe to look.

When Will saw the courtyard, he suppressed a gasp.

The garden glowed like a city at night. Every plant sparkled or glittered. One bush branched upward with stems like silvery bottle brushes. A glass cactus bloomed with ruby-red flowers. Sapphires and diamonds formed a gem-paved path that wove its way through the flower beds. Each plant was the most beautiful thing Will had ever seen until he gazed at the one next to it.

But none of them were as beautiful as the woman tending the azure roses in the center of the garden.

Persephone's peach-colored dress shimmered in the light, the fabric stitched with tiny green vines that flowed and spiraled down her sleeves. Her dark brown hair framed a face so soft and gentle that the roses seemed to bend toward her, aching for contact.

The stories about Persephone's beauty did not do her justice.

As the goddess drifted deeper into her garden, Will finally managed to peel himself away and turn back to Nico.

"You okay?" whispered Nico. "I know it's hard to see her for the first time."

"She's the most gorgeous person I've ever seen," he said in awe.

"Calm down, Night Light."

"What? I'm not wrong."

"I didn't say you were."

He raised an eyebrow. "Are you jealous that I find her attractive?"

Nico wrinkled up his face. "Ew, *no*, Will. I'm trying not to be weirded out because that's my *stepmother*."

"Oh," said Will. "Right. Sorry."

"But yes, you're correct. She's stunning. I guess I'm just used to it by now."

Will shook his head. "We're *told* of her beauty, but that's nothing compared to actually *seeing* it."

"Okay, okay, enough of your bisexual chaos for the moment," said Nico. "We have to figure out how to get past her and pick some fruit without getting caught."

Will thought for a moment. "Can't we just dart in and grab something near the gate?"

Nico shook his head. "All the good fruit-bearing plants are in the center of the garden. In fact, I'm starting to wonder . . . what if Menoetes is setting us up to fail?"

"I was worrying about that, too," Will admitted. "But I think he really wants that fruit. If we're the only way he can get it, why set us up for failure?"

Nico sucked in a deep breath. "Okay. We'll just be as careful as we can. Get in, get the fruit, then get out. Hopefully Persephone stays on the far end of the garden for a while. Keep close to me, okay?"

Will nodded, and the two of them tiptoed through the gateway. They veered to the right, crouching behind a thick row of hedges with silver leaves. Will, still completely under the spell of the place, reached out and touched one.

"This is incredible," he whispered. "How does all of this grow here without sunlight?"

Nico gave Will a familiar look: something between annoyance and concern.

"It's just like the trees Menoetes showed us," Nico said. "Life finds a way to persist, even in the land of the dead."

A thought came to Will. "It's kinda like you, then."

Nico's eyebrows furrowed. "What?"

"You found a way to survive even in Tartarus. You're one of the only demigods who ever has."

"I was kidnapped by two fame-craving giants. It was hardly heroic."

"Hey, don't do that." Will touched Nico's face, stared into his dark eyes. "You *survived*. You continue to survive. You've been through more in your fifteen years than most people will endure in an entire lifetime."

Nico looked away, but Will knew this grumpy ball of darkness—*his* grumpy ball of darkness—and he refused to let Nico off the hook.

"I don't always understand you, Nico," he said, "but I do know that you're resilient. And in that sense, you are *just* like this garden."

Nico shifted uncomfortably. "We shouldn't be talking. Trying to be sneaky, remember?"

Still, he didn't protest Will's assessment. He even sounded a tiny bit pleased.

Will decided that was progress. Nico *had* been through a lot, but as Will watched the crystal petals floating to the ground from a nearby flowering tree, he felt a renewed sense of hope. This place seemed impossible. Yet here it was, thriving in a land of darkness and sorrow.

He supposed that darkness and life *could* coexist. . . .

Nico touched his shoulder. "I think she's gone inside. Let's move."

They followed the gem path through a grove of trees that looked like skeletal hands, which were both awe-inspiring and a little frightening. Each new sight took Will's breath away, like the velvety vines draped from the boughs of an amaranthine oak, or the veranda covered in moonflowers and surrounded by emerald prickly pears.

Nico guided him toward the center of the garden, where a large orchard encircled a three-tiered fountain. A syrupy-sweet odor hit Will's nostrils.

"What's *that?*" he asked.

"The pomegranate trees," Nico said. "Menoetes didn't specify what *kind* of fruit he wanted, so why not a pom? They're Persephone's signature fruit, after all."

Will frowned. "If you eat one of Persephone's pomegranates, aren't you're stuck in the Underworld forever?"

"Pretty sure that doesn't apply to creatures who are *from* the Underworld," Nico said. "But even if it did, it might be kind of romantic. Like sending a message: *You're stuck with me.*"

"I think we need to work on your definition of *romantic*, my love."

Nico's ears blushed. "Let's grab a couple of poms, then head back to the donkeys. Sound good?"

When they reached the pomegranate trees, Will nearly lost himself in the beauty of their emerald leaves and glittering fruit, festooning the branches like ruby ornaments, just begging to be plucked.

"Perfect," he murmured to himself.

Nico walked up to the nearest tree and grasped at a pomegranate. His hand went right through it.

For a moment, Will thought he was seeing things, his head swimming from the heavy perfume of the trees. But then Nico tried again. Again. *Again.* Each time, his fingers went right through the fruit like he'd turned into a shade from Asphodel.

"What's wrong?" Will asked.

"I don't know!" Nico hissed. "This doesn't make any sense."

He tried other pomegranates on different trees with no luck whatsoever.

Will's nerves tingled. He thought about what Nico had said—how the fruit wasn't as dangerous for creatures from the Underworld.

"Have you ever actually picked one of these before?" he asked.

Nico scowled. "Well . . . no. I was just given some seeds."

Will looked at the red fruit hanging above him. Maybe they were meant to be picked only by potential victims from the world of sunlight. He gulped and stretched out his hand.

His fingers grazed the smooth, cool rind. The fruit was so large it barely fit in Will's hand.

He pulled.

The pomegranate came off the branch with a gentle snap. Will was filled with the urge to dig into its flesh, to seek out all the juicy seeds and devour them. . . .

"Will." Nico's voice shattered the spell. The son of Hades looked as if he was *immediately* going to leave mortality behind. "How did you *do* that?"

Will shrugged. "I just . . . picked it?"

"Well, *don't* eat it. Pick a few more, and let's get out of here!"

Will grabbed another pomegranate, tucked it under his arm, then plucked a third and turned to hand it to Nico.

Nico shook his head. "If I can't pick them, I suspect I can't hold them, either." He opened one of the pockets of his leather bomber. "Can you do the honors?"

Will stuffed one pomegranate into Nico's jacket pocket, then slipped the other two into pockets on his own shorts.

"Oh my gods," said Nico. "I can't believe your cargo shorts are coming in handy."

Will beamed. "Told you so."

Nico didn't waste any more time. He grabbed Will's right hand and pulled him along, retracing their route. Every time they came to an intersection on the path, Nico froze, carefully inspecting their way forward.

Will's heart was pounding. He was both afraid and a little exhilarated. He felt like a little kid again, running through the aisles of the New York Public Library on Forty-Second Street and Fifth Avenue while his mom tried to catch up.

If only she could see him now, dashing through Persephone's garden.

Near the gate, Nico let go of Will's hand. "I'll make sure the coast is clear," he whispered. Then he slipped past the bottlebrush plants and out the gateway.

Will waited, anxiety coursing through his veins. He heard something rustle in foliage up ahead and thought, *Please let that be Nico.*

The figure stepped out from behind a thick bush of pink oleanders.

It wasn't Nico.

It was *her.*

CHAPTER 24

Will didn't move. He *couldn't* have moved even if he wanted to. He was transfixed by Persephone's beauty.

She raised a finger to her lips. Her eyes were the rich brown of freshly tilled soil, ready to burst into a million colors. Will couldn't turn away. He was mesmerized. He was also afraid.

His heart pounding fiercely, he glanced over at Nico, hoping he'd tell him what to do.

But Nico was *frozen*, crouched in a sneaking position, still as stone.

"Look at me, son of Apollo."

Her voice . . . Oh, gods, it was sweeter than the scent of the pomegranates. Will gulped and faced Persephone.

She brushed a strand of her dark brown hair out of her face. As she drifted forward, Will's mind and heart clashed. He felt he should run away as fast as he could, but he was also drawn to her. She was vibrant. Shining. *Alive.*

She was so unlike everything else here.

"How are you doing this?" Will said, his voice full of awe.

"I can do many things." Persephone was now just a few feet from him. "Especially here, in my garden."

She stepped closer until her nose nearly touched his. "In which you're currently trespassing."

Will sucked in his breath. "I can explain. It's— It's important, what we're doing."

"And what is that, exactly?"

Will found it terribly hard to pull his gaze from hers. Should he tell her the truth? Lying to gods was usually a futile exercise, and in this case? Well, he and Nico had been caught red-handed in Persephone's garden.

"I can see the gears turning in your demigod mind, Will Solace." Persephone pointed to the bulging pocket on his cargo shorts. "I obviously know you're stealing from my garden. The question is *why*."

"It's a quest," he said. "We need fruit from your garden to progress to the next part."

Persephone frowned. "And I assume my husband has not assigned said quest."

"Uhhh, no?" Will gestured at his companion. "Nico could probably explain it better if you'd just free him."

"But I'm talking to *you*, son of Apollo," she said, annoyance crossing her face. "Besides, *you* are dating my stepson. Am I not allowed to speak with you?"

Will gulped. "No! I mean yes. Of course you're allowed to!"

"So now Will Solace is telling me what I'm allowed to do in my own garden."

Will thought he was going to pass out. "I'm— I'm not—"

"Relax, demigod." Persephone smiled, and suddenly the whole garden seemed warmer. "Some of us still have a sense of humor, and I like to use mine from time to time."

Will couldn't relax, though. Persephone began to pace around him, and if he wasn't currently in the Underworld, he would have wondered when the bright overhead lights were going to flick on. This felt like an interrogation!

"You know," she continued, "I haven't always treated Nico as he deserves to be treated. It was hard for me to look upon him. His very face reminded me that Hades had betrayed me and had a child with someone else." Persephone maintained her smile, but it did not reach her eyes. "We gods can be very jealous, you know."

Will nodded, afraid to speak.

"But over the years—and especially recently—I have had to reexamine my perception of Nico. He is . . . well, he is not always what he seems. There is more to that boy than what I saw on the surface."

Despite his galloping nerves, Will found his voice. "I know that," he said. "It's been the best part of knowing him—how often he surprises you."

"But do you see the depths within him?" She gazed intently into Will's eyes. "Do you realize who he really is?"

"Yes?" he said, though he hadn't intended for it to sound like a question. "I mean . . . He's a very complicated person."

Persephone raised an eyebrow. Even that small gesture sent a jolt of terror through Will.

"But . . . ?" she said. "I sense you want to say more."

How did she know that? Did she know he was thinking about how being with Nico wasn't always easy?

The words tumbled from his mouth.

"How do you do it, Persephone?"

"Do what?"

"Love someone from the Underworld."

This time, she actually looked surprised. "That is quite the question, son of Apollo."

"I'm sorry," he said, raising his hands. "If you'll just let Nico go, we'll return the fruit and leave and—"

"You know love is a difficult choice, right?"

His hands fell. "What?"

"Oh, certainly, there are people in this world for whom love comes easily or abundantly. It is instantaneous, like it was for Narcissus."

"Sure," said Will. "But I—"

"And there are, of course, those who experience no romantic feelings whatsoever."

"Right, but—"

"But no matter what form love takes, no matter how much or how little you have, you must still *choose* to cultivate it. In friendships, in romantic relationships, in *life*."

He frowned. "But that doesn't really answer my question. Plus . . . Didn't Hades kidnap you?"

"Comparing your situation with mine will not be very helpful," she said. "You are right. I was brought here against my wishes. I only came to love this place—and Hades, too—after I began to appreciate the time away from my mother."

"Demeter," said Will.

"If someone ever tries to force you into a relationship, I highly recommend running far, far away. That is not love, Will. My circumstances were unique, and in that uniqueness, I found something I did not expect. But there are aspects you may relate to."

Persephone sat down on a carved jade bench next to the oleander bush. She patted the space next to her. Will glanced at Nico, still frozen in the gateway. He imagined his boyfriend thinking, *Oh, sure. Take your time. Have a nice chat with my stepmom. I'll just stand here.*

Then, not having much of a choice, Will joined the goddess.

"It was an adjustment," Persephone said, staring out at her

garden. "When I came to this place, I missed the sun, as I'm sure you do, too."

"So much," he said. "I don't think I've ever been this long without it."

"Beyond that, though, I had to reconsider everything I believed," she went on. "About light and dark. About life and death." At this, she gestured to Nico. "He has all those things within him, just like his father. It took me too long to see it because I was blinded by jealousy."

"But I already know all that," said Will. "I don't think Nico is just *one* thing."

Persephone seemed to ignore him at first. "A god or demigod so surrounded by death . . . they seem to appreciate life more than anyone else. They *understand* it, even if they don't always drift *toward* it."

Her words hit him like the Gray Sisters' taxi. "You think so?" he said. "Because . . . sometimes Nico doesn't seem like that at all."

"That is because you and I are creatures of the daytime. Creatures of the light. It is sometimes very hard for us to see and appreciate the darkness."

"Appreciate the darkness?"

Persephone rose and crossed to a large flowering tree. She plucked an illuminated pink flower with long, elliptical petals. "It's beautiful, is it not?"

Will held out his hand, and she passed it to him. Once it touched his palm, the petals slowly opened, and he gasped. In the center of the flower, there was a stone—pitch-black, so dark that it seemed like a shard of absolute nothingness.

"These are a special breed of night-blooming cereus, Will," explained Persephone. "I grow them because they only open in the presence of darkness."

"Darkness?" His eyes widened suddenly. "In *me*?"

"Yes, absolutely. Do you think that because you are a child of Apollo, there is no darkness within you?"

"I guess not," he said, examining the stone in his hand.

"There cannot be light without darkness, nor darkness without light. You must have the contrast for both to exist."

She helped Will stand, and he passed the stone back to her. "But with Nico . . . It's hard, Persephone. I want the best for him, and he seems to disappear into his darkness, like he's hiding in a place where he doesn't *want* my light."

"Then why not offer him your darkness?"

It was a simple question, but once again, Will felt like he'd been knocked flat. He stood there, slightly ashamed that he had not considered meeting Nico on his own level before, and also frightened about what it might mean to do so.

"I cannot tell you how to love someone, Will." For the first time, Persephone sounded sympathetic. "But as I said before: it is a difficult choice. You have to *choose* to continue loving someone. Feelings aren't enough."

"That's a lot to think about," he said sheepishly. "What if I'm not ready?"

"I can answer that with a question: Do you *understand* Nico?"

He gazed into Persephone's eyes, then looked back to Nico, who was still frozen.

"Not completely," said Will, turning back to Persephone. "I've never met anyone like him. But . . . I *want* to understand him."

The goddess of springtime smiled, and Will felt like the sun was beaming down on him.

"You and Nico will make a fine couple," she said. "As long as you keep trying to understand."

Will dug his hand into his cargo shorts pocket and presented one of the pomegranates. "Here," he said. "I'm sorry we took this."

"Keep them. A gift from me for the two of you." She winked. "But don't tell Nico I said that. Let's just keep this little interaction between us."

Persephone stepped behind the oleander and was gone in an instant. Will heard a rustling to his left, turned, and saw Nico waving at him.

"Psst!" Nico hissed. "What is it? What are you looking at?"

He shook his head. "Nothing. Thought I saw something."

"Then come on!"

Will hurried to Nico, his mind still reeling from what he'd experienced.

Offer him your darkness. The words unfolded inside him like cereus petals.

"You sure you're okay?" Nico asked. "You look like you just saw a *daimon.*"

"I'm fine," Will said, and he was surprised to find that he meant it. He kissed his boyfriend on the cheek. "Let's get back to Menoetes before someone catches us."

They climbed on their donkeys and burst into a gallop, leaving Persephone's garden and Hades's palace behind.

CHAPTER 25

Nico was staring at a very odd scene.

Menoetes leaned against one of his nectar trees, laughing so hard tears streamed down his face. Screech-Bling stood next to him, staring into the distance like a nervous mom waiting for the school bus. Down in the pastures, a herd of black cattle seemed to be doing marching-band maneuvers—pinwheeling, prance-stepping, and re-forming columns in perfect synchronization. In front of the bovine troops stood a tiny figure in a foam cheese-wedge hat—Hiss-Majesty, waving a tree branch like a baton.

When Nico's and Will's donkeys came to a stop, Menoetes didn't even acknowledge them. Instead, he cupped his hands around his mouth and yelled to Hiss-Majesty, "Amazing! Now bring them back!"

Hiss-Majesty clicked a series of commands in Troglodytish, and the entire herd marched double-time toward the orchard.

Nico hopped off his donkey. "Um . . . what's going on?"

Menoetes wiped the tears from his eyes. "Turns out that little troglodyte has a knack for herding cattle!"

"They have many talents," Screech-Bling agreed, his face alight with joy. "And the cattle churn up many tasty grubs and worms from the soil as they march. It is a win-win!"

Menoetes and the trog CEO gave each other a complicated fist-bump/secret handshake like they'd been friends for years.

"*We* were productive while you were gone," Menoetes told Nico. "Did you get what I asked for?"

Nico slowly reached into his pocket. He worried his hand would drift right through the pomegranate, as it had in his stepmother's garden, but his fingers touched a very solid fruit.

What was that about? he wondered. Why couldn't he touch the fruit in the garden but Will could?

When Nico brought out the pomegranate, Menoetes's eyes gleamed with hunger. His jet-black tongue flicked across his lips.

"Just one?" he asked wistfully.

Will produced the other two.

"*Three?!*" Menoetes sounded like he was about to burst into tears. "That is more than I expected!"

And then he opened his mouth and threw in the first pomegranate.

"Wow," Nico said. "So . . . you're not worried about being stuck here forever?"

"Why would I be?" Menoetes let out a loud burp. "I love it here. I don't ever want to leave, and I'm sure Geryon will feel the same. We would never be accepted aboveground. Where would people like us fit in? I have a job here that I like a lot. I'm in love. Why would I ever want to throw that away?"

Will stared wistfully into the distance. "But you're not worried about what you might miss out on in the mortal world?"

Menoetes grunted. "Every so often, sure. But I've been working for Nico's father now for a long, long time. This is what I'm accustomed to. It's where I feel at home. And it's where Geryon is."

Nico felt a chasm opening in his heart. He loved what Menoetes had just said. But . . . what was this aching sensation? Was Nico *envious* of the bull-man?

Nico knew that for practical reasons Will would never offer to stay here for him. That was fair. The Underworld had been negatively affecting Will since they'd arrived. But there was something about Menoetes's confidence in Geryon that felt distant to Nico . . . out of reach.

Nico's fingers found their way into the pocket of his jeans, where they traced the image embossed on the coin.

Maybe he was overthinking this. Maybe the Underworld was starting to wear on *him*, too.

Meanwhile, Will was telling Hiss-Majesty and Screech-Bling how he and Nico had managed to sneak into Persephone's garden. Will did a great job making it sound much more suspenseful than it was, dialing up the tension as though they'd come much closer to getting caught by the goddess. He looked genuinely nervous.

"I am impressed." Menoetes turned to Nico. "I know you have complicated feelings about Geryon, and I must admit I do not blame you, but still, you got this fruit, at great danger to yourselves."

"We kind of *had* to," said Nico. "You know, the whole quest thing?"

Menoetes shook his head. "You could have retrieved just one pomegranate. Or you could have unearthed an entire skeleton army and forced me to let you pass!"

Nico rolled his eyes. "Now you're just being dramatic. I could still summon some skeletons if you like, though."

Menoetes gave a hearty laugh. "You are a funny one, Nico. Maybe the funniest of Hades's children."

"Hazel's pretty funny," Will offered.

Nico elbowed him in the ribs.

"Regardless," Menoetes continued, "I would like to offer you something besides just safe passage through my land. I can provide you with information."

Nico's pulse jumped. "What information?"

"About your quest, of course," said the bull-man. "I know what you're up to. You're not the only one hearing his voice calling from Tartarus."

Nico was pretty sure what was left of his soul had evaporated out of his body. "I'm sorry, *what?*"

"Many of us down here can hear him from time to time," said Menoetes. "He is . . . loud. Sorrowful. We learn to tune out those who are suffering because we *have* to. I mean, the Fields of Asphodel and Punishment are basically white noise to me at this point." He sighed. "But *he* is different. Because . . . well, he's not *dead.* He's a living being in terrible pain, calling out, aching to be listened to."

Rage swept through Nico, so encompassing and intense that it wasn't until Will cleared his throat that Nico realized he was summoning multiple skeletons from the ground. He let out a deep breath, and they collapsed into heaps of bones.

"Sorry," he said. "I just hate knowing Bob is in pain."

"I do, too," said Menoetes. "Bob is pretty legendary around these parts. What he did for Percy and Annabeth . . . Those of us who care about the Underworld *and* what happens in the mortal world won't forget that. But after that incident with the Doors of Death, we're all prohibited from entering Tartarus. So none of us can go confront her."

"Her?" said Will. "You mean—"

"Nyx." Menoetes spat on the ground. "She's obsessed with Bob. He represents *everything* she hates."

"That's what we figured," said Nico. "I met her once, a while ago."

"I hope I never meet her," said Hiss-Majesty, shaking their head. "She sounds terrible."

Menoetes's head drooped. "Nyx believes that what is born in darkness must remain in darkness. The problem is . . . Bob willingly chose to remain Bob rather than return to being Iapetus. That is why she has detained him."

"Detained him . . . how?" asked Will.

Menoetes stared into Nico's eyes. "Do you remember your time in Tartarus?"

Nico winced. "Unfortunately."

"Do you remember the regeneration blisters?"

"I always thought of them as zits."

Menoetes snorted. "That is appropriate. Being inside one is rather like drowning in a boiling whitehead."

Will clutched his stomach. "Thanks for that."

"It is an experience most monsters and demons have had," the bull-man continued grimly. "At any rate, a few weeks ago, a demon who works with me got trampled to death by the cattle. This in itself was not a big deal. He just regenerated in Tartarus and clawed his way back here. But while he was down there . . . he saw Nyx standing over a very large regeneration blister, berating the entity inside who was trying to be reborn, telling him he would never break free until he relented. It was Bob."

The two trogs yelped in horror and hugged each other.

Nico had to clutch Will's shoulder to keep himself steady. "No. That's too cruel, even for Nyx."

"I'm afraid it is true," said Menoetes. "Nyx is holding Bob in a *permanent* regeneration cycle until he chooses to become Iapetus again."

Nico's fury rose again, but Will—blessed, illuminating Will—squeezed his hand. A radiant calmness passed up Nico's arm and spread into his chest.

The kind act warmed Nico, both in the literal and the figurative sense, but then he began to worry. "Will, you need to conserve your energy."

"I just thought you might need the reminder."

"Of what?"

"That I'm here. That I know you're upset."

Nico pulled Will close, still vibrating with residual anger. "I didn't mean to raise the dead. I'm just . . . so, so mad."

"You should feel what you need to feel," said Will. "I don't want to diminish that. I don't even know Bob, and *I'm* furious, too."

Nico stared at Will. Wow, where had *that* come from?

Screech-Bling clicked and hissed in outrage. "What is happening to Bob is wrong. No one should be treated like that. And for—SCREEK—what? Having the courage to change?"

Hiss-Majesty nodded. "We troglodytes love to adapt. We are always changing! For example, who knew that I would love herding cows?" They glanced at Will, clearly hoping for approval, and were rewarded with a beaming smile.

"I doubt there's ever been a finer cowherd with a finer cheese hat," Will said. Then he turned to Menoetes, and his expression hardened again. "So where do we find Bob?"

"Yes, that is the information I wanted to give you," said the bull-man. "Deep in Tartarus, there is a hut that belonged to a reformed giant."

Will frowned. "You mean . . . like Geryon?"

Menoetes seemed to consider that. "Yes, I suppose so. This giant is well respected here in the Underworld, for he opposed the Maeonian drakon and helped the demigods close the Doors of Death."

"Percy mentioned him," said Nico. "Damasen?"

"Yes! That is the giant. When you emerge in Tartarus from the troglodytes' shortcut, follow the trail to the left until you reach the swamp. There you will find Damasen's hut. And once you do, Bob should not be far away." Menoetes gave Nico a somber look. "I hope Damasen has regenerated. He was killed fighting the drakon, but if he has been reborn, I am sure he would love to help you."

"We'll do our best to find him," said Will.

Screech-Bling adjusted his powdered wig. "We should leave soon, demigods. The shortcut is not far."

"Make sure to refill your nectar before you go," added Menoetes. "You will find no more of it where you're going."

"Thank you," said Nico. "For helping us. You didn't have to."

Menoetes shook his head. "I did. And not just because you brought me tasty pomegranates. We can't let Nyx get away with torturing Bob. What if this is just the start of her tyranny?"

His words dug under Nico's skin. He hadn't even considered that Nyx might be torturing others down in Tartarus. Nico knew she was setting a trap to kidnap and torment *him*—and possibly Will, too. That was one thing. At least they were choosing to face that danger. But other entities who were just trying to be reborn, maybe to *change* into something better . . . Nyx had no right to make them suffer.

For the first time, Nico wished the prophecy had been *longer*. All it warned was that someone would have to leave something of equal value behind. That wasn't enough! It could mean so many things! Nico had to stop the goddess of night, but he needed more clues about how to do it.

He remained frustrated and nervous as the troglodytes guided them out of the farm. His last glimpse of Menoetes was the bull-man's red-tinged silhouette, waving at them from the top of the hill, his cattle still standing at parade rest behind him.

Soon the farm was lost in the gloom as the troglodytes led them into the stretch of dark hills—part of the Underworld Nico had never visited. He had no idea what awaited them at the shortcut, nor what Tartarus would be like on his second visit.

However, as Will walked alongside him, Nico worried most about what the abyss would do to his boyfriend. Had this whole trip been a mistake? Should they have brought a third demigod like questers were supposed to?

Nico walked on, full of questions with no answers.

"The first time we kissed?" Will's eyes looked hazy and unfocused. "I . . . Yes, I remember. Why do you ask?"

Nico forced down his growing sense of panic. Will's condition kept swinging from *almost fine* to *ready to keel over*, but the trend was definitely downward. If this kept up, they would never make it down the river, much less to Tartarus.

Meanwhile, Gorgyra loomed over them on the dock. Nico tried to ignore the fluttering of the nymph's gown in the chilly breeze, the whispers swirling around him, yearning for more secrets.

"Because the stories help." Nico tried to sound confident. "It won't take long. Then we'll get in the boat and go."

Will nodded. "Okay . . . Well, if I remember correctly, it wasn't that long ago."

"No, it wasn't," Nico agreed.

Will watched Gorgyra drifting around them, like a teacher monitoring a test. He put a hand on Nico's leg. "We don't have to talk about this now, Nico."

"Yes," said Nico. "We do."

The whispers from Gorgyra's gown reached out again:

You were so alone then.

Will you be alone again?

Nico pushed them away. "It was after Jason died." He willed his voice to stay even, not to give in to the rising sadness in his chest.

"Yes," said Will. "Just like with Leo, you were distraught. But not angry. Not that time. You were more . . ." He sighed. "I'm not sure what to call it. I didn't know what to do."

The dock boards creaked under Gorgyra's feet. "Do about what?"

"About me shutting down," said Nico. "Like, completely. I wasn't even crying over Jason's death. It didn't seem real to me. How could he just be *gone?*"

"And Jason meant a great deal to you, yes?" said Gorgyra. "He was the first to truly accept you."

"Exactly. And I wasn't there to help at the end. I couldn't save him!"

Hot tears poured down Nico's face. He turned away from Will and Gorgyra, suddenly ashamed by his display of grief. But the whispers followed him, threads of loneliness and desperation wrapping around his heart, pulling him back.

You wish for him to return, they said.

You resent that he left you.

You are worried that this one will leave you, too.

That last whisper was a punch to the gut. Nico sobbed, because that *was* his biggest fear, wasn't it? That's what he worried awaited them at the bottom of the plunge: Will would die. Will would sacrifice himself.

Will would be left behind.

"I've got you," Will said in his ear. Then his boyfriend's arms wrapped around him, holding him tight. Nico turned until they were face-to-face, staring into each other's eyes. Nico was supposed to be nurturing Will, not the other way around, but Will always seemed to know when Nico was most vulnerable. There wasn't pity in Will's face, just concern. Just care.

Nico leaned forward and kissed him.

It wasn't a long or particularly romantic kiss. Their lips met. Will reached up and held the back of Nico's head. It was brief, it was sweet, and it was what Nico needed.

It was also exactly what Will had done for Nico that day outside the Hades cabin, shortly after they'd learned of Jason's death. Will had kissed Nico for the first time in a moment of impulsiveness, something Nico didn't know Will had in him. The kiss had been just like this one, short and sweet. Then Will had pulled away, worry on his face, an apology tumbling from his lips.

Nico had stopped him. Then kissed him *back*.

In a moment so full of grief and rage and sadness, Will had given him . . .

Light.

Now Will pulled away. "I'm right here," he promised. "For whatever you need. We have each other."

Nico didn't mean to laugh. It came out as a frail, brittle sound. Only a few days ago, he'd joked to Annabeth that her advice sounded like a Hallmark card. Now he felt like he was living in one.

He was worried Will might take offense. Instead, his boyfriend only looked concerned.

"What is it?" Will asked, wiping away Nico's tears.

"Nothing," he said. "I just . . ."

He glanced over Will's shoulder and his voice died. Gorgyra now stood at the end of the dock, moving her hands as if working a loom. Below her, the River Acheron churned, threads of dark water weaving themselves together into a thick band, which Gorgyra pulled toward her.

Will turned to watch. He and Nico sat there—Nico's arm around Will's waist—as Gorgyra gathered cords of woven water, stitching them into her dress. Only when the last thread disappeared into her gown did Nico realize what she was doing: rescuing lonely souls trapped in the River of Pain, adding them to her collection. When she was done, her chest heaved with exertion. Her gown's fabric had turned cloudy, whispers filling the air as the older souls greeted the newcomers.

Gorgyra staggered under their weight. Instantly Will and Nico rose to help her, their own problems forgotten.

"I'm fine," she promised, though her face was drained of color. "The souls called to me, and I had to help them. It seems your tender moment drew them here."

"I'm sorry," said Nico.

"No, it is a *good* thing," Gorgyra said. "Lonely souls finding one another is *always* a good thing."

She gestured to the boat. "She is yours. You have more than earned her. Take care of her, and she will guide you straight into Tartarus."

Nico's heart leaped—not because he was anxious to get to Tartarus, but because they might finally be making some progress.

Will shifted next to him. "But . . . I didn't finish the story."

Gorgyra's smile was weak but still warm. "I believe you just showed me."

The boat bobbed precariously as Nico climbed in. He hoped Will had good sea legs. The only ship Nico remembered spending a significant amount of time on was the *Argo II*, and that had flown more than it had sailed.

This trip was with Will, though. That changed everything, even if their destination was the basement of the universe.

Gorgyra watched them pensively as their boat drifted away from the dock. What was she thinking? Did she believe that they'd make it?

Nico reached in the pocket of his jeans. He took out the coin, running his fingers over the embossing until he'd traced every bit of it.

"You brought my gift," said Will, smile lines crinkling around his eyes. "Great minds think alike."

He reached inside the collar of his shirt and pulled out his gold chain.

On it glinted Nico's ring.

CHAPTER 26

The trogs led them farther into darkness.

There'd always been a comforting glow to the land of the dead. Well, comforting to Nico, at least. But here, far beyond where he'd accidentally been sucked into Tartarus a couple of years ago, that glow was fading.

Perhaps he should have asked Hades about the boundaries of the Underworld. How far did it stretch? Were there other subterranean lands beyond the black walls of Erebos? Other ways into Tartarus that Hades had never talked about? But of course, Nico couldn't have risked posing such questions. He had to accomplish this mission without his father's knowledge.

If he survived, though, he would ask his father about Tartarus . . . and so much more.

The mini adventure to Persephone's garden had mysteriously invigorated Will, but now his newfound energy seemed to be fading. He struggled to keep up. Whenever he fell behind, Hiss-Majesty would zip to his side, offering words of encouragement and nourishing lizard jerky. Nico was glad that at least Hiss-Majesty didn't try to herd them like the cattle. He didn't relish the idea of double-time high-stepping all the way to Tartarus.

As they traveled, the shadows became longer. Skeletal cacti stretched their brittle arms toward the acidic clouds overhead. Packs of rogue spirits drifted over the parched land. Where were the spirits headed? What were they doing out here, so far from the fields? At one point, Nico and company had to wait on a low ridge while a pair of drakons moved along a ravine, spitting fire at one another. Nico wondered if somehow he and his companions had already crossed into Tartarus, because it was beginning to feel like it. . . .

"How much farther?" asked Will, panting. "I thought you said it was close."

"Just over the next ridge," said Screech-Bling. "You'll be able to hear it soon."

"Hear what?" Nico pulled his bomber jacket tighter. All he heard were the whispers of the dead being carried on the cold wind—voices that caressed Nico's ear, begging for an audience.

"Not much farther," said Hiss-Majesty, their voice low. "From here, the path is steep. Watch your step."

Which was precisely when Will fell.

He pitched forward, his left shoulder smacking hard against the dirt, then began rolling downhill like a floppy log.

"Will!" Nico cried, which was not his smartest move.

Down in the ravine, the drakons turned their long necks in his direction.

"Get Will!" cried Hiss-Majesty. "We shall buy you time!"

Both the troglodytes leaped into to action, sprinting straight toward the drakons.

"Look at me!" shouted Screech-Bling, waving his arms at the monsters. "I am your worst enemy!"

"I can herd cows!" yelled Hiss-Majesty.

By the time Nico caught up to Will, the son of Apollo had rolled to a stop on a small plateau about halfway down the hill. Nico knelt next to him, checking him for injuries. Will's eyes lolled back in his head. His arms were covered in cuts and scrapes.

"Will!" Nico resisted the urge to shake him. "Will, can you hear me?"

His boyfriend muttered something unintelligible.

Healing wasn't Nico's specialty—that was Will's thing. Nico had a few vials of nectar and squares of ambrosia on him, but he wasn't sure those would even help. He was about to rummage through Will's pack for the battery-operated sunlamp when an ear-splitting roar rang out. Nico looked up to see both drakons blast Screech-Bling with white-hot fire.

Nico screamed. He rose, drawing his sword, but then glanced down at the motionless Will. Nico couldn't leave him here undefended.

"Go!" said a familiar voice.

Nico turned. With a rush of relief, he found Screech-Bling standing next to him, wreathed in steam, his tricorn hat singed. Otherwise, he looked fine.

"H-how?" Nico stammered. "You trogs must be indestructible!"

Down in the ravine, Hiss-Majesty had taken the CEO's place as chief drakon-wrangler, zipping between the monsters, yelling out herding commands like "Attention! Forward march! Left face! Your other left!" The drakons ignored these instructions, stomping and blowing fire in annoyance.

"Tough, but not indestructible," Screech-Bling said, a puff of smoke escaping his right ear. "Go help *Hiss*-Majesty! I will watch over the son of Apollo."

Nico sprinted downhill toward the drakons.

He dove and rolled to avoid a splash of fire, then slammed his sword into the foot of the nearest drakon. As Nico feared, his blade didn't do anything other than notify the creature of his presence. Drakon scales were notoriously hard to penetrate. Nico's earlier determination to protect Will now gave way to a terror-filled desperation. There were two impervious drakons versus one very pervious Nico. He didn't like those odds.

He wove his way between the legs of the first creature, hoping to confuse it, but then his own legs were swept out from under him by the tail of the second.

Hiss-Majesty was instantly at his side. "Up, son of Hades!" Their small, strong hands pulled him to his feet. "We must defeat them!"

Nico swung his sword above Hiss-Majesty's head as the first drakon charged them—but something felt wrong. His sword was utterly weightless in his hand. The blade passed through the drakon's shoulder joint as if it were empty air.

For a moment, Nico wondered if he was back in one of Epiales's nightmares, battling a hallucination.

Then the drakon collapsed like a broken card table. The monster stared at its severed leg with a look of absolute shock, which Nico found completely understandable. *How did that sword slice through drakon scales?*

The creature howled as its body disintegrated, wafting away in a cloud of dust. Nico turned to face the other drakon but found, to his great surprise, that it was retreating into the gloom.

Hiss-Majesty doubled over, panting heavily. Their green skin was covered in a sheen of moisture.

"That was very tiring," they said. "I was not sure I could do it."

Nico stared at his blade, still smoking with drakon blood. "What did you do?"

"I am very fast. I guided your sword."

Nico's eyes widened. "You—you *what?*"

"Sometimes speed can do what pure strength cannot." Hiss-Majesty removed their cheese hat and used it to sponge the sweat from their face. "I must rest a moment."

Nico started laughing. Drakons were nearly impossible to defeat, yet Hiss-Majesty had found a way to do it in *seconds.*

"You were amazing!" said Nico. "You just . . . and then you . . . I've never . . . !"

Hiss-Majesty looked uncomfortable with this praise. "Let us go check on our friends. Unless there are more drakons to fight?"

Nico clapped them on the shoulder. "I don't think any drakon is going to come within five miles of you now."

When they reached the trail, Nico was happy to see Will sitting upright, munching on an ambrosia square. Screech-Bling sat nearby, applying some sort of grease to his blistered skin. Apparently, the fire had hurt him worse than he'd let on.

"Hey," Will said sleepily. "What happened?"

Nico planted a kiss on Will's forehead. "Well, you passed out, *Screech*-Bling got torched, and *Hiss*-Majesty defeated a drakon."

"I— Wait, what?" Will glanced over at Screech-Bling. "Are you okay?"

"I will be fine." The CEO scooped a handful of goop. "Our salve is very good for burns. Top-rated SPF—skink protective fat. You have none in your medical kit?"

"I think I need to correct that oversight," Will admitted. Then he turned to Hiss-Majesty. "And did Nico just say you defeated a *drakon?*"

"I only assisted." Hiss-Majesty kicked at the dirt. "It is not as big a deal as the son of Hades is making it out to be."

"You defeated a *drakon!*" Will said. "That is *absolutely* a big deal!"

Hiss-Majesty blushed a deep shade of emerald.

"How are *you* feeling?" Nico asked, inspecting Will's cuts and bruises. "You took a nasty tumble."

"I'm fine," said Will. "Nothing that can't be fixed with some nectar or ambrosia."

Nico frowned at the bleeding spot on Will's knee. "Seriously, did you *have* to wear shorts?"

"They're comfortable!"

"Not when they don't protect you in a fall!"

Will pulled a small red plastic case from his knapsack. He popped it open and rummaged through the medical supplies: disinfectant pads, gauze, bandages.

"Let me do that." Nico took the kit from Will.

While the troglodytes kept watch, Nico disinfected his hands, then cleaned out each of Will's cuts and scrapes, the way Will had taught him to do after the war with Gaea. He found a small gash on the back of his boyfriend's right leg, then some swelling on his left elbow. Will winced and jerked away when Nico touched the area.

Nico applied some antibacterial salve on the deeper cuts and wrapped them with gauze. He made a sling to hold Will's elbow stationary for the time being. When he was finished, Will looked like he had gotten in a fistfight with a hurricane.

"You did really good," said Will, inspecting the bandages. "Thanks."

"I had a good teacher." Nico sat back. "But you don't seem to be as healing as fast as usual. Should I be worried?"

Will shook his head. "I sort of expected that my healing abilities would be diminished down here. These are just scrapes and cuts. I'll be fine."

But would he? They *still* weren't in Tartarus yet, and quite literally everything down there would be worse than up here in the

Underworld. Nico felt trapped between his concern for his boyfriend and the urgency of their quest. Maybe this was yet another reason why going on a quest without three demigods was a bad, bad idea. Had they been doomed from the start?

Nico helped Will up as Screech-Bling—now completely recovered—packed up his SPF supplies and Hiss-Majesty jumped around them excitedly. "We are very close!" they said. "I cannot wait for you to see the shortcut!"

Nico wanted to grumble about how very *long* this journey to the shortcut had been, but he kept his thoughts to himself. Will started off limping, but within a few minutes, he was more limber. He looped his free arm around Nico's shoulders, hobbling slower than Nico wanted to be moving, but Nico also appreciated the closeness.

We're going to get through this, he told himself. He had to believe it.

The climb up the next ridge was tougher. All Nico's adrenaline from the drakon fight was gone. A dull soreness seeped into his muscles. Halfway up, Will was huffing and puffing so badly they decided to rest while Nico pulled out the sun-therapy globe. Naturally, the batteries were starting to die, and judging from the waxy sheen of sweat on Will's face, his internal batteries were dying, too. While still standing, Will put his hands on the back of his head so he could breathe more deeply.

Nico struggled to put new batteries in the globe. He dropped one, which rolled merrily down the hill.

"Oh, come *on*," he muttered.

"Just grab another," said Will. "Don't worry about it."

Nico wasn't sure they would find any extra triple-A batteries for sale in Tartarus, but he fished another from Will's pack. Once the globe was glowing at full strength, he handed it to Will.

"Thanks, Nico." He sounded . . . defeated.

At the crest of the hill, Will sat to rest, and Nico noticed a dark red stain spreading across his boyfriend's midsection.

"Will . . ." Nico tried to keep the fear out of his voice. "What happened there?"

Will looked down at his gut and frowned. "I . . . I don't know. That can't be right."

Unfortunately, the wound was very real. When Will lifted his shirt, the long red curve across his abdomen looked like someone had tried to draw a frowny face there with a razor. Nico cleaned and dressed the wound, but his fingers wouldn't stop trembling. Maybe the cut had happened when Will fell down the hill, or before that, in Persephone's garden, or as they passed through the orchard of Menoetes. But Nico couldn't shake the feeling that the wound had simply *opened*, as if Will's body was unraveling from the inside under the stress of being in the Underworld.

As Nico wrapped Will's abdomen in gauze, he noticed that Will's other wounds were all bleeding through their bandages. Children of Apollo were usually even quicker to recuperate than most other demigods. Something was *deeply* wrong if Will's wounds weren't closing.

"Hey." Will's hand touched his face. "You're worried. Upset. I get it. But I'll be fine."

Nico frowned. "You're *not* fine. Your cuts . . . This shouldn't be happening."

Will sighed. "We knew it was a risk for me to come here."

"But we haven't even—"

"Gotten to Tartarus yet," Will finished. "I know. But I'm tougher than you think."

He leaned against Nico's shoulder. "I'll just keep up a steady regimen of nectar and ambrosia. You'll keep the wounds clean. Maybe I can rest here a second before we continue."

"Demigods!" Screech-Bling shouted from the other side of the summit. "You can see it from here—the next step in your journey!"

Nico kissed the top of Will's head. "Be right back."

He joined the troglodytes, who wore matching solemn expressions as they gazed down at the flat expanse beyond the hill.

Far below, a massive river roared and churned as it rushed over jagged rocks. The water looked like . . . well, water. It didn't have a strange-colored hue, at least. It wasn't made of fire. But the sight of it unsettled Nico nonetheless. Those vicious rapids cut across the dark plains and then . . .

The river dropped into nothingness.

Nico shivered. "There's no way we can cross that."

"No," Screech-Bling agreed.

Nico raised an eyebrow. "So what are we supposed to do?"

Hiss-Majesty pointed to the drop-off, then made a hand gesture like a plane going into a nosedive. "It is the fastest way."

"I really hope you're kidding," Nico said.

"What's going on?" Will shuffled up to them, his limp much more pronounced. The sun globe glowed in the crook of his arm. Given the terrible chill in the air, Nico worried about Will in his cargo shorts. Couldn't that boy have just worn a pair of jeans for once?

But there was no protecting Will from what was in front of them—no hiding the truth or sugarcoating reality.

Will's eyes traced the course of the river. "Is that our shortcut?"

Nico nodded. "Afraid so."

"I don't suppose the entrance to Tartarus is on the other side of the river, and there's a convenient bridge somewhere?"

Nico smiled in spite of himself. "Apparently not."

"It is the Acheron," said Screech-Bling. "The River of Pain."

The name sent a chill down Nico's back. "No."

"Yes," said Screech-Bling.

"I mean *no*, there has to be a better way."

"There is not," said Hiss-Majesty. "And we have looked. This is the best!"

"Excuse me." Will raised his hand. "First-time caller, longtime listener. Remind me why the Acheron is so bad?"

Hiss-Majesty faced him. "Five rivers run through the Underworld, son of Apollo. You have already seen the Styx, which is merely spicy."

"*Acid dissolving your bones* spicy," Will said. "But yeah."

"And you know of the Lethe," said Screech-Bling. "The River of Forgetfulness, where Iapetus became Bob."

"And I told you about the Phlegethon," Nico added, "which I drank from."

"Right," said Will. "The River of Fire."

"The fourth is the Cocytus," said Screech-Bling, "the River of Lamentation, which mostly runs deep in Tartarus."

"With luck, we can avoid that one if we're careful," Nico said. "But the fifth river, the Acheron . . ."

Nico gazed down at the raging torrent. He didn't want to tell Will what those waters could do. Will already looked miserable, though he put on a brave face and didn't complain. But Nico feared that what they were facing now would break his facade.

Will stood straighter, probably sensing Nico's hesitation. "So it's the River of *Pain*. I can deal with pain."

Screech-Bling adjusted his scorched tricorn hat. "If only that's all it was, Son of Apollo." Hiss-Majesty whimpered in agreement. "The Acheron is also the River of *Punishment*."

Will gave Nico a look that clearly meant *Explain*.

"Sometimes . . . Sometimes when souls arrive in the Underworld, they have done such horrible things that they're not even fit for the Fields of Punishment. They have to be cleansed . . . in the Acheron."

Will cupped his sun globe a little tighter. "And I guess this cleansing is . . . painful."

"The pain is not just physical," said Screech-Bling. "It will rip your soul to pieces. It will find every bad thing you have done, every bad thought, and make you feel agony and guilt until you have been purified."

Will gulped. "And then . . . you can get out?"

"Oh, no," Screech-Bling said. "By then you will have dissolved into a fine sediment of eternal misery, still conscious, but probably not sane."

"Even standing on the banks of the Acheron will affect you," Hiss-Majesty warned.

"And you two will not be standing on the banks. You must go in."

Will took a step back. He started shaking his head. "Okay, Nico, I–I can't go in that water. Maybe you're right. There's got to be another way."

"Well," said Screech-Bling, "you won't actually—"

"Hold on." Nico felt an unexpected surge of irritation. "Will, *you're* worried about going in the Acheron? If anyone could come through that river unscathed, it's you. You've never done a single terrible thing in your life! You help people!"

Will took another step back. His eyes looked haunted in a way Nico had never seen. "I'm worried about *both* of us, Nico. And you're just as good a person as I am. I know you've had a tough life, but—"

"A 'tough life'? It's been more than just tough, Will."

"Son of Hades—" Hiss-Majesty tried to interrupt.

"That's not what I meant!" Will continued. "But you haven't done anything you deserve to be *punished* for."

"How do you know?" shouted Nico. "Do you know everything I've been through? What I've had to do just to survive?"

"No! Because *you won't tell me!*"

Silence fell between them. Nico was reminded of the time Will chastised him for not helping in the camp infirmary last year. This wasn't just the weight of the Underworld pressing down on Will, making him say things he didn't mean.

Will's bitterness and frustration were real.

Before Nico could find a response, Hiss-Majesty tugged at the sleeve of his bomber jacket. "Um, Son of Hades, we were not done explaining the shortcut."

"What do you mean?"

Hiss-Majesty pointed upriver. "You will not have to swim. She can help you."

A few hundred yards from the precipice, a small thatched hut squatted near the riverbank. A well-worn path led to a rickety pier, where a white boat like a large canoe was moored. On the ground outside the hut sat a woman with pale blue skin, the muted colors of her gown rippling in the light of a cooking fire. She was too far away for Nico to see her face, but she had clearly noticed them. She raised a hand and waved to her onlookers.

Great, Nico thought. Will and I just had an argument in front of Ms. Shortcut.

"We cannot accompany you any farther, demigods," said Screech-Bling. "This is where we must part."

Hiss-Majesty nodded sadly. "She cannot help *us*."

Nico wasn't quite sure what that meant, but he felt ashamed that his last moments with the troglodytes had been spent arguing with Will. His face burned.

"Thank you both," he told them. "For all you've done for us."

Screech-Bling doffed his tricorn. "You will always be a friend of the troglodytes. When you return, we will welcome you with open arms!"

Then Hiss-Majesty stepped forward, bashfully holding their cheese-wedge hat.

"You have helped me find much more than my proper hat, demi-gods," they said. "I have found my calling. I am not sure when I will see you again, because I have . . . I have decided to stay with Menoetes and herd cattle!"

Nico imagined Menoetes's entire herd in matching uniforms with sequined pants and plumed hats, marching to the barn each evening in perfect lockstep. The thought made him smile.

"You will make an excellent cattle-herder," Will said. Tentatively, he touched the troglodytes' faces, and a warm glow spread from his fingers across their skin. "Thank you both for your kindness, for taking care of me, and for getting us this far."

The trogs stood a little straighter.

"You honor us," said Screech-Bling.

"I will never forget you, Will Solace," Hiss-Majesty said with a sniffle.

Then the trogs exchanged a look, as if silently agreeing that stay-ing a moment longer would lead to ugly sobbing, and vanished in a cloud of dust.

Nico remained silent, stewing in his shame and irritation.

"I'm sorry, Nico." Will broke the tension. "I didn't—"

But Nico waved off his apology. He didn't want to risk talking about it while he was still so upset.

"Let's go meet our shortcut," he said. Then he turned and walked toward the mysterious woman with the boat.

CHAPTER 27

The woman was unlike any nymph Nico had ever seen. Her soft, round face, wispy hair, and coy smile reminded Nico of Juniper, the dryad at Camp Half-Blood. Her gown was made of the same sort of billowing gossamer fabric. But unlike the nature spirits in the world above, this woman's eyes and skin were tinged blue instead of green. Her plump lips were the darkest indigo. Her gray dress seemed to whisper with plaintive voices, similar to the damned souls woven into his father's robes.

As Nico approached, she barely glanced up from her cooking fire.

"You seem intrigued," she said, as if they were resuming an old conversation. "Or confused."

"Both," said Nico.

"You and your friend look exhausted. Please, rest by my fire."

Nico turned to see Will stumbling down the decline. He felt a stab of guilt. He shouldn't have walked away from Will like that, no matter how angry he'd felt.

Nico stretched out his arm as Will got closer. He mouthed an apology.

Will nodded and took his hand. But his eyes said *We'll talk more later.*

As they settled in by the fire, the woman poked the embers with a branch of ebony.

"You two have had a long journey," she said. "I do not get very many visitors out this way."

"Can I ask your name?" Nico said.

"Of course." Her smile was warm, but with an edge of loneliness. "I am Gorgyra."

The name rang no bells for Nico. He glanced at Will, but his boyfriend shook his head.

"I'm sorry," said Nico. "We don't know who you are."

"I did not expect you to." The whispers in her gown grew in intensity until Nico could almost make out what they were saying. "I imagine there are no stories told of me in the upper world, since very few have ever made it here."

"And where is here?" Nico asked.

"At the edge." She cast her gaze downstream, where the River Acheron vanished over the precipice. "Like most things, the Underworld has an end. You have reached it."

Will coughed. "And . . . if we needed to go beyond the edge?"

She jerked her gaze toward him. "Why would you seek that?"

"We're heading to Tartarus," Will said, and Nico couldn't help admiring the determination in his voice. "Our guides said the river . . . They said *you* could provide a shortcut."

She studied him carefully, the whites of her eyes etched with veins of sapphire. "Your guides were correct. You could gain access to Tartarus by following the Acheron over the brink and plunging into the darkness. But why would you ever do that of your own volition?"

Nico looked at Will. Without speaking, they had a whole conversation comprised of raised eyebrows, frowns, and shrugs. Each knew what the other was thinking: *Can we trust this person?*

Nico decided to get more information. "Is the drop survivable? Like . . . in your boat, for instance?"

The corner of Gorgyra's mouth twitched. "Survival is such a relative term here in the Underworld. My husband and I have *survived*. But is that the same as living?"

"Your husband?" Will asked.

"Acheron." Gorgyra gestured toward the rushing water. "Go say hello."

Nico's mouth felt dry. "He *is* the river? Or the god of the river?"

The sadness in Gorgyra's expression was almost unbearable. "I'm not sure there is a difference anymore. Over the centuries, he has lost his physical form and his sense of self. One can only absorb so much pain from others. The souls who are consigned to his waters . . . Their sins and wrongdoings are so overwhelming, they forget all that was ever good in their lives. And so has Acheron."

Nico watched the current flow. He wondered how much pain Will, as a healer, had absorbed from others over the years. How much had Nico himself asked him to carry?

Suddenly, Nico didn't want to bring his boyfriend any closer to that riverbank. He wanted to run back to the sunlight of the upper world.

"We have to try." Will's tone didn't waver. His eyes were locked on the white boat. "Gorgyra, is there any way we can borrow that?"

She made a sound somewhere between a grunt and a laugh. "You are brave to ask . . . or foolhardy. The difference is subtle, as is the difference between life and survival. But you are jumping ahead of me, young demigod."

She stood, and the whispers of her gown rose to a crescendo. Nico was used to deceased souls begging him to listen, but these had a particularly strong pitch of desperation. As the gray fabric swished and shifted, Nico knew his suspicions were correct: each thread was a soul. Each thread had once been a person, and each thread was still *self-aware*.

"You can hear them, can't you?" Gorgyra rested her fingertips gently on Nico's shoulder.

"Yes." Just admitting it brought a wave of sadness crashing over Nico.

How could Gorgyra stand those voices? Why would she choose to wrap herself in their desperation? But at the same time . . . wrapping oneself in desperation wasn't new to Nico. He'd been doing it his whole life. A part of him welcomed the rush of sadness. At least it was familiar, and the familiar was not frightening.

"Nico?" Will clenched his hand around his sun globe, as if ready to throw it at their hostess. "What is she talking about? Who is *them?*"

"You have nothing to fear." Gorgyra smiled her sad, caring smile. "I am not here to trap you. I am not going to hurt you. Like so many others, you have found me because you need me."

She ran her hands over the gown, and the whispers finally became clear in Nico's mind:

I'll never find anyone who loves me.

Why don't I get a family?

What's wrong with me?

Why couldn't she just feel the same about me?

What did I do wrong?

Do I not deserve to be loved?

Nico wept.

He wasn't sure how much time passed before Will removed the

sling and wrapped his arms around him. "Gorgyra, what are you doing?" Will's voice was full of fear and confusion. "Stop it!"

"It's not her," Nico sniffled. "She told the truth. She's not hurting me."

Nico reached out and stroked the smooth fabric of the nymph's gown. The voices seemed to embrace him, recognizing one of their own.

"Lonely souls," said Nico. "That's what your dress is made of, isn't it?"

Gorgyra nodded. "I began to weave this gown long, long ago, when Acheron left for the last time. Deep down, I knew he would never return. So I began plucking souls from his waters. It wasn't long before they began to seek me out, yearning to find . . . well, to find the others."

Will shivered. "I thought the souls in the Acheron were guilty of terrible crimes. Why would you want them near you?"

Gorgyra smoothed her skirts. "Not all the souls are so terrible. Those I collect are the lost, the remorseful, the ones whose greatest crimes were against *themselves*."

"I—I don't understand."

Gorgyra arched her dark brows. "Do you not, Will Solace? Self-doubt. Despair. Fear. Guilt. Shame. So many ways we do harm to ourselves . . . and convince ourselves we do not deserve a place in the fabric of the world. I try to show these lonely souls that even here, at the edge of eternal darkness, there is a chance for hope. Is that not what has brought you and Nico here as well?"

Nico and Will exchanged another look.

"How do you know our names?" Nico asked.

"Oh, names are the *least* of it," Gorgyra said. "When you spend every day listening to souls, you learn that they have a great deal to say. Even those of the living . . . like so."

She raised her hands, and then she *tugged*.

Nico gasped. Something shifted deep within his chest, as if she had reached into him, roped his heart, and pulled it. A faintly glowing thread curled through the air between him and Gorgyra, who had the opposite end laced between her fingers.

Questions vibrated along the thread, echoing in Nico's mind:

Does he love me?

Will I ever find my place at Camp Half-Blood?

Who could ever find me lovable?

Next to him, Will gasped. Nico turned to see another thread snaking toward Gorgyra, this one anchored to Will's chest. His eyes were red and watery.

"Stop it," Nico croaked. "Stop!"

"As you wish." Gorgyra lowered her hands. As quickly as it started, the sensation ended. The thread went slack, then wound itself back into Nico's chest. Will collapsed, panting.

"I will not take threads without consent," said the nymph. "I only wished to demonstrate that I can hear you. I *want* to hear you. There is a yearning in both of you, and it begs to be heard."

Will shuddered. "The darkness . . ."

Nico wasn't sure why Will had said that, but as he stared at his boyfriend, he recognized the expression on Will's face: loneliness. Had anything been more of a constant in his life?

Nico scowled at Gorgyra. He didn't appreciate their souls being yanked around like marionettes. He wondered if they should just fight this woman and take her boat . . . if they even had the strength to beat her.

Gorgyra's pained smile told him she could read his feelings, and she would find such an attempt both sad and predictable . . . two things Nico did not want to be.

"What do you want from us?" Nico asked. "We need your boat. Do we have to complete some kind of quest to get it?"

"Not in the way you think," she said softly, and sat down again by the fire. "The boat will help you survive the plunge, yes. It will not completely shield you from the effects of Acheron, but it will make the voyage . . . possible."

Will pulled himself upright. He leaned against Nico's shoulder for strength. "And what do you want in exchange?"

Gorgyra gazed into the flames. "There is only one currency among the lonely . . . to help us feel part of the texture of the world again. And you need to share it as much as I need to receive it."

Nico growled. "Enough with the riddles—"

"We'll do it," Will said. He faced Nico. "We can't turn back now."

Nico made a mental note not to let Will do the negotiating if they ever bought a first car together. But he also knew that Will was right.

"Fine," he said. "If it will help us get to Tartarus, we'll do it. What do you want, Gorgyra?"

Nico did not like the way the nymph smiled.

CHAPTER 28

"**N**ico di Angelo, why don't you tell me a story?"

Nico bristled at that. A story? *Any* old story? That seemed too easy after everything they'd been through. After all the suffering.

He looked to Will briefly, and his boyfriend arched an eyebrow. He looked tired. *Too* tired. And his bandages . . .

Nico's stomach roiled. The gauze strips were soaked through with blood again.

He turned back to Gorgyra. "A story about *what?*" he asked.

The nymph examined Nico's face, then Will's. Was she going to pull soul threads out of them again?

Nico felt something brush his knuckles. He glanced down and saw that Will was trying to hold his hand. He opened his fingers and let Will slip his in between.

Nico's heart sank. Will's grip was *very* weak.

Nico had to do this. He *had* to finish what they had started.

The whispers called out to him.

And then Gorgyra did, too.

"Tell me about the two of *you*," she said.

CHAPTER 29

Now they sat on the dock, their feet dangling above the Acheron's current.

All their stories had been told, except for this one . . . and whatever happened to them afterward, assuming there *was* an afterward once they dropped over that precipice.

Nico turned the coin in his fingers. "I always keep this with me," he said.

"Same," said Will. "I mean your ring, that is."

The dock boards creaked as Gorgyra came closer. "Tell me about them."

Her tone reminded Nico of Mr. D—and not in a bad way. When he helped Nico unpack his nightmares, the wine god could be surprisingly gentle and patient. The memory made Nico ache for Camp Half-Blood.

"We traded keepsakes," said Nico. "After Nero."

Will and Nico did their best to relate the final battle with the resurrected Roman emperor. Given Gorgyra's isolation, she'd only heard snippets of what had transpired aboveground, and what she *did* know came from souls she had collected.

The victims of the war.

This meant the two demigods had to back up a few times to explain things, especially once Will mentioned Apollo.

"Your father was *in* the battle?" she asked. "Why was he getting involved in mortal affairs?"

Then they had to explain the whole *Zeus punished Apollo by sticking him into the body of a sixteen-year-old boy named Lester Papadopoulos* thing, which Gorgyra found deeply, deeply amusing. "The gods can be quite funny when they want to be," she allowed.

Finally, Will got to the part of the story he wanted to tell. "After watching my father go off to fight Python, I wasn't sure I was ever going to see him again. There was something so *final* about his departure. . . . It got me thinking about what was important to me."

He leaned against Nico. "Then, once Nero and Python were destroyed, I asked Jake Mason to make me something special."

Nico held up the coin for Gorgyra to see. It was a dull bronze color, but the embossing was extraordinary. On one side, Jake had managed to perfectly replicate the stylized sun tattoo that Will had on his pectoral—every beam, every angle, every detail. On the other side was the helm of Hades.

"It is beautiful," she said. "What does it mean?"

"Us," Will said. "Together. Two sides of one coin. I gave it to Nico so if we ever got separated, he would know I was thinking of him, no matter where he was."

Nico smiled at the memory. "Will came to me just before dinner on the night we heard the prophecy about Bob. I could tell he had something important to say because he always gets all bashful beforehand."

Will stuck out his tongue. "I'd never given anyone a gift so personal before."

"And you did great," Nico assured him. "It was *so* sweet. In exchange, I gave him my ring."

Nico pointed to the silver skull ring that Will was running back and forth across its chain. "I'd had that ring for a long time, but it needed to be with Will. So he'd always know how I feel about him."

Will tucked the ring back inside his shirt, then tapped where it lay against his chest. It was such a small gesture, but it felt enormous to Nico. After everything they'd been through since they'd left Camp Half-Blood, it was a reminder that he was loved. *Really* loved. Sure, he and Will had things they needed to discuss. Sure, they often disagreed. But an invisible string connected them nonetheless.

Nico gazed down the Acheron, to the point where it dropped out of sight. He would have to steel himself against the coming onslaught—not just of the River of Pain, but of Tartarus itself. He remembered the despair; he remembered the doubt. It would be magnified for Will, and he would need Nico to be there for him.

Nico curled his fingers around the coin. He dreaded the upcoming journey, but he also felt the residual warmth of the stories they had shared. They clung to him, wrapping around him like a protective layer.

From Gorgyra's dress, the voices reached out to Nico one last time, but now he heard something besides devastation and fear. . . .

Hope.

You might just make it, one said.

You keep that one close.

Someone like that is a rare find.

You are not alone.

The whispers dissipated and returned to Gorgyra's gown, turning the fabric a luminous pink, like imperial topaz.

"Thank you, Gorgyra," Nico said quietly. "The stories were to give us strength for the journey, weren't they?"

"They were," she said, her voice raw with emotion. "But it is I who should be thanking you. You came and visited an old nymph. You offered me kindness, and you showed me that love and companionship still exist in the mortal world." A sad smile grew on her lips. "It is easy to forget that when you collect the souls of the lonely."

Will reached over and squeezed Nico's hand. The color had returned to his face.

"And the boat?" Will asked their host. "What should we do with it when we reach Tartarus?"

"If you are successful in your quest, the boat will return to me."

Will peered downstream at the raging waterfall. "How? That looks like a pretty one-way trip."

"You misunderstand the nature of the Acheron. Its course is not one-directional. This is the River of Pain. Like life, it flows in a circle."

Will scrunched up his face. "This sounds like a complicated geometry problem."

"Pain is a part of all lives, mortal and immortal," said the nymph. "It is inescapable. We *all* must navigate this river to get where we want to be."

"Shouldn't we aim to avoid pain?" Will asked. "Or at least mitigate it?"

Nico shook his head. "You know it's not that simple."

"Pain helps us learn," said Gorgyra. "It is unfortunate, but we rarely forget the lessons taught to us in moments of pain."

"Pain is inescapable. . . ." Will sounded like he was talking mostly to himself. "I guess that's hard for me to wrap my mind around because I'm a healer. I'm always trying to *reduce* pain."

His tone reminded Nico of their trip to Persephone's garden . . . how dazed Will had acted when they emerged from the gates, as if he'd been shaken to pieces, then put back together in a slightly different pattern. What had happened to him in there?

Nico didn't ask. He quickly hopped into the boat, then supported Will as he shakily climbed aboard. As they sailed away from the dock, Gorgyra watched in silence, her silhouette becoming smaller and fainter until it dissolved into the dark haze over the river, as if she had been reabsorbed into the community of lonely souls.

The current picked up speed. The white boat rocked back and forth under their legs. The roar of the waterfall got so loud it rattled Nico's teeth.

"I guess this is it," he said.

"I guess so," said Will.

"We have to go over that thing."

"We do." Will's knuckles were white as he gripped the gunwales. "Like, is there a technique to riding a boat over a waterfall *without* dying? Do we just fall into Tartarus?"

Nico shrugged. "Where's Lil Nas X when you need him?"

"Who?"

He glared at Will. "Really? You've never seen the video for 'Montero'? We'll address that hole in your education later."

Will laughed—maybe the only time anyone had ever laughed while sailing the River of Pain. "It's a date. I like the idea that we'll have a chance to share more stories. I'll hold on to that . . . in case things get worse."

Nico swallowed his fear. As their boat edged ever closer to the abyss, he knew there was no "in case." In Tartarus, things *always* got worse.

CHAPTER 30

Near the drop-off, the voices raged even louder than the water.

These were not the whispers of lonely souls, like in Gorgyra's gown. These were angry. Resentful. Frightened. Terrified.

And they were in pain.

She made fun of me! a voice called out. *Why am* I *the one being punished?*

I'll do it again. You can't stop me. No one can.

Will clutched his ears. "I can't keep them out."

You deserve to be here, said another voice. *This is where you belong.*

"Will," Nico said, "I know it seems impossible, but you have to try to ignore them."

"How?" His face was scrunched up. "They're so *loud*."

"Not the voices. Try to ignore the memories."

"What does *that* mean?"

Nico struggled to answer, but he could barely suppress his own tortured thoughts.

He saw Minos and his army of spirits sucked into a void in the floor.

He saw himself slaying Kronos's demons in Manhattan—cutting down monster after monster with his Stygian iron sword.

He saw his sister Bianca lying in his arms as the life drained out of her. . . . And even though this had never happened, the memory was *real*. It was exactly how he had always felt about her death: helpless, useless, completely guilty.

The voices hissed. *You have killed so many. You are a murderer.*

Nico tried to shake away the accusations. He held out his hand for Will.

"The river is turning your memories against you," he said. "I know it's awful, but . . . you're *Will Solace*. I've never known anyone as good as you in my entire life. Hold on to that."

Will shuddered. "If you say so."

They clung to each other as the boat picked up speed. The keel began to turn sideways, and Nico instinctively reached for an oar. Something told him they would have to face this drop head-on.

You've killed so many, Nico di Angelo, said the voices. *What's a couple more?*

Will groaned. "But I've killed, too," he slurred. "So many dead by my hands—"

"No, you're a healer!" If they were on any other river, Nico would have splashed his boyfriend's face with water, but here that would have been a very bad idea. "We've been through *three* wars in our lifetime. Of course we've had to fight. Of course we've lost people. But you've done everything you could to save our friends and family."

"But I let you kill," Will mumbled. "I let you do it."

The comment punched Nico in the gut. Then the voices rushed in, pushing their advantage. *So cavalier with life,* they chided. *You take it away so easily. You distribute death like a badge of pride. Even when you tell your boyfriend you love him, you give him a ring in the shape of a skull.*

Nico tried to focus. "You—you aren't responsible for me, Will."

Will's eyebrows stitched together in anger. "Maybe I am. I let you kill Octavian. I shouldn't have allowed that. I contributed to his death. I'm a *murderer*."

"That's the Acheron speaking," Nico insisted. "You need to ignore it."

"You don't even feel bad about killing him, do you?"

"I think about it all the time! Now grab the other oar, please—we're starting to spin!"

Nico's words were like a crack of lightning in a thunderstorm. They were enough to snap Will out of the trance, and his blue eyes locked onto Nico. "The oars—"

"Grab that one!" Nico yelled as they slid toward the terrible maw of darkness.

Murderer. Don't try to fight the truth.

Will took hold of the other oar. "What now? We can't just row over the—"

"Lock your feet under the thwart," Nico ordered, wondering how he knew this to be right. "Turn the prow downstream and hold on!"

He'd barely gotten out the words when their boat slid over the edge of the waterfall. Time seemed to slow, as it does at the top of a roller coaster, as if the universe were teasing them: *Should I drop them to their deaths, or not?*

"I *hate* this," Nico grumbled.

Then they fell into nothingness.

CHAPTER 31

The first time Nico fell into Tartarus, it had somehow seemed to last a long time and no time at all, as if time had become elastic. But right then, as he and Will plunged through the void, it seemed to take days.

It was hard to talk. Hard to think. Hard to do much of anything except hold on and be terrified. Did either of them fall asleep at their oars? Maybe. Nico's memory was a patchwork of nightmares and darkness.

At one point he drew his sword—he wasn't sure why—and held it above him as if he could intimidate the abyss into releasing them. The blade's dim glow illuminated the boat, enveloping him and Will in a violet halo.

But then the darkness closed back in, its black tendrils swarming the sword like antibodies attacking a virus, and snuffed out the sword's light.

After that there was nothingness once again: just the free fall and the roar of water, pain, and voices.

Will had never experienced darkness like this.

He could feel it *inside* him, as if he were breathing it, consuming it.

And it never ended.

It was not like night. His eyes would have eventually adjusted to that. He could see *nothing* here—not the boat, not the waterfall cascading around them, not even Nico beside him on the bench. Only the warmth of Nico's shoulder pressed against his told him that his boyfriend was still there. Every so often, Will thought Nico might be trying to say something, but it was impossible to be sure in the thunderous roar of the Acheron and the torrent of screams from the tortured souls.

He tried to summon light from within himself . . . the faint glow that usually came so easily. But here it was impossible. This place seemed to drain him of his willpower.

That thought almost made him laugh. Because it was literal. His "Will" power wasn't there. It was gone. He just . . . existed.

But he existed with Nico. His sole comfort was that he wasn't alone.

He had Nico.

And together they fell.

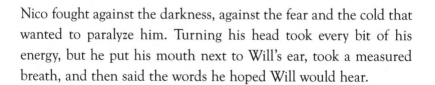

Nico fought against the darkness, against the fear and the cold that wanted to paralyze him. Turning his head took every bit of his energy, but he put his mouth next to Will's ear, took a measured breath, and then said the words he hoped Will would hear.

Three words.
A promise of *hope*.

The words tingled in Will's ear.
They ignited his heart.

"I love you."

And they fell.

Nico noticed a tint to the darkness below—something between red and black. It grew, and as it did, so did the heat.

At first, he found it welcome—like the warmth of a spring day.

Then it felt like the dead of summer.

Then like a furnace, a pit of lava, the middle of the sun.

He had a silly fleeting thought: Maybe this will recharge Will!

But the only thing the heat seemed to recharge was Will's need to scream.

Will began to float off their bench . . . upward? Sideways? Nico wasn't quite sure because the boat was twisting and spinning through the void, and his sense of orientation had gone haywire.

The oars forgotten, Nico grabbed Will and held him tight, his legs straining to stay anchored under the thwart beam.

"I'm here!" Nico told him. "I've got you!"

"But *that*!" Will yelled, his eyes fixed on something below them. "What about *that*?"

Nico followed his gaze, and he absolutely hated what he saw.

The red-tinted darkness had now resolved into deep ruby sky, punctuated with menacing darker clouds of . . . Oh. As their boat punched through one, Nico realized the vapor droplets were blood. Great. On top of all its other selling points, Tartarus had blood clouds. Nico didn't recall those from his last trip.

And below the clouds was the rapidly approaching terrain—which they were moments away from smashing into.

"I don't know what to do." Nico said it softly at first, to himself; then he looked at Will. "I don't know how we survive this."

The wind blew through Will's bushy hair. In the fiery light of Tartarus, his bronze skin seemed to glow again, each whisker on his cheeks a filament of gold. Nico found it completely unfair that even as they dropped to their deaths, Will still looked stunning.

"Nico," Will said, his tone suddenly confident, infused with sincerity, "if anyone can save us from this, it's *you*."

And in that moment, Nico pushed aside his panic and his fear, because . . .

Well, Will Solace believed in him.

The voices of the Acheron had dispersed as the waterfall broke into a loose funnel cloud of rain, but their words still rang in Nico's head: *So cavalier with life. You distribute death like a badge of pride.*

A solution sprouted in his mind.

He was in Tartarus. Death was all around him.

It was time to use that to his favor.

"Will, hold on to my feet."

"What?"

"Just do it!"

Will grabbed him by the ankles. Nico spread out flat with his belly pressed against the bow of the boat, his head sticking over the prow like he was sledding in the Winter Olympics, skeleton-style . . . which only seemed appropriate. The ground kept rushing up to meet them—a depressingly familiar terrain of jagged hills; fleshy, pockmarked plains; and bubbling, poisonous swamps. From the base of the waterfall, the Acheron snaked away through a deep canyon, but Nico had no faith they would hit the water, if that was even a survivable option.

He *had* to make his plan work.

Nico opened his mouth and screamed—unleashing all his power, his desperation, his will to live. Far below, the ground splintered in a web of fissures. Skeletons began clawing their way out of the soil—thousands of human, animal, giant, and monster bones cobbling themselves together, climbing atop one another to form an ever-growing scaffold of undeath. Nico commanded them into the shape he needed, and the skeletons complied.

When the boat hit the top of the bone ramp, Will screamed, but he kept his grip on Nico's ankles. Their canoe skittered down the slope perilously fast and bumpy at first, but the bones reshaped around their hull, slowing and guiding their descent. Moments later, the boat skidded to a gentle halt on the banks of the Acheron.

Nico rolled out of the boat and collapsed on his back, gazing up at the bloodred clouds in Tartarus's sky.

That's when he heard the laughter.

Nico sat upright, worried that some horrible demon had already found them. But it was *Will*, sitting in the dirt, hugging his belly as tears streamed down his face.

His giddiness was infectious. Nico couldn't help it. The enormity of what they'd just survived hit him, and the only thing he *could* do was laugh.

"Nico, you—" Will dissolved into giggling. "You just built a half-pipe of the dead."

"I'd like to thank Tony Hawk," he said, "and all the dead who made this moment possible."

Right on cue, the towering slope of skeletons collapsed into a lifeless mountain of bones.

Nico crawled over to Will and rested his head on Will's thigh.

"Welcome to Tartarus," Nico said. Then he passed out.

CHAPTER 32

As Nico slept, Will ran his fingers through his boyfriend's dark hair.

He wasn't alarmed that Nico had passed out. He knew Nico would need a serious nap after summoning so many dead. In fact, Will was feeling strangely upbeat and excited. When Nico woke, Will could reveal that—ta-da!—he had brought Kit Kat bars. The candy did wonders to help Nico recuperate after shadow-travel, so Will had made sure to stow some in his knapsack, carefully sealed in a Ziploc bag labeled IN CASE OF EMERGENCY, EAT CHOCOLATE.

He clung to that idea: He could help Nico. He could contribute to this quest. He was more than just a powerless child of sunlight in a death pit of eternal gloom.

Because otherwise, he wasn't sure he could handle what was happening to them.

They were actually *in* Tartarus. In every direction, the desolate landscape stretched as far as Will could see—the terrain drenched in the color of blood from the thick, gelatinous clouds that hung overhead. Did it *rain* here?

He did not want to know the answer. Having fallen through

those clouds, he did not want to experience their version of a thunderstorm.

The plains were pockmarked with craters, as if Tartarus got a lot of meteor strikes. A few hundred feet from the banks of the Acheron, a craggy red hill was covered in sickly orange bubbles, almost like . . .

Almost like zits.

These were the regeneration blisters Nico had told him about—the pus-filled pods from which monsters were reborn.

Goose bumps rippled up Will's arms.

This place was *wrong*.

When he breathed, the air felt *sticky*. Not like humidity—more like melted ice cream running down his hand in the summer. And the smell . . . It made him think of rotten eggs left out in the sun, then blended with dog poop, then put *back* out into the sun.

It also hurt. The air hurt.

Will felt a new level of sympathy for young Harley back at Camp Half-Blood, who struggled with asthma. Will wondered if this was how he felt during a severe attack. The idea of standing up, much less hiking across this horrible landscape, was enough to bring Will to tears.

Nico stirred. Will thought he might be rousing, but instead he turned and settled again.

Will wondered how long he should let him sleep. He felt terribly exposed sitting next to a bright white boat in an otherwise-monotonous red-orange landscape. He wasn't sure what to be on the lookout for, or where danger might come from next, but Nico needed rest.

So Will kept watch. And while Tartarus was deep beneath the land of the dead, he discovered it was full of life.

In the crimson clouds overhead, something with enormous wings flapped by. A flock of smaller somethings chased after it, fluttering and screeching. In the distant hills, just at the edge of Will's vision, shadows moved across the ridgelines, and Will couldn't help thinking about the packs of slavering wolves Nico had described.

Every so often, the land itself grumbled like it had indigestion. Will wouldn't have been surprised if that were the case, given the number of monsters it was constantly spitting out.

Somewhere in this nightmarish world, Bob needed their help.

Will shivered. He didn't get how this place could be so hot and still make him feel so cold.

After a while, his legs started to fall asleep. As gently as possible, he moved Nico's head off his thigh and onto his knapsack. Nico barely stirred.

Will stood up and stretched his legs until the pins and needles faded.

Exhaustion tugged at the edge of Will's consciousness, but he had to stay awake, and he didn't want to wait around doing nothing. He already felt terrible about how much Nico had been forced to look after him in the Underworld. Will wasn't used to that. *He* was the caretaker and the healer. It was literally his job as a child of Apollo.

And yet all the powers that made up Will's sense of self were so limited here. He couldn't even heal *himself* effectively. It was only due to rest and Gorgyra's kindness that his bleeding had stopped. Speaking of which, he should probably change the bandages, but . . .

He glanced down at Nico, snoring softly, and completely unsheltered.

Will had another idea. He walked over to the boat. He put his hands on the gunwale, then squatted and gave it an experimental tug. He didn't want to strain himself—Nico would not appreciate it if Will reopened his wounds—but the hull was surprisingly light. It was good nymph workmanship, just like the canoes at camp.

Will went to work as quietly as he could. He collected rocks and bones—the plentiful building supplies of Tartarus—and made a low wall near where Nico was lying. The effort left him winded and sweaty, but it felt good to be doing something productive. Finally, he was able to turn over the boat, resting the starboard gunwale lengthwise against his wall, and—voilà!—he had constructed a crude shelter for Nico with an upside-down boat for a roof. It wasn't much better than a lean-to, but if those clouds did decide to rain blood, acid, poison, or some other vile liquid, at least they would have some cover.

Will was pleased with himself. He imagined Nico waking up and being amazed. Will could say, *Welcome home, honey!*

The idea was so ridiculous it made him feel giggly again, but also warm and satisfied. He tried to hold on to those sensations. Even *feelings* were hard to come by here—unless they were something akin to despair or anger or fear. *Those* came easily. And how could they not? Will was in a place that seemed to spend every moment thinking up new ways to kill him.

Wasn't that how Annabeth had described Tartarus? For a brief moment, Will wished she and Percy were with them, but then he discarded the thought. He wouldn't wish this place on his worst enemy. . . .

And just like that, his despair came creeping back.

They had no idea where Bob might be.

Their only lead was to find the giant Damasen's hut, but it wasn't like there were signposts here in Tartarus for Menoetes's suggested trail. No maps or travel guides. Will tried to imagine what a tourist brochure would look like. *Come visit the geysers of suffering! Free tours of the acid-rain fields!*

He didn't know where to go. His boyfriend was out cold. He didn't know what he was supposed to do aside from build houses out of rocks and boats. And on top of everything else . . . Oh, gods, he'd accused Nico of murder, hadn't he? All his deepest grievances, and his guilt about Octavian's death, had come pouring out when they navigated the Acheron.

When Nico woke up, Will would have to apologize. They'd have to talk it through.

They could get past it. They had bigger problems to deal with. But Will's disappointment in himself was enough to trigger an emotional landslide.

The sheer absurdity of this quest hit him in full force. They never should have come here, at least not without more support. And if—a big if—they somehow managed to find Bob and rescue him, how were they supposed to climb back *out* of Tartarus?

There were so many unknowns. They piled up like the bones Nico had summoned to break their fall. Will knew *nothing*. All he could do was wait for Nico to wake up and tell him what to do, then lug Will across Tartarus like an overstuffed duffel bag.

Heat rushed to his face. He'd been a huge burden on Nico since they'd entered the Door of Orpheus, and that wasn't fair. This quest was already a terrible gamble for Nico. He shouldn't have to take care of Will on top of everything else.

Will was a counselor. A leader! He was supposed to take the initiative.

A thought nudged his mind, just a gentle push in a new direction. He gazed again at the closest hill, dotted with its orange blisters.

It was only a few hundred feet away. Will calculated that he could make it to the top and back in less than five minutes, without Nico ever being out of his sight. At least that would allow him to gather some information—maybe get a better view of their surroundings and find out more about those regeneration pods. As a healer, he had to admit they fascinated him. Who knows? They might have healing applications for demigods.

He glanced at the boat one more time, then pulled his hood over his head. He'd have to be quick, but this was doable.

Will hummed to himself as he started walking. His legs were still sore, but they weren't *that* bad. The worst part was the noxious air coating the inside of his throat and nose every time he breathed. He pulled the drawstrings of his hoodie, yanking it tight enough to form a makeshift mask. That helped a little bit, and it reminded him of feeling like a turtle. . . .

Had that been yesterday? How did time pass down here?

His aching intensified as he started to climb the hill. The red soil glittered and crunched under his feet like broken glass, and Will decided he didn't dare stumble here.

Keep a lookout, he told himself. *Stay vigilant.*

He glanced back to check on the boat. He felt a brief stab of anxiety when he didn't see it . . . but no. The boat was exactly where he'd left it. Nico was safe. Will had just been looking too far downstream. The terrain was so disorienting here. Will would have to remember that.

He started up the hill again. As he approached the first regeneration blobs, he realized they were a lot creepier up close. He could see the dark silhouettes of monsters floating inside, and every time they moved, the bubbles pulsated and shook. Nico's description of them—as zits—wasn't quite right. These blisters were more like embryonic sacks, and they were very much alive.

Fascinated, Will squeezed himself between two of the pods, trying his best not to make contact. A terrible heat emanated from the protrusions, and he stopped to remove his hoodie and stuff it into his knapsack. After a few more steps, he realized that the pods were clustered more densely toward the summit, which made climbing *really* hard.

Still, he had to keep going. A few more feet and he should have a much better view of their surroundings.

He was almost to the top when he slipped on a patch of loose gravel. His back heel slid straight through the membrane of a pod.

It was easily the grossest sensation Will had ever felt, like stepping in a rotten pumpkin that happened to be filled with battery acid. He pulled his foot free, but the yellowish goo had coated his shoe and was smoking against his bare shin.

He yelped and kicked, then pulled out a sleeve of his hoodie and used it to wipe away as much of the goo as possible. Unfortunately, his shin was already red and blistering. So much for the goo having healing applications . . .

He had no time to recover, though. From the punctured blister something small, dark, and slimy clawed its way out of the fluid. It lifted its sticky head and let loose a terrible squawk.

Will froze. "You're *kidding* me!"

Because he recognized that Celestial bronze beak, those beady red eyes, those razor-sharp feathers. He was face-to-face with a goo-covered Stymphalian bird.

The demon bird cocked its head as it studied Will. It cooed—a normal pigeon-y coo, that is—then tapped the ground with its beak.

"Nice birdie." Will held up his palm. He meant it as a gesture of peace, but belatedly he worried he might be signaling *Here! Exposed flesh to eat!* "Stay right there."

The bird cooed again, then hopped closer to Will.

He pulled his knees to his chest. His heart was hammering, but he tried to stay calm. "Sorry if I woke you early. Really, I love demon pigeons. You're cute, aren't you, buddy?"

The bird screeched—a sound like metal nails on a chalkboard—and then leaped at Will.

He kicked at it and rolled sideways.

But when he got to his feet and crouched in a defensive stance, the bird was nowhere to be seen.

Will scanned the hill, certain that the bird would swoop down on him at any second. Where was it? Had it simply flown off?

Then he heard a sickening *gurgle*, and his stomach dropped. He turned slowly toward the regeneration blister and found the bird staring at him. . . .

Along with two *other* birds that had just been extruded from the break in the membrane. More dark shapes were inside the pod, stirring and wriggling toward the exit that Will's foot had conveniently provided.

Of course. He couldn't just wake up *one* Stymphalian bird. He had to go and wake up an entire flock—the very same creatures that had tormented him and his mom in Washington Square Park.

"Oh, *no*," he said. "I—I don't suppose we can talk about this."

The demonic birds screeched and lifted into the bloodred sky, more and more of them pouring out of the broken pod.

Will tried to run up the rest of the slippery slope. He darted to the left and dodged more bubbles, hoping to put some distance between him and the winged terrors.

He had never wanted to be a fighter. Not in the Battle of Manhattan or the Siege of Camp Half-Blood, not even in Nero's tower. He *loved* being a healer.

Yet here he was, alone on a hill in Tartarus, surrounded by vicious Stymphalian birds. Why, oh why hadn't he honed his archery skills? Why had he not considered that he might get separated from Nico and would need his own weapon?

He heard fluttering above. *Close* above. He dove to the ground, but it was pointless. A group of birds attacked him, pecking his scalp and tugging at his clothes.

"No!" he cried out. "Go away! Find someone else to attack!"

But there was no one else, and even if his screams woke up his boyfriend, Nico would never be able to reach Will in time to help. As Will he tried to crawl away, he realized he never should have left Nico's side. He shouldn't have been so arrogant and reckless.

The Stymphalian birds pulled at his sleeves, his shoes, the hems of his shorts. His backpack was ripped off his shoulders. Will curled up as tightly as he could, but he knew it wouldn't help. Those bronze beaks could tear him to shreds.

But . . . why weren't they?

More and more of the creatures swirled around him, cawing with exultation, pecking at his clothes. And then . . . Will was rising. The cursed birds weren't trying to kill him. They were *lifting* him off the ground.

He screamed, but it did no good.

He swatted at the birds and kicked his legs, but the flock was everywhere now—a living cloud of angry feathers and claws.

As they carried him up and away—five feet off the ground, ten feet, fifteen—he looked down in despair, hoping Nico had heard the noise and was coming to his rescue. But instead, he saw something even more terrifying than his own predicament.

Crouched near the boat, as if getting ready to lift it, was a tall creature with furry legs and pointy horns.

Then Will was swallowed in a black storm of feathers and transported into the poisonous skies of Tartarus.

CHAPTER 33

When Nico woke from his nightmares, he was convinced he had fallen into another dream.

He didn't know if Nyx was still trying to invade his subconscious to . . . do whatever it was she was doing. That still confused Nico. Was she trying to draw him into a trap? If so, did she not realize she didn't *have* to? Nico would have come for Bob regardless, so the whole thing was perplexing.

His nightmares were weirdly predictable. It was as if his brain were a Magic 8 Ball and someone had shaken it, plucked whatever memory floated to the surface, and then twisted it, warping the past to fit the same dream narrative: Nico needed to listen. He needed to tell the truth. Blah, blah, blah. It was all very repetitive, and he much preferred his usual chaotic dreams over this.

So when he opened his eyes and found himself in a dark space, he wasn't frightened or startled. It was merely the next chapter in his boring dream journey. Was he back in the jar? Who was going to open it this time?

More light came in, and Nico blinked as his eyes adjusted to the shadow above him. Well, *partial* shadow. There was still a red haze everywhere. Wait. He was in Tartarus! And was that Will's face? No, he thought he could make out horns. . . .

Maybe this wasn't a dream after all.

Nico rubbed at his cheeks and sat up, promptly smacking his head on something that fell away from him.

The horned figure grunted. "Why were you under a boat?"

"What?" said Nico. Just to his left was a lone Kit Kat bar. Where had *that* come from?

And then he saw the white boat on the ground behind him.

The boat. For some reason, Nico had been sleeping underneath the canoe Gorgyra had lent them. Had they crashed? No, not that Nico remembered. He'd been with Will when—

Will.

Where was Will?

Nico felt panic rising in him as he quickly sprang upright, his sword in his hand. "Who are you?"

The creature stared at him in confusion. He looked like . . . like Grover. So . . . a satyr? No, his horns were strangely shaped. They were much, much bigger than any Nico had ever seen, and they curled up on the sides of the creature's face, which was that of a pale human with boyish features. Below the neck, he quickly became . . .

Actually, Nico wasn't sure. He was furry like satyrs usually were, and there were hooves at the end of his two legs. Was he part goat? Part sheep? Around his waist he wore only a long, tattered cloth held in place by a thick band of leather.

The satyr-ish being looked down at the boat, then back to Nico. "Have you seen the child?"

"The what?" Nico said.

"The child. I'm looking for him. I'm supposed to protect him."

Protect, not *eat*, thought Nico. Well, that was a point in his favor.

Nico scanned the grim landscape that extended in every direction. Was the creature talking about Will? Nico didn't see his companion anywhere. Where had he gone?

The creature shook his head. "I keep losing him. One second, I think I have him, then—BOOM!—gone."

"Who are you?" asked Nico.

"I am Amphithemis," he said. "And you?" He narrowed his eyes. "Are *you* the child?"

"No! I'm just . . . I'm Nico. Not a child."

"Would you help me find the child?"

Nico's nerves prickled along his skin. Something about this seemed very, very wrong.

"Speaking of finding someone, have you seen my boyfriend?" he asked. "Tall. Bushy blond hair. Looks like both a camp counselor and a surfer. Maybe we can help each other. . . ."

Amphithemis shook his head. "I am not sure I know what a surfer is, but I have seen no one." He shuffled in place, scraping one of his hooves against the dirt. "I have not seen anyone else in a very long time."

Nico thought of Gorgyra's loneliness and a pang of sadness hit him. Amphithemis was even deeper in the Underworld than she was! "No kidding," he said. "Gods, where *is* Will? He wouldn't just wander off. . . ."

"Perhaps he, too, is looking for this child," said Amphithemis, his face lighting up.

"No," said Nico sadly. He bent down and picked up the Kit Kat bar. "We're looking for . . . someone else." He didn't want to reveal too much to this stranger, especially when he knew so little about the creature. He took a step closer to Amphithemis and examined his face. "If you don't mind me asking," he said, "what kind of being are you? You remind me a little of a centaur I know, but you don't walk on four legs. So, a satyr?"

"I am actually both," he said. "A Lamian centaur in name, but more like a satyr in nature. In fact, that is how I found you. We satyrs have a knack for finding demigods."

That *was* true. Grover had found a number of them over the years, and satyrs were known for bringing unclaimed demigods to camp.

"Can you sense another demigod nearby?" Nico asked excitedly. "He's a son of Apollo."

"Apollo?" Amphithemis sniffed the air. "Hmm. The scent is light. Perhaps too light. But yes, there is another demigod in the vicinity."

"Excellent! Can you help me track him down? Then maybe both of us can help you find this child."

But Amphithemis was still sniffing the air. Suddenly he lunged at Nico and began smelling his neck.

Nico jumped back. "What are you doing?"

"I smell him on you," said Amphithemis. "And others. Other living things who are . . . lost. Children. I smell *children!*" At that, he shook his head violently. "No, no, I must find the children, must find them!"

Nico kept backing away, his hands up. "I'm sorry," he said. "I haven't seen or been around any children lately. I'm just looking for my boyfriend."

Amphithemis glared at him. "Which god is your parent?"

"Well, it's—"

"Answer me, boy!" Amphithemis demanded, his eyes flashing red. "I refuse to help a son of Zeus or Hera!"

"Then don't worry! My father is Hades."

"Hades?" At the mention of the god of the Underworld and the dead, Amphithemis visibly calmed, his shoulders drooping. "Oh. Well, that is fine."

Nico finally stopped backing away from him. "Why not Zeus or Hera?"

"The child," Amphithemis muttered. "Zeus sent me after the child, and I think I lost him. Can't find him, can't find him. *Where* is the child?"

Nico stepped closer. "And Hera?"

The Lamian centaur gave him a rage-filled look. "She interfered. She turned me into *this*." He gestured at his body. "I was once a river spirit. Incorporeal. And now . . . now I'm part human, part ox, and . . ."

Amphithemis was lost in thought again. He started circling Nico, mumbling to himself. How long has he been down here? Nico wondered. If Zeus had sent Amphithemis to guard a child, he'd clearly failed. But who did Zeus want to protect, and why were they down in *Tartarus?*

Nico hadn't really interacted with Hera, but he knew enough to fear her temper. So that checked out. But there wasn't enough time to put all the pieces together—Nico *had* to find Will.

"What if we help each other?" he suggested once more, to get Amphithemis back on track. "I think that would be beneficial to both of us."

"Yes, yes," said the centaur. "Yes, two are better than one, and two can find the child."

"Well, it can be *three* if you help me find Will first."

"Three for the child," said Amphithemis, and he scratched at his chin. "Yes. Much better odds. Better odds of finding him."

Without warning, the centaur sniffed near Nico's neck again. It was definitely not Nico's favorite thing, but he didn't want to upset Amphithemis, especially if the centaur could help track down Will.

After a few seconds, Amphithemis turned his nose up into the air.

"Oh, yes, I think he is close," he said. "Very."

The centaur's movements were jerky. He lurched to the side and ran to the bank of the Acheron. "I know, I know," he said to the water. "I have made many mistakes. But I think they shall be no more. I will succeed this time!"

He waved at Nico, beckoning him. "Come," he said. "We must cross the River of Pain to get to him."

Nico hesitated. He didn't think Will would have gone that way. How could he have crossed without a boat? Then again . . . this was Tartarus. It was entirely possible that Will's mental stamina was not what Nico's was, and this place could have led him astray.

Nico had a horrible thought. Had Will been drawn into the water and . . . ?

He shook his head violently. No, he would not think that way. The centaur believed Will was on the other side, and it wasn't like Nico had any other information.

He walked over to Amphithemis but stopped short of the edge of the bank. "So, how do we get across? Should we get the boat?"

The centaur looked at Nico as if he'd just spoken gibberish. "Um, we *walk* across," he said, like it was the most obvious thing in the world.

And that is exactly what he did.

There was no reluctance. No uncertainty. Amphithemis waded through the rushing water—which came up to his thighs—and then stood on the other bank, staring at Nico. "Well?" he said.

Nico's mouth was still open. "I'm sorry, did you just casually walk through the *Acheron*?"

"It's fine," he said. "It only affects those who need to be punished. It means nothing to me."

That made no sense. The River of Pain magnified a person's

mistakes and wrongdoings. Did Amphithemis mean to suggest he'd never made a single mistake in his entire life?

"I'm waiting," said the centaur, tapping his hoof on the ground. "We must keep moving!"

Nico grimaced and tentatively approached the edge. "Well, here goes nothing."

The river whispered to him, begging him to give himself over to it.

This is where you belong.

Nico unwrapped the Kit Kat he was holding and greedily gobbled it up, hoping it would give him some strength. Will had to have left it for Nico; that was exactly the sort of caring thing his boyfriend would do. Nico clutched that thought tightly as he stared at the rushing waters.

He recalled the nightmare Epiales had given Will: Nico jumping into the Styx, leaving Will behind. The terrible irony was not lost on Nico. Had Will left *him* behind?

There was no point hoping an answer would come, and Amphithemis was now stomping his hoof like he was keeping time in a demonic Broadway musical.

So Nico held his breath and leaped.

Nico's plan had been to quickly jump to the other bank, but once his legs were submerged in the Acheron, the current grasped him and sent intrusive thoughts into his mind.

Nico remembered every monster and demon he'd ever killed. He remembered the dead he had raised. He remembered all the people he'd been unable to save.

Jason. Bianca.

His mother.

"Come on!" yelled Amphithemis, his hand extended. "What's taking you so long? I'm losing the scent!"

Nico trudged his way through the River of Pain, then reached for Amphithemis's hand. The centaur pulled it back at the last second, so Nico ended up pitching forward and flopping onto the opposite bank.

"The child," Amphithemis said. "The child. Where is the child?"

"We'll find him," said Nico, gasping and rolling over onto his back. "Just let me catch my breath first."

Amphithemis danced around him, hopping from one hoof to another. "Who are you? Do you know where the child is?"

Nico scowled at him. "I already told you my name."

"Where did you come from?" The centaur dropped to all fours and approached Nico, then sniffed his now-wet jeans. "You were in the river. River washed away the scent."

Nico's eyes widened. "What? No!" He quickly removed his bomber and held it out to Amphithemis. "Smell this. Will's scent is definitely still on it."

"Who is Will?"

Nico scoffed. "My boyfriend, remember?"

The centaur tentatively sniffed one of the sleeves. "Oh, yes. Yes, I smell them. Children. The children are near."

And then he bolted away from Nico.

"Hey, wait up!" Nico called out, pushing himself up and slipping on his jacket. He was a little woozy at first, but he soon found his footing and chased after Amphithemis.

The centaur was running wildly, his nose in the air, sniffing every which way. Why would Nico's boyfriend have come this direction? *Oh, Will*, he thought. *What ridiculous idea did you get in your head?*

Then: *What ridiculous idea did this place put in your head?*

Amphithemis darted helter-skelter, sniffing every rock and bone they passed. He muttered to himself the whole time, and Nico couldn't make out what he was saying. He seemed . . . determined.

This mission Zeus had given him was clearly his sole purpose in life. It wasn't like Zeus handed out assignments regularly, so it had to be important to find this child.

"Here, here," said Amphithemis loudly, and he came to a grouping of stones, each of them pitch-black like volcanic rock. "The child was here."

Nico panted as he walked up to him. "Will was here?"

"The children. The children were here."

Nico wasn't quite sure what he was looking for. Or *at*, for that matter. Where had these stones come from? Unlike where Nico had been when he'd woken up, there was nothing else here on this flat plain. Nico twisted around and peered back at the river. He could still see the boat on the other side, and off to his right was a set of hills.

He thought he saw movement there. Was he imagining it? Maybe Tartarus was playing tricks on his mind already.

He gazed back at the volcanic rocks, and this time, he was *sure* he saw something move.

And it looked like a mouth snapping shut.

Nico froze and focused on the spot. "Shhh," he said to Amphithemis. "I think something is here."

There was a soft rustling sound, and out of the corner of his eye, he spied something dart past. Nico was only quick enough to catch a pack of shadows moving together into the distance.

"This isn't Will," said Nico. "He's not here!"

"Who's Will?" said Amphithemis, scowling at Nico. "Who are *you*?"

"What?!"

Amphithemis took a tentative step forward. "I'm trying to find the child. I think I lost him. Do you know where he is?"

Nico squeezed his eyes shut, then opened them. "Am I dreaming? This is a dream, isn't it?"

"Do you have him?" Amphithemis snarled. "You have him, don't you?"

Nico began to back away. "I don't know who you're talking about!"

The centaur's eyes widened. "I know! I know his name! Dionysus!"

The ground rumbled underneath Nico's feet, but he remained frozen in place. "What did you say?"

"Dionysus!" Amphithemis's tone was more certain. "Yes, yes, the baby Dionysus!"

No, no, no, thought Nico. This *is* a dream. This is Nyx! She's trapped me in another nightmare!

Without a word, Nico turned and ran. He ignored Amphithemis's shouting and pumped his legs, his boots slapping the dirt. He tried to leap as far as he could from the bank of the Acheron, but both his feet slammed into the water. The voices cried out, first in shock, then in oozing relief, grateful that Nico had returned. They begged him to join the others, to cleanse himself of all he'd done wrong, but he slogged through the current, stumbling and getting a mouthful of the river. He spat it out, but he could still feel the poisonous thoughts slithering down his throat, begging him to stay.

You deserve this.

You are a murderer.

You belong here.

Nico climbed out the other side of the Acheron, then crawled toward the boat. He was convinced that if he reached it and returned to where he'd woken up, he would somehow break the spell Nyx had cast over him.

He had to wake up.

But as he grabbed the gunwale of the boat and lifted his leg to climb in, he heard a splash behind him. He spun to see Amphithemis stomping his way.

"Stop running!" the Lamian centaur cried. "It's useless!"

"You're not real!" said Nico. "This is all a dream!"

Amphithemis stopped short, his face aghast. "Excuse *you*, but I am very much real!"

"No, you're not." Nico scooted backward until his legs hit the boat. "None of this is."

"Where is Dionysus? Where is he, boy?"

"At *camp*!" Nico screamed. "And he isn't a baby!"

Amphithemis scrunched up his eyebrows. "That is *impossible*. Zeus ordered me to protect the child! It is my sacred duty!"

Nico was at a loss. "Amphithemis, he's grown-up. He's *been* grown-up for thousands of years! He's the director of a camp for demigods."

The centaur shook his head. "No. No, he isn't."

"I don't know what else to tell you. I literally *just* saw him a few days ago, and he's very much *not* a child."

"I don't understand," Amphithemis said, and he grabbed his own horns, then began to pull on them. "What you are saying makes no sense."

"I'm sorry," said Nico, full of pity for Amphithemis, who was on a fool's errand and didn't even know it. "What you're saying makes no sense to me, either."

Amphithemis looked like he was about to burst into tears. "But I . . . But Zeus said . . . and I–" He fell to his knees in despair.

Nico rose. This was wrong. It felt so cruel. But he also didn't understand it. Before, when Nyx and Epiales had crafted Nico's nightmares, they'd used his existing memories. Yet all this was *new*. He had never met Amphithemis before. So why send him these images? What was Nyx trying to do?

He approached the centaur. "Hey," Nico said, his hands open

in front of him. "I'm sorry. I ran because I was scared. But I'm not scared of *you*. It's just the situation that frightened me."

"Did I fail?" Amphithemis sobbed. "Did I fail the child?"

"No," said Nico. "You didn't. Dionysus is healthy and happy now."

Well, Nico wasn't sure the god was all that happy as the camp director, but he didn't think this was the right time to share that observation.

"You promise?"

"I do. He's perfectly fine."

Nico held out his hand to the centaur, who examined it for a moment.

"Okay," he said, and he reached out so Nico could hoist him to his hooves.

And his hand went right through Nico's.

It was a strange sensation, but unfortunately a familiar one, one he'd experienced numerous times here in the Underworld and even a few times aboveground.

It was the feeling of a soul passing through a body.

Nico yelped and jerked his hand back, which only upset Amphithemis more. "You said you weren't afraid of me!" he bellowed. "That was clearly a lie!"

Many things dawned on Nico at once.

Amphithemis was dead. Completely and utterly dead, and yet he was the most mortal-looking soul Nico had ever seen.

Nico was not dreaming. This was real. *Very* real.

And Amphithemis was . . .

No. Even thinking it seemed impossible. But then the centaur's eyes flashed red once again, and a look of righteous anger passed over his face.

"The child," said Amphithemis. "Where is he?"

Nico remained still. "He's not here."

The centaur tilted his head to the side. "Who are *you*? Do you know where the child is?"

It finally came together. Amphithemis was a soul obsessed with a task he could not complete, one he had died without fulfilling, and now he was repeating that obsession here in Tartarus in a never-ending cycle.

"I need to find him," said Amphithemis, spinning in circles. He stilled, then focused his bloodred eyes on Nico. "You have him, don't you? Give him back!"

The centaur screamed and leaped at Nico, and as the demigod dove out of the way, he knew the truth for certain.

Amphithemis was a mania.

CHAPTER 34

As Will struggled against the birds' sharp talons, trying to free himself, his mind went back to the hypothetical brochure.

See Tartarus from up high! Complimentary transportation via Stymphalian birds!

He tried to twist around to catch a glimpse of Gorgyra's white canoe, desperate to know if Nico was okay, but the birds dipped and guided him farther away. Below him, the landscape was covered in zits, craggy hills, and shadows of creatures Will couldn't identify.

"Okay, this has been fun!" he called out. "Love the view! You can let me down now!"

He swung an arm out and smacked one of the pigeons, which caused it to let go. The flock began to veer slightly to the right. Without any hesitation, he whacked another bird, and as he'd predicted, the flock moved even more sharply to the right.

He was *steering* them.

Will imagined himself as a captain of the sky as he hit pigeons off his right shoulder until he'd guided them back in the direction he'd come from. But more Stymphalian birds flew in, grabbing at his T-shirt, and he heard a tearing sound.

"Oh, no," he said. "Please don't—"

A few hundred yards short of his goal—he could see his back-pack sitting near a large rock—Will's shirt ripped completely off. The birds flew away with its remains without missing a wingbeat.

Will plummeted, the ground rushing up to meet him. *Love how much falling I'm doing on this quest!* Will thought. *Maybe I should teach a class at Camp Half-Blood on how to fall.*

Oh, how he missed Camp Half-Blood.

Thankfully, his fall was broken by a large monster zit. He bounced off it and hit another enormous pod like he was inside a pinball machine. Yet his relief over not plunging to his death was quickly negated by what tore itself out of the first pimple he'd crashed into.

Will saw a human hand claw through the membrane, followed by the snarling head of a *dog*.

A *cynocephalus*. Those terrible dog-headed men who'd allied with Octavian *and* Nero. And now here was one with their eyes locked on Will, sharp fangs snapping. If he didn't get out of here *now*, he was certain to become demigod coleslaw.

Yet as he turned and scrambled away, he saw more zits burst. Saw more dog-headed monstrosities rip their way into Tartarus. Saw a cloud of Stymphalian birds heading his way.

He was but one demigod in a *soup* of monsters.

Will heard the cynocephali snarl, and he dove for a nearby boulder, flattening himself against the craggy ground. His heart beat so hard he was certain the monsters would be able to locate him from all the thumping.

He'd made a terrible mistake.

He never should have left Nico's side. Never! How had he let this place get to him so *quickly*? He'd only been here a few minutes before it had put thoughts in his head, just like Percy, Annabeth, and Nico had warned. And now he was in the midst of a disaster, something had found Nico, and Will couldn't do anything about it because dog-headed monstrosities were regenerating all around him.

More of the pods popped.

More creatures slithered to the ground.

More cynocephali growled close by.

Will crawled forward and peeked around the edge of the stone he was hiding behind.

A group of slimy, goo-covered cynocephali sniffed the ground about twenty or thirty yards away. One of them pawed at a regeneration bubble until it ripped open and another member of the pack was spat out.

They were growing in numbers. Will had no weapon and no hope.

He sat up and pressed his back against the stone, then covered his mouth with his hand to mask his breathing. With his other hand, he grabbed Nico's skull ring on its chain. He clutched it tightly.

I'm sorry, Nico, he thought. *I'm sorry I let you down.*

There was a bright flash overhead, followed by a vicious cry.

Will waited for the cynocephali to find him, desperately hoping he would think of a plan before then.

While dodging the spirit's attack, Nico hit the ground hard, knocking the breath out of him, but he couldn't stop moving. He rolled to his feet and unsheathed his Stygian iron sword, but how was it supposed to help? Only Imperial gold could destroy manias. And Amphithemis wasn't even solid. In all his years, Nico had never heard of a mania in the form of a soul.

What was he supposed to do?

Amphithemis let loose a guttural growl. "Give me the child! You cannot keep him from me!"

He swiped at Nico, who ducked and brought his sword down on the centaur's arm.

And unfortunately, his weapon passed straight through the appendage, as expected.

Nico swore.

"Stay still!" Amphithemis ordered.

Nico decided to do just that. Why am I trying to fight him? he thought. He can't even touch me!

He lowered his sword until the tip of it touched the ground. "I don't have the child," said Nico. "There isn't one anymore. Amphithemis, just think for a moment. You're in Tartarus. Only one type of person ends up here."

The centaur actually appeared to consider this for a few seconds before he shook his head angrily. "I won't be fooled by your tricks, demigod," he spat. "If the dead are the only ones here, then why are you standing before me, using your magic so I cannot strike you?"

"Damn," said Nico. "I hadn't thought of that."

Amphithemis raised his arm to bring it down on Nico's head.

The demigod didn't even wince. He knew what was going to happen—Amphithemis's hand would pass through him, and they'd be back at square one.

So he didn't brace himself before Amphithemis raked his nails over Nico's face.

Nico cried out and stumbled back. His hand flew to his cheek, which was wet with blood.

Amphithemis looked just as shocked as Nico. But he soon closed his mouth and squinted at him. "Who are you?" he asked. "Do you know where Dionysus is?"

Nico slowly stuck his hand in his jeans pocket, ran his bloody fingers over the coin's embossing. *I don't know where you are, Will,* he thought, *but I'm going to find you.*

Amphithemis hunched over and held up his hands in an offensive posture. "Don't move," he said. "I don't know who you are, but I know you have the child."

The centaur launched himself toward Nico.

And Nico turned and started sprinting. He gripped the coin tightly as he headed for the ridge in the distance. Amphithemis screamed as he chased him, and Nico knew he wouldn't be able to outrun a centaur. It was only a matter of time before he got caught.

He had no plan. He had a sword that was useless, Will was missing, and they weren't any closer to finding Bob or Nyx.

On the ridge, there was a bright flash, and Nico saw numerous dark shapes converging on a single point.

"Will," he breathed.

It *had* to be him.

He only managed a few more steps before Amphithemis tackled him from behind.

Will heard a splatter from behind the rock.

He nearly jumped in fright. Next there was a sickening tearing sound, then a pained cry. Had the cynocephali found another victim first? Were they eating each other? He fleetingly wondered if this had bought him some time, and he suddenly knew he couldn't just sit there and wait for them to attack first.

He was a demigod! The son of Apollo! And his boyfriend needed him *now.*

There was another grouping of stones a few yards away, so Will pressed his hands and feet into the ground and sprang forward, racing to the rocks and diving behind them. He was overjoyed to see his backpack sitting there, and he quickly pulled out his hoodie and put it on. Then he hoisted the pack onto his shoulders. Another bright flash illuminated his surroundings, so Will poked his head above the rock.

He could not believe what he saw.

An entire pack of cynocephali were fighting a large, translucent, glowing *cat.* The feline hissed and growled at one of the dog-headed monsters, then swiped an enormous paw at it, drawing blood. The big cat leaped onto the cynocephalus and tore at its neck, then jumped out of the way as another member of the pack tried to attack. The cynocephalus on the ground jerked around a bit, and then its body dissolved.

The cat turned in Will's direction, and he was able to see its fierce front fangs, which hung down below its bottom jaw, red with the blood of cynocephali. It had a spotted pattern over its coat, making it look a whole lot like a—

Wait.

Like a saber-toothed tiger.

"Small Bob?" Will said, rising.

The feline's ears perked up, and then it bounded in his direction. For a moment Will believed he'd made yet another terrible mistake, but the cat skidded to a stop in front of him and *shrank.* Seconds later, it was a . . . a cat. A regular house cat with an orange-and-brown calico coat, and it was *purring*, slipping in and out of Will's legs.

"You're kidding me," muttered Will.

He wanted to kneel down and pet it—because it was *evil* not to pet a cat that was being so friendly—but he had a more immediate problem to deal with.

The other cynocephali were closing in.

The lead one lifted its top lip in a growl as it advanced. Will quickly counted, and once he got to twelve, he realized that maybe he had a better use for his time.

"Small Bob," he said. "If you can understand me, I need you to do that saber-toothed-tiger thing again."

The cat purred and rubbed his head on Will's leg.

"Right now would be great!"

Small Bob meowed.

"Any second now!"

The cynocephali circled Will, and the leader lowered its head, preparing to pounce.

"Please don't scratch me," said Will as he bent down and picked up Small Bob. He pressed the cat to his chest with his hand covering Small Bob's other ear, and with his free hand, he put his fingers to his lips.

The lead cynocephalus leaped at him.

And Will let loose an earsplitting whistle.

The cynocephalus dropped in mid-jump and cried out in pain while the flock of Stymphalian birds fell from the air. The rest of the dog-headed men tumbled all over themselves and one another, giving Will what he needed—a temporary advantage. He let go of Small Bob, who jumped out of Will's arms. Before the cat hit the ground, there was a flash, and Will could see the skeletal outline of

Small Bob as he *grew*, his legs and paws and body swelling and elongating until a full-fledged saber-toothed tiger hit the packed earth.

Small Bob wasted no time. He decimated as many cynocephali as he could while they were incapacitated, and Will stood there in shock, watching the spirit-like cat lay waste to nearly a full pack of dog-headed monsters. Blood spilled on the ground, and the dead cynocephali disappeared, sent back to regenerate here in Tartarus again. Small Bob had killed nearly all the creatures when a new sound rang out from down the hill.

A voice.

"Get back here!" it snarled.

And there, darting in between some intact regeneration pods, was Nico and his glowing purple sword.

"Nico!" Will called out, his heart leaping in both excitement and terror. He briefly glanced back to Small Bob, who was fighting three cynocephali at once.

"You seem to be doing just fine here," Will told the cat. "I'm gonna go save my boyfriend!"

Small Bob roared. Will thought it sounded a lot like a roar of encouragement.

Will sprinted down the hill, nearly colliding with Nico moments later. To his dismay, Nico's face was red, and there were three slash marks on his left cheek. Will wanted to sweep his boyfriend up in his arms, shower him with kisses and hugs and healing, but there was no time for that. The creature he'd seen lifting Nico's boat earlier was now at the bottom of the hill and rapidly approaching.

"Where is the child?" it demanded. "WHERE IS HE?"

Nico grasped Will's hand the second he was within reach, but he didn't stop moving. He yanked Will up the incline, practically pulling the son of Apollo's arm out of its socket.

"Ow!" Will cried. "Nico, what's going on? What child is he talking about?"

"Not enough time!" Nico screamed. "Go!"

Will followed Nico up the hill, where, unfortunately, they were met with another chaotic scene. Small Bob had indeed taken out two more cynocephali, but now he was limping. His front left leg was injured. Even worse, though, was the revolting sound of more regeneration pods tearing open, their contents spilling out.

The demigods stumbled to a stop. "Will, what is *happening?*" Nico asked, panting.

At the sound of Nico's voice, Small Bob turned his head. Without any hesitation, he turned back into a calico cat and bounded over to Nico, limping the whole time. He leaped onto Nico's leg and climbed it.

The cat settled on Nico's shoulders.

"I'm sorry, is this—?" said Nico.

"Nico, meet Small Bob," said Will. "Small Bob, you seem to already know who this is."

"Stop!"

Will turned to see an out-of-breath satyr trudging up to them. At least he thought it was a satyr. But why were its horns so big?

"Don't . . . move," panted the creature. "I need . . . to find . . . the child."

Will looked from this newcomer to the one remaining cynocephalus, who examined them all and clearly realized that he was outnumbered. He slunk away to a freshly burst pod and lay down to wait for his packmates to revive.

"I am so lost," said Will. "What child?"

"Will, meet Amphithemis," said Nico. "He's looking for Dionysus."

"Yes!" said Amphithemis, standing upright. "Yes, I'm looking for the child. Have you seen him?"

"Just for the record," said Will, "that didn't help me understand this any better."

Nico, now cradling Small Bob, leaned closer and whispered a single word in his ear. "Mania."

Will's eyes opened wide, and he cautiously watched Amphithemis pace back and forth.

"Zeus will be so angry with me," the newcomer said. "So angry. I cannot disappoint him!"

"Zeus?" Will glanced at Nico. "I'm still confused."

"Not now," Nico said. "What are we supposed to do about *them?*"

Nico jerked his head to the right, and Will's heart sank when he saw that five regenerated cynocephali had appeared. They would soon be ready to mount an attack, and Will still had no idea what to do about the odd standoff they were in. Nico had a sword, at least, but Small Bob was licking his injured paw. Would the cat even be able to fight again? And where were all those awful pigeons?

Will looked back at the pacing satyr creature.

And once the idea came to him, he just *acted.*

"*They* have him," said Will, pointing to the cynocephali. "They took the child."

Nico gripped Will's hand. "What are you doing?"

Will ignored him. "Those dog-headed creatures," he insisted. "They stole Dionysus."

Amphithemis seemed to raise himself higher. "The child . . ." he said softly, and then his face transformed into a portrait of fury. His eyes flashed red and he said, "They have the child, don't they?"

Will nodded. "You have to save him!"

"Will, don't—" Nico began.

But the son of Apollo lunged at Amphithemis. "Go!" he bellowed. "What are you waiting for?"

With a terrible shriek, the satyr creature launched himself at the waiting cynocephali, snarling and biting and slashing with his nails. Will watched as Amphithemis chased the retreating monsters, a swarm of murder pigeons above his head, shouting about a child and Zeus. Soon, they were all just a distant echo.

Will slumped against Nico, resting his head on his boyfriend's shoulder. "Nico, I'm sorry," he said, wasting no time in addressing his regret. "I shouldn't have left you."

Nico pulled away. "Why did you do that?"

"Leave you? Because you were sleeping, and I thought—"

"No, I mean just now. Why did you send Amphithemis after them?" He scratched Small Bob behind the ear. "It's not his fault he's the way he is."

"What are you talking about? I just *saved* us!"

"But now he's going to continue wandering Tartarus *forever*!" said Nico. "His spirit has clearly been trapped down here for millennia."

Will's mouth dropped open. "What was I supposed to do? You told me he was a mania. I thought they were bad!"

Nico sighed. "I mean . . . sometimes, yeah. Like when Reyna's father lost it, and she had to kill him. But it's not like they can help it! I could have . . . I could have—"

"You could have done *what*, Nico?" said Will. "You don't have any Imperial gold. What exactly *were* you planning on doing?"

"I don't know!" said Nico. "I didn't really get a chance to think about it, since you sent him off after a bunch of monsters."

"So why are you mad at *me*?"

"Who said I'm mad?" Nico yelled.

"Well, excuse me for trying to save our lives!" snapped Will.

"I'm sorry, weren't you the one who abandoned me? Under a *boat?*"

The guilt smacked Will in the chest, and he tried to swallow it down deeper. "Look, I'm sorry," he said quickly. "I was trying to—"

"And what exactly could *you* have done?" Nico shot back. "You left me alone and defenseless!"

Nico's eyes filled with tears, and Will's stomach sank. "Nico, I'm sorry!" he said again quickly. "I don't know what came over me. I just . . . I just got this idea in my head. It came so easily, and it was like I couldn't think of anything else." Hot tears poured down his own face. "I thought if I found something that could bring us to Bob, you'd be proud of me. It was so *stupid*, I know. I never should have left you, but I didn't realize that this place had tricked me until I was surrounded and—"

Then he burst into sobs, fear burning through him. He had lost Nico, hadn't he? He'd made a mistake so awful that Nico was going to leave him behind, abandon him in this terrible nightmare, and he *deserved* it, he'd earned it, this was where he was supposed to be, and . . .

Nico put Small Bob on the ground and approached. He wrapped his arms around Will and held him while he wept into Nico's shoulder. Will let it all out until he had basically soaked Nico's bomber jacket with tears and snot.

"I'm sorry," said Nico. "I shouldn't have snapped at you. The truth is, I figured this place had gotten to you and you hadn't *actually* abandoned me."

Will pulled away, sniffled, then wiped his nose with the back of his hand. "I did leave you a Kit Kat bar."

Nico barked a laugh. "You did," he said. "And it was delicious. Thank you."

Nico helped him sit down next to one of the rocks he had hidden behind, and Small Bob came scampering over, leaping into Will's lap. The cat immediately began purring so loud and hard that he kind of felt like a portable massage gun, which Will's sore legs absolutely needed.

While Small Bob got settled, Will told Nico everything that had happened since they'd been separated, including his brief flight on Stymphalian Airlines. "I don't know how you managed alone," he said after catching Nico up. "I was by myself for maybe twenty minutes, and I thought I was never going to survive this place."

"Well, we still have farther to go," said Nico. "So don't get too excited."

"Does it feel weird? To be back here?"

Nico surveyed the lava plains in the distance. "A little," he said, his eyes aglow in the light of the burning magma. "But it's also . . . I don't know, familiar? I spent a lot of time here, so I'm not sure there's much that can surprise me anymore." He chuckled. "Well, I guess I can't say that. I've never seen a mania spirit before."

"I'm sorry I acted without thinking it all the way through," said Will. "You were right—Amphithemis doesn't deserve a fate like that. His soul should be put to rest."

"Well, I don't even know how I would do that," said Nico. "And at least we're safe . . . for the moment." He looked around suspiciously at the nearest regeneration pods.

Will sat forward and rummaged through his knapsack until he grabbed hold of his med kit. After pulling it out, he situated himself so that he was facing Nico's left side, while Small Bob hopped into Nico's lap.

"Let me get those scratches on your cheek," Will said, opening some antiseptic pads to disinfect his hands. "How'd you get them?"

"Ugh," Nico groaned. "Amphithemis."

Will paused. "But I thought you said he was a spirit."

"He was. But he became solid when he was angry at me, hence these."

Will frowned. The boundaries between life and death, solid and incorporeal, seemed so blurry here. Tartarus and the Underworld were not as black-and-white as he'd thought.

He told Nico to hold still, then delicately dabbed at the cuts on his face. Nico jerked a bit at first but mostly cooperated while Will cleaned the gashes. Will gave Nico a sip of nectar, applied ointment to reduce scarring, and held gauze against the area, humming while he did so. It was another melody his mother had composed long, long before Will had been born, but it was a comforting one. As he did so, Nico pressed his cheek into Will's hand and closed his eyes.

They remained like that for a while, the only sounds Small Bob's rhythmic purring and Will's haunting healing melody. Will loved how at peace Nico looked, especially since it was so rare that he ever did. He was always scowling or fretting about something wrong in the world around him. But right here, right now, Nico was in the moment, and it gave Will a sense of accomplishment.

He also hoped Nico believed that Will would never actually abandon him.

Guilt still ate at Will, even as he removed the gauze pad and admired his work. The cuts had mostly healed, but Nico could end up with some light scarring on his cheek. Later he would ask Nico if he wanted them erased, but Will suspected Nico was going to be okay with them. They kind of added a bit of mystique to his face. And it was a nice face, too. Nico's eyes fluttered open, and Will gazed deep into them.

"I'm sorry," he whispered.

Nico shook his head. "No, no, we're not doing that again," he said. "I know you didn't mean to leave. And I know you were still looking out for me, or else you wouldn't have left that Kit Kat behind."

Will leaned against the rock and wiped sweat from his face, a wave of exhaustion pouring over his body. "Okay," he said. "Would you mind if I rested for a moment? Just to recuperate a little before we go on?"

Nico nodded, then looped his arm around Will's shoulder, pulling him in so that Will's head came to rest on Nico's sternum. Small Bob, still curled up in Nico's lap, remained alert. This was hardly a safe place for them to stop, Will knew, and they had to stay vigilant. But for now he let Nico and Small Bob keep watch as Will drifted off to sleep to the calming rise and fall of Nico's breathing.

CHAPTER 35

Nico didn't know what to do or where to go next.

The lava fields churned below him, and the land sloped gently downward. Menoetes had told him to "follow the trail to the left until you reach the swamp," but Nico hadn't found any such trail yet. Nico assumed, though, that they needed to go deeper into Tartarus. Were they headed to the Doors? Was that where Nyx had Bob imprisoned?

The ground shuddered, and Nico waited to see if Will would wake up, but he continued to snooze soundlessly. Had that shudder been Tartarus taking a breath? He hoped the protogenos would remain in slumber—he had no desire to face him like Percy and Annabeth had, especially not since he already had Nyx to contend with.

He wondered if Nyx had sent Amphithemis his way. He hadn't told Will this part, but manias were technically born from her. It was possible that the centaur's arrival had been a coincidence, but Nico couldn't really believe that.

At the same time . . . why? Why would she do that if she was waiting to torment Nico herself? That part didn't make sense. Shouldn't she want him to reach her as quickly as possible?

It was yet another unknown among so many others. He ran his fingers through Will's hair, and his boyfriend stirred.

"Shhh," said Nico. "Go back to sleep. We're safe for now."

Will yawned. "Nah," he said, rubbing his eyes. "I just needed a quick nap."

He sat up slowly, and Small Bob woke up, too, arching his back and yawning. Nico noticed that Will's skin looked a little waxy, like it had in the Underworld prior to them finding Gorgyra. "Eat some ambrosia," said Nico. "Please?"

Will smiled at him. "Your cheek looks better," he said, rummaging in his knapsack. "And the scars might be kinda cute."

Nico rolled his eyes. "Don't start with that."

"Well, it's true!" He munched on an ambrosia square. "It'll also make you more intimidating."

"Now *that* is much more interesting," Nico said. "I could always go for *more* intimidating."

Will scoffed. "Like you need it."

The two of them sat in silence as they watched the spurting, hissing magma. It was Will who vocalized what Nico had just been thinking.

"I don't know what we should do next, Nico," he said. "This place . . . It feels like it goes on forever."

"I know. It's hard to wrap your mind around."

"Now I get what you meant before. About how Tartarus presses down on your spirit. I don't know how else to describe it, but it's . . . it's *heavy*."

Nico nodded. "I know this is hard for you," he said. "Being down here for all this time. But you're doing pretty well, all things considered."

"You think so?"

Nico leaned over and kissed Will's temple. "Yeah, I do."

"I think *we* are doing well," Will said. "You realize we basically just had our first real fight, right?"

Nico raised an eyebrow at Will. "Did we?"

"I don't know. Things felt a little intense before I fell asleep."

"They did," said Nico. "I was annoyed. And scared. And confused."

Will cuddled closer. "Me, too, Nico. And it's like this place is pushing us to that point."

"Yeah. It . . . It does that." He went quiet. "And I think it's worse when you're alone."

Will sighed. "I'm really sorry I left you."

Nico leaned away. "No, no, that's not what I was referring to. I was talking about the time I was here before."

"Oh," said Will, and his face fell. "It's one thing to hear you talk about it and another to actually *experience* it. You were in Tartarus for days! I've been here maybe a few hours, and I'm already losing it."

"No, you're not," said Nico. And then, much quieter: "Not yet, at least."

Will pushed himself up and held out his hand. "Then we keep an eye on each other," he said.

"Deal," said Nico, taking Will's hand.

Will struggled a bit helping Nico up but brushed it off with a dismissive wave. "I'm fine," he said. "Just tired."

"This is me keeping an eye on you," Nico said, smirking. "*Are* you okay?"

Will grimaced. "Better than before, I guess. But . . . I haven't been without the sun this long in my entire life, and it's starting to wear me down."

Nico knelt and pulled the sun-therapy globe from Will's knapsack. "Then maybe it's time for you to recharge!"

Will laughed. "Oh, I'd forgotten about that!"

He took the globe from Nico and switched it on.

Nothing happened.

"Batteries must have drained," he said. "They were new, too." He tossed the globe to Nico, then dug around in his bag for the second extra set he brought. But even after replacing the dead ones, the globe didn't turn on.

Nico frowned. "Maybe it got damaged."

There was a moment when Nico thought that Will was about to panic. But the son of Apollo quickly smiled and put the globe away. "Perhaps we should just get going, then. The sooner we find Bob, the sooner we can leave, right?"

"True," said Nico. "But I . . . don't actually know how to get out of Tartarus yet, though."

"We'll figure it out later." Will turned around and looked out toward the boat. "What should we do with that?"

"Good point," said Nico. "I'm not sure. I guess we're supposed to take it with us? Or maybe come back to it?"

"But we have no idea how far we're going," said Will.

"I know. I just wish I knew the way to Damasen's hut. Where's the swamp?"

There was a loud meow at Nico's feet. He looked down at Small Bob, who yowled again.

"What?" said Nico. "Are you hungry? Thirsty?"

Small Bob meowed, then darted down the hill toward the boat.

"What's he doing?" asked Will.

"I don't know. I don't speak cat."

"Ha-ha. You know that isn't what I meant."

Small Bob stopped just past a couple of craters left behind by exploded regeneration pods. He let loose a long meow, then trotted away again.

"I can't believe I'm going to say this," said Will, "but does he want us to follow him?"

"I've seen stranger things in Tartarus," said Nico. "Let's go."

Nico took Will's hand and led the way as they chased Small Bob. Every so often the calico would pause and look back at the two of them, which pretty much confirmed Will's theory. At the same time, Nico resisted the urge to celebrate. It was possible that Small Bob knew where his companion was, but it was just as possible that the cat was leading them somewhere else. However, it wasn't like Nico and Will had a ton of information to go on.

Moments later, they arrived at Gorgyra's boat. Small Bob stood on his rear legs to try to look inside it, meowed, then sat and whipped his tail back and forth.

"Okay, we made it to the boat," said Will, who was slightly out of breath. "Now what?"

"Well, what did Menoetes say about Damasen's hut?" said Nico. "He told us to follow the troglodytes' shortcut to the swamp."

Will raised an eyebrow. "Maybe he meant that *literally*."

"Huh?"

"Like, the troglodytes' shortcut was the Acheron, right? So, what if we're supposed to literally follow it to the swamp?"

"Oh!" Nico widened his eyes. "Because it might take us to the exact swamp he was talking about."

Will nodded enthusiastically. "I think that's our best option right now."

"Meow!"

Small Bob pawed at the air.

"I think Small Bob just voted yes," said Will.

"Let's do this, then," said Nico, and he lifted the cat into the white canoe. "We'll need to push it into the water together. You up for that?"

Will nodded, but he still looked a little sick.

"Keeping an eye on you," said Nico.

Will swung his knapsack around and took a swig of nectar, which was the last bit left in the first of two bottles. He screwed the lid back on and put it away. Within a few seconds, the color returned to his face, and he took a deep breath.

"I really don't want to go back in that river," he said, "but it's now or never."

Nico smiled. "I'll be right there with you."

That seemed to be enough for Will. He closed the distance between them and planted a kiss on Nico's lips.

"Together," he said.

"Together," Nico whispered.

With Will's help, Nico dragged the boat over to the bank of the Acheron, and the agonized, pain-stricken voices called out to him once more, like he'd tuned in to the universe's worst talk radio show. He ignored them as they both shoved the canoe into the water. Nico gripped the stern as hard as he could, and Will took a deep breath before hopping in.

His boyfriend gasped. Grimaced. Shook his head.

"Hurry, Nico," he grunted. "Get in!"

Nico kept pushing the boat while bracing his legs on the bank, and soon it started moving, floating on the Acheron, while tormented voices called out to Nico, assuring him that he, too, would have his own place among them. He vaulted over the hull and rolled over onto his back, breathing hard.

You are the ghost king, a voice said.

I am, Nico thought.

This is where you belong.

But then Nico raised his head. Looked at the other two passengers. Will, whose face was strained as he reached down with a shaking hand to grab at him. Nico took it, gripped his boyfriend's hand tight, and thought, *No. This is where I belong.*

Then Nico lay there, staring up at the bloodred sky, while the three of them drifted down the River of Pain.

CHAPTER 36

E ventually, the voices of the punished souls became a sort of background noise for Nico. Though they were certainly more insistent, they reminded him of his own internal voice, the one that always told him negative things about himself. What difference did a few thousand more make?

He sat up and gestured for Will to join him. Will, still shaking, quickly crawled over and twisted around so his back was against Nico's chest.

"I'm going to close my eyes," Will said. "This place . . . I don't like looking at it. It's getting more and more intense."

"I got you," said Nico. "Just rest. Recuperate. I'll wake you once Small Bob does anything."

The calico meowed, then hopped into Will's lap.

Will went silent then, only moving as he breathed. Nico suspected that the protective layer over Will's vision—kind of like the Mist, but for demigods in Tartarus—was fading. That wasn't good. It was actually very bad. An unfiltered view of Tartarus felt like beetles invading your mind, and Will was already so weak.

But Nico . . . well, he'd done this before. So he was better able to withstand the signs of a slumbering protogenos as they drifted down a river full of agonized souls.

He finally saw the source of the lava fields far in the distance to their left. There was an erupting volcano spewing magma and black ash up into the blood clouds, and from there, flows of lava spread in every direction, much like . . .

Oh.

He gulped.

The lava flows spread over Tartarus like *veins.*

This was the protogenos's circulatory system, carrying fire and hatred throughout his body.

Nico was thankful that Will was asleep and not observing any of this.

Not yet, said a voice from the river. *But he will. And then you two will give yourselves over to us.*

Nico shook his head. No, they wouldn't. They were here to free Bob from Nyx, and Nico would do anything it took to fulfill this quest and rescue his friend.

But as the Acheron led them away from the lava fields, Nico still wasn't sure if that was true. The final lines of the prophecy jabbed at him. He still hadn't figured out what that part meant. How would he be required to leave something behind of equal value?

It couldn't be Will.

It couldn't be himself.

It just *couldn't.*

The river began to bend toward Nico's right, and that was when the sky started changing. The bloodred sky took on an orange hue, then a yellow one. Mountains rose on either side of the Acheron farther downstream, and they looked horrific, as if they were made of bones and knives, jagged and sharp. As the river approached them, Nico could also see the clusters of regeneration pods spread all over the base and lower half of the mountains. He wondered what kinds of monsters were going to break free from them, but then he was immediately glad he wouldn't be around to find out. On either side of the banks of the river were bone-white Joshua trees, thorny bushes, and the skeletons of cacti.

This was a wasteland within Tartarus. Nico wasn't sure which part of the body this represented, but he wanted to suggest that Tartarus use some moisturizer.

And Will and Small Bob slept on.

The mountains rose ever higher. Nico realized that the Acheron was set to pass between them, and his senses tingled. Something was wrong. *Terribly* wrong. He twisted around as best as he could without waking Will and saw . . .

Shadows.

Shadows were darting between the skeleton trees and cacti.

Something was following them.

Nico tried not to panic. They were on a fairly fast-moving river, and it was also wide enough that most creatures wouldn't be able to access the boat without plunging into the deep waters. But . . .

They were about to lose their advantage.

As the boat floated toward the next pass, the walls of the mountains rose high above them. Nico recalled Percy's stories of facing Scylla and Charybdis with Clarisse La Rue, and he knew that *this* predicament was far worse.

This river was in a narrow canyon, and the Acheron thinned to a width only slightly larger than the boat's. Anything that wanted to ambush them could do so now.

Nico looked back one last time.

He thought he saw something lurking behind the trunk of a cactus.

He wasn't sure, and that was a million times worse.

"Just stay alert," Nico whispered to himself.

His left arm was looped around his boyfriend, his fingers interlocked with Will's. But his right hand now crept toward his sword, and his fingers grazed the pommel.

The boat entered the mountain pass.

Nico kept his eyes on the steep inclines, dancing from one side to the other. There were jet-black scrub plants growing on the sides, as well as bushes with sickly brown leaves shaped like long needles. The stone of the mountains glistened, and Nico was sure that if he reached out and touched it, it would be wet and sticky.

Like an organ.

Like something that was alive.

He pulled out his sword and brought his right arm around so the blade was now resting just over Will's body.

He heard a splash behind him.

It was small. Nothing too large, then. And to Nico's left, a few pebbles rolled down the mountain and softly plunked into the Acheron.

He glanced up, gripped his sword tighter.

The eyes were small and glowed in the yellow hue of Tartarus. There weren't many of them tucked up behind the needle plants, but they were there. Watching. Waiting.

Waiting for what, Nico did not know.

But they didn't attack the boat. The river surged, and they picked up speed, twisting through a sheer gorge before the Acheron sloped down.

Nico held Will tightly as the boat bounced along the river, and then they returned to a slow drift once the Acheron straightened. Behind him, the short rapids petered out until they were a dull roar, and then . . . nothing. The canyon was deathly silent.

"I really hate this," Nico whispered aloud.

The tension was unending. Nico wasn't sure if he was imagining the sound of something entering the water behind him, but he also didn't want to risk taking a look back and leaving himself vulnerable to an attack from either mountainside. Every so often he'd catch a creature hiding in the shadows, its small, beady eyes glowing as it watched them, but nothing made a move.

Meanwhile, Will began to stir in Nico's arms. He wasn't waking but struggling in the midst of a dream. Nico wished he could pull the nightmares from his boyfriend's mind and take them on himself so that Will could sleep restfully. He needed it.

You need it, too, said the river. *Why don't you join us? Why don't you rest forever?*

Nico inhaled deeply, trying to still his racing heart.

Soon, though, the twisting, turning canyon gave way to an opening. An *ending.* The stone walls on either side no longer towered over the boat. It was only once they'd passed the other end of the canyon that Nico allowed himself to look back.

He spied a few sets of glowing eyes peeking around the trunk of one of the bony Joshua trees.

Who were they? What did they want? Why hadn't they attacked?

He glanced down at the dark waters of the river but saw nothing following him.

Nico settled, facing forward, and Will continue to twitch and kick softly in his arms.

The Acheron flowed, and they flowed along with it.

Will woke when Nico started coughing.

Will drifted from his nightmares into consciousness. Nyx or

Tartarus—he wasn't sure which, nor did he think it mattered in the end—had sent him images of Nico, furious. "You left me behind!" Nico had spat, and he'd backed Will to the edge of the cliffs that overlooked Erebos, Hades's palace, and the fields of the dead. "Now it's *your* turn."

And Nico had shoved him.

Over and over again.

Will had believed he was falling, but it was only once his eyes were open and had adjusted to the yellow-green light that he realized he was no longer dreaming. The feeling of Nico trying to hold in a cough had shaken him awake.

He leaned forward and spun around, and that was when Nico doubled over, coughing hard and deep. Before Will could react, before he could comfort his boyfriend, the gases hit *him*, too.

Will's eyes stung, then welled up with tears, blurring the sickly landscape on the banks of the Acheron. His lungs quickly filled with the bitter, thick air, and he started coughing as well. But it didn't help. No matter how hard he coughed, he couldn't expel the foulness.

"Nico," he groaned. "Where are we?"

Small Bob sat on the bow of the ship and meowed at them.

Nico spat a thick blob of phlegm onto the floor of the boat, and it was tinged with brown. "Inside," he slurred. "We're inside."

Will wiped at his eyes and clung to the hull. He peered out into landscape, but everything was coated in a terrible mist, greens and yellows mixed in a sickening cloud. He could see the slick, moist stone ground, but nothing else.

He gazed behind them and thought he saw a pair of glowing eyes, but the mist swallowed up whatever it was.

Inside.

Inside.

Something was too familiar about that. Will crawled forward and lifted Nico's head, which had drooped to his chest.

"Inside *what?*" he choked out. "What's inside, Nico?"

Nico's eyes rolled in his head before they focused on Will.

He had never seen Nico so scared before.

"You know," Nico breathed out. "The mist."

Will was beset with another bout of horrific coughs, and he fell back, his right shoulder hitting the opposite bench and ringing out with a dull pain.

The acidic air clung to his lungs.

It coated his skin.

Which then began to *blister.*

The bumps were small at first. His arms were itchy, but as soon as he brought the fingers of his other hand up to scratch, the lumps became prominent. He cried out and bolted up and saw that Nico's outstretched hand was bubbling with them, too.

It was like . . .

Like they were being digested.

It all came to him then, and it felt as if something had been lifted from Will's consciousness, some sort of gauze that had been there since they'd fallen into Tartarus on this very boat. He had never seen Tartarus for what it truly was. Everything before this had only been what his mind had been able to handle.

Will crawled forward. How had Nico described it?

Tartarus was alive.

Oh.

They were *inside* the old god.

And this . . .

This was his digestive system.

Tears flowed out of Will's eyes. No. No, this couldn't be happening.

This couldn't be true. But his skin ached, his lungs struggled to fill themselves with air, and his eyes burned.

They were being consumed.

Tartarus was *alive*.

Will felt his mind start to crack, to shatter. The pained voices in the river cried out to him, reminding him what a horrible person he was, showing him how many monsters he'd killed, how many campers and demigods he had failed to protect. His fingers were in his bushy hair, pulling it over and over again, and he clamped down on the scream building in his throat.

It was Small Bob who saved him.

Will felt claws in his shirt, on his chest. Small Bob's face loomed in his, and he meowed loudly.

"Huh?" Will tried to grab the cat, but the furball darted off toward the bow of the boat.

"Meow!"

"What is it?" Will struggled toward him.

The cat continued to mewl, so Will pulled himself up and peered over the hull.

The Acheron was widening, but that didn't interest him. The shadows in the mist, however . . . ?

Will squinted. Within the clouds of acid, he could just make out twisting shapes that rose out of the ground. The boat slowly drifted toward them until . . .

He knew.

He knew what they were!

"Nico!" he cried, then coughed. "Nico, I think we're here!"

He turned quickly and Nico groggily pushed himself off the bench he was leaning on. "What?" he said. "What is it?"

Will pointed as Small Bob mewed again. "I know those trees!" he said. For a moment, the name escaped him, but then he was finally able to blurt it out. *"Mangroves!"*

Nico squeezed next to Will and spat again. "Which means . . ."

Small Bob meowed.

"It's a *swamp*," said Will.

Right then Small Bob leaped from the boat and landed on the shore. He kept pace with the boat, yowling loudly.

Nico groaned as he stood slowly. He stepped out of the canoe to follow Small Bob and waded his way to the banks of the Acheron.

The voices hissed and cried out.

You can't leave.

You can't escape what you've done.

Failure.

Join us.

Come join us.

Nico stumbled, and Will spun around. He needed to land the canoe, moor it to something, so he could climb out. All he had to do was stick out an oar and . . .

The oars.

No!

He had completely forgotten them. They must have fallen out when he had flipped the boat to make a shelter for Nico!

Panic filled Will. He looked back at his boyfriend, whose figure was getting smaller on the riverbank.

So Will grabbed the gunwale and he, too, jumped out of the boat, keeping a tight grip as the Acheron's freezing waters ran over his bare skin. He was finally ready to admit that wearing shorts had not been the brightest idea. An unbearable pain ripped through his body, and this time it felt like the souls of the punished were clinging to his legs. The boat was being pulled downstream by the current, but Will held on to it as he took a tentative step toward the bank. Then, with a scream of frustration and agony, he heaved the canoe onto the shore. He dragged it with jerking movements until it rested completely on the mossy ground.

Only then did Will allow himself to collapse.

He lay there, staring up at the diseased sky, his every breath a painful rasp. Thankfully, Nico soon arrived.

"Will," he breathed out. "Will, you're okay."

"I hate this place," said Will, struggling to sit up.

Nico actually laughed. "It's really terrible, isn't it?"

This time, even Will couldn't resist. He fell into laughter with Nico until the son of Hades was doubled over, coughing into Will's chest.

"We look hideous," said Will. "Like Aphrodite's worst nightmares."

Small Bob trotted up to them, and Will was suddenly overcome with emotion at the sight of the cat. He held out his arms, and Small Bob crawled into his lap, where he promptly curled up and started purring.

"Thank you, Small Bob," said Will.

The three of them sat there while Will and Nico caught their breath, which still hurt from the acidic air. But it wasn't as bad as it had been a few minutes ago. By the time Will felt rested enough to rise from the ground, he'd noticed that the greenish-yellow mist only hung lightly in the mangrove forest. He could make out the twisted roots of the trees and now saw there were other plants, too: thin reeds with puffy ends shooting out of the ground; a leafless clump of bushes, their branches covered in thorns. Dark vines with small gray flowers hung from the mangroves.

"So this is the swamp," said Will. "It's sort of . . . peaceful here."

"Peaceful?" Nico spat out some more phlegm. "*Really?*"

"I don't know! In its own way. It's so quiet here. And the longer I'm in the Underworld, the more I have to accept that it's nothing like what I thought it would be."

Nico raised an eyebrow. "What do you mean?"

He gestured to the mangroves. "It's like in Persephone's garden. There's no sunlight at all, and yet these plants all seem to be *thriving.*"

Nico fidgeted in place. "Well . . . yeah. Like I said before, life finds a way, even here."

Will stepped closer to Nico. "I've been kinda closed-minded, haven't I? That bothered you," he said. "And so have a lot of other things I've said, right?"

Nico shrugged. "It's not a big deal."

Will rolled his eyes. "I knew it!"

"I'm fine, I promise."

"Nico," he said, "I can always tell when you're upset, and we're in a place where *being* upset is actually a very bad thing."

Small Bob mewed softly at Will's feet.

"See? Even the cat agrees with me."

Nico looked like he was going to give Will a sarcastic reply, but he pressed his lips together, then sighed. "I just feel like sometimes you haven't been willing to see the Underworld through my eyes," he finally said.

"Through your eyes?"

"I don't know. It's complicated. I get why this place scares you, and it's not like I *love* Tartarus or anything. But the Underworld is . . . well, it's like a second home for me. And it hurts to hear you talk about it like it's evil. Death isn't evil. It's just . . . death."

Will thought about that for a moment. Nico did have a point, and Will's mind immediately offered up a memory: the sight of Persephone, glowing with beauty, amid a garden that was the most picturesque thing Will had ever seen. Her words came back to him, too. *A god or demigod so surrounded by death . . . they seem to appreciate life more than anyone else.*

The Underworld was populated by death. That didn't make it evil.

The troglodytes had helped them. So had Menoetes. And Amphithemis . . . He was more victim than assailant.

There was so much *life* in this place dedicated to the end of it.

Maybe that's what Nico meant. Somehow, the Underworld was like . . . like a spark of hope in the darkness.

"I know it's not all evil," Will said finally, and he took Nico's hand. "It's just . . . I guess it's hard for me to adjust to it all. But . . . I'm trying. Do you believe that?"

Nico examined Will's face. "Yeah," he said, and it warmed Will's heart. "I think you are."

"I still think Tartarus sucks," Will said.

Nico chuckled. "Oh, I agree. It's—"

"MEOW!"

They both looked down to Small Bob, who stood facing the Acheron. He was hissing, his back arched, tail up in the air.

Will's heart flipped in his chest when he followed Small Bob's gaze and saw, on the other side of the river, a pack of cynocephali.

The dog-headed monsters approached slowly, their lips curled up in growls and snarls. The leader—was it the same one Will had narrowly escaped earlier?—paced back and forth, eyeing the river, clearly trying to determine if it should wade in.

"Oh, great," said Will. "They followed us!"

Nico let go of Will's hand and grabbed his sword. "I think I spotted them a few times along the way," he said. "I wasn't entirely sure what was tracking us, but it had to have been them."

Nico's voice didn't sound entirely certain to Will, but it didn't matter. He quietly counted the pack. "Seven," he said. "Seven of them, three of us."

Small Bob hissed again.

Will glanced at Nico, but he didn't seem fazed at all. He had a mischievous grin on his face.

"What is it?" asked Will.

"Our odds aren't seven to three," he said. "Ours are *much* higher."

Nico lifted his sword, blade down, then called out a summoning as he plunged the tip of it into the mossy terrain.

Immediately, the ground rumbled, and Will stepped back as a crevice formed in front of him. A bony hand poked out stiffly from beneath the dirt, and soon more bones appeared as skeletons rose from their resting place, and . . .

No.

Something was off. Will sensed it.

Before Will could stop Nico, before Nico could realize what he'd done, the truth revealed itself.

The bones were not the dead, not in the way Will and Nico understood them. Will knew this as soon as the first creature's head broke free of the earth, then pushed itself upward.

Its head was crested with sharp, serrated bones. Femurs and jawbones, ulnae and humeri. Some were absolutely not human.

When the monster fully emerged, it stood on two legs but otherwise looked like something between a goat and a woolly mammoth, its body covered in shaggy, matted fur, its eyes slitted and red. It roared, a piercing, horrifying sound that made Will clutch his ears, certain his eardrums would rupture if it went on any longer.

The monster spotted the cynocephali across the Acheron. The dog-headed creatures howled and barked, but Will watched in shock as the towering monster easily stepped over the *entire* river, then swung its crested, bone-covered head down and cleaved three of the cynocephali in two with just one movement.

"We should go," whispered Nico, his hand now on Will's elbow.

Will wasn't going to argue. He turned with Nico toward the mangrove forest, and . . .

Another one of the woolly mammoth–goat monsters burst out of the swampy forest. It crushed a tree under its hooves, then blew its rotting breath into the boys' faces with a roar.

"Dam it," said Nico.

CHAPTER 37

Small Bob glowed brightly enough that Nico could see his skeletal outline. Nico watched as the cat elongated, then grew in height, until there was a full-size, snarling, illuminated saber-toothed tiger next to him.

Well, that's the coolest thing I've ever seen, he thought.

Nico glanced back at the first woolly mammoth–goat monster, which was making quick work of the remaining cynocephali. They didn't have much time before the odds would be . . .

He grimaced. It didn't seem accurate to say two-to-three, given that the "two" were enormous monsters Nico had never seen before.

He had to focus, despite the fact that his inner voice was screaming at him. He'd sensed the dead beneath the ground and foolishly raised them, unaware that the bones weren't bodies, but attached to . . . those things? What even were these creatures? What monster collected the dead and fashioned their bones into *weapons*? A part of him wanted to take back everything he'd just said to Will about the Underworld not being evil. Because these things seemed pretty evil to him.

"What do we do?" asked Will. "I don't have any weapons."

"Maybe you can Care Bear–stare them?" Nico suggested.

"Them? Nico, what are these things?"

"I have no idea! I've never seen them before!"

Will hesitated. "I'm not sure I should use my abilities just yet."

The monster took another thundering step toward the demigods, crushing the mangrove roots beneath it.

"How 'bout now, then?!" said Nico.

"What about Nyx? What if I only have enough power for a single shot?"

Nico glared at him. "What? Why would you say that?"

"I'm *exhausted*," said Will. "I don't know what I have in me!"

The first shaggy monster roared, and both boys watched as it opened its mouth—revealing a truly unfair number of teeth—and chomped down on the head of the final cynocephalus.

"Well, that was awful," said Will.

Small Bob growled next to Nico, and he reached down to pet his head. "Kitty, I don't know what strategies you have, but I'm willing to try anything."

The saber-toothed tiger licked Nico's hand, and it was strangely very much like being licked by a house cat, just rougher.

Small Bob crouched as the monster examined them. The woolly mammoth-goat thing lowered its head just like Small Bob had, and the two creatures locked eyes.

Come on, Nico thought. *You can do this, Small Bob.*

The monster made the first move, charging the tiger. Nico grabbed Will and yanked him out of the way.

It was just in time for Small Bob to leap *up*, rather than to the side. He landed on the creature's neck, under the ridge of bones, and bit down on a fleshy spot. The creature cried out in pain, and Nico knew this was his only chance. He sprang forward, his sword ready, and jammed its point into the monster's leg with a quick and deep jab, then ripped it free. The monster immediately stumbled, falling on its bleeding knee, which was when Nico heard the impossible.

"Leave Carl *alone!*"

Nico spun around to find that the other shaggy creature had stepped back over the Acheron.

And had spoken.

"That's unfair!" the monster said. "He's going to get a head start!"

Carl whimpered. (The monster's name is *Carl?* Nico thought.) "Don't worry about me, Bartholomew! I'll *still* beat you this time!"

"You're *cheating*, bro!" Bartholomew yelled back. "You're just jealous my collection is *better!*"

"What in Hades's name is going on?" said Nico, lowering his sword. "You two can *talk?*"

Bartholomew scoffed. "That's a fine question to ask *after* you just stabbed my bro in the knee!"

Small Bob hopped down off the monster's back and slunk over to Nico, his maw soaked with blood. Moments later, he turned back into a calico. A very *confused* calico.

"Nico, I know Tartarus is a bizarre place," said Will, "but please tell me I'm not hallucinating."

"You're not hallucinating," he said.

"Are they *talking?*"

Carl panted on the ground. "I *am* right here," he said. "You don't have to talk about me like I've already died, dude."

Bartholomew plodded over to his friend. "But you're about to," he whined. "Did you plan this? Is this a setup, bro?"

"Oh, so you think I somehow found this guy and brought him to Tartarus so he could resurrect us?" Carl laughed weakly. "Even you know that's absurd, bro."

"Could someone *please* explain to us what's happening?" Nico cried. "What *are* you two?"

Bartholomew lowered himself to sit next to Carl. "We are *aeternae!*" he said. "Surely you've heard of us."

Nico shook his head, but Will was nodding.

"Alexander the Great wrote about you!" said Will excitedly. "You killed a bunch of his men over in India."

Carl grunted. "Gods, he was so *annoying.*"

"Always said he never lost a battle," added Bartholomew. "And yet we easily destroyed, like, half his army without them killing a single one of us."

"I guess *we* don't count," whined the other aeterna.

Bartholomew snuggled closer. "You count to me, bro."

"Bro," said Carl. "That's . . . That's so nice of you to say."

"Am I drunk?" said Will. "I'm drunk. Menoetes put wine in the nectar, I know it."

Nico ignored Will. "I'm . . . I'm still lost. Why are you *mad* at Carl for dying?" Then he turned to Carl. "And why do you seem to *want* to die?"

"Oh, bro, it's so cool!" said Carl. "When we die, that's when we collect bones for our defenses. I'm gonna get so many more bones than Bartholomew, dude!"

"Only because you're getting a head start!" screamed Bartholomew. "Now I gotta go find a battle that will end in my death, dude. Those dog-headed monsters were, like, *way* too easy, man!"

At the exact same time, both Carl and Bartholomew turned their heads to Nico, then looked down at his glowing Stygian iron sword.

"Bro," said Carl.

"*Bro,*" said Bartholomew.

"Oh, no," said Nico. "No, no, no. Don't even think of it."

"It'll be so easy!" said Bartholomew. He then fully lay down and stretched out his neck. "Just make it real quick, and then it will be a fair race."

"I'll still beat you, dude," said Carl.

"As *if*. I'm gonna find so many bones that my *bones* will have bones!"

"Oh, yeah?" Carl coughed, and blood trickled from his mouth. "My bones won't just have bones, but while you're asleep, they're gonna *steal* your bones."

"Bro, I'd like to see you try!"

Will's jaw was practically on the mossy ground. "I think I may never recover from this."

"I'm not going to kill you, Bartholomew," said Nico. "I just thought you were going to kill us. That's the only reason we attacked Carl."

"Bro, it's almost time," said Carl. "I'll see you on the other side!"

"Not fair!" cried Bartholomew, and he raised his head, glaring at Nico. "Come on, dude, just kill me!"

Nico dropped his sword, his face twisted in bewilderment. "This is too much," he said. "I can't *willingly* kill someone like that!"

"Why not? You basically killed Carl. What's one more?"

Will tugged on Nico's bomber jacket. "Let's just go, Nico."

At that, Bartholomew fully rose and roared at both of them. And once again, Nico *really* hated how many teeth were in his mouth.

"You don't have a choice!" the aeterna bellowed. "If you don't kill me, I'll eat you both!"

Which is the exact moment when Nico realized that Small Bob was no longer around. He looked down, then around him, and then he was too late.

Small Bob—now back to saber-toothed-tiger form—leaped from behind and clawed his way up Bartholomew's body. The aeterna roared, but mostly because he was surprised.

There was nothing Nico could do as Small Bob ripped out the monster's throat.

He fell to the ground alongside his friend.

"Bro," Carl groaned. "You did it."

"Just for you, bro," said Bartholomew.

"You're the coolest, dude."

"No, *you* are."

Moments later, there was silence. Small Bob trotted over to Nico, looking quite pleased with himself. He shrank until he was back to a calico cat, then rubbed his blood-covered face on Nico's boots.

The bodies of the two aeternae sank into the earth of Tartarus. The last thing Nico saw of Carl was a lone, bony hand, disappearing into the dirt, its thumb raised in approval.

"Let's never tell anyone about this," said Will.

"Oh, most definitely not," said Nico.

"Meow."

Small Bob began walking toward the swamp, stopping halfway there to turn back and mewl at Nico and Will.

"I think he wants us to follow him," said Nico evenly.

"I think I'm dreaming," said Will. "Did Epiales just give us a fever dream?"

Nico didn't answer. The two of them slowly followed Small Bob into the swamp, leaving Gorgyra's boat behind.

The blisters on their skin had begun to heal, but Nico picked at one of them as they trudged through the muddy undergrowth. Even with no sun in the sky above, the swamp felt just as muggy as a summer afternoon in Manhattan, when all the heat got trapped in between the buildings and cooked the people down below. Sweat poured down Nico's face constantly, running into his eyes and stinging them.

It was clear Will wasn't doing much better. His skin had fewer blisters on it, but it had returned to its previous waxy sheen. Nico had to slow his pace so Will could keep up, and even then Nico wasn't sure how much longer Will was going to last.

The swamp was dense, dark, and oppressive. The greenish haze was gone, but high in the mangrove trees there was a yellowish mist that smelled of sulfur. The water below was a deep brown color, and all sorts of slimy creatures slithered away from them.

Small Bob kept a much faster pace, darting so far ahead that Nico often lost track of the cat until they managed to stumble upon him, and then he'd bound away again. Nico knew he should be more vigilant about what awaited them in the swamp, but exhaustion was beginning to numb his senses, too. He heard things rustling nearby, yet he didn't look. It felt like something was close behind them, but he couldn't bring himself to turn back. He moved forward, one pained step at a time, because if he stopped, if he hesitated, he would simply cease moving entirely.

They walked for hours. Nico soon had to grasp Will's hand and tug him along. They stepped over gnarled roots and trudged through thick mud that threatened to hold them in place. The swamp hummed with a terrible energy. Was it the creatures who hid in the darkness? Or was it a sign that they were trampling through a living thing, an organ or another part of Tartarus that was just as alive as everything else?

"I wish Small Bob could talk," said Will, breaking the long silence. "So he could tell us how much farther we have to go."

"You're doing well," said Nico. "Every step we take brings us closer to Bob."

"How come those boneheaded weirdos could talk but not Small Bob?" Will said, continuing as if Nico hadn't spoken. "Like, where's the justice in that?"

Nico chuckled. "Yeah, that does seem pretty unfair."

Will started to say something, but he snapped his mouth shut.

"What is it?" asked Nico.

He squeezed Nico's hand weakly. "I love you, Nico," he said, and his voice shook on Nico's name.

Tears sprang to Nico's eyes. He could hear the pain in Will's voice. "I love you, too."

"I don't mean to get sappy in the middle of the most cursed swamp in the whole universe."

"You totally do."

Will nodded. "I one hundred percent do," he said. "I have to."

Nico tugged him forward again. "Why?"

Will hesitated, then said, "Because I can feel it all slipping away."

Nico froze, and Will's boots sloshed in the wet mud. "What?"

"I don't know how else to describe it," he said, his lips moving slowly. "It's like . . . like who I am, and what I've done . . . it's hard to remember."

Nico could feel his own exhaustion pulling at his bones, beckoning him to remain still, to drop to the ground.

But he couldn't give in to it. Not after all this. Not with Will in this state.

"Come on," said Nico. "We have to keep going."

Small Bob meowed from the twisted roots of a nearby mangrove, and Nico guided Will in that direction.

"I can't say I'm going through what you are," Nico said. "But think about what Percy and Annabeth told us. We have to keep reminding each other of our lives before. That's how we're going to survive this, Will."

"Before?" Will groaned. "I can't grab on to any one thing. It's all a soup in my mind."

"Then let me remind you," said Nico. "Or we can talk about the stories we shared with Gorgyra."

"Gorgyra." Will said her name sleepily. "Her dress was weird."

"It was," said Nico, smiling.

"It was full of voices."

"Don't think about those. Think about what we told each other."

"They said I belonged with them," said Will. "That I was lonely, even with you."

Nico's heart sank. "What?"

"Not all the time, Nico," said Will, shooting him a sad look. "Just sometimes. When I'm not sure if you've let me in."

Nico didn't slow down, even though he wanted to, even though he needed to know what Will meant. But . . . he already knew, didn't he? As much as this trip had revealed some of Will's uncomfortable thoughts about the Underworld and the darkness in Nico, it had also revealed that Nico often shut Will out. Of his past, of his feelings, of the things that scared him.

"This relationship stuff is hard," said Nico softly.

Will nodded. "Yeah, it is," he said. "I didn't know you had to, like . . . always work on things. But you do, don't you? Every part of it . . . is a *choice*."

Small Bob leaped across the path they were on and jumped over a downed mangrove. Nico helped Will over it first, then hopped up onto the trunk. On the other side, Will had his arms out to help Nico down.

"Will, you're exhausted. Don't worry about me."

"I got you," said Will. "Just like you've had me this whole quest."

Nico eased himself into Will's arms, and soon they were both locked in a tight embrace.

"Is it okay if I tell you I'm scared?" Will said into Nico's shoulder.

"Of course."

"Because I'm scared of what's coming."

Nico pulled away. "Of Nyx?"

"Maybe a little," he said. "But more . . . more the prophecy. And what you'll have to leave behind."

Will's upper lip quivered, and Nico stilled it with a kiss.

"It's not going to be you," he said, "and it's not going to be me."

"You promise?"

Nico hesitated for only a second, then blurted out, "I swear on the Styx."

Will's eyes went wide. "Nico, why did you say that?"

"Because I meant it!"

"But what if that *is* how you have to save Bob? Now you can't!"

Nico shook his head, then pulled Will along once more, desperate to get past this awkward moment. "We'll figure it out when we get to that point."

He could tell Will had more to say, but his boyfriend fell back into silence.

So Nico filled it as they walked. He started with the stories they'd told Gorgyra, even recounting Will's own past to him. His companion didn't speak the entire time, but Nico knew that Will needed this more than he did.

He reminded Will about the infirmary.

The trading of trinkets.

That first kiss.

Nico then shared parts of his childhood he'd never talked about before—good parts. He spoke of Bianca, his Mythomagic set, the Lotus Hotel.

Nico described as much brightness as possible. He imagined

himself as a sun that shone on Will and cast him in warmth. He *had* to, because shadows swallowed them on all sides, gnarled roots threatened to trip them up, and thorny vines hung menacingly from the branches.

They walked.

Finally, Nico couldn't keep talking anymore. His throat was dry, and his tongue was sticking to the roof of his mouth. He so desperately wanted all this to be over.

But the swamp kept going on and on and on. The only sound Nico heard aside from their footsteps was Will's labored breathing.

It was getting worse.

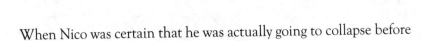

When Nico was certain that he was actually going to collapse before Will did, Small Bob started yowling repeatedly.

Nico's eyelids were drooping again and again, as if they weighed a thousand pounds. His vision was beginning to blur at the edges, too. Sleep threatened to take over his body, but he couldn't stop here. Everything was dark and wet and muddy, and Nico had no idea where he was. What if Small Bob got too far ahead? What if they had doubled back the way they had come?

So when Small Bob's cries reached Nico's ears, he let go of Will's hand, then began to lightly slap his own cheeks. "Stay awake, Nico," he said. "Stay awake."

"Is that Small Bob?" said Will. "Or is there some sort of cat monster calling out to us, announcing that we're about to be its next meal?"

Nico walked toward the sound of Small Bob and found him perched on an enormous root. The calico looked up at Nico and purred loudly.

"What is it?" he asked. "What did you find?"

Small Bob turned his head to the side.

The trees were sparser in that direction. Beyond them, there were no more mangrove roots and no more yellow mist.

"Will . . ." Nico said, practically vibrating. "Will, I think we're here."

Small Bob bounded forward, and Nico chased him, dragging a stumbling Will behind him. The trees parted, and Nico gasped as they burst into the clearing.

To his right was an enormous oak. It leaned so far to the left that Nico wasn't sure why it hadn't completely fallen over. He noticed it grew not from the ground but out of a frighteningly large drakon skull.

But there, in the direction the tree pointed, was a hut. It had a strange dome made of green leather and . . . were those bones? Maybe. The dark entryway was on the side facing where they'd exited the swamp, and Nico almost slipped on the mossy rocks as he scrambled toward it. Two large femurs were situated on either side of the door, their top ends stained black.

"Damasen!" Nico called out. "Damasen, we are friends! Are you here?"

He heard Will say something behind him, but Nico didn't stop. He needed this. *They* needed this. After so much pain and suffering, they had to have this win.

Nico skidded to a stop in front of the hut. He tore free his sword, holding it aloft so it would illuminate the darkness, and stepped inside. . . .

His heart dropped to his feet.

Will shuffled up next to him. "Where is he?" he said. "Where is Damasen?"

Nico wanted to cry.

"The hut is empty," he said. "He's gone."

CHAPTER 38

"Gone?" echoed Will. "What do you mean?"

Nico slumped against the doorway. It just seemed so unfair.

"No one has been in here for a long time. He must not have regenerated yet." Nico couldn't keep the defeat out of his voice. "All these monsters we've seen, and somehow, Damasen has taken over a *year* to regenerate?"

"Well, we have shelter, at least," said Will, and he swung his knapsack around. He dug inside and pulled out a box of matches.

Nico watched as Will moved slowly about the room, looking for something to light until he ended up igniting a pile of bones and strips of dried drakon skin in the center of the hut. The flames rose *without* smoke—which Nico didn't know was even possible—and cast an orange-and-yellow glow on Damasen's hut.

It was clear that someone had once lived here. There were rugs spread all over the floor, and near the back, a bunch of sheepskins were heaped up in what must have been a bed for . . . well, a giant. If Nico had curled up at the head, he wouldn't have even been able to see the foot. Damasen had also bolted racks to the walls. Whether they were for hanging weapons or drying food, Nico wasn't sure, because they were empty now.

And the giant wasn't here to answer any questions.

Nico drifted toward Will, who stood next to the fire. Will was transfixed by the flames, his eyes unmoving and focused.

"You okay?" Nico asked.

"I just forgot what this felt like," said Will. "It's not the sun, but . . . it's nice."

As Will appeared to be recharging, Nico felt himself plummeting in the opposite direction.

"I'm tired," he muttered.

"I know," said Will. "Maybe it's finally my turn to take care of you."

"Back to our old roles, eh?" Nico smiled. "My little Night Light."

Will groaned. "We're not starting that now."

"My little Care Bear."

"Please stop."

Nico gave Will a tight hug. "My little sun-therapy globe."

"All right, all right," said Will. "Go get some rest. Now."

"*Yes*, Field Medic Will Solace," said Nico.

He left Will by the fire and made his way over to the back of the hut. His body became heavier and heavier as he walked, and he practically collapsed on the sheepskins. They smelled faintly earthy, but mostly just stale. Another sign that it had been a long, long time since anyone had been here.

He did not drift off to sleep immediately, though, even if his body wanted to. Will's back was to Nico, and his shadowy outline remained still. From this angle, it almost looked as if his boyfriend were aflame.

Nico felt a wave of affection toward him, maybe because the two of them were getting closer to locating Bob. But he also wondered, as sleep finally began to claim him, if it was because Will was *trying*. He wanted to understand Nico, even the parts that seemed difficult or sad. All Nico needed was to be seen and heard by someone he cared for, and Will was making the effort.

Will glowed next to the fire like one of the torches on Erebos.

And it was hard even for Tartarus to stamp out that kind of hope.

Nico dreamed of his mother.

She did not turn into a horrible monster. She did not reveal a mouth full of extremely sharp teeth. (Why did that *always* happen in nightmares?) She did not give him a cryptic message disguised in dream logic.

It was nighttime, and Nico stood next to his mother on a balcony overlooking the canals. She'd convinced a friend to let her and Nico sneak into a lush, unoccupied apartment so they could watch the *festa notturna* on the water below. An enormous floating stage approached, decked out in ribbons and silks, a full orchestra upon it. Flanking it were two smaller barges with singers belting out complex melodies and harmonies.

It was one of his favorite memories of Maria di Angelo.

He couldn't quite see because the stone guardrail came up to Nico's eye level. But then he felt his mother's hands under his armpits, and she lifted him up. "*Stai attento,*" she said as she placed him on top of the railing.

"Bianca!" he cried out. "*Guarda!*" Then he pointed to the floats.

Nico turned, but his sister was not with them.

"*Mamma?*" he said, twisting to the other side. She was not there, either. He was alone on the balcony.

Alone.

The river called out to him.

This is where you belong, it said. *You do not deserve their love.*

And then he felt the hands on his back.

Heard the words in his mother's voice.

"You will never make it back."

She shoved, and Nico fell.

He woke suddenly.

The fire in the center of Damasen's hut was still flickering. It sent shadows dancing along the ceiling, and Nico watched them as he regained his breath.

He sensed warmth nearby and turned his head. He was met with a shock of blond hair and Will's soft snoring.

Nico's heart was racing. A part of him wanted to wake Will and tell him about his dream. It wasn't an impulse Nico was familiar with—he was more accustomed to keeping things to himself. And he also knew that Will absolutely needed to sleep. They *both* did.

So he resolved to talk to Will later, once they'd both gotten some rest. Would it make Nico feel better? He wasn't sure. But if he wanted Will to understand him better, he also had to open up more. It was a two-way street.

He fell asleep again, his hand lightly caressing Will's arm.

He plummeted from the balcony over and over again.

CHAPTER 39

Nico woke to Small Bob licking his cheek.

He opened his eyes slowly, and the calico's face loomed close to his.

"Okay, okay," he said. "I'm up."

He sat as Small Bob scampered away, bouncing over to the still-flickering fire. It didn't seem to have gone down while Nico and Will slept, and yet there was a chill in the air. He glanced down at his boyfriend. Will was clearly in deep sleep—his mouth was open, and there was a small line of drool on the sheepskin. So Nico leaned over, kissed him on the forehead, and decided to let him rest for a while longer.

He took a sheepskin with him and wrapped it around his shoulders. Even with his bomber jacket on under the sheepskin, it was still cold. *Much* colder than it had been when he'd first entered Damasen's hut. Even when he walked over to the fire and stood next to it, he could still see his breath.

It was probably going to get worse.

Nico heard a scuffling sound behind him, and he turned to see Will approaching.

"Go back to sleep," Nico said.

"I'm up," said Will. "Once I'm awake, it's hard for me to fall back asleep."

Nico held out his sheepskin, and Will huddled beneath it.

"You think this cold is Nyx's doing?" Will asked, rubbing his hands together.

Nico nodded. "She must be close," he said. Then: "Which means Bob must be close."

"Should we just find her now? You know, get it over with?"

He raised an eyebrow. "Get it over with?"

Will yawned. "You know what I mean."

In truth, he did. Nico knew that facing Nyx was going to be awful no matter what happened, so he, too, wanted to get it over with.

"Mrrow!"

They both looked up to see the shadowed form of Small Bob in the doorway.

"Well, clearly *he* thinks it's time for us to go," said Nico, reaching for Will's hand. He squeezed it once. "You ready, Will?"

Will squeezed back. "If I'm being honest . . ." he said, then sighed. "No. Not really. But I don't have much of a choice at this point. We're practically on Nyx's doorstep, aren't we?"

Terror fluttered in Nico's heart. He could see himself back there again, beyond the walls of Nyx's home, the Mansion of Night looming and seeing deep into his soul.

He was going to have to return there. He knew it.

"Let's just go," he said, dropping Will's hand and turning from the fire to head toward Small Bob. Will went over to collect his knapsack.

The cat was cleaning himself at the entry to the hut. He looked up at Nico and mewled pitifully.

"I know," said Nico. "I don't want to do this, either."

Small Bob rubbed his head against Nico's boots.

Moments later, Will stood next to Nico, his hand outstretched. In it was a small Ziploc bag full of Golden Oreos, a granola bar, and a banana.

"What's this?" asked Nico.

Will rolled his eyes. "Nico, it's *food*. We still have to eat down here."

"You packed these ahead of time, didn't you?" Nico began to peel the banana. "Seriously, what else do you have in your magic bag?"

Will didn't laugh at that, though. "Not much, actually. I think the batteries I brought fell out somewhere, and there's not much nectar or ambrosia left."

Nico breathed in deep. "Well, we're almost there. Just a little farther to go, and then . . ." He let the thought die, not wanting to speak any outcome aloud.

So he dropped the sheepskin from his shoulders and followed Small Bob as the cat bounded off into the swampy darkness.

For the first few hours (Were they hours? How much time had passed in the mortal world?), the demigods' spirits weren't as dire as Nico had expected. Sleep seemed to have greatly helped Will, who was no longer limping along. The blisters had healed on both their faces and arms, and Nico's mind felt clear for the first time in ages.

After they left the clearing around Damasen's hut, Small Bob led them through a soggy woodland. The air was chilly here, too, and a light dew coated the green and brown grasses that grew in clumps like hair on a giant's head. Though Nico hadn't traveled through a swamp the first time he was in Tartarus, he wondered if this was part of the same forest he'd been in before finding the Mansion of Night.

But he mostly felt disoriented. He had no idea which way they were heading, and he longed to be back in a world with the cardinal directions. Here? It was just *down*.

As they trudged over the uneven ground, Will hummed to himself. It was a lilting melody, and Nico got lost in its rising and falling.

"Another song of your mom's?" Nico asked once Will stopped.

He nodded. "Yeah. This is gonna sound cheesy, but I think I remember Annabeth and Percy saying cheesy stuff helps."

"Lay it on me, Will. I'm your grilled cheese."

He stepped over a thorny rock, then squinted at Nico. "I think your metaphor needs work," he said. "Anyway, it makes me feel like Mom's here with me. Like, I *know* she's not, but whenever things get scary and hard, I hum her songs. And I know she's somewhere, thinking of me."

"Good," said Nico. "Let's have more of that."

"Do you do anything similar?"

Nico hopped up on a fallen tree, then pulled Will over it. "No, not really," he said. "Father's not the sentimental type."

Will was silent for a moment. "I was asking more about your mom."

The comment shocked Nico so much that he misstepped and his foot landed in a pool of freezing-cold muck. He shook off his boot.

"Sorry," said Will softly. "I'm not trying to pry. I'm just curious, since you don't, um, talk about her all that much."

Nico felt a brief flash of irritation, but this time, he pushed past it. Will wasn't being obtuse or rude about Nico's past—he genuinely seemed to want to know more about him.

So Nico smiled at his boyfriend. "It's okay," he said. "It's just that . . . well, I didn't get much time with her before Zeus killed her."

"I'm sorry. I shouldn't have brought—"

Nico held out his arm and stopped Will. "But I do have memories of her."

He told Will about his most recent dream, explaining that the memory at the heart of it made him feel loved. "I sometimes have to remind myself of that," he said. "That people *did* love me when I was younger."

Will seemed to chew that over in his mind. "Because it's harder for you to remember that when things get dark, right?"

He nodded. "Yeah, that's more or less it."

Small Bob meowed at them, as if he was saying, *Stop being sappy and follow along!*

So they continued, doing their best to avoid the sharp, angular stones in the forest, as well as the mysterious puddles of lightly glowing liquid. Will asked more questions. Did Nico's dream bother him? Why did he think Nyx or Epiales changed it the way it did? Did he have other nice memories of his childhood?

"Sure," said Nico. "Some are easier to recall than others. It's hard, though, because sometimes I feel like all of that was so long ago."

"Because of the Lotus Hotel?"

He shook his head. "I don't think that's it. When I started talking to Mr. D about the whole PTSD thing in the summer, he told me it's actually really common for those of us who are dealing with it to feel as if our lives happened to someone else."

"To someone else?"

"It's a way for my mind to protect itself, basically. If it happened to someone else, it's not as painful to me. I don't have to relive things like . . . well, you know."

Will clutched Nico's hand. "You don't have to say it. Let's just stick to positive memories while we're here, okay?"

"Deal," said Nico.

Hand in hand, Nico and Will walked through the forest, trading stories, reminding each other that there was a world above them where they had friends, where they were loved, where they had something to return to.

Nico was thankful for this because it allowed him a temporary distraction from a fact that was creeping into his awareness.

He was certain that something dark and shadowy was following them again.

The landscape changed. Over and over again.

The trees thinned, and a low, cool mist settled over a long plain of brown and sickly-green grass. It reminded Nico of staring at Long Island Sound: the water seemed to go on forever. Yet this plain was motionless, and it slanted downward just enough that he felt like at any moment he might slip and then slide into the deepest part of Tartarus.

Nico pressed on through the grass, following Small Bob. His calves ached first. Then his head. He couldn't even settle into a rhythm that allowed him to mindlessly follow Small Bob. It was as if Tartarus wanted to make sure that any being who dared to traverse his body would be exhausted with every step.

And for Will it was worse.

He lagged behind at times. His natural glow had been extinguished, and he was once again back to looking like he'd been dipped in wax. At one point, Nico ordered him to stop and eat some ambrosia.

That was when they discovered it was the last piece.

"Save it," said Will. "In case something happens."

Nico didn't have the heart to tell Will that something *was* happening, right now.

They walked. The mist dissipated as if Tartarus himself had sighed and blown it away. They were in a clearing in a field, and bumps rose over Nico's flesh.

He knew this place.

Where had he seen it before?

Nico froze as they approached the center of the clearing. The name came to him immediately.

"Akhlys," he whispered.

"Gesundheit," Will said drowsily.

"No, it's a name. Akhlys, the protogenos I saw a while ago," he said. "We've talked about her before, remember? She appeared to me in a dream . . . ?"

"You mean like Nyx?"

"Exactly like her. Nyx is her mother."

Will groaned. "How many children does Nyx have?"

"Quite a few," said Nico, trying not to lose patience with Will's memory lapse. "But this one . . . she doesn't seem to be here."

"Is that good?"

"She's the protogenos of misery and poison."

"Sounds like a yes," said Will. "Well, let's not hang around and wait for her to show up."

Nico looked behind them. He sensed it again—someone was watching them. Still, it was hard for him to locate a source. They were traveling over the body of a protogenos, so they were *always* being watched. What was this, then? Why couldn't he escape it?

Small Bob led them out of the clearing, and the decaying field gave way to a large, dusty flatland. Will started coughing, and a few times, they had to stop while he spat up dirt. But they trudged along, and Nico's whole body seemed to be throbbing in pain. Soon, he'd slowed down to Will's pace, which made Small Bob impatient. He kept darting ahead, meowing, then rushing back to the two of them.

"We're trying!" said Nico after the third time the calico cat yowled at his feet. "I can't really see anything, so we have to move slowly."

"Are you arguing with a cat?" joked Will.

"Maybe," snapped Nico. "What's it to you?"

"Nico . . ." Will said his name softly, a gentle admonishment.

"Sorry. It's getting to me. This place, I mean."

"I know," said Will. "It's like . . . like Tartarus is reaching inside my brain. I can feel something rooting around there, pulling my memories out."

"We can't have much farther to go. We have to be close."

"Do you *know* that?"

Nico didn't answer. Of course he didn't know. But Menoetes had said that Bob was being held near Damasen's hut.

Will stumbled, grabbing Nico's arm to keep himself upright. Nico swayed for a few seconds, then used his free hand to wrench Will up.

"How much farther?" Will asked.

"Let me ask the cat," slurred Nico. "Hey, cat! Where is Bob? Are we there yet?"

Small Bob came bounding back out of the darkness, and he sat at Nico's feet. His purring was so loud that Nico could feel it through the soles of his boots. He looked up and saw . . .

His stomach dropped.

Darkness. Darkness *everywhere*. The dusty plain dropped away in the distance, and it was as if reality blinked out of existence beyond it.

"Nico," said Will. "What's going on?"

"We're here," he said. "Er . . . at least I think we are."

"Where?" Will spun and looked around him. "There's nothing here."

Nico pointed a shaking hand forward. "There."

Will followed the gesture; then he gazed back at Nico. "I don't get it. What are you pointing at?"

And then, as if a terrible maw into eternal nothingness weren't just a few yards away, Will started to walk forward.

"Please don't!" Nico begged, and he lunged forward, grabbing Will's arm and pulling him back. "You can't!"

"What are you *doing*?" Will screamed, and he shook off Nico's hand.

Nico grabbed him again, only to discover that something was revealing itself out of the darkness.

The dirt plain extended ahead in a narrow, sloping trail, and at the end of it was a doorway of black stone. On either side of the trail—nothing.

It was the same path he had traveled the last time he was here.

Except . . . this wasn't the right place. Nico had come out of a thick, dark forest the time he'd found the path to Nyx's home. What was *this*?

"Will, can you see that?" Nico asked. "Please tell me you can see it."

"See what?" said Will, his voice rising in alarm. "I just see . . . dirt. Some grass. The same thing we've been seeing for hours!"

Small Bob darted forward, and Nico watched as the cat negotiated the narrow path easily, then stood next to the stone doorway at the end. He meowed like he was saying, *Well, hurry up, bozos!*

"Will, I need you to trust me," Nico said. "The veil must still be over your eyes."

"The what?" Then Will's eyes widened. "Wait. You mentioned that before, didn't you? That only you could see Tartarus for what it really was?"

"Yes. Exactly. And now I can see the path to the doorway I found the last time I was here."

"But, Nico, I think that veil or Mist or whatever it is . . . It's already burned away. I know what Tartarus is. I *can* see him now for who he is."

Nico scratched at his head. "Then why can't you see the path to Nyx's palace?"

Will shrugged. "Maybe she doesn't want me to see it."

That filled Nico with a whole new dread. Had he gotten Nyx's plan wrong? What if Will had nothing to do with it?

"I dislike every part of this," Nico groaned.

He heard Will sigh beside him. "We're going to have to go down that path, aren't we?"

"Yep."

"A path I can't see."

"That's the one."

"A path that I'm guessing crosses over a dark and evil pit."

"You guessed right."

Will took off his knapsack and handed it to Nico. "Well, if I fall off, I don't want to take what few supplies we have with me."

"Will!" said Nico, glaring. "Don't say that!"

"It's also so I can hold on to the bag as I walk behind you, Nico."

"Oh." He frowned. "Okay, that makes sense."

"I'm not *that* dramatic," Will said, then curled his lips in a smile. "That's your job in this relationship."

"Oh, be quiet," said Nico, but he couldn't help but grin. "Just hold on tight and stay directly behind me, okay?"

"I can do that," said Will.

Nico sure hoped so. He gingerly approached the point where the dirt path extended out over the void. As he got close, Will gently tugged on the bag.

"You okay, Will?" he asked.

Will hesitated. "I can hear the pit. Speaking to me, that is."

"Ignore it. Or at least try."

"It's telling me to jump."

"Well . . . don't?"

Will actually laughed at that. "I have no plans to."

The toe of Nico's boot inched over the edge. For a moment, he wondered if the path was an illusion, if as soon as he took a step forward, he'd plummet into Chaos, dragging Will with him.

"Nico?"

"Just hold on," he said.

One foot in front of the other. That's what he had to focus on. He shook off his nerves and began walking. Each step was intentional and careful, and soon he was firmly above a void that did not end. Nico did his best to steady his shaky knees while crossing this perilous tightrope. He kept his eyes locked on the doorway ahead—if he looked down, he'd probably lose it and pitch over the side from vertigo. He inched closer and closer, and every so often, Will pulled down on the bag to keep his own balance.

As they neared the doorway, Nico saw that it, too, was swirling with darkness. Pinpricks of starlight gleamed through the passage. Then the darkness spun away, and Nico spotted something new beyond it.

"Nico," said Will. "Oh, gods, Nico."

Will could see it, too.

Nico reached for the stone arch of the doorway only to shriek as it gave way and hundreds of black beetles crawled over his hand and up his arm. Oh, gods, he'd forgotten what this place was made of! He jerked back hard, *too* hard, and the backpack crashed into Will. Nico moved with the speed of lightning, whipping around and snatching the front of Will's hoodie as he started to fall backward.

The fabric stretched.

He heard the seams tearing.

"Nico!" Will cried out, and he grabbed Nico's arms for support.

Nico yanked him up and caught him in an embrace, tears pouring down his face. He held Will tight there at the end of the path as the void begged Nico to let go, to give over the son of Apollo.

"I got you," he breathed into Will's ear. "I got you."

After a moment, the two of them turned toward the doorway, and there was no hesitation any longer. They both ran through the arch, and there, on the other side of it, pulsing and shaking, was an enormous regeneration pod. Its fleshy membrane was practically clear, and inside, struggling within a yellowish goo, was Bob the Titan.

CHAPTER 40

Nyx's garden was exactly how Nico remembered it. The opposite of Persephone's garden—something beyond death, beyond rot, beyond life. Every branch of every tree and bush was twisted and gnarled like a bad nightmare, and all of it clicked and chittered with the sound of trillions of swarming insects.

Small Bob let forth an anguished cry and ran to his friend. Nico followed, overwhelmed by the sight of Bob inside one of those disgusting pods. He dropped to his knees at the base of it.

"Bob," he said. "I'm sorry it took me so long."

Nico watched Will approach the pod, his hand outstretched. He laid it gently on the bulging surface and hummed.

Inside, Bob thrashed about, and Will jerked away.

"He's still alive," said Will. "But . . . this isn't like the other pods."

Nico wiped the tears off his face and stood. "No, it's not," he said. "Look." He pointed at the transformation.

Within the regeneration pod, Bob was not just trying to escape. He was *changing*. In one moment, he was Iapetus, his orange jumpsuit in tatters, his wild white hair pulled in every direction. He opened his mouth and screamed at Nico and Will, but they couldn't hear anything.

Then, in the next moment, Iapetus was torn apart.

Will gasped as they both watched. The Titan was nothing more than a soup of flesh and threads, and then he slowly coalesced. His uniform—the one Hades had given him after he'd become Bob— began to stitch itself together. Bob's body formed next, muscles and sinews stretching, and then there he was, his silver hair parted down the middle and softly glowing.

"Bob," said Nico, and he placed his hand on the membrane.

Bob did the same, and for a moment, they made a connection.

You came, he said. *My sun and star.*

Of course I did, Nico replied, unsure what the other part meant. *We shouldn't have left you down here.*

I didn't know if you'd heard me crying out to you.

Nico laughed. *Well, the prophecy was a nice touch. That made it easier.*

Bob startled. *What prophecy?*

Bob pulled his hand back, and Nico heard his cry of pain as he was torn apart and remade into Iapetus. The Titan screamed in fury.

Once he was Bob again, Nico reestablished the connection.

Get me out of here! Bob begged.

Nico unsheathed his sword and stepped back. "Watch out, Will!" he cried, and then he raised his Stygian iron blade and brought it down swiftly on the pulsing membrane of the regeneration pod.

The blow promptly bounced off.

Nico was thrown back by the force, and he landed on his butt. *Hard.*

"You're kidding me!" he screamed. "How is that possible?"

He got up quickly, then thrust the point of his blade at the pod. It was like trying to stab concrete.

"This doesn't make sense," Nico said, lowering his sword to his side. "How?!"

"Let me try," said Will, and he raised both his hands and placed them on the pod. He hummed a low melody, which rose in volume. Will stopped for a moment and glanced at Nico. "You should cover your ears."

Nico complied after sheathing his sword. Even with his ears plugged, he heard the piercing note that rang from Will's mouth.

But still nothing happened.

Bob pressed his agonized face against the membrane. His lips were moving, so Nico placed his own hand back against Bob's.

You need to get out of here! It's dangerous!

We know, Nico replied. *We know Nyx is behind this.*

But Bob was shaking his head. *No, not just her.*

This time, Nico spoke aloud. "It's *not* Nyx?"

"What?" said Will in alarm.

It is, said Bob. *But they're coming. You need to leave.*

Nico backed away from the Titan, his heart racing.

Will was in his face. "What, Nico? What did he say?"

He didn't have time to answer. They felt the rumble beneath their feet, and Nico spun around, trying to locate where it was coming from. The dark, bitter garden stood still, except for the leaves that fell from the trees with each roll of thunder.

"Nico, what's happening?" said Will, panic on his face. "Is that Nyx?"

"He said 'they're coming,' whoever 'they' are," said Nico. "We don't have much time. What are we supposed to do?"

"I don't know! Those other pods . . . I broke them by accident when I used my power. So I don't get why it's not working now!"

"And my sword is Stygian iron. I don't get it, either."

Bob—now as Iapetus—pressed both of his hands against the side of the pod. He was mouthing something to Nico, and Nico rushed forward, slamming his own hands against the membrane.

My sun and star, he said again.

What? said Nico. *What does that mean?*

It must be both of you.

Then the Titan shrieked as he was torn apart again.

Bitter, frustrated tears poured down Nico's face. This couldn't be it. This couldn't be how they lost.

A terrible roar echoed from somewhere in Nyx's garden.

"Nico, what was he saying?" asked Will.

It must be both of you.

Nico pulled his sword from its sheath at his waist, and it glowed. It *hummed.*

There was another roar.

It was *closer.*

"Will, he said it has to be *both* of us," said Nico.

Will hesitated at first, but an epiphany dawned in him, and his eyes went wide. "Together," he said.

He reached out and wrapped his hand around Nico's, the one that clutched the hilt of the sword.

They pointed it at Bob's regeneration pod.

And Will began to sing.

It was his mother's song, the one Nico had first heard earlier in this quest. But this time, as each note left Will's mouth and echoed through Nyx's garden, it illuminated him. Will burned with the brightness of a thousand suns, and that energy passed through Nico, through his Stygian iron blade.

Will sang, and Nico burned. He burned like a red giant, a star ready to explode and engulf all of Nyx's realm.

The blade grew longer until the tip of it pierced the membrane of the pod, and Nico cried out as he sliced downward, sending goo gushing everywhere. As Bob slid out of his fleshy prison, complete with his broom, Nico and Will let go of the sword, which smoked and clattered to the ground.

Bob used his wide broom to push himself to his feet, and he coughed up the nasty goo from the pod. Nico and Small Bob rushed to his side, not caring that their friend's coveralls were dripping with slime. Nico wrapped his arms around Bob's shoulders and squeezed.

"You're free!" he said. "You're free, Bob."

Bob breathed heavily, his whole body shaking. "You listened to me," he said, dropping the broom so he could gather his cat into his arms. "Thank you."

"I'm just sorry we didn't get here sooner."

"What about the other one?"

"What?" Nico pulled back.

Bob pointed.

Nico turned to see Will doubled over, panting. "I'm fine!" he called out, then stood upright. "Just a little tired."

Will's eyes widened as he looked past Nico.

Nico spun around.

It was Nyx, her smoky wings raised in the air and her body swirling with darkness, and Nico could easily imagine that she was wearing the most horrible smile on her void of a face.

"Welcome back, Nico di Angelo," she said. "I've been waiting for you."

She folded her wings . . .

. . . to reveal an army of monsters waiting behind her.

CHAPTER 41

There were chimeras and basilisks.

Cynocephali and telkhines.

Dark pegasi and pit scorpions.

It was like a Tartarus version of "The Twelve Days of Christmas."

Hypnos stepped out from behind Nyx's left wing, and from the other, Nemesis emerged, a sad look on her face.

"Sorry, kid," she said. "Duty calls."

Every monster Nico had ever encountered and more awaited Nyx's command, snarling and yapping, growling and hissing.

All but one of them.

A human-looking person was standing next to one of Nyx's vampire horses. He wore a black uniform with red trim, and his gray hair looked exactly as it had the last time Nico had seen him. And this time, he was *not* a nightmare conjured up by Epiales.

Nico's mouth dropped open. "Dr. Thorn?"

His old vice principal from Westover Hall—his accent still thick, his tone still furious—spat on the ground. "I've waited too long for you," he said. "You are the last demigod who shall escape me."

"No," said Nyx, glancing down at him. "Now is not the time."

But Dr. Thorn didn't listen. He roared in Nico's direction, and then his body began to change.

It all happened so fast. Dr. Thorn's arms and legs became the furry appendages of a lion, and from his rear sprouted an enormous scorpion tail, leathery and brown. He sent numerous missile-like spikes toward Nico, who rolled out of the way just in time.

"Oh, I don't think so," said Nyx.

Nico watched in horror as she pointed a finger at Dr. Thorn. From it, a dark smoke erupted and surrounded the manticore's body, and then . . .

Well, it was like Nyx had encased Dr. Thorn in a black hole. The manticore screamed, "Come *on!* I've been planning this revenge for years!"

Then he folded in on himself and disappeared.

Will helped Nico up. "Who was *that?*" he asked.

"Nico di Angelo," said Nyx, before Nico could answer Will. "You succeeded in bringing me another demigod! The brochures must have worked!"

Nico raised an eyebrow. "The what?"

"The travel brochures!" she said. "The last set of demigods who came through here said I wasn't advertising enough, so Hypnos helped me design some to spread throughout the Underworld!"

Hypnos drifted forward and held out a few leaflets.

Nico took one. Across the front of it were the words SO YOU'RE THINKING OF VISITING TARTARUS . . .

Beneath it was a black rectangle.

"Uh . . . what's this?" said Will, pointing to the cover.

"That's the pit," said Hypnos proudly. "I think it's a rather flattering depiction."

"I think it's ridiculous," said Nemesis. "Mother, those demigods were making *fun* of you."

But Nyx wasn't hearing it. "We should expect a boost in tourism any day now," she said, dismissing Nemesis with a wave. "Just you wait and see."

Nico tossed the brochure aside. "We're not here to visit."

It was as if he hadn't spoken. Nyx examined Will's face, and her dress swirled. "You know, I am glad Nico got you here, son of Apollo. Even though I tried to trick you into falling into Chaos. How do you mortals put it? You're the cherry on top of the Saturday."

Nemesis hid a laugh in a cough. When Nyx glared at her, she shrugged. "Sorry," she said. "You know how weak I get when I'm in Tartarus."

"It's *sundae*," corrected Will. "And you'll regret that I'm here once we escape with Bob."

"Oh, you have no idea what you've set in motion, Will Solace!" said Nyx. "This will make Nico's sacrifice all the more worthy."

This time, Bob arose. "There will be no sacrifice," he said, and Nico could easily imagine him as a Titan. "I will walk out of your realm with these two demigods, and you will leave us alone forevermore."

Nyx laughed, and when she did so, it sent a horrible chill through Nico's body, like his blood had been flash-frozen. The stars in Nyx's dress sparkled, and Nico found his gaze getting lost in her void.

Fight her, Nico told himself. *You can't lose when you're so close to rescuing Bob.*

"You underestimate what I have done," said Nyx. "You do not understand why I have gathered all of my children here."

"You already told me," Nico said through gritted teeth.

Will tugged on the sleeve of Nico's bomber jacket. "Nico, let's just leave. We can't win here."

"Your boyfriend is correct," said Nyx. "There is no winning here for you. Not only are you outnumbered, Nico di Angelo, but you will ultimately choose *not* to fight."

Nyx took a step forward, and Nico's heart raced.

"Impossible," he said. "I would never choose you or this place."

"My darling," said Nyx, and she moved closer, her wings fluttering. "You already have."

Nico's sword was at his feet. He bent down and picked it up; it was still warm to the touch after they'd freed Bob.

He pointed it at Nyx. "No, I have not," he said. "And now I've got a Titan on my side. Just let us go, Nyx. It's the easiest solution."

Nyx rolled her eyes. Well, Nico wasn't quite sure that's what she was doing—he *felt* more than saw it. Still, he could tell she was annoyed, and she waved a hand in his direction.

"Fine, then. Kill the son of Apollo and the Titan."

At her word, the telkhines in the front charged.

The sea demons looked a little silly, what with their dog heads, flipper hands, and flopping rhythm as they galloped toward Nico, Will, and Bob. Nico wondered if they knew that. They certainly didn't inspire the kind of fear Nyx was hoping for. He kept his sword up, not sure which one he'd attack first, and out of the corner of his eyes, he saw Will bringing his finger up to his lips.

Before the telkhines could do any damage at all, Bob stepped forward. He raised his enormous broom high, then swept it to the side. With that one swoop he managed to smack the telkhines so hard that they flew off into Nyx's garden, howling as they sailed through the air.

"You are a bully," Bob said to Nyx. "I won't let you hurt my friends."

Without a word from Nyx, more monsters charged forward. The basilisks slithered over the ground, and Bob stomped on one of them, grinding his heel into the dirt. Small Bob was now a glowing saber-toothed tiger, roaring and hissing, tearing at the throats of telkhines and wolves. Nico cried out as he brought down his Stygian iron blade and chopped a basilisk in two. He turned and watched as Will slammed a large rock into the head of a snapping cynocephalus.

"Behind me!" Nico called to Will. "We have to do it together!"

Will's face broke out in a smile, and he twisted out of the path of a manticore's spines. Nico swiped and slashed as Will started singing. Nico felt the notes vibrate in his sword, and he channeled them through the iron until the blade began to glow purple and hum again.

He stabbed another basilisk as Bob roared and tossed a bloodred pegasus at Nyx. She didn't even flinch. The creature simply disappeared within the void of her dress.

Nico didn't let the disturbing image distract him from the onslaught. He slammed the tip of his blade into the ground. "I am the ghost king!" he cried, and the earth erupted beneath him. A hand clawed at the dirt, and then the dead began to pull themselves up, one after the other. Soon Nyx's army was *very* occupied with the many skeletons that were assaulting them. A rotting human ripped a pit scorpion in half, and Bob used the handle of his broom to impale them both, creating the world's weirdest kebab in the process.

Nico pointed his sword at Nyx and . . .

Smoke rose from the end of it. The purple glow was intact, but it no longer hummed with Will's music.

"Will?"

He turned around to see Will's face twisted in rage. "I'm sick of you tormenting my boyfriend through his dreams!" he cried. "Leave. Him. Alone!"

Before Nico could stop him, a ray of light shot out of Will. It crossed the space between him and Nyx in an instant, and Nico could tell the primordial goddess was genuinely shocked. The beam hit an upper joint on one of her wings and she shrieked loudly. Her wing was singed, and she pulled it tighter to her body.

"I . . . I got her," said Will. .

Then he dropped like a sack of potatoes.

"Will!" Nico sprang forward, but he wasn't quick enough.

Will's head smacked the ground, and he groaned, his eyes fluttering. "Nico," he slurred.

"I'm here," said Nico, cradling Will's head with one hand. "I'm not going anywhere."

"No, you're not," said Nyx, and then, just as before, Nico was lifted into the air. His sword fell out of his right hand, and he thrashed against Nyx's hold.

But it was no use.

"Now," she said, twisting Nico around until he stared into those horrible burning eyes of hers, "are you ready to accept your fate?"

"No!" he screamed. He shut his eyes tightly, but he couldn't get the image of Nyx's non-face out of his thoughts. "There's nothing you could say or do that would make me give up my life!"

He opened his eyes and saw Will's limp body on the ground on his right. To the left he saw Bob thrashing and flailing as he was swarmed by pit scorpions. He turned back to face Nyx, whose very posture was a promise.

She would do anything to force him to stay in Tartarus.

Nico's skin tingled all over. He knew that more dead were about to rise. He hoped they'd be enough to at least distract the goddess.

But nothing happened. Nyx threw back her head in a laugh. "Oh, Nico, you really should have read my brochure," she said, then cackled more. "I mean, it *literally* spells out that there is no greater force of darkness in the world than me. Did you think your paltry trauma and your brooding gothic sensibilities were any match for *this?*" On the last word, her wings extended.

A chariot appeared out of the shadows around Nyx, and her two vampire horses whinnied and reared. From the void that was her body the goddess pulled a whip made of fiercely burning stars. She snapped it toward Bob, and the end of it wrapped around one of his legs. When she yanked it, he flipped over, slamming into the ground.

"I *am* the darkness," she boomed, and Nico felt like he was being screamed at by a black hole. "And you will *never* return to a world you don't belong in."

CHAPTER 42

Nyx squeezed.

Darkness bloomed in Nico's vision, but only for a moment. There was a loud cry somewhere near him, and then he went tumbling through the air. He slammed into the ground and saw bright flashes, but he knew this might be his only chance to escape Nyx. He scrabbled against the earth while gasping for breath, then went straight for Will, who now sat upright, rocking back and forth.

"Will!" he called out, and his boyfriend looked up at him.

"I can hear it," Will said.

There was another crash, and Nico turned back to see an enraged Bob tackling Nyx.

A broom handle was sticking out of her torso.

She yanked it out and tossed Bob aside. "You think you can hurt me, you useless Titan?"

Bob smiled.

And Small Bob leaped from behind and began to claw Nyx's head. The goddess shrieked as she tried to pull off the tiger, and her horses flipped out, bucking and jumping as they, too, screamed.

Nico reached Will and cupped his boyfriend's face in his hands. "Are you okay?"

"I can hear it," he said again, and tears poured down his cheeks as he pointed behind Nico.

Nico spun around, and he cursed himself.

He had forgotten.

There, beyond the monsters, beyond Nyx, beyond Nemesis and Hypnos, was the house.

The Mansion of Night.

Even at this distance, Nico could still sense it. It was alive. It spoke to a part of his mind, deep and buried and afraid.

And unfortunately, Will was transfixed by the ever-moving mansion. "It's alive, isn't it?"

Nico quickly clamped his hand over Will's eyes. "Don't look at it."

But Will pushed him away. "It wants me."

Nico removed his hand and stared deeply into Will's eyes. "Don't let this place get to you," he said. "That's what Nyx wants. She wants me to give myself up, but I made you a promise, Will."

"I can't," said Will, and his body went limp in Nico's arms. "Tartarus has drained me, just like you said it would."

"Then we'll get you out of here. We'll feed you some ambrosia—"

"Only one piece left, remember? Save it for yourself," said Will weakly. He coughed, clutching his chest. "I think this is how the prophecy is fulfilled."

Nico tried to lift Will, but he was like an enormous rag doll.

"No, this is how it has to happen," said Will.

"It's not! Neither one of us is staying here!" Nico reached into his pocket and produced the coin. "This isn't you speaking. It isn't the Will Solace I know. You're a child of Apollo! You would *never* give up this easily!"

Will tried to look past Nico to the horrible house that was calling to them both. But then he locked eyes with Nico and . . . he changed.

He slowly reached into the collar of his hoodie and pulled out his chain. There, dangling on the end of it, was Nico's skull ring.

"We made a promise," said Will softly. "I . . . I remember."

Nico nodded. "*Both* of us get out alive."

"Yes," he said, and then Will came back to him, light returning to his blue irises.

And then: panic.

"Nico," said Will, paling. "Nico, we can't die here. We just *can't.*"

Nico had never been so happy in his whole life. "We won't," he said.

"But what about Bob?"

Nico glanced back to their friend, who was still trying to over-power Nyx. Only this time, Hypnos was at her side, his hand raised, trying to will Bob to sleep. It was clearly a lot harder than he'd anticipated, as his features were twisted in frustration.

And the other monsters . . .

They weren't doing *anything.* They were scattered around Nyx's garden, watching the fight unfold with interest but not moving. Not even Nemesis, who was leaning against a blackened tree, her arms crossed over her chest. She looked exhausted.

Why weren't they attacking Nico and Will, who were easy pickings at this point?

The other shoe hadn't dropped.

What was Nyx planning for them?

"Will," Nico said, standing. "Will, we need to get out of here." He saw his sword lying on the ground and snatched it up.

There was a loud roar behind Nico. They were both shocked to see Bob running toward them.

"We must go!" said the Titan, and Small Bob in calico form bounded at his heels. "This distraction won't last long!"

"Distraction?" said Nico.

Then he smelled it.

Something was burning.

To Nico's great horror, the Mansion of Night was now on fire.

Flames lapped at the eaves of the house, and a nightmarish screaming rose in Nico's mind. It was high and piercing, and he knew it came from the burning insects that made up the foundation.

"How did you do that?" shouted Nico, finally yanking Will upright.

"It wasn't me," said Bob, panting. "Give me the son of Apollo!"

Nico handed Will to Bob, who easily hoisted him on his shoulder.

"Go!" the Titan screamed. "We must escape now, or we will never leave!"

"Say less!" said Nico, and with Small Bob still at his heels, he ran for the stone gate. He glanced back to see Nyx wailing at the bonfire as some of her minions struggled to calm her down. Other monsters shrieked along with her, and a pack of cynocephali clutched their dog ears with their hands.

"I feel like I'm floating," Will said dreamily, pulling Nico's attention back to their escape.

Nico heard Nyx order her army to stop them, but this time he didn't look over his shoulder. Moments later he passed through the dark entryway. The long path over the pit of Chaos seemed even narrower than before, but that was probably because Nico was sprinting across it, desperate to reach the other side and get as far away from this place as possible.

Yet he slowed. Ahead of him, there was an eerie glow at the end of the path. Was something else on fire?

"Go!" Bob shouted from behind. "Do not stop, Nico!"

No, no, something was wrong.

Nico jogged to the end of the path and absolutely *hated* what he saw.

The earlier inconsistency finally made sense. The first time he'd found Nyx's realm, he had stumbled upon it out of a dark and starless forest. The second time, he and Will had discovered it in the middle of a clearing.

And now Nico was standing at the edge of a cliff, looking down upon the convergence of two rivers. One was absolutely the Phlegethon, and it was the source of the unnerving glow. The other, he knew, was the Cocytus.

The River of Lamentation.

The two rivers flowed down toward the pit of Chaos, then smashed into one another about fifty feet from where Nico stood. The sound was horrible: pain and punishment clashing, the heat of the Acheron meeting the frigid waters of the Cocytus and hissing. They slammed against the cliffside, and as they did so Nico could hear the souls trapped in them. Crying out. Begging for respite. Beckoning to Nico to jump in.

"It moves," Nico said softly, and he backed away from the cliff's edge.

Bob set Will down next to Nico, panting. "What . . . did . . . you . . . say?"

"It moves," he repeated. "Nyx's realm. It's never in the same spot in Tartarus. That's why it's so hard to find!"

"That's convenient," groaned Will, whose skin was deathly pale. "Hopefully, we'll never have to find it again."

The four of them stared down at the converging rivers in a collective silence of dread.

"We must go in," Bob said matter-of-factly.

"In *there*?" said Will. "Do we have to?"

"I don't know that we have any other choice," grumbled Nico. "It'll be awful, but not impossible."

"This quest has involved a lot of falling," said Will. "I would like to be on solid ground for the rest of my life after this."

Bob picked up Small Bob and rubbed his face against the cat's head. "I missed you, my friend. Are you ready?"

Small Bob mewed, and for a moment, warmth filled Nico's heart. Here was Bob the Titan, alive and reunited with his friends.

They had done it.

And then Nico was immediately reminded that no, they had *not* in fact completed the quest.

Nyx's furious shriek split the air around them, and Tartarus cracked with thunder.

Fear tore through Nico's body as he watched smoke pour out of the stone archway across the pit, and soon Nyx and her chariot materialized in the endless darkness above the rivers. Her vampire horses pulled her forward, and once they made landfall on the cliff-side, she seamlessly stepped from the dissolving chariot. Her starry whip cracked alongside her, and in her eyes Nico saw . . .

Rage. The rage of dying stars, the rage of the darkest night, the rage of destruction.

"How *dare* you!" she screamed, and her voice shook the very belly of Tartarus. "You think you can hurt me?"

"I don't care what you think or what you do, Nyx," said Bob defiantly. "You will let me and the demigods leave without any more interference."

"After you set fire to my home?" she yelled. With a flick of her wrist, her two vampire horses came forward. "Shade, Shadow, if any of them so much as twitch, devour them."

"Your quarrel is not with us," said Bob. Then he pointed

behind her. "Why don't you ask one of your children what really happened?"

Nico saw that Hypnos and Nemesis had also made the crossing, and they were joined by a third sibling.

The now-regenerated Epiales.

"Don't try to distract me," said Nyx. "You have nowhere to go. I will capture you again, and I will force *all* of you to choose!"

"All this talk of choosing is so *boring*," said Nico, mustering all the strength he had left to appear truly disinterested. "You did all this to force Bob to choose to be a Titan? Give it up, Nyx! You're never going to succeed!"

"He can never stop being Iapetus!" she screeched. "This new name, this new personality . . . it's all a *lie*!"

"She's right, Nico," said Bob.

"What???" said Nico and Will in unison.

"About the first part," he said. "I can never stop being a Titan. It is a piece of my past."

Then Bob—with Small Bob growling at his side—stepped toward Nyx.

"But what Nyx does not know is that it is possible to *change*," he said. "Because she never has. She has spent eternity as the Queen of Darkness, the protogenos of night." He turned to address her directly. "Has it never occurred to you to be anything *different*?"

"Why would I be?" Nyx snarled. "I am perfect as I am. The entirety of existence *requires* me. What would the world be without night?"

"And so you trapped Bob?" yelled Nico over the roar of the clashing rivers. The cliff's edge was way too close for comfort. "Just because you don't want to change doesn't mean everyone else shouldn't either! How does that make any sense?"

"How does it make any sense that no matter what obstacle was thrown at you, you still came here to Tartarus, knowing this was a trap?" countered Nyx.

Nico's stomach flopped like a fish on a hook. "What?"

"You and your boyfriend have known throughout your entire journey that this was a trap," she said. "And yet you still came. You still fought my children when they tried to stop you."

"Hey, you *told* me to do it!" said Epiales, shuffling forward, their appendages pulled close to their body.

"Be *quiet*, child!" barked Nyx.

Epiales shrank back.

"You persisted, Nico," continued Nyx, "because it is in your nature. You are drawn to the darkness. You are drawn to others in pain. It is *all* you know."

Nico swallowed his fear. "It's not all I know," he said, but even he had to admit he didn't sound too convincing.

Nyx lowered her wings and glided forward. Nico instinctively took a step back, then stopped. He looked over his shoulder.

The edge of the cliff was *way* too close.

"As you cower before me," said Nyx, "you know I am right."

"Remember what you told me," said Will, gripping Nico's hand tightly. "Don't listen to her or this place, Nico. We'll find a way out."

"Even if you do, Nico di Angelo isn't leaving," she said. "Isn't that right, my child?"

"I'm not your child." Nico seethed. "My mother is Bianca di Angelo, and she loved me and my sister."

"And where are they now?"

It was like she had slapped him across the face.

Don't give in to her, he thought, and he felt Will squeeze his hand again. *It's what she wants.*

Still, Nico couldn't stop the tear that rolled down his cheek. "They're dead," he said. "They have been for a while."

"And it burns you up inside, doesn't it?"

She moved closer, and Bob took a step in front of Nico.

"No more," he said, and he gritted his teeth. "No. More."

But Nyx ignored him. "I reached out to you through your dreams," she said, speaking directly to Nico. "Do you remember what I told you? What I asked of you?"

"To listen," Nico said. "We figured that out long ago, Nyx. We know you were goading me down here."

She shook her head. "That wasn't all I said."

Then she looked at Will.

He braced himself next to Nico. "What is she talking about?"

Nico had forgotten. He'd never told *anyone* about that part. It seemed like such an inconsequential detail.

He repeated the words from the dream he'd had the night before leaving on this quest, the same words that had come from the mouth of Cupid in the image of Will.

" 'When the time comes, tell me the truth.' "

"Well, Nico?" said Nyx, smiling. "When are you going to tell him the truth? When are you going to tell him that you doubt it all?"

Terror spiked Nico's heart. "What?!"

"Nico, what does she mean?" asked Will in alarm.

"I don't know!" he said.

"Yes, you *do*," said Nyx, her voice slimy. "You know what you feel in your heart. You know you don't belong in the world above. You *never* will."

"She is trying to confuse you as she tried with me," said Bob, still standing his ground in front of Nico. "She tried to torture me into making another decision. But, Nico, she couldn't break me. Do you know why?"

"Why?" said Nico, his pulse racing.

"Because I called out to someone I knew would listen," he said, and he reached down to pet the top of Small Bob's head. "I told Small Bob that one day a boy would come down here looking for me, and that he was to guide you to me. I *knew* you would hear me."

Small Bob meowed, then leaped up and climbed the sleeve of Bob's uniform to sit on his shoulder.

"As long as I live," said Bob, "I will fight for you, Nico di Angelo. Nyx can never have you."

Nyx yawned, then glanced back at her three children. "It's so touching, isn't it?" she said. "They think they can change what I've set in motion."

"It seems futile," said Hypnos. "Shall I put them all to sleep?"

Nyx shook her head. "No. They need to be awake for the last piece."

"I can give them a good nightmare," said Epiales.

Nyx groaned. "I said *no*, Epiales."

The demon grimaced and slunk back again, this time hiding behind Nemesis.

Nico examined her face, but there was no expression on it. Nemesis had helped him before. Why wasn't she doing anything now?

"Just give up, Nyx," said Will. "You and your children will never be able to stop us!"

"Maybe not," said the Queen of Darkness, and her gown swirled about her as she floated backward. Her chariot returned, and two reins appeared and looped around the necks of Shade and Shadow. "But I think Nico's will."

Nico's world spun. "What did you just say?"

"I am the mother," said Nyx. "Haven't you heard? I can create demons of anything I want."

He sensed them before he saw them. It was the same sensation he'd felt on the stairs past the Door of Orpheus. And on the plains overlooking Erebos. He recalled the passage through the stone cliffs as they passed down the Acheron, Will asleep at his feet, all those eyes observing him.

Now shadows moved out from behind Nyx's chariot, and he saw them again.

Those eyes.

They *glowed*.

There were so many of them. Ten? Twenty? He wasn't sure. At first, they looked like little blotches and smudges, like someone had taken a brush with black paint and dabbed it against a canvas. But as they got closer, Nico saw arms. Legs. Spikes. Some had protuberances from their backs; another had tusks jutting from the sides of its mouth; yet another had something like antlers growing from its head, its body long and sleek like an otter.

They approached with jerky, unsure movements, hesitant to be near Nico, and he felt his knees go weak, his stomach pitch downward. He could hear Will next to him, asking him what was going on, but Nico couldn't answer, couldn't do anything but fall to his knees as the shadow creatures snapped at one another, jostled and shoved and snarled, and Nyx seemed to tower over them all.

"Nico," she said, "you should finally meet your children."

CHAPTER 43

"I literally do not understand what's happening," said Will, and he knelt in front of Nico. "What are those? She can't be serious about the whole 'children' thing, can she?"

Nico swayed. *This can't be real.*

But it was.

Bob raised his broom. "I can destroy them in a heartbeat," he said. "Just give me the word, Nico!"

But the son of Hades rose quickly, his hands up. "No!" he cried. "You can't!"

"Why not?" said Will, his eyebrows stitched together in confusion. "Nico, we have to *leave.*"

"You know what they are, don't you?" said Nyx softly, and she cast her gaze down upon the baby demons at her feet.

Nico looked up at her face.

A fragment of a memory struck him then. He had no context, no details—just a gut feeling that he'd seen this before: Maria di Angelo staring at him like this when he was much, much younger.

"Cacodemons," he said.

"Cactus what?" said Will.

"I told you about them," said Nico. "That's what Nyx creates—cacodemons."

"Oh, right," he said. "Her children. Personifications of negative emotions and feelings."

Nico glanced over at Nyx's other children.

Hypnos, who could put anyone to sleep in an instant.

Epiales, who had filled both Nico's and Will's minds with the most horrible of nightmares.

Nemesis, who was obsessed with retribution.

And now . . .

"She made more," said Nico.

"I can see that," said Will.

"From *me*."

Will's mouth dropped open. "I'm sorry, *what?*"

"You knew without me having to tell you," said Nyx. She lowered herself to the ground and contracted until she was just barely taller than Nico. "You knew exactly what they were."

Nico stepped forward, past Bob's objections, to get a better look at the cacodemons that trailed Nyx like she was leading a parade.

"I made one from each terrible, dark part of you," she said, then nodded down at the closest one, the one with gnarled antlers on its head. "Go ahead. Meet your children."

"Nico, *don't*," begged Will. "Let's just leave, okay?"

"No," he said. "No, I can't abandon them."

He stuck out his hand.

The horned cacodemon skittered forward, its pupilless eyes glowing. It pressed its nose into his palm and sniffed him.

And memories flashed in Nico's mind:

Camp Half-Blood. The dining pavilion. Percy. "She wanted you to have this."

The forests outside camp. The pit in his stomach. Jason . . .

Nico jerked back and fell on his butt. The cacodemon skittered away.

He looked up to Nyx, tears in his eyes. "What have you *done?*"

"I sent you visions," she said. "As soon as I realized it was you Bob was trying to reach, I knew I had a chance to communicate with you as well . . . and *encourage* you to accept your true nature."

Another cacodemon approached, this one with a single eye like a Cyclops and paws like a wolf. It licked Nico's fingers.

The lid of the jar. The pom seeds. The loneliness.

"I knew you wouldn't be able to resist the call of your worst memories. That's who you *are*, Nico di Angelo. You are a demigod made up of trauma. Your very *soul* is one of darkness."

A third cacodemon—the one with tusks—pounced and landed at Nico's feet. It rubbed its head against his leg.

Percy smiles at Annabeth. Will stares at Paolo's big biceps.

"You proved my theory right with every step you took toward this place," Nyx crowed. "The second you entered the Underworld, our new children were born."

She knelt and touched each of the cacodemons, naming them as she did so.

"Grief," she said, her hand gracing the demon with the antlers.

"Guilt." That one had legs like a spider, and its touch brought forth images like Nico lashing out at Percy or allowing Octavian to die.

Sadness was a shapeless blob that showed him Maria, Bianca, the Lotus Hotel, and lonely nights in the forest surrounding Camp Half-Blood.

Jealousy was the one with tusks, who reminded Nico of how often he coveted the lives of others.

"Isolation." A cacodemon with one glowing eye sent Nico right back to the jar.

"Shame." A catlike cacodemon with needle-sharp teeth and claws scratched at his leg, and he thought of . . .

Cupid. Cupid and Jason.

There were many others, but Nico couldn't handle any more. A rage built in him. Or was it shame? Shame, because every single trauma had been trotted out before him—quite literally—for all to see? Guilt, because maybe, just maybe, Nyx was right? Or maybe . . .

Maybe his rage came from the fact that she had it all wrong.

Nico pressed his hands against the cliffside, and the ground rumbled. He heard rocks fall behind him and splash into the colliding rivers below.

"Accept it," ordered Nyx. "Accept that you prefer the darkness. You prefer suffering. You *know* it is true! Your own children prove it! Stop denying your nature!"

"No," Nico said simply and without emotion.

He rose. The earth trembled. A bony hand thrust out of a crack in the stone.

"You have no idea who I am," he said.

And then he drew his sword and charged Nyx.

CHAPTER 44

Will watched as Nyx revealed Nico's demons, and he wished his suspicions hadn't been right.

He remembered hearing something on the steps descending from the Door of Orpheus, but like Nico, he had convinced himself that his overactive (and, frankly, terrified) imagination was running wild. But now, staring at the pack of tiny demons as they approached his boyfriend, Will's whole mind was screaming at him.

This felt wrong. Like something he shouldn't be seeing. What Nyx had done to Nico was horrifying! Everyone had their own personal demons and traumatic events in their history, but *this*?

She had made them real.

She had brought them to *life*.

And now Nico didn't even have the choice to keep them to himself.

But Will had no idea what he should *do*. Attack Nyx? Grab Nico and jump into the roaring rivers below? He was generally pretty good at strategy, but he felt completely out of his element here.

"Accept it," said Nyx. "Accept that you prefer the darkness. You prefer suffering. You *know* it is true! Your own children prove it! Stop denying your nature!"

Will looked to Nico, and he watched as his boyfriend's face settled.

He knew that expression.

And he knew what Nico was about to do.

He backed up, and when Nico said "No" to Nyx, Will saw the cracks in the ground appear and begin to spread.

Nico was about to raise the dead.

There was a part of Will that would always be unnerved by this display, but at that moment, as the cacodemons scattered, he felt an immense pride.

Nico was refusing Nyx's manipulation.

He was *fighting back*.

"You have no idea who I am," said Nico.

Will's boyfriend drew his glowing blade in one swift movement, and before Will could do anything, Nico *charged*.

He swung his sword down in front of Shadow, and the horse reared up in shock. When it did, the ground underneath Nyx's vampire horse split open, and the dead *raged* forth.

"Nico's fight invigorates me!" said Bob, pressing an open palm to his chest. "Come, son of Apollo! Let us lay waste to Nyx!"

Will wasn't sure about laying waste to *anyone*—particularly Nyx's children, who were all now backing up and away from their mother rather than defending her against Nico. But as he watched Bob scream, his broom raised in the air, his cat changing back into a saber-toothed tiger, Will was energized, too.

He was the son of Apollo.

He had survived in the Underworld without the sun.

He was one of only four demigods *ever* to travel to Tartarus.

And now here was Nico di Angelo, the boy he'd fallen in love with, fighting to return to the mortal world.

It all came to Will so suddenly then: Nico might have been born to Hades. He might have suffered untold amounts of pain and sorrow. He was at home in darkness.

But that didn't mean that he couldn't choose the alternative.

Will knew that for a fact because Nico burned brightly as he fought Nyx, as he dodged her tendrils of smoke and hacked at her body. There was a ferocity in him, a power and a fury that could scorch the galaxy when he battled for those he cared for.

And he was now using it to fight for *himself.*

Even in the darkest parts of life, there was still . . . light.

Like the plants in Persephone's garden. Like Menoetes's love for Geryon. Like the ingenuity and loyalty of the troglodytes.

And no light was brighter than Nico di Angelo.

But what could Will himself do? He had no weapons; he wasn't good with a bow and arrow; he felt as if there wasn't a drop of power left in him.

Well, maybe he had to come up with his own alternative.

Maybe it was his turn to find a little darkness within.

Will screamed at Nyx, so loud and so fierce that she actually snapped her head in his direction, and Nico's cacodemons fled in terror once more, seeking refuge in the shadows.

"Leave him *alone!*" Will shouted.

And then he ran.

He had no real plan. He just had *anger.*

Will let that rage propel him forward, and he reached inside himself to find darkness. He knew loneliness, like on the nights when he'd stood at the back of a club while his mother performed. He'd experienced fear. He'd felt jealousy.

He was a child of the god Apollo, and so, with all those feelings close to the surface, Will tapped into his father's power and did something he had never done in his life.

He gave his enemy hay fever.

Nyx began to sneeze violently, and she swatted at herself. Soon, mucus poured out of her—well, Nyx didn't have a nose, but the fluid was coming out of *something*.

"What have you done?" she cried out, then sneezed again, sending more snot flying.

"Gross," said Will. "Cover your void when you sneeze, please."

Nyx snarled and let loose a command: "Children, *attack!*"

Will never made it to Nyx.

The first cacodemon—Will couldn't see which one—collided with his right leg, which sent him flying. He smacked into the ground, stars bursting in his vision as the air left his lungs. But soon there was another cacodemon, this one with enormous tusks, and it pounced on his chest and snapped at his face. Will did his best to keep it from biting him, but then there was another, and another, and another. They swarmed him, tearing at his hoodie, and one finally did clamp its jaw over his left hand.

He screamed and flung it off as blood welled to the surface of the bite.

All he could see was the darkness of their bodies.

All he could hear was Nyx laughing.

This was it. He'd failed. He'd failed them all. He was going to . . .

"STOP!"

CHAPTER  45

Nico didn't know if it was going to work, but something Nyx had said triggered the idea.

Your own children prove it.

If Nyx could command the cacodemons she created . . .

He had to try it, too.

Nico held up his free hand toward Will and the swarming cacodemons, then issued the command.

"STOP!"

There was no hesitation. Immediately, every cacodemon froze. Then they turned back to face him.

Nyx roared. "No!" she screamed. "Attack the demigod! Now!"

The cacodemons swiveled between Nyx and Nico.

Then they climbed off Will and scampered over to his boyfriend.

Will clutched his bleeding hand to his chest. "Nico," he said. "You're . . . That's . . . Oh, Apollo, I can't believe this."

The cacodemons stared at Nico, their glowing white eyes open wide, eager for his next command.

"They obey you," Bob said in awe as he reached down and helped Will to his feet.

"They do," said Nico, and he examined them. They all looked slightly different from one another. They were *unique*, even if they seemed to be made of the same swirling darkness as Nyx.

Unique and . . . *his*.

He rose.

He faced Nyx.

The words came from his mouth, from memory.

> "Go forth and find the one who calls out your name;
> Who suffers and despairs for refusing to remain;
> There leave something of equal value behind,
> Or your body and soul no one will ever find."

"I don't care about your silly poetry, child!" Nyx hissed. "Kneel before me and admit I am right. I will encase you in the same prison as Iapetus if I must!"

"No, you won't," said Nico. "This is a quest, and you didn't account for me fulfilling it *my* way."

"A quest?" The air temperature around Nyx dropped. "I do not assign *quests*. This was a trap! One you walked directly into!"

"Yes, and that was my choice," said Nico. "Bob is my *friend*, and I was *always* going to try to save him!"

Will limped to Nico's side, and Nico took his hand.

"Will was always going to come with me."

And then he looked up at Bob's beautiful face and smiled.

"And we would find the third person to be part of our quest."

Small Bob meowed.

"Okay, maybe four," said Nico.

"Do ghost cats count toward quest numbers?" Will asked.

"I don't know. I think Small Bob is the first cat to ever be part of one."

"Stop your *blathering!*" shrieked Nyx. "Children, attack them!"

The cacodemons remained still at Nico's feet.

And so did Nyx's *other* children.

"No," said Nemesis, and she buffed her nails on her motorcycle jacket.

"I'd rather not," said Epiales, shaking their head.

Hypnos yawned. "I don't really see the point."

Nyx swung her whip around her, then cracked it at Nemesis. "You are the goddess of vengeance, child! Will you not fulfill *my* vengeance?"

Nemesis shrugged. "You forget that I am more than that, Mother."

"No, you are *not!*"

Nemesis unzipped her red leather jacket and let it fall to the ground. As she did so, her eyes blazed, and then she *changed.* Seconds later, the spitting image of Zeus towered over Nyx.

"I am also the goddess of *balance,* Nyx!" she cried, her eyes glowing brighter. "Vengeance is about *balance.* There is no retribution without it."

She raised a hand, and out of the shadows, she pulled her *own* whip.

"What *balance* is restored by imprisoning the Titan?"

She cracked the whip, and Nyx actually *flinched.*

"What *balance* is preserved by forcing Nico to remain here? How is it fair for you to take his deepest, darkest fears and traumas and give them *life?*"

Nyx sputtered but was unable to speak.

Nemesis returned to her original form, then spat on the ground. "I am not one to be ordered around," she said. "I only help those who need me, and you *definitely* don't."

"Hypnos!" Nyx screamed. "Send them all into slumber! And you, Epiales, curse them with nightmares!"

The minor god and the demon traded a quick look.

"Nah, I'm good," said Hypnos. "I don't see how that would help."

"You dare defy me?" She glared at Epiales. "And what do *you* have to say for yourself?"

"At least the demigods appreciate my talents," they said, then turned their back on Nyx.

"Aaarrrrggggh!" screamed Nyx, wheeling around to face Nico again. "I don't need them. I will make you choose on my own, Nico!"

"No, you won't, Mother."

Nemesis lashed out with her whip, and it wrapped around Nyx's waist. As she cried out, Hypnos stepped forward.

"You only use me as a weapon," he said. "A tool. You can't see what else I'm capable of." He shook his head. "You won't let me be anything else! Which is why you didn't notice when I set your mansion on fire."

Hypnos raised his right hand in front of his mother's face as she thrashed about, as she shrieked in rage, and then . . .

Nyx slowed.

Her eyes flicked open, closed, open again.

"What are you doing to me?" Nyx said. "I am the goddess of night! You cannot hold me down."

Epiales drifted over to their mother, their appendages spreading out from their body.

"We know we can't," the demon said. "But we can at least buy the demigods and the Titan some time."

"No-o-o!" Nyx screamed, but the word came out sluggishly, as if her mouth was full of tar.

Epiales looked to Nico. "Thank you for helping us realize the truth, too."

"I will get you, Nico," slurred Nyx. "I will force you to choose."

"You misunderstood me, Nyx," said Nico, approaching her. "You keep saying I need to choose the darkness, but *I already have.* I'm not afraid of my past anymore. And you helped me realize that. I can't ever escape from what's happened to me. But I *can* learn to live with it."

Will was so proud he felt like he might erupt like a solar flare.

Nico shook his head at the goddess. "You want me to be controlled by my darkness, just like you thought you could control my . . . my . . ."

He groaned. Yeah, this word was going to be a problem.

"My . . . cacodemons."

Will sighed as he stepped up beside Nico. "The term doesn't exactly trip off the tongue, does it?"

"I think it's cute," said Bob. "Like Small Bob."

Who promptly meowed.

"So this is how I fulfill the prophecy," Nico said to Nyx. "I'm tired of constantly trying to fight my own demons. And now you've given me my answer."

He turned around, and the pack of cacodemons scurried up to Nico, waiting for their next command.

"First of all," he said, kneeling, "I can't keep calling you *cacodemons.* It's the worst. And I would also feel very weird naming you after whatever memory you remind me of."

The cacodemon with the antlers cooed at Nico, then lowered its head to the ground.

"So, a little bit of renaming . . ." he continued. "What if I called you . . . my Cocoa Puffs?"

"Cocoa Puffs?" said Bob.

"They're quite delicious," said Will, and he put his hand on Nico's shoulder. "And it's the perfect name for them."

Nico reached down to the antlered Cocoa Puff, who jerked away at first. Finally, the demon stayed still and let Nico touch it.

It was . . . odd. A *very* odd sensation. Soft, but without any substance. Like somehow, Nico was petting *smoke*. And then images floated up in his conscious mind.

Jason Grace, dead. Leo, dead. Bianca, dead.

This one, the Cocoa Puff of grief, howled softly.

"I have to leave something of equal value behind," said Nico. "And I think it's time I left my demons behind. So, I'm not going to control you, Cocoa Puffs. I am not going to order you around. Nyx granted you life, and I'm giving it back to you. You get to make your own choices now."

The Cocoa Puffs squeaked and growled as they looked at one another.

"I know that's scary," Nico continued. "The scariest thing in the world is that we have to make our own decisions. But you don't deserve to live a life without that option, so . . . I'm setting you free."

The Cocoa Puff with teeth and claws like needles approached next, and Nico scratched it behind the ears.

He stood across from Cupid, and his face burned with shame.

Nyx groaned loudly. "I'll . . . I'll get you, Nico di Angelo," she slurred.

"Go," said Nemesis, pulling her whip tight. "It's only a matter of time before she breaks away from us."

Nico nodded at all three of Nyx's children, then stood. He looked to Will, whose eyes were red with tears, and Bob, who was sniffling.

"Don't be dramatic," said Nico, rolling his eyes. "Let's go."

The four of them moved toward the edge of the cliff, and dread hit Nico once again. They were still *way* too high up.

"I literally forgot we had to jump into that," said Will. "At least the Acheron could heal us a bit, right?"

"Not here," said Bob, shaking his head. "The Cocytus is too potent. It is a river of hopelessness."

"You might be healed," said Nico, "but you'd never move again. The despair would be too great."

Nyx groaned again, and this time it was louder. Nico glanced back at her struggling form and saw that Hypnos and Epiales were doubled over.

"Go!" screamed Nemesis.

Nico gazed down at the rivers. "How exactly are we going to do this?"

"Like this," said Bob, and before either of them could protest, he snatched them all up and clutched them to his chest. A moment later, he leaped off the edge, and Nico couldn't help but scream as they fell down, down, down, and hit the combined waters of the Acheron and the Cocytus.

The currents rushed over him. Nico felt too many things at once: the frigid, icy water on his skin; the screams and lamentations of the dead, those who believed there was no point to existence anymore; the hopelessness; the grief; the overbearing, all-encompassing sadness; the desperate desire to live; the fear that this was it, this was what would finally take him out.

Nico resurfaced and gasped for air, and soon he felt chilled through and through, like he'd become one giant ice cube. Bob moved Nico to one shoulder, even though Nico barely fit there. As his teeth chattered, Nico saw that Will was shivering on Bob's left shoulder. Small Bob clung furiously to his Titan friend's head.

"Would l-l-love t-t-to never d-d-do that-t-t again!" Will stuttered.

"Hold on," said Bob, and a little sob broke out. "This is the hard part."

He was standing upright in a rushing river, and then . . .

He started wading.

His steps splashed in the converging rivers, and he grunted every so often, as if the currents were trying to hold him back. Nico was in awe, for the water *had* to be tormenting Bob continuously, reminding him of all he'd done throughout his long, long life. But the Titan didn't stop. He pressed on, leaning slightly forward to give himself momentum.

Bob strode toward the far bank, each step methodical and precise. He was deep in concentration, tears pouring down his face. Or was that sweat? Both, probably. So Nico leaned over and kissed Bob on the temple.

"We love you, Bob," he said. "Whatever the river is telling you . . . fight it."

Bob smiled. "Thank you, Nico," he said. "But I do not need your assistance. I shall not be sacrificing myself today. I would *very* much like to leave Tartarus and never come back."

With that, he let out a whoop of laughter, and he pushed forward, the currents racing perpendicular to the direction he walked. "I'm free!" he screamed. "I'm free!"

Will was chuckling, too, and it was an infectious sound. Nico didn't even realize until then how much he had missed the sound of his boyfriend laughing.

He had missed a lot of things.

Bob finally lifted his right foot out of the rivers and stepped onto the bank. He nearly fell over as he did, but he steadied himself at the last second, then pulled his other leg from the water. The Titan cried out in joy and quickly set the demigods on the ground. But the success was short-lived.

Because an out-of-breath Nemesis was standing right in front of Nico.

He practically jumped out of his clothing. "Don't do that!" he said. "Like, give a warning or something!"

"No time," she said, her chest rising and falling. "She's free. You need to go now."

Nemesis raised her hand toward upstream and squeezed her eyes shut tight. "I have the power of tychokinesis."

"Tyson chicken?" said Will.

She glared at him. "The ability to shift someone's luck."

"That makes more sense than frozen chicken," he said, grinning.

"Well, you will all need it," she said. "Getting out of here . . . It won't be pleasant. You'll have to ride the Acheron until it circles back to the top of the Underworld."

"We know," said Nico. "But how?"

To Nico's great surprise, a boat rounded the bend upstream. Gorgyra's white canoe.

"Promise me something," said Nemesis, sweat pouring down her face. For a minor god, she looked *awful*, which made Nico remember that she couldn't spend much time in Tartarus. "Promise me you'll never come back to this place."

"Oh, I'm ready to swear that on the Styx," said Will.

"Don't worry," said Nico. "Two trips to Tartarus is two trips too many."

The corner of her mouth turned up. "It's just that . . . well, luck won't be on your side if there is a next time."

And then, just like Nico did when he shadow-traveled, she folded herself into darkness.

Bob reached out and snagged the bow of Gorgyra's boat. "Where did this come from?"

"It's a long story!" said Nico. "But right now, we just need to get in."

Will climbed in first, and Bob and Small Bob hopped in next. The Titan shrank down as he did to fit inside the narrow canoe. Nico finally vaulted over the gunwale. Bob used the handle of his broom to push them off the bank, and the boat began to drift quickly down the rivers.

"Did we do it?" said Will, collapsing against one of the wooden benches. "Did we really escape her?"

No sooner had he finished speaking than Nyx's screech tore through Tartarus.

Nico spun around and looked up at the cliff's edge above them. One smoky tendril snaked over the side. And another. Then the rest of Nyx leaped into the air, plummeted, and slammed down onto the riverbank across from them.

No! he thought.

Nyx spread her wings wide, and the void on her dress grew. The impenetrable darkness swelled and lashed out from her body, and Nico watched in horror as skeletal bushes and stones were sucked up into it.

She had become an enraged black hole, and she was heading right for them.

CHAPTER 46

Nico frantically searched the floor of the boat. "Where are the oars?" he cried out. "Will, do you see them?"

"Nico, I'm really sorry, but I kinda . . . lost them? Back before the swamp."

"We don't need them," said Bob stoically. "We'll be fine."

Nyx roared again, then fell to all fours as the darkness she was creating grew bigger and bigger.

"Are you sure?" Nico shouted. "Because it looks like she's going to absorb us!"

The boat drifted slowly down the river, and Nyx began to crawl forward, screaming at them, her dress devouring all that it touched.

"Yes," said Bob. "She doesn't realize that we are safe."

Nico scowled at first, then realized something he hadn't noticed before.

The river wasn't talking.

He could no longer hear the lamentations of the dead. The punished weren't crying out to him.

"Will," he said. "Will, can you *hear* the river?"

His boyfriend grimaced. "No, not over Nyx."

Nyx swallowed up a chunk of landscape and reached for them.

Nico shook his head. "No, remember before? Even when we were in the boat, we could still hear the voices in the Acheron."

Will's face perked up. "Oh, you're right," he said. "Is it . . . empty? Like, empty of souls?"

"No," said Bob. "You misunderstand the nature of it. It only calls out to you if you let it."

Nico's eyes widened. "What? That doesn't make sense."

Bob looked at him impassively. "It does. You are not worthy of punishment, and you do not despair. At least not anymore."

As the epiphany crept through Nico's mind, he twisted his head around to watch Nyx claw at the riverbank. One of her hands briefly submerged in the gently flowing waters and . . .

A new scream erupted from her, and she jerked back.

Her hand was blistered and smoking.

"NO!" she cried. But she didn't stop coming. She leaped into the river, trying to grasp the stern of the boat. A terrible hiss echoed off the cliff face, and Nyx thrashed wildly. Ultimately, she had to turn around and paddle furiously back toward the shore. She rolled onto the bank, blisters rising on her body, her dress dissipating into wisps of smoke. The stars on her skin flared and then winked out.

"No," she groaned. "Impossible!"

The boat continued to float away from her, but Nico moved to the stern. "You can't enter the River of Pain," he called out to her, "because that is all *you* know."

"I will get you, Nico di Angelo!" she screamed. "I'll capture you and seal you up, and I'll force you to . . . to . . ."

She went quiet as her body, now just a wizened husk, started sinking into the ground. They watched as her still figure became darkness, evaporating into the shadows.

Meanwhile, Gorgyra's boat bobbed peacefully along the surface of the water.

Nyx would not be coming after them again anytime soon.

We're free! Nico thought.

He sat down across from Will, who asked, "Is she *dead?*"

Nico shook his head. "No. She's a goddess, remember? But Bob was right. I didn't get what he meant at first, but . . . she can't enter the Acheron. Gorgyra said that pain is the river we must navigate to get where we want to be. Well, Nyx refuses to accept that, so the river . . . it rejected *her.*"

Just then a loud screech echoed over Tartarus. Nico peered at the cliff on their left and . . .

"Oh, Hades," he said, pointing. "Look!"

Up on the ledge above them, multiple Cocoa Puffs were crying and calling out as they ran along it to keep up with the moving boat.

"What do they want?" asked Will. "Did Nyx send them?"

"I don't know!" said Nico.

"I don't think so," said Bob, and he stood slowly, his hands extended to the sides to keep the boat from tipping over. "But I'm ready to expel them if they try to attack."

The Cocoa Puffs scrambled over one another as the boat continued down the river. They kept pace with the rushing water, chirping and growling as they did so. Nico glanced at the shore on their right to make sure it was empty, and he saw only dead tree trunks and wilted grasses.

But when he looked back at the cliff . . .

It was *shrinking*. No longer did the stone wall tower over them. As the Cocoa Puffs got closer, Nico's heart raced as quickly as they did.

"What should we do?" said Will. "They can't reach us, can they?"

The current picked up speed, so the cacodemons practically rolled down the last bit of the decline to keep up. They snarled and yapped and appeared to be shoving each other aside in an effort to . . .

Oh.

Oh.

"Bob, stop the boat."

The Titan looked down at Nico. "What?"

"Use your broom or whatever," he said. "Please!"

"Nico, what are you doing?" cried Will. "They're going to get us!"

"Please, Bob!" Nico shouted.

Bob raised an eyebrow. Then he lifted his broom, spun it around so the bristles pointed up, and jammed it into the water. The boat swerved to a stop.

Nico turned back to Will. "They're not trying to fight us," he said. "They're trying to *escape.*"

Sure enough, as soon as the cacodemons caught up to them, they began to throw themselves aboard. The boat rocked back and forth as they did so, but Bob kept it steady with his broom. When the last Cocoa Puff leaped in, Nico nodded to Bob, who yanked the broom handle free.

The cacodemons cowered in the bow, shrinking away from Will. They grouped together so closely that they looked like a single blob of darkness with multiple eyes and mouths. Small Bob hissed at the Cocoa Puffs from Bob's shoulders.

"Well," said Will, moving to sit next to Nico. "Now what?"

"They're free to go where they want," said Nico. "That was the whole point of me letting them go. It's just . . . well, I didn't think they'd want to come with *us.*"

Will smiled. "Well, if they're going to be sticking around, then I want you to know that I accept them."

"Thanks," said Nico. "I mean, I don't know that they're *actually* sticking around. Maybe they just want an express ticket out of Tartarus."

"Fair," said Will. "I still like the idea of you having a perpetual band of little demons following you around, though."

"Don't you dare call it cute."

"Nico and the Cocoa Puffs."

"Don't do that, either."

"Sounds like a great power-pop band."

"I swear, Will . . ."

"Catch them opening for Paramore this winter."

Nico gently slugged Will's arm. "Glad to see you're back to being your annoying self."

Will held out his hand, and Nico took it. "Glad to see you didn't give yourself over to Nyx."

"In a way, I feel sorry for her," said Nico. "She's stuck. All she knows is pain. And I get the appeal of constantly holding on to the darkness."

"Nico, you don't have to explain her actions away."

"I'm not. I just think . . . well, it was her way of being in control. She was born of Chaos—*literally*. Her parents are Chaos and Tartarus. Her whole existence is darkness and suffering and death." He swallowed his own grief as his eyes blurred with tears. "I think I relate to that a little too much."

Will scooted close and wrapped Nico in his arms. Finally, Nico let go of the tension he'd been holding and he cried into Will. Cried with relief, cried from fatigue, cried because his life had been so very, very hard.

It was still hard.

But maybe this part . . . Maybe this part could be easier.

Nico curled up in his boyfriend's arms, and Small Bob purred at his feet. Tartarus was quiet around them. Nico wondered if maybe the old god had drifted off to sleep. . . . And then exhaustion began to pull at Nico's own consciousness.

As his eyelids grew heavy, he took one last look around them. A seemingly endless expanse of barren, arid land stretched out in either direction, like they were traveling through a sunless desert split by the river. This time he saw no monsters or creatures, no gods or protogenoi, nothing lurking in the shadows.

Even so, Nico still worried. What if something else awaited them? Could this terrible journey truly be nearing its end? It had been so torturous just to *enter* Tartarus. Surely it wouldn't be easy to leave it.

But they had come so far—too far to fail. Nico clung to that thought—alongside the reformed Titan, his ghost cat, a band of newly born cacodemons, and Will—as the canoe passed silently into darkness.

CHAPTER 47

Will wasn't surprised when Nico fell asleep in his arms. The Acheron—or Cocytus, Will supposed, as he wasn't quite sure which river this was anymore—carried them along smoothly, and the gentle current was lulling. But sleep was proving to be a little more elusive for Will.

It didn't help that there were, like, fifteen blobs of darkness staring at him with glowing eyes.

Nico's Cocoa Puffs (Wow, another great band name, he thought) examined Will. Were they trying to determine if he was safe to be around? It sure felt like that. As the boat traveled through the empty expanse of Tartarus, they watched him vigilantly while occasionally cooing or purring.

This was going to be quite an adjustment.

But so was being around a *Titan*. Will had never met Bob before, and now he was sharing a boat with him.

Oh, and Bob was weeping.

Like, full-on weeping. Tears poured down his face.

"Bob, are you okay?" Will asked.

"I am more than okay," the Titan choked out. "I am free. I'm also thinking of something I once said to some other demigods."

"What was that?"

"I told Percy Jackson and Annabeth Chase that Titans are not meant to change, that we are the same forever. But this . . . this is not true. I am evidence of that. All things can change, if given the opportunity." He smiled. "It is a lot to consider, Will Solace."

Will smiled back. "Do you need anything?"

"No, my demigod friend. You just rest."

Will glanced ahead, and the river continued into the darkness. "Do you think we're actually going to make it to the top of the Underworld?"

"I'll get you back home, Will Solace," Bob said. "You saved me. Now it is time for me to save you."

Nico stirred against his chest. "Yeah," he said. "Let others do the saving, Will."

Will hugged Nico tight. "Shhh, my little ball of darkness," he said. "We don't need your sarcasm right now."

Nico grunted a laugh. "You live for my sarcasm."

"So . . . is this it? Do we just wait until this river leads us back to the entrance?"

"Will, it really *is* okay if you just rest," Nico said. "You don't always have to be saving the world."

"I know, I know. It's just that it seems like after everything we've been through on this quest . . . this part is too easy."

"Well, now you're starting to sound like me." Nico sat up and turned to face Will. "And I get it. I really do. I'm always expecting the worst because . . . well, the worst *always* seems to come for me. I even assumed that for this quest. I was so worried even *before* we entered the Door of Orpheus."

"I know," said Will, and shame burned his face. "And I don't think I made it any easier for you."

Nico raised an eyebrow. "What do you mean?"

"This whole quest got me thinking. About you and me, and how often I thought your darkness was something to be conquered or healed."

Nico's head drooped. "Yeah. I *did* feel that sometimes."

"But now I know that it's not about conquering, or vanquishing, or any of that kind of hero talk. Sometimes it's better to learn to live *with* the darkness."

Will looked to the Cocoa Puffs, who were still watching him nervously.

"I guess I'm going to have to *literally* do that, too."

Nico looked deep in thought for a moment, and then he leaned forward quickly and kissed Will. It was short, but when he pulled away, his face was alight with joy.

"I appreciate you telling me that," said Nico. "But also . . . I like that you *want* to take care of me, Will. I haven't had someone like that in my life since Bianca and Maria, and I'd started to forget what it felt like. Until I met you. I love that you care so much for the people in your life. I don't want you to think I dislike that."

"I don't," Will said. "But maybe I need to do a better job of figuring out *how* to take care of you, rather than assuming you're just like everyone else." He took Nico's hands, which were cool to the touch. "Because you're not like anyone I've ever met."

He pulled Nico close, and this time, they kissed longer. Fuller. They only stopped because Bob's sobbing was now impossible to ignore.

"Are you sure you're okay?" asked Will, looking back at the Titan.

"I am perfectly fine," Bob said, wiping at his face. "I am crying tears of happiness for my sun and my star."

"Do you know what that means?" Will whispered to Nico as he settled back against the rear seat.

Nico cuddled up against him. "Not a clue."

Moments later, the ghost king was fast asleep in Will's arms once more. Bob sniffled softly behind them, and the current carried them all down the river. There were shadows in the distant fields this deep in Tartarus, but if they hid secrets, those secrets never revealed themselves.

Will just drifted along with it all, strange as it was—the reformed Titan on one end of the boat and the shadowy, inky Cocoa Puffs at the other. And the whole being-in-Tartarus thing. And escaping Nyx's control. And . . .

Okay, there was a lot. But this one part here—Nico using Will for warmth *and* as a pillow—nothing felt strange about that.

It was the most fitting part about this whole quest.

They both had plenty to talk about when they returned to the mortal world, and Will felt a sudden jolt of nerves flash through him when he thought about bringing the Cocoa Puffs into Camp Half-Blood. He was certain Chiron would erupt into flames on the spot. Will would have to keep his field-medic kit handy.

For now, Will allowed himself to close his eyes. Bob and Small Bob were watching over them. They were safe. Or at least as safe as two demigods could be in the lowest part of the Underworld, where monsters and demons regenerated.

Before sleep came for him, Will felt an odd softness on top of his right hand. He opened his eyes to see that one of the Cocoa Puffs—the one with a single eye like a Cyclops—had cuddled up against him. It stared at him, and he worried it would dart off like the others. But it merely observed him sleepily until its eye closed, and then it began to snore.

Will had heard love described in so many dramatic, bizarre ways over the years, but no one had described it like this:

It's like drifting down a river of pain and knowing you are safe.

It's like holding a person in your arms and realizing they are an interlocking piece of a puzzle you hadn't known how to assemble.

It's like staring into a dark and treacherous expanse, unsure of what awaits you but finding comfort in the fact that you won't have to face it alone.

It was a son of Apollo falling for a son of Hades.

It was this.

CHAPTER 48

Nico dreamed.

He was in darkness, and he heard his name being called.

Nico. Nico di Angelo.

He knew who it was, and his heart sank. Had Nyx decided to hurt him through his dreams because they'd managed to escape?

He pulled his dream blanket tighter over his head. "I'm sleeping this off," he announced. "Give it up, Nyx!"

"I don't know why you think I'm Nyx," said another familiar voice.

He slowly pried the blanket back.

He was in the Lotus Hotel once more, but . . . no, this was different. It wasn't like the dream that had tormented him all summer. Somehow, this one felt more *real*. The details weren't fuzzy around the edges. The blanket he was wrapped in . . . He ran his fingers over it. He could feel every thread, every fiber that it was made of.

"Nico."

He looked to his left.

Bianca sat next to him in bed, dressed as one of the Hunters of Artemis. She glowed vaguely, as if . . . as if . . .

As if she were a ghost.

"Bianca?" said Nico, kicking off the blanket. "What is this?"

"Calm down, Nico," she said, smiling from ear to ear. "I know you've been through a terribly difficult experience, and that's going to make this harder for you to believe."

She reached over.

She *touched* him.

Her hand was cold, but it was there, her fingertips lightly running over the back of his hand, and it sent goose bumps up and down his skin.

"This is a dream," said Bianca, "but it is also very real."

"I don't understand," said Nico, and his whole body went still.

"You will soon," she said. "An exception was made."

"An exception?" He tried to get out of the bed, but the blanket became tangled with his feet. He tumbled onto the floor, landing so that he faced the leather chair tucked into the corner.

Someone was in it.

Nico backed up until his shoulders hit the mattress, his heart in his throat.

A beautiful woman was sitting in the armchair. She wore a long black skirt that came down to her shins, and there was a veiled black hat on her head.

Even through the veil, he knew those eyes.

He had not seen them in . . .

Years.

Decades.

"*Mamma?*" he uttered, and his voice broke. His *heart* broke.

Maria di Angelo smiled down at him. "*Ciao, caro figliuolo,*" she said. "It's been a long time."

"This isn't funny, Nyx," he said, his voice trembling. "It's never going to work. If anything, you're only going to make me *more* dedicated to resisting you."

Bianca knelt at his side. "This isn't what you think it is."

She extended her hand to show him a Mythomagic figurine on her palm. Zeus. "His lightning bolts do six hundred damage," Bianca said. "He was one of your favorites."

"You loved that game," said Maria, her dark eyes sparkling beneath the veil. "Half the time it was impossible to pull your attention away from it, especially when we moved to the United States."

Nico rose slowly, then looked from Maria to Bianca and back.

"You can't be here," he said. "It's not allowed. You both . . . You both moved on."

Maria nodded. "We did, Nico. I am sorry I was never able to come back to see you before this. It is a regret I had, but . . . where I went, I *had* to let go."

"Where you *went?*" Nico raised an eyebrow at Bianca. "How is she here, then? How are *you* here? Aren't you in Elysium?"

"I am," said Bianca. "But the two of us . . . We were granted one last visit with you."

"What?" said Nico. "Granted by *whom?*"

Maria ignored that question. She stood, and the sight of her was like a crashing wave that swept Nico away. He choked out a sob, then covered his mouth.

Tears spilled from Maria's eyes. "We are not truly here," she said.

"Think of us . . . like an essence. Like the smallest drop of who we once were."

"We are still ourselves," Bianca added, and she crossed over the room to stand next to her mother. *Nico's* mother. "But this cannot last long. It is just for you."

"Just for me?" Nico wiped away his tears. "Why?"

Maria and Bianca did not answer. Instead, they both cast a glance over Nico's shoulder and smiled.

The temperature dropped, and Nico sensed another presence in the room.

He didn't want to turn around. It was Nyx, wasn't it? Or Epiales, or some other nightmare demon or god. They'd found a way into his mind, to torment him more, or . . .

"Turn around, Nico," said Bianca. "This is not what you think it is."

He gulped loudly.

But what if it was?

"You have to let go of that fear," his mother said. "Fear is not always a bad thing, but sometimes it can hold you back."

She stepped forward and placed a ghostly hand on his cheek. "Turn around," she said.

He swallowed his terror and turned.

Hades stood behind him, dressed in a black pin-striped suit. He was holding a wide-brim hat in both hands, rotating it nervously. Despite the fact that he was many feet taller than everyone else in the room, he seemed . . .

Like an embarrassed child.

But wasn't Nico the one in trouble? For defying his father's wishes? For entering Tartarus even though it was forbidden?

"Father," said Nico. "What is this?"

At first, Hades did not speak. His glittering dark eyes jumped from Nico to the floor, then to Maria.

"Go ahead, Hades," prompted Maria.

"This is my doing," Hades finally said. "This dream."

"Wait," said Nico. "If this is really you—"

"It is, my son," said Hades, cutting him off. "If you don't believe, I can prove it to you—"

This time, Nico didn't let him finish. He lurched forward and wrapped his arms around his father.

Who was solid.

Who was *really there*.

Nico had never been one to show affection toward Hades in the past, but he was raw from what he'd just been through. He was also *afraid*. If the god was here in his dream, then he had to know where Nico was in real life.

"Father," he muttered into Hades's suit, "I'm sorry. I know you said not to return to Tartarus, but I *had* to."

"I know, Nico," he said, and Nico felt his father's hands on his back, running up and down his bomber jacket.

"I promise I wouldn't have done it if—"

"I said I know."

Those words sounded more like the Hades that Nico knew—gruff and cold. He pulled away. "Are you mad at me?"

Hades sighed. "I could hardly be angry with you after I sent you that prophecy."

"*What?*"

Hades gestured to the bed. "Sit, my son. We must talk."

"*You* sent it to me?"

His father raised an eyebrow. "You have no idea how *loud* Bob was getting toward the end."

Nico sat on the edge of the bed nearest his mother, and she

immediately reached out to him. When he took Maria's hand, he trembled.

Somehow, she was both there and *not* there.

"I don't understand," said Nico. "The prophecy, Bob, *this*. What's going on?"

"Though the Underworld is my realm, I am often restricted in my movements," said Hades. He sat to Nico's left and put his hat aside, then gazed at him with his dark eyes. "I believed there was no demigod better suited to rescuing Bob from Nyx's clutches than you."

Nico barked a laugh—he couldn't help himself.

"I fail to see what is so amusing," said Hades.

Nico grinned. "I just remember a time when you were annoyed that I wasn't as good as Bianca at being a demigod."

Hades frowned. "I never said that."

"Totally did," said Nico.

"That doesn't sound like me."

Bianca hid a laugh in a cough, and Maria scowled at Hades.

"Okay, perhaps that is true," the god allowed. "But you have grown so much over the years and have proven yourself time and time again."

"But . . . Father, it's *Tartarus*," said Nico. "You know I got captured there once. You know what I went through. Why would you want to send me back?"

Hades looked to Maria again, and this time she glared at him, as if to say *I'd like to know the answer, too.*

Hades squared his broad shoulders and turned back to Nico. "Sometimes, we gods can be a bit . . . calculating. We see things in a way that makes logical sense to us, yet our actions can have disastrous consequences for mortals."

He nodded at Maria. "And sometimes, mortals end up paying the price for our actions."

"Okay," said Nico. "I get it. You're not human or mortal. Our world confuses you."

"*Sometimes*," Hades said sternly. "But other times . . . well, my child, that demigod friend of yours, Percy Jackson? He changed things for a lot of us. Made us rethink our priorities, our behaviors, our standards. I did have second thoughts in this case, but only *after* I sent you that prophecy. When you came to the Underworld with Will Solace, I was worried that I had asked too much of you."

He sighed and lowered his head. "You have lost so very much, my child. Your mother. Your sister. Jason Grace. And I worried that you would lose Will as well."

"But I didn't," said Nico.

"No, you did not." And for the first time Nico had seen in many, many years, a smile broke out on Hades's face. "You survived. You were resilient. You made me proud to be your father."

"*Vita mia*," Maria whispered, and Nico saw that she was crying.

"And so, I wanted you to have this respite. A reward to show you how proud I am." He gestured toward Maria and Bianca with his right hand. "What good is it being a god if I can't break the rules for my son once in a while?"

"We cannot be here long," said Bianca, "but we needed you to know . . . we are proud of you, too, Nico."

A tear spilled down Nico's cheek. "I miss you, Bianca, Mom. I miss you both so much."

"We know," said Maria, her wet eyes sparkling. "It has been hard, and you've been through so much heartbreak . . . and yet you have not given up. You are very strong, *caro figliuolo*."

"I once told you something, Nico." Hades picked up his hat and placed it atop his oil-slicked hair. "I hoped you would finally be the exception to a legacy of children who struggled to find happiness."

The god of the Underworld reached over and grabbed Nico's left hand. "Go," he said. "Go be with Will Solace, and now that Nyx has plucked your demons from you . . . choose happiness. Not for me, not for your sister or mother, but for *yourself*. You deserve it, Nico."

Hades went quiet, and his next words sounded like they'd gotten stuck in his throat.

"You deserve everything, my son."

Nico hesitated for a moment. "Everything?" he said.

Hades frowned. "Yes."

He gave his father a mischievous smirk. "So, if I ask for something, you'll give it to me?"

"Perhaps I did not mean 'everything' quite so literally, but go ahead. Ask."

"There's a soul in Tartarus," Nico said. "Amphithemis. Zeus sent him to protect Dionysus, and Hera cursed him with the form of a Lamian centaur, and now his soul is a mania, trapped in that place. Could you . . . could you find a way to set him free? It's not fair that he has to suffer forever."

Hades smiled. "You finally have me in a place where I can grant you whatever you desire, and your wish is to help someone else. You continue to make me proud." He adjusted his hat. "I will make it so."

Then his father stood, and Nico's heart leaped as the walls of the Lotus Hotel began to dissipate, wisping away like smoke in the wind as Hades walked into the quickly approaching darkness.

Nico turned back to his sister and mother, expecting to feel anguish and rage, expecting to beg them to stay just one more minute.

But Maria and Bianca di Angelo glowed.

And they looked so happy. Completely at peace.

"I'm glad I got to see you again," he said. "And it's time for me to let you go."

"Thank you," said Maria, and she caressed his cheek one last time as Bianca beamed at him. Then they both blew away, mist into darkness, and Nico fell deep, deep into a dreamless rest.

When he awoke some time later, the sky was a red orange. He felt warmth on his face, and he blinked, adjusting to the light and shadows.

Bob looked down at him. "Go back to sleep, my friend," he said. "You should not be awake here."

Nico sat up. Will was curled up on the bottom of the boat, surrounded by Cocoa Puffs, who also snoozed soundlessly.

And in the distance, Nico could see Erebos.

The great black walls of his father's palace were the best thing Nico had seen in a long time. A wide smile spread over his face.

"We do not need your father knowing where you have been."

"He already does," said Nico.

Bob raised an eyebrow. "And he's not going to stop us?"

"Bob, he was the one who sent me the prophecy to find you."

The Titan was silent, and then he smiled, too. "Always did like working for your father," he said.

The Acheron was bringing them closer and closer to the palace, and Nico lay back down, snuggling closer to Will. "Wake me when we need to head to the Door of Orpheus."

Bob shook his head. "Not going that way."

Nico stitched his eyebrows together. "But . . . how else are we getting out of the Underworld?"

"I am still a Titan, Nico," he said. "I still possess some of the knowledge, even if the Lethe wiped my memories. Rest, friend. As I told Will, it is my turn to take care of you."

Nico didn't argue. He put his head on Will's chest, and moments later, he fell asleep to the rhythmic up-and-down of his boyfriend's breathing.

CHAPTER 49

The next time Nico opened his eyes, everything was blue.

A soft breeze wafted over his face, and the stars came into view: tiny pinpricks of light poking through a navy blanket of sky. He wasn't sure which part of the Underworld this was, but he lay there for a few moments, just existing.

Until a seagull spoiled it all.

When it cawed loudly, Nico bolted upright. He'd somehow made it to the stern of the boat, and his Cocoa Puffs chirped at him as he looked around.

Will and Bob were both awake, sitting together on a bench in the canoe, facing front. That's when Nico figured out where they were, because on the horizon, the sun was beginning to rise over the Long Island Sound.

They were out of the Underworld.

They had made it!

Well, they could thank Bob for that. Nico stretched his arms above his head, and Will turned at the sound of him yawning.

"Morning, sleepyhead," he said. "Welcome back to the land of the living."

"Ha-ha," said Nico. "Funny joke."

Will scooted over to join Nico on the rear bench. "You missed Bob's waterworks display."

"Another one?" Nico said, leaning his head on Will's shoulder. "I feel like I need to cry some more to catch up to him."

"You are welcome to join me," said Bob, running his enormous hand over Small Bob, who was curled up in his lap. "This view is worthy of a good cry. I did not think I would see the sun or stars again."

The Titan lifted his head and took a big whiff of the brisk sea air. "To be alive in the world once more . . . It is beautiful."

He quietly wept while Small Bob purred.

Nico examined Will's face. His boyfriend looked significantly better. His skin was no longer waxy, and the bags under his eyes were starting to fade.

"I'm guessing I don't look like I'm close to death anymore," said Will.

"That's right," said Nico. "But I still find you attractive anyway."

"I'm pretty sure I spent the last few days looking like a pile of melted Play-Doh."

"Nonsense. You were more like soggy ambrosia."

"Your little pile of soggy ambrosia," said Will, blowing Nico a kiss.

Nico watched as the north side of Long Island grew in the distance until he could make out details on the shoreline. Trees. Docks. The garish, impossibly huge houses of rich families, their estates sprawling along the coast in both directions. And there, far, far to the west, he could see the outlines of skyscrapers and towering apartment buildings. He couldn't make out the Manhattan skyline, but that didn't matter. Those were buildings. Buildings constructed by humans.

He truly was back in the world of the living.

Bob guided the boat through Long Island Sound to the beach, to Euros Creek southward into camp. Each sight they came upon—from squirrels rushing up the trunk of an oak to reeds wavering on the banks—thrilled Nico. He wouldn't say he was becoming a *nature* person or anything like that, but he was overjoyed to be back in a world that wasn't actively trying to kill him or Will.

Nico finally let loose his own waterworks when he saw Peleus trotting alongside them in the forest.

They were home.

They were home!

The dragon that watched over the Golden Fleece at Camp Half-Blood kept pace for a while, then darted off into the trees. Next two dryads cried out in shock at the sight of the boat and its strange inhabitants. They ran off, too, probably to tell the others.

The others. Oh, Hades, who else was at camp right now? How much time had passed since they'd gone through the Door of Orpheus? The air was chilly but not freezing, so it had to still be fall.

Will tapped Nico's arm. "Look," he said, pointing ahead.

The creek was coming to an end at Canoe Lake, and there, standing on the edge, was Chiron.

Nico had never been so happy to see his centaur friend. He didn't even wait for Bob to guide the boat to shore—he hopped over the gunwale, water soaking his boots, and splashed his way over to Chiron. He wrapped his arms around the activity director's waist.

"Nico," said Chiron. "You're . . . You're hugging me. Are we hugging now? Is that a thing we do?"

"Shut up, Chiron," he said. "Just hug me back."

The centaur did.

It felt wonderful.

Chiron stepped away, and his eyes went wide. "Oh, my."

Bob the Titan stepped out of the wooden boat, and it was then that Nico remembered just how ridiculously tall Titans were. He loomed over all of them, and one of the nearest trees came up to his chest.

He held out his hand to help Will. The son of Apollo jumped to the ground and wobbled for a second.

"A real-life Titan," said Chiron. "At Camp Half-Blood."

Nico wished he could have bottled the gasp Chiron let out when the Cocoa Puffs hesitantly emerged from Gorgyra's boat. The one with antlers peeked over the edge, then hopped over and scurried to Nico's side.

Chiron reared, then slammed his front hooves down on the ground. "Nico, what are *those*?"

"It's a long story," he said. "But . . . uh, Chiron, I'd like you to meet my Cocoa Puffs."

Chiron's mouth dropped open. "Your . . . what?"

More and more of Nico's cacodemons poured out of the boat until they formed an inky blot of a group at his feet. A couple of them yipped and jumped up toward his hands.

"Sorry, Cocoa Puffs," he said. "I don't have any food."

He raised an eyebrow and turned to Will. "Wait, what do they eat?"

"You're asking the wrong person," said Will, shrugging. "I didn't even know anything like them could exist until a few days ago."

Nico turned back to Chiron. "How long have we been gone?"

"A week," the activities director said. "A very long week, I imagine."

"Very, *very* long," said Nico. "And it would have been a lot longer if we hadn't had the boat!"

"Um . . ." said Chiron uncertainly. "Do you by chance mean the one that's now drifting away?"

Nico spun and saw that Gorgyra's white canoe was indeed floating out on the creek, heading toward Long Island Sound.

Will groaned. "That's the second time we've lost that boat," he said. "I hope Gorgyra isn't mad at us."

"You need not worry," said Bob. "These things find their way back home."

He knelt so he was closer to Nico's height. "And I must go find mine. It is time for me to leave."

"Stay a while," said Nico. "Let me show you around the camp."

"Yes, you are very much welcome to," said Chiron. "I, for one, would love to chat with you about all sorts of things."

Bob shook his head, and Small Bob leaped into his arms. "I must head west. It is where I belong."

Then he smiled. "No, that's not quite right. It is where I *want* to go."

He hugged Nico tightly, then held his arms out for Will. "Thank you, Will Solace, for helping me obtain my freedom."

"It was my pleasure," said Will. "Well, actually, I was miserable most of the time, but, Bob, I'd do it again if it meant saving you."

Small Bob meowed loudly at Will.

"And you, too, Small Bob," he added.

"Where exactly will you go, Bob?" Chiron asked.

"I have no idea." The reformed Titan rose and looked to the west, and when he did so, beams of sunlight hit the back of his head. Nico thought they looked like points on a crown. "But that is the best possible reality for me. I now have choices when I used to have none."

He raised his hand to Will, Nico, and Chiron, and then he strode off through the forest, Small Bob glowing at his heels.

After a short silence, Chiron cleared his throat. "You boys managed something impossible," he said. "Mr. D and I are eager to hear how you accomplished such a feat, but first let's get you both a nice hot meal."

"Yes, please," said Will. "I'm tired of nectar and ambrosia."

"There will be more of that in the future to facilitate your healing," said Chiron, scanning their faces. "I see you're both a bit dinged up."

He reached down and lifted Nico's chin. "Do you need to visit the infirmary first, son? I'm sure we can fix that slash on your cheek."

"Nah," said Nico. "There's nothing to fix. I like it how it is."

"In the meantime, though, how do bacon, eggs, and toast sound?"

"Sunny-side up?" asked Nico.

"I like my toast dark," said Will.

The demigods grinned at each other.

Chiron looked down at them with a serious expression. "I just want to say how deeply, deeply proud I am of both of you. Dionysus will probably not admit as much, but he feels the same way."

"Thanks," said Nico.

He reached down and laced his fingers between Will's.

Will sent a warm glow into Nico.

And Nico accepted it.

CHAPTER 50

A small gathering of dryads and nymphs greeted Nico and Will as they entered the dining pavilion, and Mr. D had to shoo them away to even get close.

"My two *favorite* demigods have returned," he said, and he held his arms open and embraced both of them at the same time.

"Favorite?" Will said into Mr. D's armpit. "I thought you didn't even *like* demigods."

"Oh, I don't," he said. "All of you could fall to the bottom of the sea and I wouldn't care. But I'd prefer if you two were the last to drown."

"I can't believe I missed you," said Nico, grinning. "It's great to be back."

"I must hear *everything*," said Mr. D, gesturing to a table piled with fresh, steaming food. "Eat up, and commence with the story-telling, because what I've already heard sounds *phenomenal*."

"Already heard?" said Will. "But . . . we *just* got here."

"News travels fast in our world," said Chiron, sitting at the head of the table. A couple of dryads darted up and began to pour chalices of nectar for everyone. "And bits and pieces of your exploits have floated to the surface, so to speak."

Mr. D glanced down at Nico's feet and the Cocoa Puffs ducked behind them. "I am especially eager to hear about . . . whatever *they* are!"

Nico thought Mr. D looked like he was about to explode from excitement, and it was honestly a complete delight.

Will led Nico to the table, and they sat next to each other. There were fluffy eggs, glistening bowls of fruit, a towering stack of fresh pancakes, and a platter piled high with crispy vegan bacon. Nico was certain he was going to eat every morsel.

"Well, where should we start?" he said after scarfing three flapjacks in rapid succession.

Chiron's mouth was open a little bit. Mr. D's eyes were wide, like he was a demigod in the armory.

"The beginning, Nico," said Mr. D, sitting opposite Chiron. "Obviously."

And so Nico and Will took turns sharing what had happened over the course of the previous week. Nico would speak when Will needed to eat, and Will would take over when Nico's eyes went all glassy as a new plate of food was placed on the table. Nico expected to feel exhausted after everything that had happened, but he realized how badly his heart, soul, and mind had missed being here, in Camp Half-Blood, among people who cared for him.

He would always have a soft spot for the Underworld. It was his second home. But his *first* home—and this was what Nyx couldn't understand about him—was the mortal world.

He had spent so many years resisting companionship, friendship, and love. He'd refused to stay in one place and hadn't allowed anyone to get close to him. No matter how hard people tried to show

Nico that they cared, he had chosen loneliness and isolation instead.

And as he listened to Will recount Chaos's pit and the show-down with Nyx, Nico told himself that his past self had been trying to stay safe. After so many years of disappointment and pain, he had come to expect the worst. But now he'd . . .

There was a soft chittering at his feet. The Cocoa Puffs had gathered under the table, and they looked at him expectantly. The one-eyed cacodemon licked his lips with a glowing tongue.

So Nico grabbed a fresh plate of pancakes and quickly placed it on the ground. He did his best to ignore the frenzy that erupted as the Cocoa Puffs feasted, but Chiron finally looked under the table and scowled.

"Those things are what Nyx created out of you?" he asked.

Nico nodded. "She's created cacodemons all her life," he said. "It's not that surprising that she would do it again."

"So, you're basically a father to a bunch of cacodemons," said Mr. D. "This might be my favorite part of this story. It's so *chaotic*."

"Excuse you," said Will. "They're the Cocoa Puffs. Get it right."

"I don't understand the reference, and I refuse to learn what it means," said Mr. D. "But Cocoa Puffs it is."

Chiron rubbed his goatee. "What an ingenious way of fulfilling the prophecy," he said. "I must admit . . . I was worried." He gestured to Mr. D. "We were *both* worried."

"Speak for yourself," said Mr. D, popping a grape into his mouth. "I always knew that Nico would emerge victorious."

Chiron scowled at the director. "Anyway, I think you did something scary and risky, Nico, but I'm glad you were willing to give up that part of yourself."

"Well, not completely," said Will. "If I learned anything from this quest, it's that eradicating the past isn't really possible. Or healthy, for that matter. It's better if you learn how to live with it."

He reached down and petted the Cocoa Puff with tusks. "And I think Nico is going to do a wonderful job of that."

Heat rushed to Nico's face. "Thank you," he said quietly.

Will put his hand on Nico's left leg and squeezed.

Nico sat back, his hands on his bloated belly, and he realized it had been a long time since he'd last been this full. He'd always been known as the demigod who wouldn't eat. Why had he let himself get to the point of starvation over and over again?

Because it was what he was used to.

But Nico's life was changing. *Had* changed. What he was used to now was different than what his life had been like even a year ago. Back then, the idea that he could be in a relationship seemed impossible.

Things changed.

That wasn't a *bad* thing.

But something needled at Nico as he sat there, watching Will's animated storytelling as he described Tartarus to the two directors. Something was missing. Incomplete. There was a thread left that still needed to be pulled.

He looked down at the Cocoa Puffs. They, too, had gorged themselves and were now napping under the table. Mr. D rested his chin on his hands and stared at Will dreamily, soaking up every detail of the Underworld.

The Underworld.

There it was.

The other piece.

Nico stood and excused himself. "I'll be right back," he said to Will. "There's something I need to do."

"Of course," Will said. "Meet me in my cabin when you're done?"

Nico nodded, and then he wandered away from the dining pavilion.

He headed for the Hades cabin. It was eerie being in the clearing with all the gods' cabins; there were so many more of them than there had been when Nico had first arrived at Camp Half-Blood.

Yet another sign of how much had changed.

The door to Hades's cabin creaked as he opened it, and it smelled a bit stale inside. It still amused him that it had been decorated as if every child of Hades was a teenage goth, but there was a comfort in the dark decor. He made his way to his part of the cabin and lifted his mattress to pull out a drachma.

Then he sat on his bed and took a small crystal and a drachma from a pocket on the inside of his bomber jacket. He opened the window shutter and held the crystal up to the sunlight. In the rainbow that formed, he tossed the coin, while reciting the offering.

And then he said: "Tahlequah, Oklahoma. Piper McLean."

Moments later, there was an image of Piper, smiling, the morning sun illuminating the two brown braids that sat on either shoulder. Next to her was a brown-skinned girl with dark hair in a pixie cut. The stud in her nostril sparkled.

"Nico!" said Piper. "Wow, this is a surprise. You haven't met Shel before, have you?"

Nico shook his head and promptly burst into tears.

After some consoling—which Nico thought was probably really hard to do over Iris-message—Piper asked Shel to give them some space.

"No, it's okay," said Nico, wiping at his face. "She can stay."

Piper raised an eyebrow. "Are you sure?"

He smiled. "If she's important to you, she's important to me."

"It's okay," said Shel. "I don't have to be here."

"Stay," said Nico. "Maybe you can help."

"What's going on?" asked Piper. "Is there an emergency? Did something happen?"

"No emergency anymore," he said. "I just got back from a quest."

"A quest?" Piper's eyes widened. "Oh, no."

He started with the prophecy during the summer, after they'd defeated Nero. He had to stop every so often so that Piper could explain something to Shel, who listened attentively, nodding.

He told them about the quest. The journey into the Underworld. Epiales, the troglodytes, Menoetes, the garden, and the Acheron. Both girls were transfixed once he got to the plunge into Tartarus and the nightmares that awaited him and Will.

When he'd finished, he was exhausted. This was the second time that morning he'd had to summarize what had happened to him and Will, and his boyfriend wasn't even around to do half the work. But Nico needed to do this by himself, especially once Piper asked him why he had reached out to her.

"Not that I don't like hearing from you," she said. "It's just that . . . well, we haven't spoken in a long time. Not since . . ."

Silence fell on Piper's side of the message, and Shel pulled her close in a hug.

"That's kind of the point," Nico said. "Because I *should* have reached out to you after . . ." He sighed. "After Jason died."

Piper turned away for a moment, and when she looked back to Nico, her eyes were red and glassy.

Shel kissed her on the temple. "I'll be right back," she said, standing up.

"You don't have to leave," said Piper.

"I know. But . . . this is something you two should discuss alone. Come find me once you're done."

Shel disappeared, and Nico smiled at Piper. "I like her. She seems nice."

"I like her, too," she said with a wry smile. "She's never been weird about my grief over Jason, either."

"I'm glad you have someone to share that stuff with. I've learned the hard way that I shouldn't bottle up my feelings."

"Nico, after all you've been through—and not just on this quest—I think it's understandable to *everyone* why you've tried to protect yourself. I don't think it's irrational or anything."

"But you were *right there*," he said. "You were grieving the loss of someone you loved so much, and I didn't even think to drop you a message. That wasn't right."

She nodded. "I mean . . . yeah, maybe it was a little weird. To be honest, I expected you to reach out to me at some point, but then it never happened, and life changed so much for me. I guess I kinda forgot?"

"Well, I'm sorry to open old wounds, but this experience got me thinking. I really want us to be better friends, but I knew that couldn't happen unless we talked about Jason."

"I appreciate that," said Piper. Then: "I really miss him, Nico."

"Me, too," he said, a lump forming in his throat. "There are days when I forget he's dead. My mind thinks he's on a quest or something, and he'll just come waltzing into Camp Half-Blood with you, Leo, Frank, or Hazel. And I know that's partially because I'm still getting over it—I'm adjusting to him not being here. But I'm also realizing that maybe I'll never get over it completely. A part of me is always going to hurt because he's gone."

"That part *does* get smaller." She flicked her braids over her shoulders. "The more you live life, the more your life sort of grows around the hole in your heart. And sometimes a person comes along and helps you build a whole new room in your heart, and you get to fill that with love and memories."

"You mean Shel?"

She tilted her head and smiled. "Well, I was referring to Will Solace, your smokin'-hot boyfriend, but yeah, Shel, too."

"How are things going with her?"

"Really good," said Piper. "It's a lot of firsts. First relationship with a girl. First time I'm with someone who's Native like me. It's really freeing, Nico. We have this shared language and experience even though we haven't lived identical lives."

"That's amazing!" he said. "I'm really happy for you."

"It's weird sometimes, too. Dad is still wrapping his mind around the whole thing."

"Oh, no," said Nico. "Is he being judgy?"

"No, not really," she said. "I think he's just had a hard time seeing me as one person, then having to accept that I'm something else. To be honest, even I struggle with that."

"Struggle with what?"

"Well," said Piper, shifting in her chair, "I really loved Jason. I was genuinely attracted to him. So suddenly realizing I was attracted to a girl was a bit of a shock to me, too. Dad doesn't have a problem with that at all. He told me that if he had even an inkling of homophobia in him, he couldn't have worked in a place like Hollywood. Almost no one there is straight."

Nico laughed. "So . . . is it a label thing?"

"Yeah, I guess. Like, I thought I was straight, and I'm clearly not. But . . . does that make me bi? Pan? If I never find another man attractive again, does that mean I'm a lesbian?"

Nico didn't answer at first. "I think, after what I just went through," he said eventually, "the best thing I can say to you is that we are not only one thing forever. We're allowed to change at any point in our lives. We don't have to be stuck with a label someone else assigns us. Gods, we don't even have to stick to a label we give ourselves. So, you can be bi or pan or a lesbian or queer, and tomorrow you may have a better sense of who you are, or tomorrow you can be a big ole queer mess and figure it out fifty years from now."

"I should tell my dad that the next time he asks," she said, laughing. She put on her best imitation of Tristan McLean. " 'Piper, dear, how should I describe your relationship?' 'Well, Father, I am a big ole queer mess.' "

Nico guffawed, maybe for the first time in his life. "Perfect."

After they spoke for a few more minutes, Shel popped her head back into the room and said something inaudible.

"I gotta go, Nico," said Piper. "We're going on a long hike today, and we need to be on the trails soon or it'll be a billion degrees while we're out there."

"Hope you have fun," he said. "The very idea of hiking even one yard makes me want to perish, but you do you."

She giggled and waved. "Don't be a stranger, Nico di Angelo."

"It was nice meeting you!" Shel said.

He waved good-bye to them, and the Iris-message evaporated.

Nico lay back on the bed, relief coursing through him. He'd been afraid of what Piper's reaction would be to him calling out of the blue, but he now knew that he'd had no reason to be so anxious. Of *course* she was going to understand complicated reactions to grief! But that was what Nico had to work on—always anticipating the worst.

Maybe he should bring that up with Mr. D. Nico would be interested in talking further with the director about Tartarus, but even more so if they could come up with other things Nico could do to help his mind.

Being so open to change now . . . well, it scared Nico. But it also thrilled him.

He hadn't intended to, but he quickly slipped into a dreamless, exhausted sleep.

CHAPTER 51

Nico awoke suddenly and in a panic.

Oh, no, he thought. Will! I told him I would meet him!

He wasn't sure what time it was when he bolted from his cabin, but it was still *very* bright outside, and there wasn't quite as much of a crispness to the air. He rubbed his eyes as he crossed the clearing to the Apollo cabin, rushing past the hearth in the center. When he shoved the front door open, he realized he should have knocked first, especially since he was met with the shocked faces of Kayla and Austin over Iris-message.

"Nico!" Austin called out. "Oh, we're so glad to see you!"

"Where are the Cocoa Puffs?" asked Kayla, eyes wide. "I really want to see *them*."

Nico glanced over at Will, who shrugged. "Last I saw, they were still fast asleep in the dining pavilion."

"Later, then," Nico told the two demigods. "You guys mind if I talk with Will?"

"Oooooh," said Kayla in a sultry voice. "How *romantic*."

"Shut up, Kayla," said Will, grinning. "I'll talk to you both soon, okay?"

Nico waved to them as the Iris-message dissipated, then joined Will on his bed. "I'm sorry," he said. "I meant to come immediately after talking to Piper, but I passed out as soon as I was done."

"Don't worry about it," Will said. "I knew you'd come back." He grabbed Nico's hand. "So, Piper . . . Everything okay?"

"Yes," said Nico, smiling widely. "Very much okay."

"And *we're* okay, too, aren't we?"

"Yup," he said, leaning into Will's shoulder. "I feel like you and I have talked more today than we have in the last year, so we don't need to have another long talk right now."

"Agreed," said Will.

They rested there for a few minutes, and then Will cleared his throat.

"But one more thing," he said.

Nico laughed and shoved Will away from him. "You love talking!"

"I can't help that I'm an extrovert!"

Nico plopped back onto the bed. "Okay, so what's the last thing, then?"

Will lay back so that he was parallel to Nico. "I just wanna make sure you know that I'm not trying to change you or anything. I think the whole Nyx thing dredged up a lot of stuff in our relationship."

"Yeah, I know," he said. "In both directions."

"Well, we're talking about *me* right now, so stay on topic, Nico."

"I'm sending you back to Tartarus tomorrow."

"And now I know how to get back, so nice try!" He paused. "Well, I don't actually know how Bob managed that last part, but that's beside the point. What I was *trying* to say was that I don't want a version of you that I've made up in my head, and I don't want to treat you like you are a *literal* ball of darkness or anything, either. And I think sometimes I have."

"But I also fed into that," said Nico. "My problem is that I never let anyone believe that I was anything *but* a ball of darkness. Even though deep down I wanted to have friends and be cared for. But I couldn't let go of all the hurt and pain I was in."

"Maybe having the Cocoa Puffs is going to help. I don't know, the idea that your personal demons now live outside your body is kinda cool."

"Oh, it's very cool," said Nico, and he propped himself up on one hand so he could face Will. "I'm already planning on not telling anyone else about them so I can use them to scare the living daylights out of people on a regular basis."

"Wow, Nico," said Will. "Why are you like this?"

"Childhood trauma," Nico said, nodding.

Even Will couldn't resist how funny that joke was. It pleased Nico to see him able to laugh at something that dark, and he took it as a sign—Will really *was* trying.

Well, so would he. Nyx had unintentionally taught Nico that he could no longer live shackled to his past. He didn't have to let his pain define him. There was another option, one he'd not been able to see before Will Solace, the son of Apollo, came into his life and shone his brightness on him.

Nico was not afraid of the light anymore.

He and his boyfriend lay on the bed in silence, his leg looped over Will's and his fingers tracing the lines on Will's palm. No one had ever loved him like Will did, and that was no longer terrifying. How could it be? How could acceptance and respect and desire be anything but the best things for Nico?

His life had been ruled and nearly ruined by gods and demons, by wars and prophecies, by doubt and fear. But as he watched Will drifting off to sleep, none of those things mattered anymore.

There was a creak at the door, but Nico did not look. He heard the patter of tiny footsteps on the wooden floor, then felt each of the Cocoa Puffs hop up onto the bed. They found a place to cuddle up with Nico, Will, or one another. It was strange—a year ago, this was not something that Nico could ever have imagined.

He had no idea what the future held or what crisis would rear its head next and threaten the safety and well-being of the world. They were demigods—all that came with the territory.

But this was the first time in Nico's entire life that a certain sensation filled his whole body, stitched itself to his bones, buried itself in his heart.

Nico smiled.

The future held hope.

And he clung to it.

GLOSSARY

aeterna (aeternae, pl.) a giant that stands on two legs, is covered in shaggy fur, and has a crested, bone-covered head

Akhlys the Greek goddess of misery; daughter of Nyx; a protogenos

ambrosia the food eaten by the gods, usually presented in small cubes; demigods eat it to heal their injuries and regain strength

Amphithemis one of the horned Lamian centaurs

Apollo the Greek god of the sun, light, healing, disease, plague, music, art, poetry, archery, reason, knowledge, truth, and prophecy. He is the son of Zeus and the twin brother of the goddess Artemis. Zeus once punished Apollo by stripping him of his godly powers and sending him to earth in the form of a mortal teenager named Lester Papadopoulos. To regain his place on Mount Olympus, Apollo had to go on a quest to restore the Oracles and face his archenemy Python (see the Trials of Apollo series).

Ares the Greek god of war; the son of Zeus and Hera, and half brother to Athena

***Argo* II** the fantastical ship built by the demigod Leo Valdez, which can both sail and fly and has Festus the bronze dragon as a figurehead. The ship was named after the *Argo*, the vessel used by a band of Greek heroes who accompanied Jason on his quest to find the Golden Fleece (see the Heroes of Olympus series).

Artemis the Greek goddess of the hunt, archery, wilderness, forests, the moon, radiance, maidenhood, and childbirth. She is a daughter of Zeus, and she and her twin brother, Apollo, are known as the "Twin Archers."

Athena the Greek goddess of wisdom

Athena Parthenos a giant statue of Athena; the most famous Greek statue of all time

Bacchus the Roman god of wine and revelry. Greek form: Dionysus

basilisk a small green snakelike monster that is venomous and breathes fire. The name means *little crown.*

cacodemons Nyx's personifications of negative emotions and feelings

Camp Half-Blood the training ground for Greek demigods, located on Long Island, New York (see the Percy Jackson and the Olympians series)

Camp Jupiter the training ground for Roman demigods, located in California between the Oakland Hills and the Berkeley Hills

centaur a race of creatures that are half human, half horse

Cerberus the three-headed guard dog of the Underworld

Chaos the first deity; the primordial mass the protogenoi emerged from. Also, a shapeless void below Tartarus where faded gods sleep in eternity.

charmspeak a blessing bestowed by Aphrodite on her children that enables them to persuade others with their voice

Charon the ferryman who transports souls to the Underworld

Chimera the monstrous offspring of Echidna and Typhon. It has the head of a lion with a blood-caked mane, the body of a giant goat, and a serpent for a tail, a ten-foot-long diamondback.

Chiron the immortal centaur who is the activities director at Camp Half-Blood

Cupid the Roman god of love

Cyclops (Cyclopes, pl.) a member of a primordial race of giants, each with a single eye in the middle of their forehead

cynocephalus (cynocephali, pl.) a dog-headed monster

Damasen the giant son of Tartarus and Gaea; created to oppose Ares; condemned to Tartarus for slaying the Maeonian drakon

Dante an Italian poet whose fourteenth-century epic poem *The Divine Comedy* helped establish the Italian language used today; his depiction of hell in *Inferno* had a lasting influence on Western literature

Demeter the Greek goddess of agriculture; a daughter of the Titans Rhea and Kronos

demigod the offspring of a god and a mortal

Diocletian the last great pagan emperor, and the first to retire peacefully; a demigod (son of Jupiter). According to legend, his scepter could raise a ghost army.

Dionysus the Greek god of wine and revelry; a son of Zeus. Roman form: Bacchus

Doors of Death the doorway to the House of Hades, located in Tartarus. The Doors have two sides—one in the mortal world and one in the Underworld.

drachma the silver coin of ancient Greece

drakon a gigantic yellow-and-green serpentlike monster, with frills around its neck, reptilian eyes, and huge talons; it spits poison

dryad tree nymph

Echidna the daughter of Gaea and Tartarus; the "mother of all monsters"

Elysium the section of the Underworld where those who are blessed by the gods are sent to rest in eternal peace after death

empousa (empousai, pl.)   a vampire with fangs, claws, a bronze left leg, a donkey right leg, hair made of fire, and skin as white as bone. Empousai have the ability to manipulate the Mist, change shape, and charmspeak in order to attract their mortal victims.

Ephialtes   a giant created by Gaea to destroy the Olympian gods during the First Giant War. He and his twin brother, Otis, were made to be the banes of Dionysus and Bacchus.

Epiales   the personification of nightmares; child of Nyx

Erebos   the great black walls of Hades's kingdom; the personification of darkness and mist

Eris   the Greek goddess of strife; daughter of Nyx

Favonius   the Roman god of the West Wind

Fields of Asphodel   the section of the Underworld where people who lived neither a good nor a bad life are sent after death

Fields of Punishment   the section of the Underworld where people who were evil during their lives are sent after death to face eternal punishment for their crimes

Furies   Roman goddesses of vengeance; usually characterized as three sisters—Alecto, Tisiphone, and Megaera; the children of Gaea and Ouranos. They reside in the Underworld, tormenting evildoers and sinners.

Gaea   the Greek earth goddess; mother of Titans, giants, Cyclopes, and other monsters

Geras   the Greek god of old age; son of Nyx

Geryon   a fearsome three-bodied giant and grandson of Medusa

Golden Fleece   the fleece of Chrysomallus, a flying ram sired by Poseidon; it has powerful healing abilities. The fleece currently resides at Camp Half-Blood on Thalia's pine tree to help strengthen the borders. It is guarded by the dragon Peleus.

Gray Sisters   three old women—Anger, Tempest, and Wasp—who share a single eye and a single tooth and operate a taxi company that serves the Greater New York City area; daughters of the minor sea gods Keto and Phorcys

Hades the Greek god of death and riches

harpy a winged female creature that snatches things

Hera the Greek goddess of marriage; Zeus's wife and sister

Hermes the Greek god of travelers; guide to spirits of the dead; god of communication

House of Hades a place in the Underworld where Hades, the Greek god of death, and his wife, Persephone, rule over the souls of the departed

Hunters of Artemis maidens who have sworn to the goddess Artemis that they will join her in the Hunt and reject love for the rest of their lives; in return, they gain eternal youth

Hyperboreans a race of giants from the north, usually peaceful and friendly to humans

Hypnos the Greek god of sleep; son of Nyx

Iapetus one of the twelve Titans; lord of the west; his name means *the Piercer*. When Percy Jackson fought him in Hades's realm, Iapetus fell into the River Lethe and lost his memory; Percy renamed him Bob.

Iris-message a form of video communication used by gods and demigods that transmits via a rainbow. The service is managed by Iris, the Greek goddess of the rainbow.

Keres a Greek spirit of violent death; child of Nyx

Kronos the youngest of the twelve Titans; the son of Ouranos and Gaea; the father of Zeus. He killed his father at his mother's bidding. Titan lord of fate, harvest, justice, and time.

Labyrinth an underground maze originally built on the island of Crete by the craftsman Daedalus to hold the Minotaur (part man, part bull)

Lamian centaur one of twelve spirits of the Lamos river who were sent by Zeus to guard the infant Dionysus

Lotus Hotel and Casino an establishment in Las Vegas, Nevada, where guests lose track of time and never age; Hades stashed Nico and his sister Bianca there before World War II and they stayed there for a few decades

Maeonian drakon a drakon from Lydia that attacked the village of Maeonia (in modern-day Turkey)

mania a spirit personifying insanity, madness, and crazed frenzy

Mansion of Night Nyx's palace

manticore a creature with a human head, a lion's body, and a scorpion's tail

Menoetes the guard of Hades's cattle

Minos king of Crete; demigod son of Zeus; every year he made King Aegeus pick seven boys and girls to be sent to the Labyrinth, where they would be eaten by the Minotaur. After his death, he became a judge in the Underworld.

Minotaur a monster with the head of a bull and the body of a man

Mist a magical force that disguises things from mortals

Mythomagic a card and figurine game based on Greek mythology

nectar the drink of the gods; like ambrosia, demigods consume it to heal their injuries and regain strength

Nemesis the Greek goddess of retribution; daughter of Nyx

Nero one of the evilest emperors in Roman history, infamous for being malevolent, ruthless, and bloodthirsty

New Rome University a college in a community near Camp Jupiter where demigods can study in peace, without interference from mortals or monsters

nymph a female deity who animates nature

Nyx the Greek goddess of night; one of the ancient firstborn elemental gods

Oracle of Delphi a speaker of the prophecies of Apollo

Orpheus a gifted musician trained by Apollo himself; he sang his way into the Underworld to try to retrieve his dead wife

Otis a giant created by Gaea to destroy the Olympian gods during the First Giant War. He and his twin brother, Ephialtes, were made to be the banes of Dionysus and Bacchus.

pegasus (pegasi, pl.) a winged divine horse

Persephone the Greek queen of the Underworld; wife of Hades; daughter of Zeus and Demeter

pit scorpion a huge monster scorpion summoned from Tartarus during the First Titan War

Poseidon the Greek god of the sea; son of the Titans Kronos and Rhea, and brother of Zeus and Hades

protogenos (protogenoi, pl.) a primordial god; a member of the first race of immortals to come into existence; born from the void of Chaos. A protogenos can be banished from manifesting in the world physically, but their consciousness can never be destroyed because they are sentient aspects of the universe itself.

Python a huge serpent with purple scales, lamplike yellow eyes, and the ability to grow and discard wings, limbs, and extra heads on a whim. Nemesis of Apollo.

River Acheron one of five rivers that run through the Underworld; the River of Pain; the ultimate punishment for the souls of the damned

River Cocytus one of five rivers that run through the Underworld; the River of Lamentation; its water is freezing cold and filled with millions of heartbroken voices

River Lethe one of five rivers that run through the Underworld;

the River of Forgetfulness; drinking from it will make someone forget their identity

River Phlegethon   one of five rivers that run through the Underworld; the River of Fire; it keeps the wicked alive so they can endure the torments of the Fields of Punishment

River Styx   one of five rivers that run through the Underworld; the River of Hate; polluted with human trash; oaths made on this river will bring something worse than death to the oath bearer if not fulfilled; heroes who bathe in the Styx and survive will become invulnerable except for a small spot on their body that, if struck, will kill them instantly; the river in which Stygian iron is cooled to make it indestructible

satyr   a Greek forest god, part goat and part man

Scylla and Charybdis   two monsters who lived on either side of a narrow channel of water

shadow-travel   a form of transportation that allows creatures of the Underworld and children of Hades to travel to any desired place on earth or in the Underworld, although it makes the user extremely fatigued

Sisyphus   a spirit in the Fields of Punishment who received one of the worst punishments Hades ever gave a mortal soul. In life, he was a murderer who tried to cheat death. After death, he was tasked with rolling a boulder up a hill with the condition that he could go free once he had finished. But every time he gets to the top of the hill, the boulder rolls back down to the bottom.

Stygian iron   a magical metal forged in the River Styx, capable of absorbing the very essence of monsters and injuring mortals, gods, Titans, and giants. It has a significant effect on ghosts and creatures from the Underworld.

Stymphalian bird   a man-eating bird with a beak made of bronze; its feathers are sharp and can be shot at humans

Tartarus consort of Gaea; spirit of the abyss; father of the giants; the lowest part of the Underworld

telkhine a sea demon with flippers instead of hands, and a dog's head

Titans a race of powerful Greek deities, descendants of Gaea and Ouranos, who ruled during the Golden Age and were overthrown by a race of younger gods, the Olympians

Triumvirate an organization headed by the three worst Roman emperors in history: Nero, Caligula, and Commodus; it profited from such events as the Second Titan War and the Second Giant War

troglodyte one of a race of cave-dwelling reptilian humanoids who enjoy eating lizards and wearing hats

Virgil a Roman poet who acts as Dante's guide in the Italian writer's fourteenth-century epic poem *The Divine Comedy*

Zeus the Greek god of the sky and king of the gods

Other Books You May Enjoy

by Rick Riordan

Daughter of the Deep

THE KANE CHRONICLES

The Red Pyramid

The Throne of Fire

The Serpent's Shadow

MAGNUS CHASE AND THE GODS OF ASGARD

The Sword of Summer

The Hammer of Thor

The Ship of the Dead

by Mark Oshiro

Anger Is a Gift

Each of Us a Desert

The Insiders

You Only Live Once, David Bravo

Star Wars Hunters: Battle for the Arena

Into the Light